"If you need a good laugh, then grab this one . . . Engaging and fun, filled with surprise twists and turns around every corner. I truly look forward to finding out what trouble the cosmic troublemakers will cause next."

—*The Eternal Night*

"Fabulously wicked." —*Midwest Book Review*

"A sensational read full of humor and romance. You'll be burning through the pages while you follow . . . all the hijinks and scorching sex. *Wicked Fantasy* is a great read and I enjoyed every minute of it. Nina Bangs has created a story with outrageous and hilarious characters and a romance that will make you wish for your own fantasy at the castle. It goes on my bookshelf as a keeper. Enjoy!"

—*Night Owl Reviews*

Wicked Pleasure

"Wicked fun from start to finish . . . A side-splitting, sexy tale that dazzles and delights." —*The Best Reviews*

"Another terrific Nina Bangs humorous, action-packed paranormal romance . . . Readers will enjoy this wicked tale." —*Midwest Book Review*

"A delightful comedy." —*The Eternal Night*

Wicked Nights

"Paranormal romance filled with humor and sex . . . and with the right touch of suspense . . . Action-packed. Readers will enjoy this wicked tale and look forward to novels starring Eric's siblings, a demon and an immortal warrior, that will surely sparkle with fun." —*The Best Reviews*

Wicked Edge

Nina Bangs

BERKLEY SENSATION, NEW YORK

THE BERKLEY PUBLISHING GROUP
Published by the Penguin Group
Penguin Group (USA) Inc.
375 Hudson Street, New York, New York 10014, USA

Penguin Group (Canada), 90 Eglinton Avenue East, Suite 700, Toronto, Ontario M4P 2Y3, Canada
(a division of Pearson Penguin Canada Inc.) • Penguin Books Ltd., 80 Strand, London WC2R 0RL,
England • Penguin Ireland, 25 St. Stephen's Green, Dublin 2, Ireland (a division of Penguin
Books Ltd.) • Penguin Group (Australia), 707 Collins Street, Melbourne, Victoria 3008, Australia
(a division of Pearson Australia Group Pty. Ltd.) • Penguin Books India Pvt. Ltd., 11 Community
Centre, Panchsheel Park, New Delhi—110 017, India • Penguin Group (NZ), 67 Apollo Drive,
Rosedale, Auckland 0632, New Zealand (a division of Pearson New Zealand Ltd.) • Penguin Books
(South Africa), Rosebank Office Park, 181 Jan Smuts Avenue, Parktown North 2193, South Africa •
Penguin China, B7 Jiaming Center, 27 East Third Ring Road North, Chaoyang District,
Beijing 100020, China

Penguin Books Ltd., Registered Offices: 80 Strand, London WC2R 0RL, England

This is a work of fiction. Names, characters, places, and incidents either are the product of the author's
imagination or are used fictitiously, and any resemblance to actual persons, living or dead, business
establishments, events, or locales is entirely coincidental. The publisher does not have any control over
and does not assume any responsibility for author or third-party websites or their content.

WICKED EDGE

A Berkley Sensation Book / published by arrangement with the author

PUBLISHING HISTORY
Berkley Sensation trade paperback edition / March 2012
Berkley Sensation mass-market edition / February 2013

ISBN: 978-0-425-25520-9

BERKLEY SENSATION®
Berkley Sensation Books are published by The Berkley Publishing Group,
a division of Penguin Group (USA) Inc.,
375 Hudson Street, New York, New York 10014.
BERKLEY SENSATION® is a registered trademark of Penguin Group (USA) Inc.
The "B" design is a trademark of Penguin Group (USA) Inc.

PRINTED IN THE UNITED STATES OF AMERICA

10 9 8 7 6 5 4 3 2 1

ALWAYS LEARNING   **PEARSON**

To my stepbrother, Christopher E. Brady,
King of Humility and Emperor of the Entire Universe.
(He insisted that I use his complete title.)
You could always make me laugh, and for that alone you deserve this.
You also beat me at every board game we ever played.
I have not forgotten.

Prologue

He'd needed this downtime away from the Castle of Dark Dreams. Two weeks to just kick back, waste a few losers, and relax with a drink.

He leaned against the oak's trunk and savored his scotch and water as he watched the dumbass crouched beside the reservoir. Edge had followed the guy's progress from the moment he'd come up with the idea to poison the city's water supply until now. Homegrown terrorists, had to love them.

Not that Edge didn't sort of admire the guy. He'd whipped up a poison no amount of testing would detect until it was too late. The death toll could reach into the millions. Now the formula would die with him. Too bad. Another great scientific mind pissed away by an idiot.

There was a time when Edge would've applauded that kind of grand gesture. But then the Big Boss had reined him in, forced him to change his methods. Edge downed the rest of his drink. *Let's hear it for the good old days.* Nowadays he was reduced to one kill at a time. Hey, you took your fun where you could.

Edge narrowed his gaze as the man . . . No, as *Mark*—didn't want to ever depersonalize his victims—pulled vials of the poison from his backpack and set them on the ground.

Now was the time to act. Edge chose an image from his mind, focused on the reservoir, and changed thought to reality.

A giant squid rose from the water's depths, big enough to swallow Chicago if Chicago had been on the menu. It wasn't, so the squid settled for Mark. One massive tentacle reached out to wrap around his body. It lifted the man into the air and then dragged him beneath the water. The squid disappeared, leaving only a few ripples on the surface. Mark's body would be found, a victim of drowning. But they'd never find the squid. It was once more only an image in Edge's mind.

Edge shook his head. He'd made it happen too fast. Mark didn't even have a chance to scream. He'd just stood there bug-eyed. What fun was that? But at least the guy died in a unique and interesting way. See, death didn't have to be boring.

Edge wandered down to collect the vials. He stashed them in Mark's backpack. He'd dispose of them later. Then he headed back to his car.

That was his last kill for now. Vacation over. Time to return to his crappy role-playing-slash-managerial job.

He took a last look at the reservoir before driving away. How did he *really* feel about Mark's death and all the ones that had come before his? The truth? Edge closed his eyes. He felt freaking tired.

1

"How ugly and horrible are they? Do they coat your skin with slime? Does their stench make you nauseous? Do you feel like you're walking into the bowels of hell?"

Passion sighed. Of all the heavenly contacts they could've assigned to her, why Hope? Once a day she'd have to listen to this idiocy in her head.

She could picture Hope sitting in her little cubicle surrounded by the neutral colors Archangel Ted loved. Ted, along with everything else in heaven, was bland and boring. Okay, so Passion could include herself in the bland and boring category. She accepted the reality of her existence. But she'd looked into enough human minds to know their vision of heaven was a fantasy.

Humans. Sure, they could get sick and die. Fine, so they suffered heartbreak and other emotional traumas. But from Passion's viewpoint, things were a lot more exciting on the mortal plane. Could anyone blame her for trying to spice up her own world? Guess that was a resounding yes.

She supposed the final straw for Ted was when she'd talked the other angels in her department into painting their cubicles lime green. In her opinion, Ted had some serious control issues.

So here she was, on the outside looking in.

And you have only yourself to blame. If Passion had been a better angel, she wouldn't have drawn this punishment— a still-to-be-determined amount of time spent living on earth as a human. No powers, no friends, forced to check in once a day with Hope-the-heavenly-drama-queen. The only good thing? The Council of Justice had at least given her some privacy. Hope couldn't read her thoughts; she could only hear what Passion spoke out loud.

"They're . . ." *Way too beautiful.* Evil should appear in shades of muddy brown or black. But no, just look at them. The Seven Deadly Sins shimmered and flowed around the Castle of Dark Dreams in vibrant jewel tones. Totally gorgeous. Totally *tempting.*

Oops. Wrong reaction. "They're . . . awful, disgusting, but sort of exciting." Hmm, maybe she should explain that last word just in case Hope got the wrong impression. "I mean, it's *exciting* to think about all the peace, harmony, and massive heavenly vibes I'm going to bring to this place." There, that was better. Didn't want anyone taking away the only thing she had left, her ability to see the colors of sin.

"Oh." Hope sounded disappointed. *"Well, keep in touch."* She broke the connection.

"Absolutely." Passion knew her smile wasn't kind. *Note to self: work on sweet and sincere smile.* Hope and the other angels had gotten used to her supplying their daily entertainment. Too bad. Passion wouldn't be there to amuse them for a while because she'd be busy earning her way back into heaven.

She had to be the perfect angel. Sure, she'd always longed for more . . . variety in her existence, but she sure hadn't planned on getting that variety as a powerless and frighteningly vulnerable mortal. She could actually *die,* as in never-coming-back die. She shuddered.

Passion crossed the drawbridge, avoiding glancing

down at the moat's black water in favor of staring up at the castle—a keep with four square towers complete with a curtain wall. The whole thing gleamed white, a color symbolizing goodness and light. Fake. Goodness and light didn't live here.

She'd take care of that by the time she left. She narrowed her eyes as she strode through the open gate and across the courtyard, headed for the doors leading into the great hall. Spotlights lit up the night around the castle. No threatening shadows warned the innocent about what waited inside. Righteous anger drove her as she reached for the door. She'd smite the wicked and save all those poor souls inside who . . .

She paused. No powers, so no smiting. Damn. Passion closed her eyes. No cursing. Ted hated cursing. So many things to remember. But she could do this. Opening her eyes, she pulled the door open and stepped inside.

Someone spoke. "Ah, another person who didn't bother to check the schedule and has chosen instead to annoy the hell out of me by showing up at the last moment." Dramatic sigh. "But I live to serve, so I'll probably be able to stick you in somewhere. All the choice parts are gone. How do you feel about playing the lowly maiden who serves the queen? Not a virgin. The virgin part was taken by a woman who obviously has only a faint memory of that particular condition."

"Virgin?" Startled, she looked at the speaker. A wizard? A short one. Gold-trimmed blue robe, tall conical hat that added at least a foot, and all of it decorated with gold suns, moons, and stars. He'd topped everything off with a long, pointy gray beard that matched his narrowed gray eyes.

"Yes. The part is gone." The wizard looked down his nose at her, which was tough to do when she was taller than he was. "If it's any comfort, you'd fit the part better. Pale hair, pale skin, pale eyes, and uninspired pale clothing. You, my dear, are the definition of unawakened. Avoid Sparkle Stardust at all cost. Now, do you want the lowly maiden part?"

"No." What was he talking about? She glanced around. People in medieval-type costumes wandered the large hall. Too bad the Council of Justice had kicked her down here without full disclosure. All they'd said was that the castle needed help. This place was her ticket back home.

"You look confused." The wizard glanced at his watch. "As much as I'd love to waste more time explaining the obvious, I have a fantasy to direct. Feel free to gawk. If you care to wait until this fantasy concludes, you may buy a ticket to the next one, over there." He pointed to a small table by the door with a TICKETS sign taped to the front of it. "And you might want to read that." He gestured toward a sign on the wall above the ticket table.

Bemused, she watched him turn to walk away. Violet, the color of pride, swirled around him. No kidding. Too bad there wasn't a color for bad-tempered old farts. She took a deep breath. *Get rid of unkind thoughts.*

Passion didn't know how other angels did it. They wore their perfection like a pair of comfortable old shoes. Her shoes pinched her toes and left blisters on her heels. She constantly wanted to kick them off. Well, she'd kicked them off a few times too many.

She looked at the sign. Fine, so she was in an adult theme park called Live the Fantasy. The Castle of Dark Dreams was one of the park's attractions. It was a hotel as well as a place where nightly fantasies were played out. The first fantasy began at seven P.M. That would be right about now. She should get out of here and find the registration desk for the hotel part of the castle, but she couldn't resist taking a peek at the fantasy.

A long table with people in costumes seated around it rested on a raised platform at one end of the great hall. Passion assumed the major parts like the queen were played by the castle staff. They'd guide the fantasy. The public could buy tickets to play lesser parts. Made sense.

It only took moments for the fantasy to capture her. What could she say, heaven didn't get cable, and she was easily amused.

Mesmerized, she followed the tale. A demon was killing the castle's people. The queen's greatest hunters couldn't catch him. So the virgin offered to sacrifice herself for the good of all. She'd lure him into their clutches with her virginal beauty and purity. Hah. Passion was seeing lots of blue swirling around Ms. Untouched. Lust. Passion couldn't read her mind, but she'd bet there weren't a lot of chaste thoughts bouncing around in that head.

The wizard had been right about the virgin. If the demon was smart, he'd run like crazy. She'd eat him alive.

Of course, the dumb demon fell for the trick. She heard the virgin's not overly convincing screams coming from one of the darkened hallways along with the demon's snarls and the shouts of the hunters. A few minutes later, the virgin led the parade back into the great hall followed by the triumphant hunters surrounding the cage of the captured demon. The queen called the virgin and her hunters forward to praise them, and Passion got her first look at the demon.

A voluminous cape and hood covered him from head to toe. All she could see of him were his hands clenched around the cage's bars. Well, that was disappointing. She was all ready to be awed by the pure evil carved into his face, the demonic gleam in his eyes. Passion felt cheated.

Then he turned his head toward her. She sucked in her breath. Wow, just wow. The hood shadowed his face, but that didn't lessen the impact. Nothing said savage predator like strong slashing brows, a full mobile mouth drawn into a snarl, and amber eyes that shone with every wickedness she'd ever imagined and some she hadn't dared.

And he'd fixed his gaze on *her*. Passion looked away first. She realized her hands were shaking as she pushed a strand of hair from her face. Time to get out of here.

But even as she started to move toward the door, Passion realized something. She'd been so focused on his eyes that she'd barely noticed the color swirling around him.

Oh, no. It spread horror in a slick coat of ice over her soul. *Black*. Not one of the Deadly Sins. This went beyond those. It was rage, greed, and all the others taken to the final act. *Death*. This man was beyond redemption. She shuddered. What could she do to yank the castle from the brink with him dragging it down? Passion didn't know.

She pushed the door open but couldn't resist one look back. A thin band of blue had joined the black. Lust. Males thought about sex a lot. She wondered if he had a specific target for all that hunger, or if it was simply his normal state of being. Passion had no experience with lust. Didn't *want* any experience. She sighed. Yeah, lying was a sin too.

Once outside, she drew in a deep breath of clean night air. She'd escaped. And that's exactly how she felt even though he was the one in the cage. She'd have to toughen up if she wanted to do any good here.

But she would need some time to get used to everything. The only experience she had of the mortal plane was what she'd seen and heard in the minds of the souls she'd visited. Even though she'd been focused on easing their worries and nudging them down the path of goodness and light, she'd absorbed enough knowledge to blend in.

Blending wasn't the problem, though. Heaven didn't generate much emotion, nothing even close to what she'd felt as she stared at the demon. She'd better get a handle on her feelings fast. Ted always said that logic was what made angels superior beings, and that humans were beneath them because they were slaves to their emotions. So, no more out-of-control emotions.

Passion scanned the courtyard. People who must be arriving for the next fantasy stepped around her to reach the door. She moved out of their way. She was sure if she went back into the great hall she could find a door leading to the hotel lobby. Did she want to do that? *And take the chance of locking eyes with the demon again?*

She walked around the outside of the castle. And as she walked, she worked on her story. No luggage because the airline had lost it all. Passion was glad that at least the Council had given her a credit card and some cash. She'd have to go shopping tomorrow. Maybe buy some clothes in brighter colors. Not that she was letting the fake wizard get to her. What she looked like didn't matter as long as she did her job.

She thought again about the demon with his amber eyes and his lust and . . . Maybe she'd buy herself a few *sexy* things. She had to fit in here, not draw attention to herself. And she couldn't change evil if she couldn't get near it. Those who embraced all that was wicked would be more willing to accept her message if she dressed like them. Not that she'd enjoy dressing like a slut. *Hello, your conscience here. Run that thought past me again.* Okay, so maybe she'd enjoy it a little. There were times when Passion despaired of ever living up to heavenly standards.

Edge went up in flames for about the five hundredth time this year, or at least it felt that way. As the fake flames rose around him, he thought about the woman.

He'd felt her stare, different from the others in the hall—tentative, intrigued, with no sexual response at all. Amazing. Edge had no illusions about his effect on women. They might not know what he was, but they all reacted to the power they sensed. They always claimed his face or body or—God forbid—his mind attracted them, but it went beyond that. No matter what humans wanted to believe about themselves, the promise of violence drew them. Just look at the top-rated TV shows. Lots of blood and death. Not that he was complaining.

The women never stayed long, though. Eventually their primal instincts kicked in, the ones that recognized him as a predator. And they ran. Smart ladies.

The flames roared around him, hiding him from the celebrating queen, virgin, and assorted other idiots. With a casual flick of power, he dematerialized.

He reappeared in the dressing room. Stripping off his cape and hood, he returned to thinking about the woman. Colorless, but with the promise of beauty if someone took the time to nurture it—tall and slender with long, pale blond hair that would flow over his body like cool spring water. And she'd gazed at him from light green eyes that hid nothing. Those incredible eyes said that he was the most amazing thing she'd ever seen. How could any man resist that message?

She wasn't taking part in a fantasy. Was she staying at the hotel? He hoped she wasn't just making the rounds of the park's attractions and then going home. Time to talk with Holgarth.

Edge found the wizard being his usual snarky self with customers waiting for the next fantasy to begin. "Have a minute, Holgarth?"

The wizard turned to glare at him. Edge didn't miss the customers' relieved expressions.

"Why wouldn't I have a minute? I have nothing to do but make sure the lifeblood of this castle, its fantasies, keeps running like the well-oiled machine I've made it after years of endless toil, sacrifice, and—"

"Oh, shit." Edge started to turn away.

"But I suppose a minute won't disturb my schedule too much. What do you need?"

Edge thought about the giant squid, even now peeking over the edge of his consciousness. Nah. If he offed the wizard, they'd try to kick him out of the castle, and he wasn't ready to leave. Bad stuff would happen.

"There was a woman watching the fantasy. Tall, long blond hair—"

"I offered her the part of the lowly maiden, but she wasn't interested." Holgarth's expression turned sly. "It was too far beneath her, I think. She's more than she appears."

"Explain." Edge never underestimated the wizard's shrewdness.

"Just a feeling." He shrugged. "She seemed confused by everything that was going on, but I sensed a purpose in her. I don't think she was a casual visitor to the castle." Holgarth looked thoughtful. "There was something about the way she looked at you, as though she'd never seen anything like you in her life." The tiny twitch of his lips was his version of a wide grin. "And of course she hadn't."

"Did she say where she was going?"

"No." Holgarth was already turning back to his cowed customers. "You've had your minute. I now have to choose the shining hero who will slay the dragon in the next fantasy." He swept his possible hero candidates with a contemptuous stare. "Where is St. George, or even Harry Potter when you need them?"

Edge snorted his disgust at Holgarth's lack of helpful information and headed for the door leading to the hotel lobby. Once in the lobby, he glanced around. She wasn't there, so he walked to the registration desk.

"Who checked in today?" This was a long shot. If she *was* a guest, she could've checked in days ago. The only thing he had going for him was the size of the hotel. The castle didn't have as many rooms as a normal hotel, so there wouldn't be that many guests arriving on any given day. But she might not even be staying in the hotel, in which case he was screwed.

And when did she become so important? Not important, just an interesting side trip. He needed something to break up his routine, and women didn't usually catch his interest. It had been so many years . . . He shook the thought away to concentrate on Bill's answer.

"Only a few new guests. A middle-aged couple, a guy here for the fishing tournament, and a woman who checked in a little while ago."

"The woman. How old?"

"Twenties, long blond hair—"

"What room?" The hunter in him stirred.

"One-ten. No luggage. She said the airline lost her bags."

"Name?"

The clerk grinned. "Passion McBride."

Edge returned his grin before moving away. More and more fascinating. Who named their kid Passion? No luggage. He checked his watch. Still early enough for her to be up. He stopped in the lobby store that carried clothing and bought a few things. Then he headed for the elevator, faster but not as authentic as the winding stone staircase in the great hall.

Once in front of her door, he knocked and waited.

She opened the door and began speaking before she even looked at him. "I didn't call for . . ." Then she saw him.

Edge watched her eyes widen and her lips part as she stared. Shock became her. She looked beautiful, vulnerable, and tempting all at once. If he leaned forward and put his mouth over those full lips, she'd really have something to be stunned about.

He controlled himself. First he'd slip into her mind to see if there was anything he needed to know. But as he reached for her thoughts, he slammed into a solid wall of *no*. What the . . . ? Humans couldn't deny him, even when they tried. And she *was* human.

Edge narrowed his gaze on her face. Nothing in her expression hinted she was actively trying to keep him out. Strange.

"You're . . ." She spoke the word on a soft exhalation of wonder and maybe a little fear.

"Not a demon." *I'm much, much worse.* He smiled his most reassuring smile.

She didn't look reassured. "I know that." Her gaze dropped to the bag he held.

"I'm Edge. I help manage the Castle of Dark Dreams when I'm not bringing death and destruction to the locals." Truer than she'd ever know.

"Oh." She looked surprised.

"When I checked in at the registration desk, Bill told me you'd lost your luggage. We always want our guests to have a comfortable stay, so I picked up a few things you might need tonight." He held out the bag.

"Thank you." She smiled as she accepted his offering.

There were smiles, and then there were *smiles*. Edge had seen some of the best over thousands of years—sexy, innocent, calculating, and his very favorite, the you'll-die-happy ones. Passion McBride's smile *was* the best. It was innocence wedded to knowing, sensuality wrapped in unlimited possibilities.

He wanted everything that went with that smile. Just for a night. Because that's how long his interest usually lasted. Besides, the few times he *had* hung around for more than a night, things had ended badly. He'd learned his lesson.

She glanced into the bag. "A nightgown, robe, slippers, and toiletries. You're a lifesaver."

When she looked up, her smile had warmed and some of the shock had left her eyes. But not all of it.

"I have about an hour before I do my second fantasy. I'm hungry. Bet you are too. Let's go down to the restaurant, and I'll buy us dinner." He tried to look nonthreatening, a lot tougher than looking demonic.

Now would be when she'd say she was married, or that she didn't go anywhere with men who scared her witless. Because he *was* frightening her. He could see the fear resting right beneath the shock. Interesting. Women never sensed his threat until further into a relationship. Not that a marriage or her terror meant anything to him. Nothing much had mattered to him for a very long time.

"Why?" Her question was straightforward.

He studied her before answering. No guile in her eyes. She wasn't fishing for a compliment. Edge thought about lying, but for whatever reason told her the truth. "You interested me when I saw you watching the fantasy. There was something different about you. I like different."

She looked horrified. "No, I'm not different. I'm just like everyone else. Do you really think I look different?"

Okay, this was weird. "Hey, if you say you're ordinary, then you're ordinary. I'd still like to buy you dinner."

She seemed to relax a little. "I guess I could eat something." She nodded. "I'm Passion. You can tell me about your job at the castle over dinner."

He'd rather impress her with his *real* job, but he had a

feeling her "ordinary" human mind would explode from that particular disclosure. He didn't want to lose her that quickly.

A few minutes later, they were seated in the restaurant. He waited impatiently while the waitress took their orders before asking his first question. "So what brings you to Galveston and the Castle of Dark Dreams?"

She glanced past him out the window with its view of the Gulf of Mexico. "I've had lots of stress in my life lately. I wanted to spend a few weeks relaxing someplace with a water view. And castles fascinate me. So this is perfect." She offered him a quick smile before looking away again.

A lie. She really needed to work on her technique. Avoiding eye contact was a dead giveaway. He was immediately intrigued again. Why would she want to keep her real reason for being here secret? Cheating on her husband? Somehow he didn't think so.

As though she knew what he was thinking, she looked directly at him. "My turn to ask a question. Why have you allowed darkness to take you?"

2

Uh-oh. Passion watched Edge's gaze sharpen. Her question had just popped out. She was too impulsive. Thoughts became words with no waiting period between them. Not smart in a place where evil walked. She was human, and she could die.

As for the evil . . . Passion knew it stared across the table at her. She didn't need any color coding to tell her that. It was there in the wicked slant of his lips and the layered secrets hidden in those amber eyes. And it fascinated her more than was safe if she ever intended to return home.

"Why would you think darkness has taken me?" He leaned forward, and a few strands of his tawny hair fell across his eye.

Impatiently, he raked them back with fingers that seemed too long and elegant to belong to a man as dangerous as she suspected he was. *All the better to wrap around your neck.* His smile mocked even the idea that he was wicked, but his eyes looked wary.

And that wasn't good. Passion needed everyone in the

castle to see her as clueless and nonthreatening. "Nothing, really. Just a feeling. I guess seeing you as a demon affected me more than I realized." She shrugged. "But feelings don't mean much, do they?"

He seemed to relax. "Glad you don't take them too seriously, because I'm a pretty laid-back and happy guy. A *good* guy."

Right. He was also a big fat liar. She could sense the tension and need for violence surging just below the surface. What *was* he? Because he sure wasn't human. She might be missing her usual powers, but her instincts never failed her.

Everything about him was just *more*. He wore a touch-and-you-*will*-get-burned warning any woman would recognize. The blond strands in his hair shone beneath the restaurant's dim lighting. Thick, and looking so soft she wanted to reach out and . . . No, definitely wasn't going there. Anyway, his hair almost brushed his shoulders and framed a face that hadn't lost any of its savage beauty since she first saw it.

And his eyes shouted *other*. She sensed too many years filled with too many experiences for any human lifetime.

She would've gone on to catalogue the high points of his body, but the tattoo on one powerful bicep snagged her attention. The sleeve of his T-shirt revealed half of what looked like . . . "Is that the grim reaper on your arm?"

Edge pulled up his sleeve so she could see the whole thing. "I like the symbolism—hooded, scary guy coming to cut your life short with that crazy scythe. I know most images of him show a skull inside the hood. But I like this better. You can't see a face, just a black hole. The unknown terrifies people. What do you think? Would you want to stare into death's eyes?" He seemed serious.

"Not particularly." Weird question. She'd swear he looked disappointed by her answer. Probably liked adventurous women, the ones who jumped out of planes or climbed mountains. Too bad she couldn't tell him exactly how adventurous she was.

The waitress brought their food, saving Passion from any further discussions of death as she concentrated on her meal. Passion loved eating anything with lots of flavor, not something she got at home. She'd eat even if she wasn't hungry just to experience the flavors. Guess that made her a glutton. She glanced down to make sure no orange was swirling around her.

And as she ate, she puzzled over her job here. What did the Council expect from her? She wasn't one of the avenging angels, so they didn't want her to eliminate anyone. A relief, because the thought of destroying Edge made her . . . uncomfortable. So *what*? Talk him down from where he perched on his evil ledge? Didn't think *that* was going to happen. Maybe if she—

"I don't mean to interfere"—a woman's voice—husky, sensual, and way too eager—"fine, so I *do* mean to interfere."

Passion looked up.

"I've been watching you. This is not an eat-your-own-weight-in-mashed-potatoes contest. You make a lumberjack look like a picky eater. Put down the fork." It was an order.

Surprised, Passion obeyed. She widened her eyes as the woman pulled out the chair next to her and sat down.

"Feel free to interrupt our meal and our *private* conversation."

Edge sounded irritated but resigned. He knew this woman.

"Your *boring* conversation. I was listening." The woman didn't apologize to Edge.

"Do you know how amazing you are?" The woman's eyes shone with wonder as she studied Passion. "You're the perfect blank canvas. I can paint a masterpiece on you."

Passion suspected an insult in there somewhere, but she was too busy staring at the woman to worry about it. Talk about painting a masterpiece. Passion had always wondered why lust was blue. Anything connected with sex should be a hot color. This woman was painted in every shade of sensuality anyone could imagine. Long red hair, sexy amber eyes, bloodred nails . . .

Wait, she had eyes the exact same shade as Edge's eyes. An unusual color. "Are you two related?"

Edge narrowed his eyes at the exact same moment the woman widened hers. What had she said wrong?

"What makes you think we're related?" Edge sounded indifferent to whatever she might say, but his white-knuckled grip on his glass told a different story.

"You have the same color eyes, and I've never seen that exact shade of amber before."

The woman laughed. "Do you believe in coincidences?"

Passion didn't, but she kept her mouth shut.

"Edge and I are just good friends."

Passion glanced from one to the other. The way they avoided each other's gazes hinted at something else. Love? Hate? She couldn't tell. Interesting. *Disturbing.* And she didn't have a clue why any relationship they might have should bother her.

"Oh, and I'm Sparkle Stardust. I own Live the Fantasy." She held up her hand. "Before you ask, I chose my name. I'm just not a Susie Smith kind of person." Her smile was friendly and open, promising that they could have all kinds of fun together.

Then why did Passion want to make a run for the door? She forced herself to stay in her seat and concentrate instead on the swirls of violet and yellow wrapped around Sparkle. Greed and pride. Strange, no sign of lust. Whatever Edge and Sparkle shared, it wasn't sexual. At least not at this moment. The thought perked her right up.

That worried her. If she expected to fix whatever was wrong here, she had to stay emotionally detached. Only no one had explained how to turn off her feelings.

"Passion's an unusual name." Sparkle leaned forward. "I absolutely love it."

Startled, Passion yanked herself back to the business at hand—to find out what was going on in the castle and then to stop it. "My parents loved strange names." The truth? The Council frowned on too many personal freedoms, but they did allow the angels to choose their own names. Passion had chosen one she knew would drive them crazy.

"You're staying at the castle?" Sparkle studied her nails. "The color's starting to chip. Damn."

"For a few weeks."

When Sparkle looked up from her nails, her eyes held a manic gleam. What was that about? Okay, Passion was outta here. The only person who'd given off normal vibes in this place was Bill at the registration desk. She needed to get out of the castle for a few minutes and clear her head before going back to her room to map her strategy. Once away from Edge and Sparkle, maybe she'd get her perspective back and realize she was just overreacting to everything. But she didn't think so.

Besides, there was no real reason to stay, because she wouldn't be getting any more information from Edge. He kept staring up at the exposed beams that crisscrossed the restaurant's ceiling. She glanced up, trying to see what had caught his attention. But shadows hid whatever it was. Sparkle was staring too, and she didn't look happy about what she saw.

Anger was in every line of Edge's tense body. And all that fury seemed centered on whatever crouched in the shadows above them. Not a mouse. Something bigger, more dangerous. Okay, that was stupid. Nothing was up there. She hoped being human wasn't making her paranoid.

"I think I'll go for a short walk and then get to bed early. It's been a long day." She pushed her chair back and stood. "It was great meeting both of you." Passion smiled as she looked at Edge. "Thanks for the meal."

He returned her gaze. The coldness in his stare froze her smile in place. She took a deep breath. That look wasn't for her. She sensed it was for whatever lived in those rafters. And what could that possibly be? Her paranoia was alive and well.

Sparkle waved. "Bill told me you'd lost your luggage. I'll have a surprise for you in the morning."

Secret joy filled Sparkle's eyes, and foreboding touched Passion. *Crap.* Vulgar but not a curse. She needed the real thing right now. *Damn it to hell.* There, that felt better.

She hurried from the restaurant, and she could feel Sparkle's stare drilling into her back the entire way. Passion quickly crossed the hotel lobby and didn't breathe easily until she stepped outside.

A cool November breeze revived her confidence. There wouldn't be anything here she couldn't handle. All she had to do was to find the emotional trigger for each troubled person and use it to convince him, her, or it that evil wasn't the best career path. *What about the irredeemable one? What can you do with* him? She didn't know.

Passion stared across the road separating the castle from the Gulf of Mexico. Light from the full moon gleamed on the surf rolling onto the beach. It soothed her on a soul-deep level, something her home never did. *Don't get too attached. This isn't forever.* And of course she didn't want it to be.

"Angels lose their wings here, babe. I have a whole collection of them."

Passion's heart pole-vaulted into her throat. Who was in her head? She spun in a complete circle. No one. She looked up. Nothing. She glanced down.

A big gray cat sat a few feet away from her, watching her from unblinking amber eyes that gleamed with feline superiority. Just a cat. Her gaze swept past the cat, searching for someone powerful enough to get into her head.

"Yo, back up. Just *a cat?"*

What the . . . ? Passion tried to regroup. Some kind of shape-shifter? Powerful. Wow, all kinds of colors whipped around him. He pretty much had the sin market cornered— greed, sloth, pride, and the always popular gluttony. But those sins she could handle. It was the black swirling in the background that worried her. Like Edge, he was irredeemable. She didn't even want to think about what he'd done to earn the big black.

She stared at the cat, widening her eyes and trying for the kind of shocked expression a human would have. "No. You're not real. A cat can't talk in my head." Did she look terrified, barely able to stand? Would a human scream? She considered the most effective reaction even as she reinforced the wall surrounding her thoughts.

"Cut the crap. The wall isn't working. You can't keep me out." The cat stood, stretched, and padded over to wind itself around her legs. *"Come on, sweetie, tell me why you're here. And why are you in human form? Hey, if it's any comfort, you almost fooled me."*

Giant whoop. Almost didn't count. "Who are you?" *And how did you recognize me when no one else did?*

"Ganymede." He stared up at her. *"And I recognized you because I'm just that good. Nothing gets past me."*

"What are you?" She glanced behind her. Could she make it back to the hotel if he decided angels weren't welcome here?

"You're safe with me. They took your powers away, didn't they? The bastards. Why? What did you do? Must've been bad for them to kick you out." His big amber eyes glowed with his need to know.

"You first." She backed a few steps toward the hotel. Passion didn't for a minute think she was safe with him.

Ganymede kept pace with her. *"I'm the cosmic trouble-maker in charge of chaos. Used to do the big stuff—massive storms, meteor strikes, all kinds of planet-altering disasters . . ."* He flattened his ears as his tail whipped back and forth. *"Then the Big Boss grounded me. Thought I was out of control. Now I have to stick with the smaller stuff. Messing with humans doesn't give me much of a rush, but you take what you can get."* His eyes got that sneaky-cat look. *"Sometimes I cheat when the Big Boss isn't looking, though. Gotta stay in shape in case he ever turns me loose again."*

Passion knew her mouth was hanging open. Cosmic troublemaker? Why hadn't anyone told her about him? "I never heard of you. Are there others like you? And why did you even tell me this stuff?" Uh-oh. The obvious answer was that she wouldn't live long enough to pass on what she'd learned.

His cat eyes gleamed in the darkness. *"Yeah, there're more like me. Don't know why you never heard of us. That's just weird."*

Something dark and threatening slid over her. She shivered.

"I can tell you all this because you won't pass it on. I'll know if you try." He sat down and began to wash his face with one gray paw. *"I sense you're a survivor. You won't survive if you blab. Simple."* Finished with his grooming, he returned to studying her. *"And I can reach you anywhere. Got it? Anywhere."*

Was this why the Council had sent her here? Did they know about these cosmic troublemakers? But why send *her*? Without her powers, she was pretty much helpless against this kind of evil.

She'd ask them directly, but none of the angels were allowed to meet the Council members. Archangel Ted passed on all of their messages.

She stared into the cat's eyes as the silence stretched and stretched until she expected to hear it snap. Wait. The cat's eyes . . . "Your eyes are the same color as Sparkle's and Edge's." What were the chances?

"Give the lady a Snickers bar. I'll leave it to you to figure out." He turned away from her. Then he paused. *"Just for your info, I take bribes. Ice cream, chips, and cookies will buy lots of forgiveness."* He padded toward the castle.

"Wait. I thought you wanted to know about me." Not that she wanted to tell him, but she needed lines of communication if she were to have any chance of clearing evil from this place.

He ignored her. She watched him disappear around the side of the castle.

"Well, hell." Passion felt no guilt over the curse. The situation called for it. Not here one day and a fat cat had blown her cover.

Passion thought about the cat's eyes, about Sparkle's and Edge's eyes. She widened her own eyes. Oh, no. Were they all cosmic troublemakers? Who had set her up for this? She wasn't qualified to deal with new evil entities.

Clenching her fists, she closed her eyes. "Someone had better get their ass down here to help me. This isn't punishment, it's murder. Because you know damn well I'm human and the evil here isn't the ordinary kind. If you want me dead, just say so to my face."

"I'm here, I'm here. Jeez, I'm so excited. I get to help you. Where're the bad guys? Are they ugly, slimy, and repulsive? Oh, and I have to remind you that 'hell' and 'damn' qualify as curses. 'Ass' is just an ugly, ugly word."

No, no, no! Passion opened her eyes and slowly turned.

"Hope." She was dead.

3

Edge didn't like the look in Sparkle's eyes. He'd seen that hungry, eager shine before. "Leave her alone. Don't you have other things to do?"

Sparkle seemed reluctant to pull her gaze from the door Passion had disappeared through. "Other things to do?" She sighed and transferred her attention to him. "Like keeping you and Mede from tearing each other apart along with half of Texas?"

"Trying to make me feel guilty?" He glanced up at the empty beam above them where Ganymede had crouched a few minutes ago. He'd disappeared right after Passion left. "Not working. Haven't felt guilt for thousands of years." So many memories, poking and prodding at him, insisting that he pay attention. But every time they tried to surface, he buried them under a few more layers of denial. Remorse was a weakness, an emotion he couldn't afford in his job. "And I'm okay with leaving Texas in one piece as long as I get a shot at that bastard."

His hatred for the other cosmic troublemaker rose on a

wave of red that pushed at his control, roared its demand that he kill, and scared the crap out of him.

Edge had walked the earth as a destroyer for tens of thousands of years. But he never killed in a mindless rage. He prided himself on his coldness, his methodical completion of each job. Emotion never entered into it, *couldn't* enter into it. This time it did.

"What's wrong with you?" Worry darkened her eyes. "I know you've never liked Mede, but suddenly I'm sensing real hatred. Did I miss something?"

"He's an arrogant son of a bitch."

Sparkle returned her attention to her nails. "See, something in common. Work with it. Bond over all that male ego."

"You don't get it." *He* didn't get it, but he wasn't about to discuss his unease with the queen of emotional manipulation. She'd enjoy it too much.

"Maybe not, but I do know that if war breaks out between you guys, the Big Boss will step in." She glanced at him and then looked away. "I don't want to lose either of you."

Because you love Ganymede. Edge would never understand that. *Never.* The chaos bringer wasn't any more lovable than he was, and he didn't fool himself about that. Women might be drawn to Edge's looks, but it didn't take long for them to realize that loving him would be like trying to sink their teeth into a frozen block of ice cream. The pleasure wasn't worth the pain.

"I need some fresh air." He wanted to see what Ganymede was up to.

"Keep the damage away from the castle." Sparkle waved down a waiter. "I need a drink."

Edge didn't breathe easily until he was outside. Sparkle was the cosmic troublemaker in charge of all things sexual—not a position that called for statements that ended in catastrophic ruin and death—but she wielded a mean payback when someone crossed her. He'd never underestimate her power.

Ganymede, in his gray-cat form, sat on the edge of the seawall looking out over the Gulf. Edge ruthlessly stomped on his sense of relief that Passion wasn't with him. He strode across Seawall Boulevard to join the cat.

"Did you talk to her?" Of course he had. Ganymede wouldn't miss the chance to stick his whiskered nose into anyone's business.

The cat didn't look at him. *"Yeah. Interesting."*

"Interesting how?" Edge was instantly suspicious.

"Just . . . interesting."

Ganymede's voice in his mind had an I-know-something-you-don't purr to it. Cryptic jerk. "Did you get into her head?"

"Of course." The cat finally turned his gaze on Edge. *"Did you?"*

Edge narrowed his eyes, wishing he could splatter the dumb shit all over his precious castle.

Cats weren't supposed to be able to smile. Didn't have the facial muscles for it. But damned if Ganymede didn't have a triumphant grin pasted across his furry face.

"You didn't." He gave a cat shrug. *"Hey, some of us have talent, some don't."*

Edge hung on to his temper. Barely. "What did you find out?"

Ganymede turned his attention back to the Gulf. *"Don't think I'll share that until I figure out what to do about it."*

He joined the cat in staring at the waves rolling onto the beach. "You know how much I want to kill you right now?"

"Yeah, I feel your hate. Me, I don't have time for that shit. All I want to do is destroy . . . everything. The need's been getting worse each day."

"Why?"

Ganymede washed his face with one gray paw. *"Chaos is my thing, but I've always controlled it. This time, not so much. It's like something in my head wants to break out and tear Galveston apart. Never felt anything like it."* He paused to stare at Edge. *"What's happening?"*

Edge shrugged. "Someone's messing with us?" Funny that he could talk rationally with Ganymede about this while he still burned to kill him.

"No one's that powerful."

Nothing wrong with Ganymede's sense of self.

"Sparkle wants this to be a long-distance thing. No rubble littering the castle." He clenched his fists as he gathered his power to him.

"Got it. Whatever my honeyfluff wants. But I'm either going to do some heavy damage or explode, so I'll just have to . . ." Ganymede's voice faded away as he stared fixedly at nothing.

"Same here." Edge's need to kill almost choked him.

Suddenly, Ganymede seemed a little less tense. *"Somewhere in the Himalayas, a mountain evaporated. Must be all that global warming. Jeez, that felt good."*

"And somewhere in Colombia, a drug lord died." The Big Boss hadn't ordered the hit, but Edge figured that in this case he'd be okay with some freelancing.

"The San Andreas Fault just shook her booty." Ganymede looked almost relaxed. *"Okay, I can handle my destroy-it-all obsession for a while longer. But if this crap keeps escalating, these little pressure releases won't work anymore."*

Edge closed his eyes. "Almost there. Maybe something more challenging will . . ." His eyes popped open. "Damn, that was Bain." He'd recognized his target at the last moment and pulled his punch, but he had no doubt he'd put a hurting on the demon. He raked his fingers through his hair. "I figured any demon would work and didn't check for ID."

Ganymede laughed. *"Hey, maybe I won't have to kill you after all. Bain will do it for me."* He was still chuckling as Edge started to walk away.

"Got one more thing to say to you, Finis."

Edge froze. Ganymede had used his real name. *Finis.* The end. The Big Boss had named him, and it fit his job description. Edge hated the name, and Ganymede knew it.

"You'll never be my equal. You know why?" Ganymede

didn't wait for an answer. *"Chaos bringer is who I am. It's my whole existence. Death is just a job to you. That's all it'll ever be. You'll never know what it's really like to live the dream, sucker."*

Edge didn't turn to look at Ganymede. If he did, he might do something that would piss Sparkle off enough for her to order him from the castle.

He decided to slip through the restaurant's kitchen entrance to save time. He was late for his next fantasy, and Holgarth believed the show must go on with or without one of the major players. Besides, Edge didn't want to meet anyone who would want to stop and talk. He had things on his mind.

Ganymede's ego wouldn't allow him to believe that anyone could be powerful enough to influence his emotions. But Edge didn't see any other explanation for his irrational hatred that had been building over the last few weeks. Right now, he was handling it. But how long before the fury took over and drove him into mindless battle? Sparkle wasn't kidding about them obliterating half of Texas if that happened.

He took a deep breath. He'd like to track down Passion so they could continue the conversation Sparkle had interrupted, but he didn't have time now. He glanced at his watch. Later than he'd thought. The fantasy had started.

He'd play the evil vampire in this one. Edge was seeing a trend here. Holgarth always cast him as the evil something in every fantasy. Sure, he'd lots of experience with the part, but just once he'd like to be the hero.

You're not hero material. Couldn't deny that. He headed toward the dressing room for his vampire outfit.

"We'll share your room. It'll be fun. Just us girls, doing our nails while we plot the overthrow of the unspeakable evil polluting the castle." She frowned. "Is caring about my nails pride?" She answered her own question. "Arch-angel Ted won't be able to see my nails. Besides, it's just this once." Hope was almost bouncing with enthusiasm. "I'm so excited. I can't see the colors of sin like you, so you'll have to point me in the right direction. But I still have my powers, so once you identify the wicked ones, I can delete their files permanently. I can—"

Passion closed her eyes for a moment, trying to center herself before opening them again. Hope was the heavenly executive secretary for Ted. She had access to everyone's files. If she deleted your file, you were dead to the Supreme Being, didn't exist, no paradise for you. Not that heaven was much of a blast in her opinion. But that was just her.

"No, you can't." Someone upstairs hated her. Passion didn't think she'd survive even a week with Hope as her partner. "We're not avenging angels. We're here to observe. Then we try to resolve things peacefully."

It was what Ted had trained her to do. He'd come to her bland and boring cubicle each morning and hand her a list of souls in need of saving. When he left, she'd ease into their minds, listen and observe, and then try to gently urge them along the path that Ted had specified. She'd never tell him, but sometimes Ted's paths seemed a little weird. But what did she know?

"Oh." Hope looked disappointed. "I don't think that will work, Passion. True evil doesn't respond to kindness."

"And you know this how?" Both Passion and Hope were pretty clueless when it came to any hands-on experience. Sure, they'd observed humans forever, and at least Passion had spent every working hour in their minds. But they'd never actually interacted with anyone here on the mortal plane.

Hope blinked at her. "Everyone knows that."

"Right." Passion headed for the great hall. She couldn't stand the thought of going back to her room with Hope tagging along and . . .

"Besides, from what Archangel Ted told me, there are lots of nonhumans here. And everyone knows that all non-humans are evil." Hope thought about that for a moment. "Except for us, of course."

Couldn't argue with that logic. Passion wanted to say it out loud, but sarcasm would wing its way right over Hope's head of tousled dark hair. Wasted effort. Ted frowned on sarcasm, so Hope couldn't appreciate the finer nuances of it. Passion thought sarcasm made a fine verbal weapon.

Passion stopped inside the great hall to look around. She needed a few minutes away from Hope to think. She'd even sign up for a fantasy if it gave her some moments free of Hope's eternal happiness. "They act out fantasies here. Watch, but don't talk with anyone."

Hope paused to study her. "You know, I don't get you. You called for help from above, and now that I'm here you act as though you don't need me."

Passion didn't miss the hurt in Hope's voice and immediately felt guilty. "I do need you. But we can't rush into anything. We have to study the situation before acting."

Hope thought about that and then nodded. "Okay, that makes sense." She smiled before turning to glance around her. "I think I'll take a look around, maybe catch some evildoers in the act."

"You do that," Passion muttered as she watched Hope wander away. Once she scanned the room to make sure Sparkle wasn't there, she allowed herself to relax. She'd buy a ticket for the next fantasy. That would give her about a half hour of freedom.

Buying the ticket was easy; dealing with Holgarth wasn't.

"I want to be the queen's lowly maiden." That wouldn't require much effort on her part, and she'd have time to catch her breath and make some plans.

"Absolutely not." Holgarth pursed his thin lips. "I have a wonderful part for you. You'll be the evil vampire's equally evil bloodsucking mate."

She frowned. "The queen's lowly maiden was good enough for me last time."

"That's because it was the only remaining part." The wizard straightened his pointed hat that had a tendency to slide to the left. "One should always aim as high as one is able." He offered her a contemptuous sniff. "The vampire's mate is probably beyond your meager acting ability, but since it's a brand-new part, you have no expectations to live up to."

"Why do you hate me?" *And give me one good reason why I shouldn't . . .* Passion closed her eyes, took a deep breath, and then opened them again. Violence was never the answer.

Holgarth raised one brow. Probably his version of a shocked gasp.

"I don't hate you. I treat everyone with equal disdain. Few deserve anything more. Now do you want the part?"

She didn't, but he'd insulted her acting talent. Pride was one of the deadly seven, but maybe just this once she could get away with no one noticing. "Sure. But why choose me to be the first? I'm surprised you didn't wait until someone with real acting ability came along."

Holgarth was lugging around a formidable-looking staff, and he used it to tap out his irritation on the great hall's stone floor. "I just invented the part. And you're the first because the real evil vampire is late. I'm responsible for maintaining our schedule. The show will go on with or without Count No-Show."

He glanced at his watch. "Now, as soon as the virgin— yes, there's *always* a virgin—leaves the queen's table and climbs those dark, forbidding stairs on the other side of the hall, you'll follow her. You'll intercept her on the first landing and make some suitably frightening threats involving neck-biting and blood-guzzling. As you reach for her, the heroic captain of the guard will rush to her rescue. You'll avoid a few sword thrusts from him and then allow him to skewer you."

"The fun never ends here, does it?"

The wizard glared at her. "Sarcasm is not an attractive trait." He straightened his hat again. "You have exactly five minutes to get your costume on and be back here."

"What—"

"Black cape and pointed teeth. You're already as pale as death. Oh, you might want to slap on a long black wig. The dressing room is over there." He pointed.

In five minutes she was back thinking that hanging with Hope might not be so bad after all. With a resigned sigh, she followed the giggling virgin up the dark winding stone stairs. She kept tripping over her cape, and no way could she talk around the fake fangs.

The wide-eyed virgin waited on the first landing. Her big blue eyes narrowed considerably when she realized she wasn't getting a *True Blood* or *Vampire Diaries* hottie. Tough shit. Passion winced. Those "ugly, ugly" words were coming a lot easier.

"I'm firsty, human." *Thirsty.* Passion was thinking "thirsty" in her mind, but by the time the word squeezed around her fangs, she sounded like a cartoon character.

The virgin put her hands on her hips. "Great, a vampire with a lisp. You know, I was expecting a little more than this."

Passion decided to forego the small talk and move right to the action. She grabbed the virgin.

The virgin screeched and tried to shake her off. Passion hung on. Okay, where was the hero?

"Take your hands from her, you filthy bloodsucker."

The voice was deep and so dangerous that Passion knew before she even turned around that the hero would be sporting lots of sinful colors.

He wasn't. Passion sucked in her breath as she stared at his only color, black so dark it seemed to absorb the dim light shining from the one sconce attached to the stone wall. This man—no, not a man, something else—was not only one of the irredeemables, he was . . . Passion had a horrible suspicion she was facing evil from the depths of hell. She really hoped she was overreacting.

"Make me." Now that was dumb. Whatever he was, he terrified her. Passion had to remind herself that angels had no fear. Yeah, and who had laid that lie on all of them?

"I intend to. I'm Sir Bain, and the queen has sent me to rescue this beautiful damsel."

He cast the gaping virgin a sensual glance that curled Passion's toes, and it wasn't even aimed at her. The virgin tore herself from Passion's grasp and flung herself at her rescuer. Passion didn't blame her.

Sir Bain backed up one step, just enough to make the fair damsel miss her target and end up kneeling at his feet. It seemed an appropriate place for her to be.

Then her rescuer smiled at Passion. "Shall we settle this now?"

Okay, she understood a little of what the virgin was feeling. His smile was a flash of white in the dimness, the only light in a face dedicated to the darkest evil. He had intense blue eyes ringed by sooty lashes. And his mouth was meant to be a sexual temptation to any woman who ever wondered what pleasure a mouth could bring. To add to the unfairness of giving all those gifts to one who was unworthy, he had a beautiful face framed by long, smoky dark hair.

But Passion wasn't quite as prostrate with desire as the unfortunate virgin. She saw the hunger crouching behind all that beauty. Archangel Ted had always warned them that wickedness wore a beautiful face in order to tempt humanity, but he hadn't mentioned that it also did a pretty good job on angels too.

Strangely enough, though, she wasn't really tempted. If she had to choose her evil, she'd pick one with tawny hair and amber eyes that promised all kinds of sexual excitement. *What the heck are you thinking?* She wouldn't allow herself to be tempted. She'd do her job here and then go home.

Her thoughts, as fascinating as they were, suddenly shattered as what felt like an earthquake made the whole landing shake. Before she could even gasp, an unseen force flung Sir Bain to the floor, then picked him up and heaved him against the far wall.

Unfortunately, as he fell, he grabbed the terrified virgin

to anchor himself. So when he hit the far wall, she took the impact with him. He staggered to his feet. She didn't.

Passion froze. Even as she registered the unnatural twist to the virgin's neck, along with her blank staring eyes, something was happening to Passion too. Warmth flooded her. Not normal heat, but a burn that seemed to race through her veins and then pool in her fingertips. *Life*. The word rang in her head. *Life*. It was a pounding at her temples, a blinding light right behind her eyes, an explosion of power that almost brought her to her knees.

Without realizing it, Passion stumbled toward the woman on the floor.

"The bastard. I'll kill him for this." Sir Bain crouched beside the woman's body.

He thrummed with a fury that Passion could feel scraping at her skin, trying to push her away. On some subconscious level, she recognized the deadliness of his anger. But she wouldn't be pushed back or stopped. Not by him or anyone like him.

"Move away from her." Passion's voice seemed to come from far away.

Surprisingly, he obeyed her. He stood and looked around wildly, as though he'd find the object of his anger hiding in the shadows somewhere.

Passion crouched beside the woman. She recognized death, but so recent that her soul still remained. Passion didn't know how she knew this. The how wasn't important now.

Life. The word was thunder in her head, a battering ram crashing against the wall of her mind. She swayed, willing herself to stay conscious. She had to put her hand on the woman. It was a compulsion, one she had no weapons against. Placing her palm flat against the dead woman's chest, she felt the heat flowing from her fingertips, watched in horror as a glow built around the five contact points.

Behind her, she heard Sir Bain suck in his breath and mutter a curse. One she'd never heard before. Then the woman began to breathe. It was as simple as that. Passion stared at her neck. No longer twisted, it looked normal. The woman opened her eyes.

"What the hell happened?" She pushed her hair away from her face and scrambled to her feet before Passion could help her.

I don't know. I don't freaking know. Passion had never been so scared in her long life. Fine, so fear wasn't a part of her heavenly experience. But this, this was so weird that she wanted to race screaming from the castle, beg Archangel Ted to take her home, huddle in the darkest corner she could find, and pull forgetfulness over her head.

"You fainted. Have you eaten anything lately?"

Sir Bain's tone was calm, the voice of reason in a world that had suddenly taken a hard right turn off the normal path. This was a side road that she didn't want to explore, but she couldn't find a place wide enough for her to turn around.

"No, I guess I haven't." The virgin smoothed down her white flowing dress, and then looked at Sir Bain from under her lashes.

Didn't the idiot know she'd been *dead*? And now she wasn't. Why? How? Passion felt panic bubbling up under the surface of her false calm.

"But before you carry me back down those steps, because I still feel a little weak, I want to see you protect me against that wicked vampire."

The wicked vampire who just saved your ungrateful butt. Even if said wicked vampire didn't know how the heck she'd done it. Passion rose from her crouch. Surely Sir Bain didn't intend to carry on with the whole fantasy thing?

Evidently he did, because he drew his sword and began to stalk Passion. Guess she had to play the game. She did a little of her own stalking as she offered him a few unenthusiastic hisses.

"Looks as though you could use a little help, my lovely vampire queen."

The husky male voice warmed the sensitive skin behind

her ear and sent prickles of awareness skittering down her spine. Passion's senses recognized him before she even had time to breathe his name. "Edge."

The virgin stared at the man behind Passion. She looked conflicted. Tough choice—vampire or hero. Passion knew which she'd pick.

Guess it was time for her to say something. "Abandon hope, virgin, for Edge, the master of all the kingdom's vampires, has arrived." Fine, so Passion wasn't great at improvising.

"Ah, my lovely maiden, I can almost taste your sweet blood."

Edge's voice was warm, intoxicating, and made Passion want to lick her lips. But honestly, they had to get a new scriptwriter for these fantasies, because everyone's lines were way too hokey.

"But before I dine, I'll make sure Sir Bain never rescues another virgin. Then I'll celebrate the night with my dark queen." His soft laughter didn't bode well for Sir Bain or Passion's emotional stability.

Shock over what her glowing fingertips had done warred with her sudden need to turn around and embrace all that dark promise. She never got to think through her tangled feelings.

"You bastard." Sir Bain flung his sword aside and leaped past Passion to land on Edge. The two men fell to the floor. "Did you think I wouldn't recognize your death touch? Try to kill me, will you?"

Then things really got crazy. Sir Bain became something else. Sure, he was still beautiful, but whatever she'd sensed crouching inside him made its appearance. He seemed to grow larger, his fingers curling into claws, his eyes glowing red. He peeled back his lips to snarl at Edge, and Passion would have sworn his teeth were pointed.

But Edge had his own thing going on. Those amber eyes shone with hungry anticipation. "It was an accident, but if you want to settle it this way, let's do it."

Passion didn't get to see what happened next, because

the small landing became a sound-and-light show that seemed to shake the whole building.

She could hear faint screams coming from the great hall, but they were drowned out by the shrieks of the totally freaked virgin. Passion knew what she had to do. She couldn't stop what the two men were doing to each other, but she could save the woman.

"Come with me." Passion reached for the woman's hand.

She yanked her hand away. "I'm not going with anyone from this crazy place." Frantic, she whirled in a circle, looking for the stairs. Any stairs.

But the flashes of light and booming explosions disoriented her. She stumbled into a wall and sat down hard.

Oh, for heaven's sake. Passion didn't have time for this kind of crap. Reaching down, she hefted the woman over her shoulder and raced down the stairs toward the great hall and hopefully safety.

The virgin beat a panicked tattoo on her back. "Put me down. Put me the hell down."

Passion was gasping for breath and her legs felt wobbly by the time she reached the last step. She dumped the woman none too gently on the stone floor. "I think we're safe."

The virgin had no opinion on that. She simply sat there with a dazed expression on her face.

Suddenly, a new player moved into the shocked silence that had fallen around the great hall. The quiet made the flashes of light and wall-shaking booms even more obvious. Passion had a fleeting impression of dark hair and blue eyes before the stranger turned to rally the forces.

"I'm Dacian. I'm one of the good vampires in her majesty's kingdom." He smiled at everyone, exposing fangs that looked way too real. "As you can hear, Sir Bain and the evil vampire master are battling to the death above us." *Boom. Crash.* "Meanwhile, the evil vampire's mate is trying to kidnap our virgin so that she can drain the innocent's blood."

There were a few weak boos from the audience. The "innocent" still looked a little wonky from her experience.

"And while we await the outcome . . ." He cast a meaningful glance at Holgarth-the-snarky-wizard, who was already making his way toward the stairway. "I'll capture the vampire's mate and drag her off to the dungeon."

Oh, no. He wouldn't. Dacian moved almost too fast for her eyes to follow. He would.

Before she could even yelp her outrage, he scooped her up and whisked her into the dressing room. As he set her on her feet, she was dimly aware of the raucous laughter coming from the crowd in the great hall.

"What're they so happy about?" Passion didn't find anything funny about the whole situation.

Dacian shrugged. "Don't have a clue. There's some woman out there keeping them all happy and laughing. I'm damn glad she's here tonight. What the hell happened up there, and who're you?"

Passion tried to pull her tattered dignity together as she absently noticed the violet swirling around him. Pride. Compared to the two fighting upstairs, Dacian was practically ready for sainthood.

"I don't know what happened up there. Sir Bain was doing his thing and then something tossed him across the room." She refused to tell him about her glowing fingers. "Then Edge came along, and Sir Bain went ballistic on him."

He raised one dark brow to indicate she wasn't finished with her answers.

"I'm Passion, and all I wanted to do was to try one of your fantasies. Holgarth gave me the part of the vampire's mate. I think I'm all fantasied out for the next twenty years or so. They're too intense for me."

She looked up at him from under her lashes to see if he was buying her story. "I think I want to go up to my room now."

He'd evidently decided she wasn't important in the grand scheme of things because he nodded absently. "Sure.

Go ahead. But don't give up on the fantasies, most of them are tamer than this one was."

Ha. With all the evil nonhumans cluttering up the castle, she'd bet death and destruction had permanent reservations here. She didn't answer him as she stumbled from the room. Passion knew she should find Hope first, but all she wanted to do was collapse into bed and forget tonight.

But somewhere between the dressing room and her longed-for bed, she picked up a shadow. The gray cat paced beside her as she trudged down the long hallway to her door.

"Damn, a good fight just makes me feel tingly all over. Too bad Bain didn't rip Edge's head off."

Startled, she looked down. The cat's voice in her head still felt creepy. "You saw it? I didn't see you."

"I was hanging in the shadows. You were a little busy, so I'm not surprised you didn't notice me."

"What was really going on between those two? And why do you hate Edge so much?" Surprisingly, she found she didn't want Edge to be a hate-worthy person.

"Bain was pissed because Edge was the one who heaved him across the landing. Don't blame Bain a bit. And I hate Edge because he deserves it."

He stopped and waited while she fumbled in her pocket for the big old-fashioned key they'd given her. The hotel was into authentic.

"But since I've sort of answered your question, maybe you can answer mine."

Anything to get rid of him so she could think. "Sure."

"You're not an angel, so what are you?"

Passion dropped the key and didn't even notice as it rolled into a shadowed part of the hall. She stared. Finally, she relaxed. He was crazy, of course.

She'd use it to her own advantage, though. "Then I guess I'm just an ordinary human. You're the one who assumed I was an angel, so I played along. Aren't you supposed to humor the insane?" She widened her eyes and tried to look innocent. Passion had had lots of practice at home.

Ganymede yawned, showing sharp little teeth. *"Give me a break. You're not human."* He wore a waiting-by-a-mouse-hole-for-dinner-to-arrive look in his feline eyes. *"I think you believe you are, though. Strange. A real angel would've known about me. They all do. Think about that, sweetheart."* Then he turned and disappeared down the winding stairs. The last thing she saw was that arrogantly waving gray tail.

Sighing, she bent down to retrieve her key.

It was gone.

4

Edge picked up the key and slipped it into his pocket. Then he leaned against the wall and waited for Ganymede to leave. The cat thought he was at the top of the Big Boss's food chain. But he couldn't sense that Edge stood invisible close enough to reach out and touch Passion. Even *he* couldn't see Death coming.

Edge forgot about his contempt for Ganymede, though, in the wake of what the cat had said about Passion. Angel? Not angel? What the hell was going on? Determined to find out, he waited until Passion was crouched, searching the floor for her key, before he walked back to the top of the stairs and became visible.

"Having a problem?" He tried to sound mild and non-threatening as he walked toward her.

She gasped and rose to face him. "Where'd you come from?"

"Sorry that I startled you." He wasn't. "After Bain and I settled things, I decided you deserved an apology." He didn't overlook the flash of fear in her eyes. Not surprising. His fight with Bain had been pretty spectacular.

"Is Bain okay?" She sounded concerned.

Something primitive and violent opened its eyes and tried to uncurl inside him. He shoved the feeling aside. He had no desire for strong emotions. They could be dangerous when you wielded Death's sword. "He's fine. And yes, I'm fine too. Thanks for asking."

Passion ignored his sarcasm. "You have some explaining to do." She glanced at the floor again. "I lost my room key."

At least she didn't *sound* scared. "I have a master." Silently, he drew out his key and unlocked the door.

"So you can get in anytime you want? Wow, way to make me feel secure." She didn't try to hide her eagerness to escape him.

He kept his hand on the doorknob. "I'd like to come in for a few minutes."

She glanced up at him and then away. He sensed her need to step inside and slam the door in his face, but beneath that need was something else, something he couldn't read.

"If I let you in, I want explanations." She didn't look happy about the bargain she was proposing.

He nodded, and then he dropped his hand from the door. It had to be her decision. He wasn't sure why. It wasn't as though he couldn't force her to tell him what he wanted to know and then be on his way. Edge pushed aside the sly voice in his head that suggested he wanted more than information from her.

She sighed, opening the door so he could slip inside. She didn't close the door. "We'll make this quick because my roommate will be back any minute."

When had a roommate arrived? Male or female? She slid her fingers through her long pale hair, and he followed the motion with eyes he feared were a little too hungry.

"Okay, forget subtlety. If you try to strangle me and stuff my body under the bed, I'll scream loud enough to raise the dead." She frowned. "Forget the raise-the-dead part. No one can do that."

"If I ever tried to kill you, I'd be a lot more creative than that." He smiled. "Mind if I sit down?"

She didn't return his smile. "You don't need to sit down because you won't be here that long. Oh, and I need a new key." She paced over to the arrow slit that passed for a window and peered out into the darkness.

He sat down. She wouldn't get rid of him that easily. Leaning back in one of the easy chairs grouped in the small sitting area, he spread his legs out in front of him. It felt good to sit down after his battle with Bain. The demon couldn't take him, but Edge knew he'd be hurting for at least a few hours until his body healed. Damn hell spawn.

Passion looked ticked off that he'd planted his butt on her chair, but she didn't make a big deal about it. She returned from the window and sat down across from him. He was glad that he'd taken the time to change from his bloody costume before coming up here. No need to freak her out completely.

"Did you see what happened to the woman playing the virgin?"

What did that have to do with anything? "Nope. Afraid I was busy trying to stay alive at the time. Why?"

She shrugged. "Just wondering. Bain dragged her with him when he hit the wall. She was pretty woozy. And what the heck threw him across the landing anyway? He seemed to think you did it."

"I did. And she was fine when I left the great hall. She's already forgotten about it. Holgarth took care of her."

"From what I saw of the wizard, that's not too reassuring."

She paused for a moment, and he had the feeling she was working herself up to something.

"So you were able to heave a grown man across the landing in absentia. What are you? And what *was* that between you and Bain?"

"That was an accident, but Bain didn't give me a chance to explain. He's impulsive that way." Now for the tough part. "Ganymede said he talked to you outside."

"You talk to cats too." She didn't seem surprised.

Okay, had to be careful here. "Did he explain anything?"

Passion avoided his gaze. "He might've mentioned something. Vaguely. He wasn't too clear on the concept." Sighing, she looked back at him. "He was very clear with his threats, though. So, I'll let you introduce the subject."

Edge smiled. "Probably the term 'cosmic troublemaker' came up."

"Probably."

"Do you really want to know?" He watched her grip her full bottom lip between small white teeth. When she released her lip, the wet sheen of it almost made him groan. She was as sensual as her name, but he didn't think she had a clue about it. His body tightened. Great. Just freaking great.

"I *need* to know."

An odd wording. He shrugged. If Ganymede had already flapped his kitty lips, then who was Edge to keep the secret? Besides, the worst that could happen was she'd run screaming from the hotel. A part of him thought that might be a good thing. He didn't need sexual distractions now. But the part of his body with all the overexcited nerve endings wanted her to hang around for a while.

"Ganymede, Sparkle, and I are all cosmic trouble-makers."

She nodded. "I figured that out. Same weird eye color."

He narrowed his gaze. She was taking this a little too calmly. "We were created sometime after the primordial ooze made its appearance. We've been around a long time." He didn't actually know the when or the by-whom of it. His first memory was of being exactly as he was now. No carefree childhood for him. He popped into existence and went right to work. It still bothered him sometimes when he allowed it to.

"Why didn't I *know*?" Her frustrated mutter didn't seem aimed at him.

He didn't think she'd meant to let that slip, because if

she were human, she wouldn't be expected to know about their existence.

He decided not to point that out to her. "Each of us has a . . . talent, but we all have the same goal—to spread chaos in all its interesting forms throughout the universe." If that didn't send her sexy feet heading for the door, nothing would.

"What's your talent?" She stared unblinkingly at him.

Don't tell her. And just because he really *didn't* want her to know, *didn't* want to see the horror in her eyes, *didn't* want her to shrink from him, he told her. "I'm in charge of death." No good could ever come from her thinking kind thoughts about him, so now it would never happen.

She was good. If he wasn't watching for it, he never would have noticed her flinch, her small gasp, and the clenching of her hands in her lap. Tough lady. Or maybe just stupid. Because no one who knew what he was stuck around long.

"What about Bain? He doesn't have amber eyes, but he was looking pretty freaky there at the end." Her hand trembled as she pushed a strand of hair from her face.

"Demon."

"Oh, crap." Her soft murmur was the first obvious emotion she'd shown. "Okay, losing it here. Too much weird info at one time—cats talking in my head, cosmic troublemakers, and now a demon." She widened her eyes, injecting lots of panic into her expression.

Edge didn't believe her I'm-just-a-poor-confused-human act. She was faking it. He might not allow himself any real emotions anymore other than the inconvenient lust he was feeling now—not that lust really counted because it was merely a physical reaction—but he recognized true emotion in others. "I've answered your questions, now I have one of my own."

"What?" Wariness replaced panic in her gaze.

"I heard your conversation with Ganymede a few minutes ago. So what are *you*?"

"I'm not an angel. I. Am. Human. Ganymede is deranged." She breathed deeply and then took a sharp right turn in the conversation. "So you've killed people for thousands of years?"

"Yes."

Silence. She seemed to be waiting for him to soften his "yes," drop in a few qualifiers. He didn't.

Something moved in her gaze. Disappointment? Horror? Disgust? All of the above? He didn't give a damn what she thought of him.

"Let's get back to you and the angel thing. I might not be a Ganymede fan, but if he thinks you're not human, then you're not. He doesn't make mistakes like that."

"Why don't you like Ganymede?"

"He's an arrogant dickhead."

"Got it." She stood. "You can leave now."

He noticed that she wasn't already on her way down to the registration desk to check out. That would be the normal reaction for a human. And Ganymede was right. Over the thousands of years of his existence, he'd met a few angels. They'd all recognized him for what he was and tried to destroy him. They'd all failed. He smiled at the memories.

"You think this is funny? A normal person pays to stay at your hotel and then they're assaulted by . . . talking cats and accused of being angels? This is a hoot to you?" Anger colored her cheeks and made her eyes sparkle. "I think you and your fiends, uh, friends, need to make a group appointment at the nearest mental health facility."

He couldn't help it, he grinned. How long had it been since a human really amused and fascinated him? Edge couldn't remember. "An angry angel. Love it. You should stay mad. It's hot."

She blinked. "What?"

He waved his comment away. "Never mind." He stood. "I'll let you get some sleep." He allowed himself the pleasure of imagining her in her bed, her long pale hair spread over her pillow, her hand stroking his . . .

Okay, moment of pleasure over. He headed for the door. "I'll send someone right up with a new key."

His last glimpse of her before he closed the door behind him was of her watching him from those beautiful eyes. However, the calculating gleam in those eyes wasn't quite so gorgeous. He smiled. That was fine with him. He liked scheming women. They were never boring.

He'd only taken a few steps toward the stairs when it hit him.

The killing cold dropped him to his knees, tore at his mind with clawed fingers. *Kill Ganymede.* Each word was a steel spike pounded into his brain. This wasn't hot rage. This was an icy compulsion that froze all thought. He gasped for breath as he felt his control oozing out through the holes in his head. There had to be holes. Nothing could hurt this much unless there were holes.

Edge fought to hold on to all that he'd become over the centuries. He wouldn't regress to the ravenous beast he'd been in his early years, a mindless killer. He closed his eyes and tried to concentrate. But this time he couldn't stop the force driving him to kill, couldn't hold on to the last few strands of reason slipping away.

"Are you sick, dear?"

The woman's voice wavered with age, trembling with concern. He opened his eyes.

Very old, with a halo of white hair surrounding a face creased with wrinkles. Her eyes were shadowed by worry.

"Can I get someone to help you?"

"Get away from me." He didn't even recognize the savage snarl as his. An icy film slowly crawled across his vision as he rose to his feet. *Kill.*

Passion leaned her back against the closed door and drew in a deep calming breath. It didn't work. Panic still gripped her.

Death. How did she begin dealing with him, with any of them? She didn't handle these kinds of . . . people. She worked with the small stuff—comforting, guiding the unsure toward the right decisions. All of which she did from the safety of her home. No face-to-face confrontations, just soothing strokes and whispers into troubled minds. Troubled *human* minds. She did *not* take on the physical manifestation of death. Passion didn't have the power to go mano a mano with Edge or Ganymede. Right now, she didn't have *any* power.

For a moment, an image of the virgin lying on the landing, her neck twisted at an impossible angle, flashed in her memory. No, she hadn't brought her back to life. That was ridiculous. The woman obviously hadn't been dead. With only her human senses, Passion couldn't be sure about when someone was really gone. She shoved the image aside.

She felt nauseous. Not a physical reaction she'd ever experienced before. Confusion and fear tore her stomach into tasty bits for her personal demons to snack on. They took time out from their partying to remind her that she was way out of her league here, and to suggest that if Ted wanted to get rid of her—after all, she was a major thorn in his mighty butt—this would be an excellent way to do it.

What were her options? She could try to do what she was sent here to do—work with her limited skills to turn those at the castle away from evil and let Hope send nightly reports back to home base. Or . . . she could fill Hope in on the full scope of the horror here and have her send for the avenging angels.

Passion would be off the hook. The avenging angels would destroy Edge, Ganymede, and Bain—maybe Sparkle could be saved—and that would be that.

A tiny cowardly voice in her mind shouted, "Let's hear it for the avenging angels." Her boring cubicle waiting back in her boring office with her boring boss waiting to give her more boring assignments was looking pretty good right now.

But it felt wrong on a whole bunch of levels. She'd be branded a failure, not able to cope with her assignment, a whiner who ran for help at the first sign of trouble.

Whatshouldshedo, whatshouldshedo, whatshouldshedo—

Passion closed her eyes and fought back her rising hysteria.

One truth rose above her mental chaos. She didn't want to see Edge destroyed, and that didn't make a bit of sense. He was an abomination, but . . . She opened her eyes. She felt like she was drowning in emotions after an existence without any. Is this what she'd wanted to experience as a human? It wasn't as much fun as she'd expected.

The pounding on her door interrupted her thoughts. Someone couldn't be here with her key that quickly. Turning, she opened the door.

An old woman stood with her fist raised, ready to start pounding again. "Please, get help. There's something wrong with that man." She fumbled with her purse. "I'm so upset that I can't find my cell phone to do it myself."

Passion looked past the woman to see Edge striding toward the stairs. "Edge?"

He paused, and then slowly turned to face her.

She instinctively stepped back. What stared at her had no relation to the man who'd just left her room. His eyes glowed, and Death lived in his stare. No recognition showed in those eyes.

"What happened?" Passion was proud that her voice didn't shake. "Where are you going?"

Those sensual lips lifted in a smile so evil it made her gasp.

"To kill Ganymede." Turning away, he disappeared down the stairs.

Ohmigod. She had to stop him. Passion rushed out into the hallway. "No. Wait. Don't do this." Panicked, she looked around. The old woman still stood by her door. "Go into my room and call the desk. Tell them to get . . ." Who? She couldn't ask them to page the cat. "Never mind."

The woman looked confused and frightened, but Passion couldn't worry about her now.

She raced down the stairs and into the great hall. Then she searched frantically among the milling crowd for someone she recognized. There, by the courtyard door. Dacian, Holgarth, and Hope stood talking. For once the other angel didn't look happy. Passion pushed her way through the costumed actors to reach them.

"Where's Ganymede and Edge? We have—"

"What we *have* is a situation." Holgarth pursed his thin lips. "Our stand-up comedian here"—he offered Hope a toxic glare—"made everyone laugh so hard that one of our customers flung back his head and cracked it on the stone wall. The ambulance just left. As soon as he wakes up, I'm sure the first words out of his mouth will be, 'Call my lawyer.' And then to end a perfect evening, my evil vampire hasn't shown up. Again." He slanted a speculative glance at Passion. "Perhaps you'd care to reprise your role as the vampire's evil mate? Of course, you'll have to make sure nothing unfortunate happens this time."

"Me?" She bit back her retort. Well, almost. "I hated the fantasy. Besides, it doesn't matter now. *You* play the evil vampire's mate. The wig is in the dressing room."

Holgarth looked as though she'd stabbed him in his shriveled little heart. Too bad.

There went her charity. She wondered what angelic quality she'd shed next.

"Edge is looking for Ganymede. He says he's going to kill him. We have to find Ganymede first. Where is he?" Her heart jackhammered in her chest, fear wrapped sharp fingers around her throat and squeezed. She ignored Hope's gasp.

Angels were supposed to be impartial, unemotional. *You. Are. A. Failure.* She wasn't even close to impartial. Passion was terrified for Edge. Not that she wanted to see Ganymede die, but dread for him wasn't what made it hard for her to breathe right now.

Dacian and Holgarth exchanged glances, and then Dacian spoke. "I'll search." He flung open the courtyard door and was gone.

That wasn't helpful. She wanted to search too, but she needed someplace to start. Passion skewered Holgarth with her fiercest glare, which probably wasn't very fierce. She'd have to practice her human facial expressions. *"Where?"*

"Murder? We have to stop it. Uh, who is Edge?" Hope looked bewildered but energized.

The wizard studied Passion for a moment, and then seemed to come to a decision. "Sparkle will be in her candy store this time of night. Ganymede might be there. Sweet Indulgence is on the right as you leave the park."

Passion turned to follow Dacian.

Holgarth put his hand on her arm, and the surge of power rippling across her skin surprised her. Maybe there was more to him than just some snarky old actor wearing a wizard costume.

"If they fight, run as fast as you can, as far as you can." He dropped his hand from her arm.

Well, that sounded ominous. Passion turned away from him and flung herself out the still-open door. She ran toward the park's entrance. Hope was right on her heels.

"It would be great if you explained things to me. We're supposed to be partners." Hope was breathing hard between each word. "And you were pretty ugly to Holgarth. I don't think Archangel Ted would—"

"Screw Ted. We have to stop them from killing each other."

Hope was either struck speechless by the ferocity of Passion's attack on Ted or she didn't have any breath left, because she didn't say anything else.

Passion was sucking wind by the time she raced out of the park and saw the sign for Sweet Indulgence. If she stayed here long, she'd have to work out. Only the avenging angels did much to stay in shape.

Passion stopped in front of the shop's door, and a few seconds later, Hope joined her. Thankfully, Hope was too busy gulping air to say anything.

Someone had drawn a shade over the glass door and put a CLOSED sign up. But a light was on inside, and Passion could hear voices. She tried to listen past her labored breathing.

A shrill scream from inside reached her. Female. Passion didn't try to analyze the tone. A scream was a scream. Suddenly, Dacian appeared beside her. She couldn't stop her startled yelp. How did he move that silently?

"Edge isn't anywhere in the castle."

"Someone inside just screamed." She raised her hand to ring the bell.

"Too slow." Dacian narrowed his gaze on the door, and it exploded inward.

Whoa. Passion took an involuntary step back. Hope found enough breath to shriek. Luckily, no one else was on the street.

Passion followed Dacian into the store and then froze. Oh, crap.

Sparkle was sprawled across a large display counter. Chocolates, jelly beans, and gummy bears, along with her four-inch stilettos, littered the floor. Her long red hair spread like flame across the counter. She didn't look frightened. She looked . . .

This was embarrassing. Passion shifted her attention to the man who'd been leaning over Sparkle. He'd straightened to stare at them.

Tall, shirtless, muscular with broad shoulders, he wore a scowl that made her want to turn and slink away. She got an impression of worn jeans tucked into calf-high boots and a black T-shirt lying on the floor at his feet.

She widened her eyes as she took a good look at his face. Wow, beautiful but frightening. The face of a fallen angel, not that she'd ever seen one. And that face was framed by thick blond hair that skimmed his shoulders. Wait, there was something about his eyes . . . But Passion's attention wandered from his eyes as she got a look at the blackness swirling around him. Another irredeemable one? What were the chances of there being so many in one spot?

"What the hell do you think you're doing?" His voice suggested that bad things happened to people who blew in his door.

Dacian raked his fingers through his dark hair. "Sorry,

Ganymede. Passion said Edge was on his way to kill you. Both of you are dumbasses for locking me out of your minds. I couldn't warn you, and I couldn't find him. Then Passion heard a scream." He shrugged.

"Of ecstasy, dear, all ecstasy." Sparkle slid the tip of her tongue across her bottom lip as she stared up at the man above her.

"Ganymede?" It couldn't be. That gorgeous man couldn't be the pudgy gray cat she'd met outside the castle.

"Watch it, babe. Pudgy gray cats have feelings too."

Passion sucked in a startled breath. It was Ganymede's voice in her head.

Ganymede's glare said he wasn't forgetting about the ruined door and his interrupted moment with Sparkle, but he was putting it aside while he dealt with the Edge thing. "Look around. No Edge. Nothing to worry about. He might not like me, but he knows the rules. He kills me—not that it could ever happen—and the Big Boss destroys him. Edge has scary control; don't know how he does it. Anyway, he'll get over what's bugging him." Ganymede's expression hinted that maybe they should leave before he crushed them like the squashed gummy bears beneath his feet. "When you leave, Dacian, prop that door up so we'll have some privacy."

No, he couldn't just dismiss the danger. Passion spoke up. "Edge is coming. I know he is. And he's not in his right mind. Don't be stupid."

"Stupid?" Ganymede skewered her with a piercing glare. "Be careful, angel wannabe." He took a step toward her to emphasize his threat.

God, he must be at least six foot five.

"Leave. Now. It takes time for me to shift to human form. I made the effort tonight so my cupcake and I could lower our stress levels." He turned to Dacian. "Make me lose any quality time with her tonight and I might do something. Bad." He lifted his hands and made an exaggerated sweep of the store. "And see, Edge isn't here."

"Yes, he is." The whisper came from a shadowed corner of the store.

Passion along with everyone else turned to stare as Edge glided forward. He made no sound as he moved, darkness and earthly endings trailing behind him. Power flowed from him, pushing at her, and she wanted to wrap her arms around herself to keep from shivering. At this moment, Passion didn't doubt for a moment that Death was among them.

No explanations were needed. Edge stared at Ganymede, his amber eyes shining with . . . nothing. Nobody was home in those eyes.

"Shit." Ganymede sounded more annoyed than terrified.

That was okay, because Passion was terrified enough for both of them. She'd witnessed more violence in her short time at the castle than she had during her entire existence as an angel. Of course, she couldn't quite remember how long that existence had been, but it was certainly longer than one night.

Dacian moved forward. "This isn't just a random attack of bad temper." He waved Sparkle off the counter.

She slid down and sidled away from Edge. "You don't want to do this, sweetie."

Edge didn't acknowledge either of them.

"Hate to admit I'm wrong, because being wrong doesn't happen to me, but I think Edge was right. Someone's messing with our heads. And I'm really pissed at whoever it is because they broke my string of a million years without making a mistake."

Ganymede's tone was the same snarky one Passion remembered from the seawall, but as she stared into his eyes, she saw a transformation that iced the blood in her veins.

His eyes darkened and became the eyes of the chaos bringer—ancient, timeless. Passion knew if she stared too long, they'd drag her into their depths where memories of screaming horrors lived. She jerked her gaze away. She wasn't ready for that.

"Time to die." Edge's voice was a monotone, no excitement, no emotion, just Death delivering his message.

"You can't fight him, Mede." Sparkle moved behind Ganymede and rested her hand against his back. "He doesn't know what he's doing. Besides, if you two get into it, humans will die. The Big Boss will come calling." She paused. "And I might lose you." The last was said so softly that Passion almost didn't hear her.

"Then they'll die. And if the Big Boss comes, he comes. I have the right to defend myself."

Silence fell. Energy built, expanding, pushing at the limits of the room, flowing out through the open door. The walls made creaking sounds, the storefront window shattered.

You're an angel, for God's sake, do something. But Passion had no communication lines to home, no way of summoning help. Punishment meant she couldn't contact Ted. Anything she had to say got said during Hope's nightly reports. She glanced at the other angel. "You're not being punished. Call Ted." Her order was a frantic hiss.

Hope looked at her from glazed eyes. "I can't focus. I have to concentrate. Passion, they're going to destroy everything."

Well, maybe not everything, but since she and Hope were standing about five feet away from Edge and Ganymede, she was pretty sure she'd be history. She might technically be an angel, but she was in human form. Hope would survive, though. She was still an angel in good standing.

"Damn, someone needs to do something."

Dacian's voice startled Passion. She looked at him just as he drew back his upper lip to expose impressive fangs. She gasped. His eyes shone completely black, no pupils, no white, just . . . black.

"Vampire." She was too numb to feel shocked.

He leaped at Edge, just a blur of movement. Edge didn't

even look at him. He simply held up his hand and Dacian slammed into an invisible wall.

Ganymede glanced at Sparkle. "Get everyone out of here. Fast." Then he focused on Edge.

"It won't do any good, Mede." Sparkle sounded scared. "You might be able to control *your* damage, but Edge isn't thinking, doesn't know or care what he's doing. Death running free will destroy the whole island, maybe more." She took a deep breath. "Please. Disappear until he calms down."

Passion sensed that Sparkle didn't get scared often, a testament to the seriousness of the situation. And she'd bet the other woman didn't beg often either.

"What happens, happens." Ganymede didn't look at her.

Passion saw no regret in his eyes for the woman who seemed to mean a lot to him, saw no emotion at all, just a cold focus on Edge.

Sparkle backed away from Ganymede, her body stiff. She blinked rapidly. "It's always about you and your damn pride."

Passion thought that watching Sparkle fight back tears raised the terror factor a thousandfold.

And then it began.

Cold darkness seemed to flow from Edge's fingertips, roiling blackness that coiled and crept along the floor, bringing with it an overpowering sense of heaviness. It bubbled as though something living breathed just below its surface, and Passion thought she wouldn't be able to hold herself upright, wouldn't be able to resist the power drawing her down, down, into the grave.

Ganymede wasn't wasting any time either. Wind whipped into the room from the shattered window and door. It circled him, lifting his hair, even as flames leaped up around him. Passion blinked to make sure she wasn't seeing things, but yes, the ends of his hair were glowing flame.

She was rooted to the spot. Not a good place to be now. Even if everyone else made the decision to stay and watch the disaster unfold, she should be outta here. She was the only human, the most vulnerable of them. Still she stayed. There was no logical reason, but there was a darn good illogical one. She remembered the virgin on the landing. If Ganymede killed Edge, maybe she could . . . *Give it up. By the time one of them is dead, this store and possibly all of Galveston will be in pieces and drifting out into the Gulf.* Still, she stayed.

Passion was vaguely aware of the wind outside. It had risen to gale force, and she could hear waves crashing onto the shore. The floor shook, and a display of chocolate creams fell to the floor.

Edge crouched and Ganymede did the same. Passion pressed her hands against her temples, trying to relieve the immense pressure from the buildup of power. Any minute her head would explode.

And right at the very moment the two cosmic trouble-makers would have leaped at each other, Hope ran between them.

Passion made a grab for her as she raced past, but missed. Ohmigod, they'd kill Hope. Passion started to run after her.

"Wait, wait, wait!" Hope held up her hands, as though that would stop the apocalypse about to rain down on them. "Let's talk this out."

Then something weird happened. Hope started speaking. Passion could hear her, but the words didn't make any sense. They seemed to flow together, creating a rhythm that somehow soothed Passion, made her feel almost relaxed and . . . happy. She wondered how that could be, because something bad was about to happen, and it should worry her.

But Passion couldn't seem to remember what the bad thing was. She started to smile. She even decided to hum a tune she'd heard . . . somewhere.

It might have been seconds, minutes, or even hours, but suddenly Passion blinked and looked around.

Dacian sat on the floor, carefully placing the spilled

chocolate creams back in their box. He was smiling. Sparkle leaned against the wall examining her nails. She seemed happy with them. Ganymede wasn't smiling, but he'd shed the flames and just stared at Edge.

Edge lay curled up on the floor, his eyes tightly shut and his breath coming in gasps.

Hope had stopped talking and had started to back toward the door. "I don't know what happened." Her voice shook. "I'm going up to my room." With no further explanation, she ran from the store.

Passion didn't care what had happened. Hope had somehow stopped Edge and Ganymede. But something was wrong with Edge. She pushed past Ganymede and fell to her knees beside Edge. "Are you okay?"

"No." His answer was pushed through clenched teeth.

"Try to relax." She placed her hand on his shoulder in an attempt to comfort Edge while she looked around for someone to help him.

She felt the moment his muscles relaxed and he went limp. He opened his eyes to stare at her.

"When you just touched me . . . it felt like . . ." He seemed to make an attempt to focus on her. "And that other woman, she talked and . . ." He raised a trembling hand to his face.

Passion could hear Ganymede's murmur behind her.

"If it looks like a duck and quacks like a duck, is it really a duck? Or just a cheap knockoff?"

5

Edge tried to focus, to understand. He forced himself to remember. He'd left Passion's room, and then *wham*, the need to kill Ganymede had hit him. Not like before. This time it had overwhelmed him. He couldn't resist. It had been lights out until the sound of a strange woman talking had drawn his mind back. Problem was, he couldn't remember what she'd been saying.

He fought despair. Over the thousands of years of his existence, he'd lost what he might have been, lost the future to endless death. He couldn't change that. But he'd managed to hang on to one thing that brought him pride—his control over his thoughts, his emotions. Now it too was gone. He took a deep breath. *Get over yourself. You can rebuild the walls in your mind higher and stronger. He won't just stroll in next time.* Edge turned his attention to the one person able to distract him from his own dark thoughts.

Passion. His maybe-angel had knelt beside him and put her hand on him. Why the hell was she even here? Someone would pay for letting her stay to witness whatever it was that had almost happened. He knew it was an "almost" because if he'd fought Ganymede there'd be nothing left of this store. *Or Passion.* Not something he wanted to dwell on.

Feeling protective? The thought horrified him. He never felt emotional connections to anyone. Emotional attachments were like rubber bands. They'd stretch just so far, and then they'd snap. The sting you got from the recoil was a bitch.

He returned to the puzzle of what had happened when she touched him. It had felt as though she'd reached inside him and smoothed away the pounding in his brain, the knots cramping his muscles, and slowed his racing heart. All things she couldn't possibly have done.

It took two attempts for Edge to stand. Passion didn't try to help him. Looking around, he saw that the talking woman had left. Dacian watched him warily from his seat on the floor, and Sparkle was staring at Ganymede's back. She didn't look happy.

"Got it out of your system?" Ganymede clenched and unclenched his fists, his only concession to whatever was going on inside him.

"Yeah, I'm fine." Or as fine as he could be, knowing that his control could be overridden at any moment.

Dacian stood. "Does *anyone* know what just happened?"

"No." Edge watched Passion as she moved toward the door. "We need to have a meeting, and I think you should be part of it, Passion. This can't happen again. Why the hell were you even here?"

"I go where I want to go. And I'm sorry if I invaded your private circle. It won't happen again."

Edge didn't miss the hurt in her eyes. She'd misunderstood. But that was okay, because she didn't need to know he'd been worried about her.

Ganymede nodded. "We need to talk. Let's take this over to Wicked Fantasy. I need a drink."

"I need to clean up this mess you made." Sparkle's expression said the mess included Ganymede.

Yep, Sparkle was mad. Edge wondered what Ganymede had done.

"I'll take care of it. Later. You won't be opening again tonight." Ganymede sounded impatient.

Edge winced. Sparkle's stare looked as though it could tear bloody furrows in him. He expected her to scoop up one of the glass shards from her broken window and begin slicing.

"You're right." She picked her way across the floor to retrieve her shoes. "*Nothing* will be happening here tonight." Her narrowed eyes and thinned lips promised that Ganymede may as well change back into a cat, because the queen of sex and sin was leaving the house.

No one spoke as they walked back to Wicked Fantasy, the small club Sparkle owned in the castle. A few minutes later, they were all seated around a table in a darkened corner. Bain and Holgarth had joined them. Edge spent a few minutes running through what he remembered.

"Has anyone else had problems?" Passion had seated herself opposite Edge.

"Yeah, I've had a few." Ganymede sounded reluctant to talk.

Edge knew Ganymede was *never* reluctant to talk, except when it might expose a weakness. Tough shit. At least Ganymede hadn't misplaced his brain so far.

"A couple of times in the last few weeks I might've wanted to blow something up." Ganymede shrugged. "I handled it."

Edge smiled. Ganymede wasn't going to mention the evaporating mountain in the Himalayas or the San Andreas Fault's booty shaking.

Sparkle spoke up. "Mede won't say it because he wants everyone to think he's all-powerful, so I'll say it for him." She offered Ganymede a frosty stare. "The same thing that happened to Edge could happen to him."

Ganymede looked like he wanted to argue the point but after glancing into Sparkle's eyes, he chugged his drink instead.

"Coward." Edge aimed the thought at Ganymede.

Ganymede glared at him but didn't say anything.

Holgarth *did* say something. "I realize we have a massive collection of egos here, but someone needs to point out the obvious. Someone or something extremely powerful, with an agenda as yet to be revealed, is putting the whole island of Galveston in danger. He, she, or possibly *it* has to know what could happen, and they don't care." He held up his hand. "I realize it's difficult for any cosmic troublemaker to admit, but someone out there is more powerful than either of you."

Dacian narrowed his gaze on Bain. "Well, I know it isn't me. But we've never quite figured out how much power you have, demon."

Bain laughed. "If you're lucky, you never will." His laughter died. "If I wanted to kill you, I'd do it directly. Someone's playing games. I wonder why."

Ganymede grunted. "Better hope I never find them. It'll be game over in a permanent way."

"So who would have a grudge against you guys?" Passion glanced at Edge and then looked away.

"Everyone." Edge and Ganymede spoke at once.

Edge elaborated. "Immortals are forever, and over the millennia we've pissed off lots of them. But if they're powerful enough to take our minds, then why not just come out shooting?"

"We'd better hope it's someone already at the castle, because if the bastard is strong enough to reach us over a distance, we're shit out of luck." If he'd been in cat form, Ganymede's ears would have been pinned and his tail would have been lashing back and forth.

Sparkle looked thoughtful. "I'll have Bill go over the people staying here. Since this has been happening for a few weeks, I'll have him check for anyone who's been here for a while."

Dacian said what Edge knew they all were thinking. "How do we keep Edge from going off on us again?"

Edge couldn't let that go. "What about Ganymede? Tonight I was the target. Maybe next time it'll be him." He glared at Ganymede. "And don't give me any crap about you being stronger than me. What got into my head tonight was powerful enough to take you down too." He grinned. "Of course, what challenge is there in possessing someone who only thinks about ice cream?"

"He thinks about other things." Sparkle's smile was all sexual. Then she seemed to remember her mad and stopped smiling.

Ganymede finished his drink in one swallow. "Enough. The point is, how do we keep everyone safe until we find the creep?"

Bain offered his solution. "When Rabid was turning up the mindless rage in our friend here"—he nodded at Dacian—"you guys locked Dacian up in the dungeon. Would that work again?"

"The dungeon sucked. Not a place to spend quality time." Dacian cast Edge a sympathetic glance. "But it's reinforced. It would hold you longer than any other place in the castle would. Besides, the dungeon is away from human guests. My apartment and a few rooms for visiting vampires are all you'd have to worry about."

Ganymede nodded. "Sounds like a good idea."

"I disagree." Holgarth tapped a skinny finger on the table. "The dungeon is part of my fantasies. It would disrupt my schedule." He seemed to think that was all that needed saying.

"Too bad, wizard. Everyone's safety comes first."

Bain must have a death wish. But enough of this. Edge was the only one who would control his immediate future. "Let's take a look at the dungeon, and then I'll decide."

With lots of grumbling from Ganymede and Holgarth, they all left the club and headed for the dungeon. Sparkle took her drink with her.

Okay, so the dungeon was creepy. Passion shivered.

Stone walls, a big heavy wooden door that creaked when Ganymede shoved it open, and a bunch of accessories meant to inflict pain. She reminded herself that they weren't real.

"This doesn't look too homey." Passion glanced at the wall sconces with their flickering lights meant to simulate a candle's flame.

Sparkle edged up beside her. "Oh, but think of the possibilities. See that table with the arm and leg restraints? Think about Edge stretched naked on it, open and helpless to anything you might want to do with his body."

Passion didn't *want* to get a mental picture. She fought it. Hard. She lost. Worse yet, her picture became a video. And in it, she stroked her fingers the length of his sweat-sheened body, lingering as she touched—

"How strong are the chains attached to that wall? If you can bring in a few creature comforts, I'll go with it. I might hate living here, but it'll make everyone in the castle safer." Edge sounded reluctant to admit it.

Holgarth sniffed. "Those chains were meant to withstand a vampire's strength. You'll be able to free yourself, but it will take a few minutes."

Sparkle was in her element. "We'll push the iron maiden and the other stuff against the wall. Then we'll bring in a mattress, lamp, chair, and TV. Dacian's apartment is next door, so you can use his bathroom."

"Cinn will love that." Dacian sounded grouchy.

Sparkle's gaze turned thoughtful. She held her drink in one hand while she studied Passion. "Everyone's been so busy trying to figure out who did this that we've forgotten the one who saved us. Who's the woman who talked Edge down from the ledge while she made the rest of us feel calm about the whole thing?"

Uh-oh. Passion had started to relax, thinking they'd forgotten about her. "That was my roommate, Hope. She's . . ." Her talent for lying had reached its end, because she had no answer for what the other angel was.

It seemed Edge didn't intend to let her get away with that. "It wasn't just Hope. When I was lying there, I still couldn't think. I was blind with pain. But when Passion put her hand on me, I felt this warm rush of . . . something, and suddenly I felt normal."

Passion raised one brow. "As much as I'd like to don the Super Healer cape, I have to point out that it was just coincidence. I happened to touch you at the moment your body was ready to recover. No big deal."

Edge didn't look convinced. "It was a big deal for me."

She almost slumped with relief when he looked away.

"But we still have a problem." Edge moved to the door and shoved hard. The door shook as though it were made of cardboard. "This room might slow me down, but it won't stop me. All I have to do is snap the chains, blow away the door, and leave."

"Good point." Ganymede turned his attention back to Passion.

She didn't like the gleam in his eyes. Damn. Too late to run.

"This Hope who's rooming with you must have some sort of power." Ganymede looked as though he were thinking things out as he went.

Passion shrugged as she backed toward the door. "I have to leave and—"

"Once Hope calmed Edge down, then you healed the aftereffects." Ganymede looked around as though the solution was obvious. "They have to stay here with Edge."

"No." Edge and Passion said it at the same time.

Strangely, Passion felt hurt that he agreed with her. And that didn't make any sense at all. But then nothing made sense since she'd landed here.

"Hope and I don't have any special powers. You're all just imagining things. We're paying guests, and you don't have the right to—"

Ganymede heaved an exaggerated sigh. "I'm getting really tired of your denials. I'll have to eat a quart of ice cream in front of the TV tonight to get rid of the annoying buzz."

"I don't want them here with me."

Edge's eyes were cold. No emotion, no hint that Passion was anything more than a pesky human. She tried not to take his rejection personally.

"I think it's a great idea." Sparkle had finally found a cause to get behind. "Edge spends too much time alone. This will be good for him." She narrowed her eyes to sly slits of anticipation.

Passion might not know anything about Sparkle Stardust, but she knew that expression spelled bad news for her.

"Here's the deal, Angel." Ganymede smiled at Passion. Not a nice smile. "Let's assume for the moment that you *do* think you're an angel. I've never experienced the feeling, but I assume angels have enhanced consciences." He held his hand up to stop her denial. "If Edge goes off again, and there's no one to stop him . . ."

He let the thought linger, and Passion hated him for the guilt trip she saw coming.

"Thousands of people would die during a battle between cosmic troublemakers with our power. Galveston Island would be a pile of rubble. Those who lived would be outta jobs. Hey, in this economy, it would be tough for them to survive. The government might even think it was an enemy attack and—"

Crap, crap, crap. "Fine, I'll stay. But I can't speak for Hope." Passion knew she'd just made the second biggest mistake of her life. The first had been her demand that the Almighty give her an audience because, well, everyone should at least know what their boss looked like. That demand had landed her down here.

But she *was* an angel. Turning her back on all those people would be unforgivable. Not that Passion thought that *she* could do anything, but Hope might have powers that Passion never knew about.

"Hope was terrified. I don't think she'll agree to this." *Please, please don't agree, Hope.*

"Don't I have anything to say about it?" Edge's voice dripped ice.

"Of course you do, sweetie." Sparkle leaned over to run her fingers along his arm.

Ganymede narrowed his eyes.

"But it won't be for that long. I'm sure we'll find who's doing this within a few days." She slipped her hand into his.

Passion narrowed *her* eyes.

"Besides, you won't be alone with them. Ganymede will be there too." She slid Ganymede a gotcha grin.

"No, I won't."

"Yes, you will." Edge was all over this. "You think you're safe from attack? Knowing you, you'd wipe out a few major cities before your brain engaged again."

Ganymede opened his mouth then shut it with a snap. His glare at Sparkle said she'd pay for this.

"It's going to be a little crowded. How will you squeeze four beds in here with all the torture stuff that's . . . ?" Passion's voice trailed off as she saw Sparkle's smile.

"Don't even think about it." Passion stood. "I'll go up and talk to Hope. All your plans won't mean a thing if she says no. And since she's a paying guest, you can't make her." There. That should hold them. She left the dungeon before anyone could say anything.

She'd almost reached her room when Edge caught up with her. Passion tried to ignore him.

"Look, I don't like this any more than you do. But as much as I hate to admit it, Ganymede's right. I wouldn't have believed anything could stop me when I was . . . out of control"—he winced as he said the last words—"but Hope somehow did it. I don't want to think what would've happened if she hadn't been there."

"You would've probably come out of it on your own. It was just a coincidence that Hope was talking at the time." And she didn't believe that for a moment. She remembered how everyone looked back in the store. Edge hadn't been the only one affected.

"I'll help you convince Hope."

"You will *not* mess with her mind."

He shrugged. "It's your call. Besides, if she's like you, I wouldn't be able to get into her head anyway."

Passion stopped in front of her door. "You shouldn't do it because it isn't right."

"I don't let things like that stop me." He leaned toward her, his amber eyes still cold. "We're different, sweetheart. Remember that. I don't have a conscience."

Did she believe him? She didn't want to. But what did she know? Passion didn't have the power to look into his heart. All she could go by was all the black swirling around him. That didn't lie. Could the color change? Archangel Ted would say Edge couldn't be redeemed, so don't even try. She knew she *was* going to try, though. But first she had to survive this first day at the castle. Things didn't look good so far.

Taking a deep, steadying breath, she lifted her fist to knock. "By the way, I still need a new key."

For the first time since the candy-store horror, he smiled.

Passion felt that smile as a warm breeze after the last winter freeze. It slid over her, and the night's grim events seemed to recede a little.

He reached into his pocket, pulled out a key, and handed it to her. "Forgot to tell you. When I left your room, I found this in a corner. Guess it was too dark for you to see it. I stuck it in my pocket right before the . . ." He shrugged. "Before whatever it was struck me."

Without commenting, she unlocked the door. Passion stepped inside and looked around. Hope sat on one of the beds, already in her pajamas. She'd clasped her arms around her bent legs, and her head rested on her knees. She raised her head to stare at Edge from wide, frightened eyes.

Passion made soothing noises as she walked over and sat on the end of Hope's bed. "It's okay. He's back to normal." *Whatever normal is for someone like him.* She took a deep breath. "We need to talk about what you did."

Hope shook her head. "I didn't do anything. I mean, I talked, but that's what I do when I'm nervous. You know, it drove Archangel Ted crazy."

Passion heard Edge's muffled laughter behind her. Who could laugh at a time like this? She turned her head to scowl at him. "What?"

"Archangel Ted? You're joking. Maybe I'm not up on the angelic hierarchy, but I've never heard of a Ted."

Even though Passion had tested the patience of most of the authority figures among the heavenly host, she wouldn't allow anyone else to criticize them. "We're allowed to choose our own names. There's nothing wrong with the name Ted. Humans don't know the name of every . . ." She closed her eyes. No, no, no. Passion had just admitted what she'd spent the whole day denying. She was an angel.

"So you chose your name?" Edge looked interested.

At least he didn't yell "gotcha." And no, she didn't want to explain anything to him. She quickly turned her attention back to Hope. "Maybe you're right, Hope. Maybe you had nothing to do with what happened in the store." Lying was becoming way too easy for Passion. "But the people who witnessed it believe you did."

Hope looked horrified. Even without any power, Passion knew what she was thinking. Hope had blown her angel cover.

"Don't worry, Hope. They didn't talk about what they thought you were, they were just happy you were there to save everyone." She smiled. "You're a hero."

Hope brightened. "Really?"

Edge walked over to a chair and sat. Then he leaned back, folded his hands behind his head, and stared at Hope.

His next words dragged Passion's attention from the way his T-shirt stretched across his broad chest. Not that she was staring at his chest specifically. She had to look somewhere, didn't she?

"Are you an angel, Hope?"

"You don't have to answer that." Passion knew she was too late. Because Hope *was* an angel, a good one. She wouldn't lie. *Unlike you.* Well, Passion had never claimed to be a good angel. She questioned too many things and definitely tried the patience of even those whose goodness shown supernova bright.

Hope dropped her gaze. "Yes." Her voice was soft and woeful.

Edge smiled. "Thank you, Hope, for being honest with me." He slid his gaze to Passion, his expression saying, "Unlike your roommate, who lies through her wings."

"We need your help, Hope."

His voice was almost gentle with Hope, and the resentment she felt surprised Passion. It shouldn't matter that he'd never spoken to her like that. Hope was sweet and innocent and anyone would react to that. Passion wasn't either of those things.

Hope offered him a small smile. "I don't know how much help I'd be. I mean, I'm only here to convince the wicked ones at the castle to change their evil ways." She studied him. "What are you?"

"I'm a cosmic troublemaker. I cause . . . trouble. I'm a very, very bad man, but I could be saved if someone took the time and cared enough."

Passion felt like growling. Couldn't Hope see that he was manipulating her?

Hope looked doubtful that she was up to the job. "I think that Archangel Ted needs to send more angels. This is too big a job for two of us."

Edge's smile widened as he looked at Passion.

Hope had a big mouth, not that anyone had believed Passion's story about being a normal human.

"So what do you want me to do?"

Without warning, the door swung open, and a chubby gray cat padded into the room. Then he shoved his rump against it, and the door swung shut. *"I'll take it from here. This explanation needs to come from someone with finesse."* Ganymede leaped onto the bed with Hope. *"Hey, babe, looking good."*

Hope shrieked.

Ganymede glanced at Passion. *"Is she always this excitable?"*

"When a cat is talking in her head, she is."

Ganymede sat down and began to wash his face. *"I don't think anyone's done an official intro. I'm Ganymede, and the crazy dude over there is Edge. We're cosmic troublemakers. You don't have to worry your cute little head over what that is."*

Cute little head? Sexist jerk. Passion made sure she shouted in her head so that Fat Cat wouldn't miss it.

Ganymede stopped washing his face. *"Body shape isn't an issue here. Besides, women love chubby fur balls. They think I'm cute."*

Passion snorted her opinion of that.

Edge exhaled deeply. "Look, let's get on with this. I'm tired. Having your will sucked from you and almost causing the apocalypse takes a lot out of a guy."

Hope shot Passion a desperate glance. Passion shrugged. She didn't like this idea at all, but if she were honest, having both Ganymede and Edge close would make it easier to start convincing them to choose a better life. Okay, so she wasn't too optimistic about her chances of success, but she had to try. They were her passport back home. *Is that your real reason?* She pushed the question aside.

"Here's the deal." The cat sidled closer to Hope. *"When you did whatever you did, Edge here calmed down, so we've decided that both you ladies should stay with him in the dungeon."* He rolled over onto his back and waited for his tummy to be scratched.

"In the *dungeon*?" She sounded a little breathless.

Passion couldn't believe it when Hope actually reached out and tentatively rubbed his stomach.

"It's built a lot stronger than this room." Ganymede purred. *"Will that be okay? Oh, and I'll be staying too, because I've had twinges of wanting to destroy the universe*

lately. But I'll be in this form, which is a lot cuter and less threatening than Edge's form."

Hope was struck speechless, a rare occurrence.

"Hey, you don't have to make a decision now, babe. Grab a few things, and we'll take a look at the dungeon. If you hate it, you can come back here."

Passion gathered what she'd need for the night while Hope did the same.

No one said anything until they were standing in the dungeon. Someone had pushed the torture equipment to the side. There were two air mattresses on the floor along with a lamp beside each, a few chairs, a small coffee table with a hotel phone on it, and a cart with a TV.

"Where will *you* sleep?" Passion stared at Edge before glancing around the room. Could they squeeze another mattress in here? Ganymede was a cat. He could sleep anywhere as long as it wasn't on her bed. That would just be creepy. "Do you need a litter box?" Aimed at Ganymede.

"I'll let myself out. If I'm gone for more than a few minutes, check to make sure I'm not whipping up a plague of locusts." He stared at Passion, and again she had the feeling he was laughing at her. *"And I'm a cat. Cats sleep wherever they want to sleep."*

She gave him slitty eyes.

"Okay, not on your bed. That work for you?"

Passion nodded and then looked at Hope. "What do you think? If you don't want this, say so." Part of her prayed Hope would refuse. But then she looked at Edge. She really did want to help him. *Is that all you want?* Maybe she needed to define "help."

Silence filled the room as everyone waited for Hope's decision. It didn't happen because suddenly the door swung open. Sparkle swayed in, wearing a new pair of stilettos and carrying handcuffs. She kicked the door shut with her foot and then dropped the cuffs onto a chair.

"I come bearing gifts." She slanted Ganymede an irritated glance. "Which is more than I can say for the cat. All he brought was his mouth."

Ganymede yawned. *"My mouth has been good to you. Don't knock it, sugarbunny."*

"You were listening at the door." Edge made it a statement.

Sparkle widened her eyes. "You thought I wouldn't? I knew you'd eventually get to this point in the discussion, and when I went to my suite to change shoes—I stepped in chocolate with the others—I found these." She pointed at the handcuffs. "There're lots of sexy memories attached to them. They'll make Hope feel safe."

Sparkle focused on Hope. "I don't think we were ever introduced. I'm Sparkle Stardust. This is my castle." She smiled. Wickedness shone in that smile. "And you're absolutely beautiful, so filled with wide-eyed innocence and goodness." Sparkle's lids slid almost shut and her expression turned ecstatic. "So much goodness. I can almost taste it. Between you and Passion, I've never had so much raw material to mold, to shape into something amazing."

Okay, that was creepy. Sparkle made them sound like Play-Doh projects. Passion moved a little closer to Hope. She'd been so focused on the obvious dangers posed by Edge and Ganymede that she hadn't thought too much about the third cosmic troublemaker in the castle. Maybe she should have.

Sparkle seemed to mentally shake herself and was once again marginally normal. "I knew that Hope and Passion might be a little nervous about Edge sleeping right there beside—"

"Not beside me." Hope was definite about that.

"No. I already told you not to even think about it." Passion glared at Sparkle. "He can sleep on the floor if you can't fit another mattress in here."

Edge was starting to show some interest. "I don't sleep on floors."

Hope clutched her clothes to her chest. "I can go back to my room right now."

Edge raised one brow as he looked at Passion.

"You. Will. Not. Sleep. In. My. Bed." Passion refused to form even one mental picture.

"See, I knew you'd need me." Sparkle picked up a cuff and shook it.

Edge's smile faded. "No. Whatever you have in mind for that, my answer is no."

Now it was Passion's turn to show interest. "Explain."

"We used the handcuffs with the chains embedded in the wall on Dacian. They were made to withstand a vampire's strength. They wouldn't hold you long, Edge, but if you suddenly got the urge to kill Ganymede in the middle of the night, they'd give you at least two minutes for Hope to do her thing." She glanced at the stone wall beside one bed. "Attach the cuff to the chain and then click it onto your wrist." She didn't meet his gaze.

"*No one* chains me to a wall." Edge leaned forward, his amber eyes almost glowing.

"I think this is a stupid idea." Passion forced her thoughts away from the fantasy trying to form in her mind.

"Yes. I'll do it." Hope's voice was quiet, determined. "Passion, we have to. Think of all those souls we're responsible for. We can't just abandon them to death because . . . because . . ." She didn't seem to know where to go after the "because."

Passion did. "This whole thing is crazy. If Edge wakes up in the middle of the night with death on his mind, he could kill us before he left to search for Ganymede."

"No, I wouldn't." Edge seemed sure of that. "My killing urge is pretty specific. You saw it. Ganymede was my target. I didn't try to kill any of you." Uncertainty touched his eyes. "Did I?"

Passion looked away. "No."

Ganymede was all business. "*Then I don't see a problem.*" He padded to the foot of Hope's bed and settled in.

"I sleep late. Don't make a lot of noise when you get up."
He glanced at Sparkle. "Will you bring a few of my snacks
with you in the morning, sugarlump? Don't want to get up
and not have anything to eat."

Sparkle's good humor evaporated. "You bet I will, *sugar-lump*." She headed for the door. "You know what to do,
Edge. The chain is long enough for you to turn over." She
dropped two keys beside the handcuffs. "The small key is
for the cuff. The larger one is for Dacian's door. He and
Cinn don't want to be jumping up and down answering
your knocks." She chanced a quick glance at a furious
Edge. "Passion can release you in the morning." Then she
jerked open the door and disappeared into the hall. She
slammed the door shut behind her.

Ganymede looked a little worried. *"She'll think about
how mad she is all night. Then she'll do something I'll
regret."* He looked at Edge. *"Do you know what I did
wrong?"*

Edge shrugged, his expression thunderous.

Passion decided to leave Ganymede in the dark. He
deserved it.

Hope stared at Ganymede sprawled across the bottom
of her bed. "We have a chain for Edge, but what about if
you go crazy?"

Ganymede looked insulted. *"I'm a cat. You don't chain
a cat. Besides, if I feel funny, I'll yowl and you can bop me
in the head. When I come to, you can start talking."* He
yawned. *"I have to stay in cat form. Sparkle would make
all of our lives hell if I slept on the bed in human form."*

Passion could almost see his furry cat face trying to
smile at the thought.

"I wouldn't let you sleep in my bed in human form."
Hope was pretty definite about that.

So where did that leave Passion, the angel-slut of
heaven?

Edge huffed his disgust at the chain. Everyone's attention snapped to him. He scowled at them. "Time for bed."

Passion nodded. She draped her clean clothes over a chair, grabbed her nightgown and robe, and then escaped to Dacian's shower. She did some deep-breathing exercises while she was in there. Why had she agreed to this? Oh, yeah, she was an angel and it was her duty. Finally, she could stall no longer. Putting on her robe, she opened the bathroom door and scuttled back to the dungeon.

The room would've been completely dark—no windows—if someone hadn't plugged in a night-light near the door. She could see the dim outline of Hope. She'd lain down and pulled the covers up to her chin. She was facing away from Passion's bed. The lump at the foot of her bed was Ganymede.

Slowly, Passion swung her gaze to her bed. She could see the outline of his tall shape. Edge was lying on his back, and he seemed to fill the whole bed. Passion stared at that shape until the clinking sound of the chain startled her into speech. "Are you comfortable with that chain?"

"No." His voice was an irritated growl in the darkness.

"Oh. Well, let me know when you need time in the bathroom. I'll get the key to your cuff." She forced herself to approach her side of the mattress. Taking a deep breath of courage, she slipped onto it and then clung to the edge like an insecure bat.

His soft chuckle made her feel breathless, whether from fear or something else, she wasn't sure.

"I took a shower earlier." Long pause. "I didn't get a chance to pick up anything from my room, so I only have the clothes I was wearing."

She breathed a little easier. He had his clothes on under the covers.

"I undressed in the dark." His voice was a sensual whisper. "Hope was already asleep, so I didn't offend her angelic innocence."

Passion knew he was enjoying every second of this. Evil got a kick out of torturing others. At least he couldn't reach her with his chain.

"Sweet dreams, wicked angel." His soft chuckle seemed awful close.

She felt his warm breath slide across the sensitive skin behind her ear at the same time his fingers trailed a shivery path down her exposed arm.

"How long *is* that chain?"

6

Edge laughed softly. How could he find anything funny so soon after his dark thoughts of a few minutes ago? He didn't know. All he did know was that Passion made him feel better. "The chain is long enough."

He lay watching her rigid back for ages before she finally relaxed on a huff of frustration. She flopped onto her back. "I can't sleep. You make me nervous."

He listened before answering. The cat was snoring. He'd have to point out that blemish to Ganymede. He loved punching holes in the cat's puffed-up sense of self. Hope's breathing was slow and steady. She was asleep.

"Anything I can do to make you less nervous?"

She opened her sexy mouth to answer.

"I'm not leaving."

She closed her mouth.

He watched her eyes travel over his bared chest down to where the sheet draped across his hips. "And yes, I'm naked. Sorry. That's the way I sleep." Not always. But he'd stripped bare before climbing into bed to accomplish exactly what he saw now. Even in the dim glow from the night-light, he couldn't miss her blush. Yeah, that was mean of him. He shouldn't be taking out his anger on one of the two people who'd helped him. But maybe it was better that she learn he was a bastard now than later.

"Great. I have a naked stranger in my bed." Her eyes gleamed at him in the darkness. "With a very long chain."

"I get the stranger part." He got the naked part too. "You might be less nervous if you knew a little more about me." *Probably not, though.* And where had his offer come from? He never talked about himself if he could help it.

Her gaze burned a hole in his chest, but his offer seemed to divert her attention. Too bad. He liked the way she looked at his body—with admiration and awakening hunger.

"Why do you kill?"

Wow, she went right for the jugular. "It's what I do. The Big Boss tells me who needs to die, and I take care of it."

"Can't you say no?"

Self-loathing choked him. He hated being reminded of his position, tried not to think about it. But he'd promised to answer her questions. "I don't have free will when it comes to my job, just the manner in which I get it done." *Don't ask anything else.*

"What happens if you say no?" She seemed to be over her nerves. Her eyes shone with curiosity and something more that made him uneasy.

How to explain this to her. "I've never said no."

She frowned.

"It's a compulsion, a knowing that what I'm doing is what I was meant to do. I've always understood that I was created for this job." He tried to explain something to her that he'd never spoken about to anyone else. "If I stopped doing the job, I'd cease to exist."

"That's awful." She looked horrified.

He supposed it was, but he'd sort of gotten used to existing, so he didn't fight it.

Sympathy gleamed in her eyes.

"I don't want your pity." His voice was harsher than

he'd meant it to be, but he hated the idea of her feeling sorry for him. "I don't mind my job, and over the millennia I've learned to make killing into an art form." There. That should wipe away her sympathy.

"I understand your anger." And she reached out to place her palm flat against his chest.

Edge wanted to deny he was angry and push her hand from his body. But he couldn't, he just couldn't. Her touch heated parts of him that had been cold for a very long time. His body absorbed the sensation, and roiling emotions awoke where no emotions were a second ago.

Lust. He understood it, almost welcomed the uncomplicated familiarity of it. But this wasn't an ordinary sexual hunger. He wanted her bone deep. He wanted to wrap his arms around her and taste her in every way possible—the flavor of warm woman and heated arousal as he slid his tongue over her bared body, the scent of earth magic rather than heaven, the feel of her smooth skin beneath him, touching his chest, stomach, cock. But beyond that, he wanted to sink into her, merge everything he wasn't with everything she was.

The second emotion was a lot more complex. It was a coming home to a man who knew no home, the healing of a wound none could possibly reach because he'd hidden it so well. And it terrified him. Anyone who could cause this feeling was dangerous. He rolled onto his back, and her hand fell away.

"The Big Boss doesn't beat us into submission." As a joke it fell flat. "He just reminds me once in a while that Death is who I am. It's my reason for existing. Can't argue with the facts."

"But millions of people die every day. You can't be responsible for each one."

"Wouldn't give me much time for other things, would it?" Like covering her body with his and driving into her again, and—*Stop it.* Seemed like his mind wasn't the only thing he couldn't control tonight. "I specialize. I rid the earth of the ones who're too evil to exist but are fated to live long, healthy lives."

She frowned. "What about redemption? The person you kill might regret his evil actions sometime in his future, but you take that chance away from him."

Edge thought about the guy about to dump poison into the reservoir. "Yeah, well tell that to the thousands of people who end up dead while he's deciding he's sorry."

She didn't seem to have an answer for that. Surprising. He'd thought she'd spout the official line of leaving things up to some supreme being.

Time to change the subject. The conversation was getting too deep, too uncomfortable. "So what's your story? Ganymede doesn't think you're an angel."

She sighed. "Ganymede is wrong."

"How long have you been an angel?"

She hesitated. "I don't know. Looks like we have something in common. Time doesn't have much meaning in heaven. And no big events have happened to mark my existence. I just . . . am."

Sounded boring to Edge. "What does the Supreme Being look like?" Better find out now, because he'd never meet Him in person.

Again that hesitation. "I don't know."

He turned his head to stare at her. She looked away.

"Have *any* of the angels seen Him?" Or Her, or It. A different gender or form for the Supreme Being wouldn't bother him.

"No." It was almost a whisper. "Archangel Ted passes on His messages."

Something was weird here. They'd never even *seen* Him? Then he thought about the Big Boss. Maybe not so weird. "You said you got to choose your own name. Why'd you choose Passion?"

She smiled. "Sometimes I'm not as accepting of my job as you are of yours. I have a streak of defiance that's gotten me in trouble a few times. Anyway, sensuality is frowned on at home. So when I chose a name, I picked one that was ambiguous enough that they couldn't deny my request. After all, passion can mean a strong drive for something, like a passion for doing good. But whenever anyone says my name, they think of the sexual meaning. Archangel Ted hates it."

While he tried to come to terms with her vision of heaven, she asked another question. "Have you ever seen the Big Boss?"

"No. He keeps a low profile too. I've met his emissary, though. Funny guy who rides around in an ice-cream truck." Edge thought about the Big Boss. "Whoever the Big Boss is, he's not the devil."

From her little start beside him, he figured that's exactly what she'd been thinking. "Sure, all the cosmic trouble-makers live up to their names, but the Boss holds us in check. When I was first created, I'd wipe out a village with hundreds of people just to eliminate the one evil guy I was after. The Big Boss put a stop to that."

"So now you only kill one at a time." Her voice was flat.

"Yeah." He wasn't making a great impression. But that's what he'd wanted, wasn't it?

"We need to get some sleep." She turned her back to him.

What was she thinking? Did she condemn him? Probably. Did she blame the Big Boss? Most likely. Did it matter? He closed his eyes as he turned on his side facing away from her. *Yes.*

Passion woke slowly, dragging herself unwillingly from the grip of a surprisingly carnal dream. Archangel Ted couldn't blame her for what she did in her sleep, so she'd allowed herself to enjoy every second of it. She'd never experienced anything even close to erotic at home, but amazingly, she'd known exactly what to do with the tawny-haired god—oops, sorry, Ted—with the tawny-haired, beautiful male animal in her dream.

Reluctantly, she released the dream. As awareness crept over her, she realized something was wrong.

Passion enjoyed room when she slept. She usually woke spread-eagled across her bed. This time was no different. Only one problem. This time her arm and leg seemed to be draped over something. What?

She opened her eyes. Uh-oh. Her arm lay across Edge's chest, her palm resting over one male nipple. Passion could feel it pressing into her palm. She'd flung her leg over his . . . Oh, crap. She hastily moved her leg back to her side of the bed, but not before she experienced her first feel ever of male sexual organs. Well, at least her toes had. They'd been resting against his long, hard . . . She could feel heat rising up her neck and crawling over her face. She'd aroused him with her toes. Could it get any worse? *Could it get any better?*

No, no, that hadn't been her thought. She was pure of mind and body. *Who're you kidding? Pure of mind? Give me a break.*

Okay, so she had her fantasies. She might not have interacted on the mortal plane, but she knew human thoughts. Men might not think about sex every seven seconds, but they thought about it a lot.

One good thing, the sheet had hidden her leg.

He turned his head to stare at her. "Bed hog." But his eyes were hot and hungry.

Embarrassed, she looked past him to where Hope sat up in bed with a laptop open in front of her. She'd turned on her lamp. Ganymede still slept. Passion strained to see what was on the screen. Facebook? "Where'd you get that?" Archangel Ted didn't approve of the social networks.

"Hmm?" Hope glanced at her but looked right back at the screen. "Sparkle brought it this morning when she delivered the clothes."

"What clothes?" Then she saw them draped over the backs of the two chairs. "Never mind." Passion didn't like the idea of someone coming into the room and leaving without her knowing it. But at least her face had cooled off enough for her to chance a look at Edge again. "I'll release you."

"Don't have to." He held up his cuff-free wrist.

Passion glanced at Hope. "Oh, thanks, Hope."

"It wasn't me. He was free when I woke up." She never took her eyes from the screen. "I registered as Angel Hope. I said that I could help people find happiness. Do you think I'll get any friends?"

Edge laughed. "Oh, you'll get friends."

"How did you free yourself?" Passion tried to free *herself* from the siren call of all that bare male flesh just a few inches away from her fingers. Heaven wasn't big on the senses. She needed to load up on her experiences before she went home. Right now she was hoping for tactile overload.

"If you want to keep a nonhuman as your bed prisoner, sweetheart, you really need to know what his powers are." Edge's smile mocked her. "You didn't hide the key. So when I wanted to get out of bed to stretch my legs, I just called the key to me and it came."

Wait. Her toes had been resting on bare . . . "Did you put on any clothes before you got out of bed?"

He looked puzzled. "Why should I? You and Hope were asleep."

"No, I wasn't." Hope sounded distracted. "Wow, I have a friend request already. Do you think I should ask him if he's evil? Because if he is, I can help him."

"No, don't ask him anything." Passion stared at Hope until the other angel looked at her.

"What?"

"He got out of bed naked and walked across the room naked. Didn't you think that was newsworthy?"

Hope shrugged. "I didn't look at him with lust, so what's the big deal?"

Didn't look at him with *lust*? How could she not? All that bare beautiful skin, all those rippling muscles, all that sexual temptation walking across the room. How could she freaking *not*?

Passion turned her gaze back to Edge. He returned her stare. Now that she'd calmed down enough to examine her response, she realized something.

She was in deep trouble. Hope's reaction had been the perfect angel's response. Passion's response was all volatile *human* reaction. This was not good.

She tore her gaze from his. "What will you and Ganymede do today?"

"Ganymede will stay with Sparkle. Neither of us should be alone until we track down whoever is doing this." Edge picked up his watch from beside the mattress. "Almost noon. Who'd know in this tomb." He started to climb out of bed. "I need to get dressed."

She thought about ripping the sheet from the mattress and offering it to him, but then changed her mind. Something sly and wicked suggested that she needed that sheet because it was chilly here in the dungeon.

She swallowed hard as he scooped up the clothes he'd flung on the floor last night and stood with his back to her. Oh. My. God. From broad shoulders down to tight butt and hard thighs, he was a living, breathing fantasy. Passion might never leave her cubicle again if she could just tape pictures of him like this all over it. *Turn around, turn around*.

She knew her face was flushed and her eyes wide. Hope had the same view facing her . . . And she didn't even look! The other angel was too busy staring at her laptop. Passion couldn't conceive of anyone being that . . . *good*. Okay, try dead. Someone just needed to bury her. Passion looked enough for both of them.

He slid jeans over his lean hips and didn't bother with anything else. Passion was in the middle of licking suddenly dry lips when he turned around.

Edge paused in fastening his jeans to study her. Then

he smiled, a slow, sensual lifting of his sexy lips. "No naked angels in heaven?"

"No naked cosmic troublemakers in *this* room." Lord, how would she survive another night knowing what slept beside her? Okay, she'd think positively. Maybe their search today would turn up the culprit.

His expression said he knew exactly what she thought of naked cosmic troublemakers. "I'll be next door in Dacian's shower. If you hear shouts of 'Kill Ganymede,' come running." He strode from the dungeon.

Passion got out of bed and shrugged into her robe. She raked her fingers through her hair. She could hear the shower running through the wall. *Don't think about it.* "What about breakfast?" *Hot, sexy male served on a warm croissant and lathered with melted butter.* "Don't you think it's time to shut down the laptop?" Good, she couldn't think of anything sensual about that.

"I ordered room service." Hope looked up briefly. "I registered on Twitter too. This is a lot more fun than soothing troubled souls."

"What would Archangel Ted say?" Not that Passion cared.

"He's not here." Hope was once again lost to the magic of Twitter.

"How easily we're corrupted." Her mutter didn't reach Hope.

Before she could think of anything else to say, someone knocked on the door. She stuffed her feet in her slippers and went to the door. "Who is it?" She'd learned caution. No more flinging the door open to just anyone.

"Jack the Ripper with your breakfast, madam." Holgarth's sarcasm leaked under the door and poisoned the air.

But if he had breakfast, she'd put up with him for a few minutes. She opened the door.

Even this early in the day, he wore his whole wizard outfit complete with tall conical hat. He waved the man pushing the serving cart into the room and followed him inside. He closed the door with a wave of his hand. Show-off.

Passion went over to peek under the lids once the man had left.

"I apologize, madam, but we ran out of eye of newt. We tried to substitute vampire's blood, but alas, Dacian refused to hold still." Holgarth walked over to see what Hope was so engrossed in. "Ah, Facebook. I believe the gentleman who has requested your friendship is a demon. I hope you're open-minded. Demons can be quite entertaining."

With a frightened squeak, Hope slammed the laptop shut.

Passion sighed. "I don't remember a side order of annoying wizard with my pancakes."

"Have no fear, I won't be staying. I simply came to collect Edge. I'll be his guardian for the day."

As if on cue, Edge returned. He must've taken a side trip back to his room for fresh clothes because he was dressed in jeans, boots, and black T-shirt. He oozed sensual promise. He paused when he saw Holgarth. "Don't tell me."

Holgarth raised one haughty brow. "Then I most certainly won't."

Edge made a disgusted sound. "Be prepared to go where I go, wizard." He strode toward the door.

Holgarth sighed dramatically. "It's not enough that I give my life's blood to my job each day, but now I've been ordered to babysit Death."

"Don't you want to eat before you go?" Passion forced her gaze to stay on Edge's face.

His smile was all about sexual temptation. "Oh, definitely, but I don't think what I want is on the hotel's menu." Then Edge followed Holgarth out the door.

Passion turned from the door and wondered what was happening to her. Somewhere during the last twenty-four hours she'd lost her focus. Then she remembered. "Did you report in to Archangel Ted last night?"

Hope was tentatively opening the laptop again. She looked up at Passion from wide eyes. "I forgot."

"Yes, well, if you don't do it soon, he'll just—" Passion got no further, as suddenly the temperature dropped and power vibrated all around her. "Too late."

A male voice filled their minds. *"It has come to the Supreme Being's attention, Hope, that you calmed the mind of an irredeemable one last night."*

"Irredeemable?" Hope's voice was a horrified squeak.

"How the heck did he know?" Passion wondered who the snitch was in the castle.

"You do not think like an angel, Passion. An angel accepts that the Supreme Being knows all. Humans are the ones who are suspicious, who lack trust and always suspect a 'snitch.'" Archangel Ted sounded sadly regretful.

Passion didn't believe he was regretful at all. He'd never liked her.

"The Supreme Being does not want you to interfere with the cosmic troublemakers again. They are beyond redemption."

There was a pause, and Passion could picture Ted ticking off his list of complaints for the day. *"Do you have anything to report, Hope?"*

Hope looked at Passion. Passion shrugged.

"Umm, no, Archangel Ted. But Passion and I will spend the day looking for souls to help. I'm sure there are many of them."

Try many, many, many of them. And Passion didn't have a clue where to start. Somehow it had been easier in heaven. It was like the difference between telemarketing and standing behind a counter. If things got tough on the phone, you could just hang up. But when you were behind the counter, the customer could jump over it and chase you through the store. Besides, she'd never had to deal with any hard-core sinners before. Add to that her pesky emotions that kept getting in the way, and you had a recipe for disaster.

"Very well. But I want a list of all the sinners you find,

their sins, and your plans to help them find the light. By tomorrow. And even though I don't want you to interfere in their fights, I do want you to keep an eye on the cosmic troublemakers. If they become too violent, I'll send down the avenging angels." The room returned to its normal temperature. He was gone.

Okay, this called for food. Passion piled pancakes, eggs, and sausage on her plate, poured herself a cup of coffee, and sat down on one of the chairs. "We won't be able to do all that by tomorrow, you know." She set her coffee cup on the coffee table.

Passion closed her eyes in bliss as she savored the spicy flavor of the sausage. She mourned that she'd be going back to a world of eternal dullness. *Be honest, everything is bland in heaven.* Ted had explained that the Supreme Being believed if anything in heaven was more than bland, it would distract the angels from their jobs. Look at humans; they were slaves to their senses. The Supreme Being was probably right.

"Of course we will. Archangel Ted understands our capabilities." Hope set the laptop on the bed, fixed her own plate, and brought it back to the bed, where she immersed herself once again in the world of Facebook.

If Hope thought that, then she didn't understand the situation. "We can eliminate Ganymede, Edge, and Sparkle. We don't have to worry about Bain either."

Hope looked up. "Why?"

"He's a demon."

"Demon?" Hope dropped her toast.

"Irredeemable."

Hope finally gave Passion her complete attention. Evidently, it took a demon to tip the scales against Facebook. "How do you know all this? And is there anything else you haven't told me?"

Passion studied her pancakes. She sort of felt guilty, but things had been happening so quickly she hadn't had time to fill Hope in completely. "Umm, Dacian is a vampire." She hurried on. "But he can still be redeemed."

Hope carefully placed the laptop on the floor next to her mattress and got up. "I'm getting dressed. We have a full day ahead of us."

"I think Ted said something about a plan. Do you have one? Because I sure don't." They couldn't just start knocking on doors and asking whoever answered if they were evil. "Maybe we can start by waking up the irredeemable cat. I got the feeling he didn't want to miss breakfast."

Hope had no chance to answer because someone knocked on the door. Passion went to the door and did her who's-there thing. She hoped there wasn't another smart-ass on the other side.

"It's Sparkle. I brought Mede's snacks and some things so we can get started on your transformation."

Transformation? Did that sound a little demonic? Fascinated, Passion opened the door.

Sparkle swept into the dungeon. She carried a small bag and was dragging a rolling suitcase behind her. Passion closed the door as Sparkle lifted the suitcase onto the table with the restraints. That seemed ominous. Then she walked over to where Ganymede still slept, oblivious to everything going on around him.

Sparkle pulled a large cup from the bag, removed the top, and calmly poured its contents onto the head of the sleeping cat.

Ganymede came off the bed in what had to be a four-foot vertical leap. Impressive. His outraged yowl made Passion's head throb.

"Now that you've had your drink, you can chow down on the rest of your snacks." Sparkle dropped the bag onto the bed and started to turn away. "Oh, and the store is still a wreck. I think you promised to clean up the mess. I can't open again until you do."

Passion widened her eyes. Wow, if Sparkle wanted to jump-start the apocalypse, she was doing a great job. She waited for Ganymede to blow out the walls of the castle.

But all he did was jump off the bed and head for the door. The door swung open with such violence that it bounced off the wall. *"I'm going next door to shower this crap off me. I'll get Bain to stay with me today. Let me know when you're over whatever it is that's pissed you off."* He was muttering about one-hinge-short-of-a-nuthouse-door women as he slammed the door shut behind him.

Sparkle strolled back to the table, hoisted herself onto it, and crossed her long legs. Her short black dress rode up her smooth thighs. "I probably should've controlled my temper." Her smile was all wicked enjoyment. "But that felt so good."

Passion dropped onto a chair. Talk about relieved. The door might be still vibrating, but the walls stood firm.

"You thought Mede was going to go ballistic on me, didn't you?" Sparkle looked amused.

"Yes." Passion decided not to elaborate on the black swirling around him and her expectations based on what that black meant. "Why didn't he?"

"He loves me." Sparkle uncrossed her legs and leaned forward to open her rolling suitcase.

Passion mustn't have done a good job of hiding her reaction, because Sparkle laughed. "Just because he's a hard-ass doesn't mean he can't love. I spread sexual chaos wherever I can, but I love him."

"But you—"

Sparkle waved away whatever Hope had been about to say. "The good don't own love." She unzipped her case and dragged out trays of makeup and nail color. "Tell me the truth, have either of you ever done anything bad?"

Passion shook her head. Sure, there were her fantasies, but they were in her mind. That didn't count as *doing* anything bad. She sat on her conscience to keep it quiet.

Hope looked horrified that Sparkle would even ask the question. "I've always followed Archangel Ted's rules."

"Not your Supreme Being's rules, but *Ted's* rules?" Sparkle looked at both Passion and Hope. "Am I the only one who sees anything wrong with that?"

Hope looked confused. "Well, Ted gets the rules from the Supreme Being."

Sparkle sighed. "This could be my greatest challenge." She crooked her finger at them. "Come here, ladies, and find out what it's like to be a beautiful and sexy woman."

"I don't think so. Archangel Ted said only natural beauty is worthy." Hope gathered up her clothes and headed for the door and Dacian's shower.

"Archangel Ted is an ass."

Hope was already closing the door and didn't hear Sparkle's mutter, but Passion heard it. And as wrong as she knew it was, she believed Sparkle.

Sparkle turned to Passion. "How about you?"

Since she'd started the day with impure thoughts about Edge, her goodness rating was already shot, so she may as well go for it. She took her coffee over to the table. "Sure."

While Sparkle worked on her, Passion asked a few questions. "What exactly are your duties as a cosmic trouble-maker?"

Sparkle smoothed a cleansing pad over Passion's face and neck. "I foment sexual chaos. That means I encourage people to have sex." Her gaze turned distant, and a small smile tugged at her lips. "I get particular pleasure when I bring together two people who're all wrong for each other, they have crazy sex, and then I'm able to tear them apart." She sighed. "The emotional trauma is absolutely wonderful."

"But that's not right. People's misery shouldn't make you happy." Passion drew back a little.

Sparkle sighed. "If it's any comfort, lately my track record sucks. I've brought together people who lust after each other but have nothing else in common. The odds should be against any lasting relationship."

Passion wanted to slap her silly. *Violence is wrong.* Right, no violence. Arrgh! "That's not the point. Your intent is evil."

"Hello, I'm a cosmic *troublemaker*. It's what I do." Sparkle brightened. "But good does come from it in the end. Once the woman gets over wanting to either kill the guy or crawl to him begging that he take her back, she realizes she's better for the experience. Now she has good hair, great makeup, and a hot wardrobe. She can aim higher next time."

"What about the poor guy?"

Sparkle shrugged. "I'd offer makeup and hair tips, but only a few men are secure enough in their masculinity to take advantage of my advice. They usually resort to drink."

Passion subsided. Turning Sparkle to the light would be tough.

Two hours later, Sparkle was finished. And so was Passion. Sparkle had labored over Passion's face, hair, and nails. Then she'd chosen an outfit and shoes for her and shooed her next door to Dacian's bathroom to change.

Passion couldn't have sat still for another minute. *Nothing* was worth this. She muttered her opinion of all things Sparkle related as she dressed and slipped her feet into shoes with heels she just knew were evil instruments of torture.

There. Finished. Then she glanced into the mirror for the first time. Oh. My. God. And knew that Sparkle had corrupted her for all time. No longer was she bland and boring. Her hair was a tangled golden glory around her face. Her lips, eyes, and . . . everything were . . . *Pride is wrong.* Passion's conscience was doing lots of finger wagging, but she couldn't help feeling a swell of excitement.

What would Edge think? She froze on that thought. He shouldn't be on her mind at all. She turned from the mirror and rushed from the bathroom.

She'd just gotten back to the dungeon when someone knocked.

"I'll get it." Anything to keep Sparkle from seeing her face, because Passion was sure the name Edge was blazoned across her forehead.

Hope had also returned, and Sparkle was busy trying to break down her resistance. Sparkle didn't look over at Passion.

Passion didn't bother to ask who was there, because honestly, she didn't care. She pulled open the door.

Edge was turned toward Holgarth, who stood behind him. "Forget killing Ganymede. I'm coming after *you* next time."

Holgarth sniffed. "I was not aware that I couldn't have an opinion on your suite. It's dreadful. Dull, dreary, and unfit for human or nonhuman habitation. I only made a few suggestions to drag it from the pit of deadly boring into which it has sunk."

Edge made a rude noise. "I'm finding someone else to follow me around." He turned to face the open door. He froze.

And then he smiled, a smile that flattened all her preconceived ideas of evil's power. No, not evil's power, but her ability to resist it.

Wickedness didn't come with fire and brimstone. It attacked with a sensuality so powerful she could actually feel something hot and needy inside spreading, melting away her almighty conscience until all she wanted was to wrap herself around his naked body and do what she'd never thought she'd do. And she wanted to do it many, many times.

Archangel Ted would be horrified.

"You can go back to single-handedly running the castle, Holgarth. I've found someone else to stay with today."

7

Edge had been around long enough to know that a beautiful exterior didn't say a thing about what lived inside that body. But there were some exteriors that just had to be acknowledged. He'd thought she was incredible before Sparkle did her thing, but now . . . Sparkle had underlined and highlighted Passion's beauty in case he'd missed any details.

The red dress wasn't as short as Sparkle's, but it still showed off her long legs. It showed off other things too. Edge thought it was kind of strange that the Supreme Being had showered her with so many gifts meant to seduce a man when she wasn't supposed to be about temptation. An oversight on His part, no doubt.

Maybe Edge should say something instead of just staring. "If I have to spend a whole day with the wizard here, I'll need a straitjacket. Maybe you can take his place." He tried to make his next words sound casual with no hot panting involved. "You look great. Sparkle knows her stuff."

Passion just stared.

Okay, not cool. He needed to add an addendum to that comment. "Not that you didn't look great before, but Sparkle just made everything . . . better." Edge winced. Lame. His usual flow of sensually charged compliments guaranteed to put a smile on a woman's face and her body in his bed had dried up. Maybe because this time he was trying to be sincere. Edge and sincerity were distant cousins at best.

"Of course I know my stuff." Sparkle abandoned Hope—who wore a mulish expression—to join Passion at the door. "Holgarth, you really need to work on your social skills."

Holgarth looked offended. "My social skills need no improving, madam. Can I help it if no one seems able to accept helpful criticism?" He turned away. "Since my services are not needed here, I'll return to supervising the running of the castle."

Edge controlled his urge to hurl an insult at the wizard's pointed head as he walked away. Instead, he turned his attention back to Passion. "So will you hang with me today?" He tried not to look as though her answer was particularly important to him.

"I guess I could." She didn't seem too enthusiastic.

Sparkle jumped in. "I have a wonderful idea."

Edge felt an uh-oh moment coming.

"Passion is here to help the wicked find their way back to goodness, although personally I find the wicked much more fun to be around than the righteous. That's just me, of course." She smiled at Passion, probably to lessen the sting. "And you, Edge, need to find the person responsible for your loss of control."

Sparkle waited for one of them to state the obvious. No one did. Her expression said, "Do I have to make all the decisions around here?"

"You both have to canvass the castle, so you may as well work together. You, Passion, can make your pitch for goodness and light." She frowned. "Don't make it too obvious, though. We don't want any guests complaining that holy nuts are harassing them in their rooms."

"Holy *nuts*?" Passion looked as though she wanted to comment on that, but Sparkle didn't give her a chance.

"Edge, you can just stand behind Passion and see if you get any kind of vibes from the guests. If you do, don't make a move. We're dealing with a powerful entity, and we'll have to attack it together."

"Umm, excuse me, but I'm part of this team too." Hope had joined them. "You said I was the one who calmed Edge, so wouldn't it make sense for me to go along in case he gets hit with another compulsion?"

Sparkle didn't look happy. Edge knew how she worked and what she was up to now. Sparkle wanted to give Passion and him time alone. They were her newest project. Read: victims. He could go along with her plans if this was just about sex, because he couldn't deny that he wanted sex with Passion. Anything deeper wasn't happening.

Passion touched Hope's arm. "Sure you are. Change to one of the outfits Sparkle brought, and come with us."

Hope turned to look at Sparkle's choices. "I think I'll just wear the stuff I brought. It's more appropriate for an angel." Her tone dared Sparkle to deny that truth.

"Do you mean boring?" Sparkle shrugged. "I guess we are what we want to be. Your loss."

Edge could feel Sparkle's anger. Not a good thing for Hope. Sparkle was ticked off that Hope was messing with her plans. And it didn't help that Hope had turned up her nose at Sparkle's clothes. Sparkle watched with narrow-eyed intensity as Hope carefully folded her nightgown and robe, then laid them on her bed.

Passion followed Hope back into the room. "Let me get a few things, and I'll be ready."

Edge lowered his voice. "Stop scheming, Sparkle."

"It's what I do, beautiful. You and Passion are all wrong for each other, but I can almost taste your hunger for her. And I'd bet her thoughts are nowhere close to angelic right now. A few more nights naked in her bed should do it."

And as much as Edge wanted to tell Sparkle to butt out, he didn't. Because he wanted the same thing she did.

"I wish Hope wasn't going, but I guess it's better that you have her near in case the urge to kill Mede hits you. Again." She thought about that. "Funny, but I've had the same urge since last night. Do you think the compulsion is catching?"

Edge laughed. "What did he do? I need to fill in the big blank space where my memories should be."

Sparkle avoided his gaze. "I begged him to walk away from a fight with you. He could've dematerialized and that would've been the end of it. He ignored me. He. Ignored. *Me.* Selfish bastard. Nothing comes before his almighty ego." There was real hurt in her voice.

Edge wasn't sure what to say. "He'll apologize eventually. He always does."

She sighed. "Maybe you need to point out to him where he went wrong. Right now, he's clueless. And that's just pathetic."

He didn't tell her, but no way was he involving himself in this. He might survive one of them, but both? Let's say he'd have a long recovery period. Luckily, Passion and Hope joined him, and Sparkle left.

A few minutes later, Edge was talking to Bill at the registration desk while Passion and Hope waited for him to finish. When they left, they had a list of the guests who'd been at the castle for several weeks. There weren't too many.

The first two were routine—two guys in town for fishing, and a couple on their honeymoon. All human and not much evil in the bunch. Passion looked relieved, but Hope seemed a little disappointed. Edge hadn't expected a hit on the first two. He figured their guy would be by himself.

Things got interesting after that. The third door swung open and . . . Oh, shit. It was the old woman who'd tried to help him in the hall last night.

She smiled at Hope, before looking past her to him. The old woman's eyes grew wide and she screamed. Then she slammed the door in their faces. Hope and Passion turned to stare at him.

"Human. She's not the one." When Hope still looked puzzled, he elaborated. "She saw the compulsion take me last night. When she tried to help, I scared her." An understatement. She'd seen the monster inside him.

Hope nodded and they walked to the next door. After the last response, she seemed a little more cautious when she knocked.

The man who answered was big, probably as tall as Ganymede. Edge only had time to notice his long black robe—not the expected outfit for late morning—before his gaze reached the man's eyes. Pale blue, cold, hard. He knew those eyes.

Edge tensed as he gathered his power to him. The air grew heavy with that still, charged feeling it got right before lightning struck. "What're you doing here?"

"I enjoyed my first visit so much I decided to swing by here again." His smile mocked Edge.

"You registered as Kurt Marsh. Not the name you gave last time, sorcerer." Edge was tempted to reach for Ganymede's mind, but he knew how the cat would react. He didn't want violence until he was sure this was his guy.

"Names are tools. I don't attach myself to a particular one. But if Zane makes you feel more comfortable, feel free to use it." His gaze shifted to Passion and Hope.

"Well, well, what have we here? Not humans. I love beautiful and mysterious women." His smile warmed.

Edge's surge of anger had nothing to do with last night's compulsion. He wanted to wipe that smile off the bastard's face, preferably with his fists. "You won't be here long enough to make friends. Do you have any idea what Ganymede and Dacian will do to you?"

Passion spoke up. "Don't mean to intrude, but what the hell is going on?" She felt violence creeping closer and rushed to head it off if she could.

Hope began, "Hell is a—"

"I *know* what it is. Now keep quiet unless you have any ideas about how to stop these two from tearing up the castle." Jeez, could Hope be more oblivious?

Passion immediately felt guilty. This wasn't about the castle at all. This was about Edge. Everything that Archangel Ted had taught her—patience, kindness, charity—disappeared the moment she thought Edge was in danger.

Thankfully, surprise at Passion's outburst had silenced Hope for the moment.

"Zane here showed up about a year ago with Dacian's maker and Rabid, the cosmic troublemaker in charge of anger. He'd hired himself out to help kill Dacian."

Passion couldn't hide her shock. She put out feelers. Human?

Zane raised one brow. "If you remember, I walked away without harming anyone."

"Yeah, that was only because Dacian's brother killed your boss, and you wouldn't work without a paycheck."

"Paychecks are important."

Zane sounded so reasonable that it was tough for Passion to connect him to the horror Edge was describing. She checked out his colors. Dark red. Rage, deep and violent. Not someone to mess with.

Zane looked at her. "I felt your touch, mystery woman. I wonder what you found. More to the point, I wonder what you are." He sounded intrigued.

His answer sucked the air from her lungs. No one could *feel* what she did. "I didn't *touch* you. And I'm human. What else would I be?"

"You could be many things." He narrowed his eyes. "Not vampire or shifter. Not demon or one of the fey." His smile looked almost hungry. "I *will* find out."

"That's ridiculous. There's nothing to find out." Because he'd shaken her, she probably sounded a little too dismissive.

His stare reached into her, searching. "Knowing is power. Never underestimate the unknown."

"What's to keep me from killing you right now?" Edge's expression said there wasn't much.

"No killing." Passion glanced at Hope to see if she was ready to jump into action. Hope nodded.

"Let me list the reasons." Zane didn't sound intimidated. "First, I'm powerful enough to make you exert yourself. Your precious castle would be flattened by the time you destroyed me." He slid his glance to Passion and Hope. "Others would be hurt or killed. Second, you have bigger fish to fry."

"How do you know?" Suspicion oozed from Edge.

"It's obvious. Why are you banging on doors? You must be looking for someone, someone big because otherwise you wouldn't bother to do it yourself. And last night I felt a spike in power around here. Too big for anything Holgarth or Sparkle could create. So now I'm curious." He smiled. "I think I'll stay to see what shakes out."

A growl started deep in Edge's throat. Tension and power rolled off him. She wasn't imagining the floor vibrating.

Frantically, Passion looked at Zane. "Go inside and shut the door."

Zane studied her from narrowed eyes. He hesitated just long enough for her to think he intended to continue taunting Edge. Then he nodded. Without saying another word, he closed the door.

Passion went limp with relief.

Hope put her hand on Edge's arm. He didn't shrug her off. And then she began talking.

Just like last night, Passion could hear the words, but something in her brain refused to translate. Her mind allowed only the feel of the words to reach her, a tone and rhythm that soothed her, made her feel that everything would be okay when she knew it wouldn't.

Finally, Hope stopped talking and silence settled around them. The blaze of anger had disappeared from Edge's eyes.

"Is he the one?" Passion sounded shaky, not the way she wanted to sound in front of Edge. Ted had pounded into their heads that when they visited the mortal plane, they represented the Supreme Being. Passion assumed that meant she wasn't supposed to be afraid. Fine, so she was a lousy rep.

Edge raked his fingers through his hair with a hand that shook. Passion didn't like to see the proof of how close he'd come to attacking Zane. She wanted to reach over and clasp his hand, pass on to him . . . What? She didn't have anything useful to pass on other than feelings he probably wouldn't welcome.

"I don't know. He's the most powerful sorcerer I've ever seen. Last year he showed up in answer to a call Holgarth put out for a replacement. Holgarth is powerful, but Zane made him look like a rank beginner. The bastard lifted the freaking castle off its foundation. Then once he set it down, he wiped the minds of all the guests."

"An illusion?" Hope was still staring at the closed door.

Edge shook his head. "No, I only wish it was. In the final battle, it was Ganymede, Dacian, and Bain along with a goddess and Dacian's maker against Dacian's maker, the rogue troublemaker, a bunch of vampires, and Zane. Sparkle almost died. Ganymede went ballistic. Luckily for Earth, the goddess revived her."

"Zane called up a freaking blizzard during the fight. He was the only one of the enemy who survived. I don't know how Ganymede will react to the news." He took a breath. "Right now, he's moved to the top of my suspect list."

"But he's human." Passion knew how that sounded, but no one could argue that a human wouldn't have the kind of power to control Edge's mind.

Edge turned away from the door as though if he stood there one more moment, he'd be tempted to go in after the sorcerer. "You of all people should know the power of evil. If Zane's weaving black magic, anything is possible."

Passion and Hope followed him down the hall.

"I don't think he looked that evil." Hope seemed distracted. "All that dark hair and those ice-blue eyes. I thought he looked . . ." She glanced away. "I know evil sometimes wears a beautiful face. Look at you and Ganymede."

Surprisingly, Passion wanted to come to Edge's defense. Only, she couldn't. After all, he was Death. How did you defend that? The realization made her sad.

At the next door, Edge stepped in front of them. "I'll be the one to knock from now on."

Passion opened her mouth to tell him she didn't need his protection, but then shut it. Why bother? It wasn't worth arguing over right now. She held her breath as he knocked.

The man who answered wasn't as big as Zane, but his intimidating expression made him seem larger. Brown hair in a buzz cut, hard brown eyes that looked almost black, and lips drawn into a thin line didn't say, "Welcome, neighbor."

"Kemp Hardiway?" Edge's smile was cold and assessing.

The man simply nodded.

"I'm Edge, one of the hotel's managers, and I'm doing a short survey. I just wanted to ask you a few questions about your experience here."

Kemp didn't smile in return. "I don't do surveys." He started to close the door.

Just before the door closed completely, he met Passion's gaze. And something in his stare seemed . . . familiar. No, that was wrong. Passion was sure she'd never seen the man before.

"What did you think?" Edge was still staring at the closed door.

"He's not human." Passion's intuition was pretty accurate. What was he? Violet clung to him. Pride. And he had a few streaks of red swirling around him. Anger. But that was probably because he was ticked about the survey. Only two colors was a huge improvement over Edge and Ganymede.

"I feel as though I've heard his voice somewhere

before." A line of concentration had formed between Hope's eyes. "And yet I don't recognize it."

Edge nodded. "I don't know what he is, but I didn't get a feeling of great power from him. Let's go. We have one more person on this list."

Passion was feeling a little snarky. Hope and she hadn't gotten a chance to talk to anyone. Ted would be angry with Hope's report tonight. But what could they do?

They took the elevator up into one of the towers to check out their last suspect. They could hear loud music playing even before they got off the elevator.

"Someone likes Lady Gaga. I'll have to tell him to dial it down before other guests start complaining." He stopped in front of the door. "Or maybe I'll have Holgarth do it. He's such a diplomat." Edge smiled at some mental picture.

"Who's Lady Gaga?"

Hope never paid much attention to humanity's pop culture. On the other hand, Passion loved all things human. So she was busy moving her feet to the rhythm when the door opened.

She stopped dancing and gasped. Holy angels in heaven.

Passion had an impression of tall and elegant—black boots, black pants, and black silk shirt open to expose a tempting vee of smooth flesh. He was a symphony in black, a perfect color contrast to straight, shining blond hair that fell halfway down his back. She didn't have to access her intuition on this one, because no human would ever have that face. Thick lashes framed clear green eyes, and his mouth was a temptation few women could resist—she glanced at Edge's mouth—but *she* could.

Beside her, Hope's sigh said it all.

Edge tightened his lips at their reactions. "David Wittcomb?"

The man smiled, and the earth moved. Figuratively speaking. Passion glanced at Hope's rapt expression. Not a good sign.

He didn't answer the question. "I bet you're Edge. Bain

mentioned you. Death, right?" Behind him Gaga gave way to Muse.

Tall, blond, and gorgeous had a great voice, but in her opinion Edge's was sexier.

Edge tensed.

Oh, no, here we went again. Passion spoke up before Edge could say something aggressive. "Who are you, really?"

"I don't look like a David Wittcomb?" He answered his own question. "No, of course I don't."

"Then who?" The threat of violence colored the corners of Edge's voice.

"I'm Murmur, a friend of Bain's."

"What a beautiful name." Hope's expression said she was willing to cancel her account with Facebook if it meant she could spend time with Murmur.

"Demon." Edge said it with certainty.

He nodded. "I'm the Demon of Music." His smile widened. "We'd make great partners. Music to kill by."

Black. Passion had been so mesmerized by his packaging that she hadn't even noticed the telltale color. This was getting ridiculous.

Edge wasn't buying his smile. "Why are you here?"

Murmur stopped smiling. "I told you, I'm a friend of Bain's. We have things to discuss. Check."

"I will."

Murmur transferred his attention to Passion and Hope. "Would you like to come in and dance with me?" Every word was soaked in erotic promises.

Hope started forward. Passion grabbed her arm and yanked her back. "Thanks for the offer, but we don't have time today."

"When you're ready." His tone said they *would* be ready.

Murmur closed his door. They remained silent as they walked away.

Finally, Edge spoke. "I don't feel like staying inside.

Want to go out and look at the view from the top of the castle's wall for a while?"

Hope shook her head. "I think I'll go down to the great hall to find some people to help. I have to make a report tonight, and we haven't even started our work here." She didn't look happy. "You'll have to come up with a summary of what we discovered today, Passion." She bit her lip. "I thought this would be fun. I was even looking forward to getting rid of some of the really bad guys. Now . . ." Hope glanced away. "I mean, it's different once you actually meet them. I like Murmur." Her last admission was almost a whisper. She turned and walked toward the elevator at the end of the hall.

"That's an unexpected complication." Passion was worried. If Hope, who'd been all despise-the-evildoers at the beginning, was being drawn over to the dark side, what chance did Passion have?

Edge smiled. "Hope is learning that not everything is black or white. Shades of gray, sweetheart, shades of gray." He said nothing more as he led her out to the walkway atop the wall.

Passion forced herself not to stare at Edge as they stood with their backs to the parapet looking down into the courtyard.

"We have three suspects: Zane, Kemp, and Murmur. I'm going with the sorcerer or the demon." He shifted a little closer.

Passion was only half listening. After an eternity of nothing to look at except a world done in neutrals, she was having a tough time with this plane of existence. Everything here was colored in such depth, such intensity. She had to squint against the brilliant blue of the sky, and the grass in the courtyard looked almost too green to be real. When she first saw her room, Passion had gasped at the deep richness of the wood, the jewel tones of rugs and paintings.

And the emotions, God, the emotions.

All those feelings seemed centered on this man. It

wasn't just his looks, because heaven was filled with beautiful males. But over time Ted had molded their personalities into a bland sameness. No spiked hair, no tattoos, no strong opinions about anything. Boring. They disappeared into the background for her.

But Edge was like the world around him—vivid, exciting, a feast for the senses. *Dangerous.* It frightened her to realize how drawn she was to him. If she were a mouse, she'd be dancing on the mousetrap about now. And no matter how many times she reminded herself that he was evil, she still wanted him.

She closed her eyes to keep from staring at him. The scariest part was the more time she spent with him, the less she thought about what he did, the more willing she was to make excuses. He *killed* people. She couldn't lust after someone who would never seek redemption. *Too late.*

Passion was in the middle of an inner treatise on the nature of evil when he spoke.

"So what do you think? The sorcerer or the demon?"

She opened her eyes. "I don't have a clue. But don't dismiss Kemp. He could be cloaking his power."

"Not from me."

She sighed. He wouldn't like hearing this. "Whoever is messing with you and Ganymede is more powerful than you guys. So, yes, he could be hiding his power from you."

Passion expected him to deny what she was saying. Instead, he nodded. "You're right. Sometimes I have to remind myself that I'm not the biggest and baddest in the universe." He grinned at her. "Don't tell Ganymede what I said. He definitely thinks he's all that. I don't need to be giving him any more fuel for his personal bonfire."

Passion stared, mesmerized. He had a beautiful smile, with a mouth so sensual she hurt with her need to touch it. She wanted to wrap her arms around him and slide her tongue across his full lower lip. The problem was, she wouldn't want to stop there.

And his amber eyes framed by those thick lashes. Since

she'd met him, this was the first time his smile had reached those incredible eyes. Her breath caught in her throat. She had the feeling this wasn't a man who smiled often with his whole heart. Good thing. If he aimed that smile at her even a few times, he'd bring down the wall she'd built to protect her against too much of everything.

Ted warned them at least once a day about the dangers of excessive emotion. It made you weak, unable to fight against evil. Desire and all unchecked hungers were only for the Fallen, not for the Supreme Being's children of light. Well, she was a burned-out bulb right now.

She never found out what he might have said next because suddenly the whole castle shook.

Edge made the connection first. "Oh, shit. Ganymede." He turned to stare at the Gulf. She followed his gaze. What she saw puzzled her. There was only beach where the Gulf of Mexico had been. No water. Stranded sea life writhed and fought death on the sand as far as the eye could see.

Edge grabbed her hand and pulled her to him. "We have to get out of here fast. The tide has rushed out. First sign of a big wave coming. The shaking, the tide—this has Ganymede's fingerprints all over it. Someone has to stop him or else everyone on Galveston Island is dead."

"How do you know it's Ganymede?" Fear tugged at her.

"Earthquakes and tsunamis don't happen in the Gulf. And after last night . . . What're the chances it *isn't* Ganymede? Not many beings have that kind of power."

She didn't have time to say anything before awareness winked out. It winked back on in the great hall. Passion blinked and looked up at Edge. He released her. "Did you—"

"Yes." The smiling man from a few minutes ago was gone. "I have to find Ganymede."

"No." The thought of him facing a mindless destroyer terrified her. Surprised, she realized her own mortality wasn't the issue here. And sad to say, she hadn't yet grasped the enormity of thousands of people being swept away by a giant wave. "If he's like you were last night, he'll destroy you."

Edge turned and grabbed her shoulders in both hands. He stared into her eyes. "No one else is strong enough to battle him."

"Hope—"

"I don't see Hope. Do you?"

Frantically, Passion searched the screaming people pushing and shoving, fighting to escape the castle, thinking that if they could reach their cars they could escape death. She didn't see the other angel in the seething mob. "They can't outrun the tsunami, can they?"

"No. The wave will take out the causeway and maybe wipe away everything for miles inland." He gripped her tighter. "I don't have the power to send you far enough away to escape this. But if I can't stop Ganymede, I'll leave you with Bain. He can keep you alive."

A second shudder shook the castle. A life-size suit of armor on display toppled and added its clatter to the rising hysteria.

"There has to be another way." She tried to elude him, but he grabbed her hand.

"I have to find Bain. He'll protect you if I can't." He stood still as the crowd broke around him.

He must be reaching for Bain's mind. She looked around frantically, searching for a familiar face. *Where was Hope?* She couldn't go with Bain. What if Ganymede killed Edge? She needed to be there to put her hands on him. Passion still wasn't sure if she had any kind of power, but she had to be there to try.

She didn't have to guess where Ganymede was. Suddenly, deep thunderous roars mingled with the wild screams of a jungle cat. The sounds almost drowned out the terrified cries of the crowd. The people who had been trying to squeeze through the great hall door leading into the courtyard turned and stampeded in the opposite direction.

Edge wrapped one arm around her waist and pushed his way through the crowd rushing past them toward the exit at the other end of the great hall. She and Edge ran toward the courtyard door. "I don't want to take you out there, but that's where the others will be, trying to stop Ganymede."

Finally, they reached the door. Passion took a deep breath and looked outside.

Hell had come to Galveston.

8

Nightmares were born from reality, and Edge knew this one would stick with him a long time.

Two huge gargoyles stood sentinel outside the door leading from the great hall to the courtyard. Similar gargoyles were placed at intervals along the top of the wall surrounding Live the Fantasy. Usually, they slept.

But now their roars of rage filled the park, and their huge eyes glowed yellow. Someone had wakened them. That was supposed to be Holgarth's job. He used a spell, but a massive burst of energy might have the same effect.

They'd obviously wakened in a rotten mood. And once they stopped roaring, they'd rain destruction on anyone trying to enter or leave the park. Just freaking great.

Edge figured Ganymede was the one who'd given them their wake-up call, because right now Holgarth stood with his staff held in front of him chanting as he tried to put the gargoyles back to sleep. He bore little resemblance to the Holgarth Edge loved to hate. His conical hat was gone, and his robe was ripped and stained with blood. A cut on his forehead dripped blood.

Edge didn't have to look far for Bain. The demon stood about twenty feet from Ganymede, his arms flung across his eyes. Whatever he was trying to do to Ganymede wasn't working. Swirling wind tipped with Ganymede's fire whirled around him.

A few feet away, Sparkle lay on the grass. She didn't move. God, he hoped she was still alive. Ganymede wouldn't survive losing her like this. But then, they wouldn't survive Ganymede either.

And then there was the main attraction. It normally took Ganymede at least a half hour to regain his human form. The compulsion's onslaught must have flung him out of his cat form, but not completely.

He stood naked in the middle of the courtyard, every muscle taut, power flowing from him in waves that squeezed the breath from Edge's lungs even at this distance. But Ganymede still had his claws and his cat eyes.

He held his arms outstretched, his fingers spread and tipped by fully extended, lethal-looking claws. His cat eyes shone with a maniacal need to destroy. The wind created by his power lifted his long hair from his shoulders. Every strand was touched by flame, and even the air around him was glowing. Nothing remained of the snarky, ice-cream-eating troublemaker Edge knew. This was the horror that hid behind the chubby gray cat's image.

This was the chaos bringer—destroyer of planets, source of some of earth's most horrific disasters. Over time and with the Big Boss reining Ganymede in, everyone had sort of taken for granted that the destroyer would never ride again. They'd all been wrong.

Behind Edge and Passion, a TV blared. A news flash warned that an earthquake had hit the Gulf Coast and a tsunami warning had been issued.

Edge turned to Passion. "Stay here. Don't even think about coming out to help."

Her eyes were wide with fear. "But I have to find Hope."

"No." He had to make this clear. "Hope must know we

need her. She'll find us if she can. But if you wander off, Bain might not be able to get to you in time."

She glanced at where Bain had taken one agonized step toward Ganymede. The demon's face was chalk-white and lined with agony, but he was still trying to help.

"What if Ganymede destroys Bain?" Left unsaid was, *What if Ganymede destroys* you?

Edge had to go now, before it was too late to save any of the people trying to flee the island. Traffic would come to a standstill on all the escape routes, and then the giant wave would wash all of them away. Ganymede could stop the tsunami.

Where the hell was the Big Boss while all this was happening? He could control Ganymede. For a moment, he thought of Hope. No, he couldn't count on outside help.

Somewhere in the castle alarms wailed their warning. Edge had to shout over the noise. "Then go with Dacian or . . ." He closed his eyes for a moment. "Crap. Dacian is vampire. He's still sleeping. His wife could wake him, but she's away at some plant symposium. He'll be trapped when the wave hits."

"I'll get him." And then she was gone.

He couldn't follow Passion. If he didn't stop Ganymede now, she'd be as vulnerable as anyone here. Sure, she might be an angel like she claimed, but she might not. He'd only seen one sign of unusual powers. He'd have to assume she could die.

Edge ran toward Ganymede, and with each step he pictured Passion being swept away, dying because he'd failed. He clenched his fists. He couldn't fail.

Ganymede's power slammed him, searing his skin wherever it touched. Nightmare images filled his mind— Earth dying, exploding, becoming only a cloud of space dust. And Edge knew those pictures were coming from Ganymede's crazed thoughts, his plans for Earth's future.

The closer he drew to Ganymede, the tougher it got to even move. The wind, the burning, the images that pounded at his mind gripped him with claws that ripped and shredded. The agony made him want to fall to his knees and never get up.

He stopped beside Bain. The demon didn't look good. Edge shouted to be heard above the wind. "You have to help me."

Bain shuddered and turned to look at Edge. Even that much movement made him curl his lips from his teeth in an agonized snarl. "Trying here. He's blocking everything I throw at him. I've put out a call to a . . . friend."

Edge nodded. The motion made him feel as though his brain was inside a cocktail shaker. "Let me draw from your power. Together we might stop him." Even if they neutralized Ganymede, they couldn't stop the tsunami from reaching the coast. None of them could multitask at this level.

Bain didn't say anything, but Edge gasped at the massive infusion of pure power that surged into him with incredible force. It amazed Edge that the demon still had this much left after battling Ganymede for who knows how long.

Edge didn't hesitate. He drew all their combined power into his mind and then called forth the image of the giant squid that lived there.

He knew the moment Ganymede felt his presence, because he turned those terrible eyes on Edge. Ganymede smiled, a smile that Edge had never seen on his face. It was filled with insane joy and anticipation. Edge readied himself for either instant extinction or the battle of his life.

Even as Ganymede unleashed his power, Edge mentally drew a protective wall around himself and Bain, and hoped to God it held. Then he released the squid. Not as a physical reality, but as a mental attacker that would wrap its tentacles around Ganymede's mind and hold him immobile long enough to stop the destruction until they could figure out how to bring him back.

Ganymede's power exploded into his wall and brought Edge to his knees. His mind was a crushed grape. He was sure of it. Beside him, Bain was flung across the courtyard. He landed close to where Sparkle was just sitting up.

Edge shut his eyes and concentrated. He pictured the tentacles closing, cutting off all thought, squeezing Ganymede's power-to-destroy tighter and tighter until . . . Edge opened his eyes.

Ganymede stood immobile, his eyes strangely blank.

He'd done it. But Edge didn't have time to celebrate. He had to keep feeding his power to the squid or else Ganymede would just pick up where he'd left off. The question was, how long would Edge's power last? And did it even matter if no one stopped the tsunami?

Edge couldn't take his eyes off Ganymede long enough to look around for help. And what about Passion? Where was she? What was she doing? He ground his teeth in frustration.

Passion raced down the stairs to Dacian's apartment. Thank God he'd given her a key. Once inside, she flung open his bedroom door. He lay sprawled across his bed. Beside him, the phone was ringing.

She picked up the receiver at the same time she grabbed Dacian's shoulder and started to shake him.

A woman's voice shouted his name against her ear.

"This isn't Dacian. I'm Passion. I'm trying to wake him. Any ideas?" Because Dacian wasn't budging.

The woman didn't even question why someone named Passion was in his bedroom. "Ohmigod, ohmigod, I saw what was happening on TV. You have to get him out of there. Put the receiver next to his ear."

The woman hadn't introduced herself, but Passion figured it was his wife. She did what the woman said. Passion could hear the woman screaming into Dacian's ear.

"Dacian, wake up, damn it! Wake. The. Hell. Up." She was sobbing between words. "I'm in danger. Wake up so you can save me."

The woman was lying, but Passion believed in white

lies. She exhaled in relief when Dacian stirred. Passion renewed her shaking. And as Dacian sat up groggily, Passion put the receiver to her ear. "He's up. I'll take care of him."

She hung up to the sound of the woman's fervent thanks. Then she turned to Dacian.

His eyes were wide and confused. "Cinn? Where's Cinn? She's in danger."

"No, she's fine. She was talking to you on the phone. She only said that to get you out of the bed."

He closed his eyes, and when he opened them the fear had disappeared. "What's happening? Why are you here?"

"We need to get you upstairs right now. Ganymede's gone crazy. He's created a tsunami that should be reaching us soon, and he's . . ." She shook her head. "I don't have time to explain everything. Edge is out in the courtyard with the others trying to contain him."

Dacian looked more alert now. "Where's Hope?"

"I don't know. It's a mob scene everywhere. Thousands of people are trying to escape the island before the wave reaches here." She raked her fingers through her hair. "Can you leave the castle while it's still light?"

He shrugged. "You go. I'll be right up as soon as I throw on some pants." He tried to grin. "Not even a tsunami would get me up there naked."

"Right. No naked vampires." She headed for the door. "I have to find Hope."

Passion purposely ignored his shouted orders that she stay close to all of them. She couldn't stop the tsunami, but she could find Hope.

Once back in the great hall, she fought her way into the hotel lobby. Some of the hotel employees hadn't fled like everyone else and were trying to make sure the guests got out of the hotel safely. Passion saw Bill from the registration desk guiding the old woman who'd slammed her door in their faces.

Passion rushed up to them. She ignored the woman's

horrified expression. "Have you seen the lady who was with me earlier?"

The old woman fluttered her hands as though she were trying to shoo Passion away. "I saw her a bit before this horrible thing happened. She was going out the door with a man with long blond hair." She looked up pleadingly at Bill. "Please, you said one of the guests would take me in his car. I want to leave now."

"Certainly." Bill glanced at Passion. His expression said the woman's attempt to run from the island would be doomed, but what else could he do but lead her to the car?

Passion pushed her way out the door. Where had Hope gone, and who had been with her? A man with long blond hair. Murmur? Passion almost dismissed the possibility. Hope wouldn't go off with a demon. But then she remembered the angel saying she liked Murmur.

That wasn't important right now. What *was* important was *where* had they gone? She gazed across Seawall Boulevard and its bumper-to-bumper traffic crawling along. The beach? Passion had nowhere else to look.

The cars were pretty much stopped, so she wove her way around them as she crossed the street. Then she took the steps down to the beach. Frantically, she glanced both ways. There. A man stood on the beach gazing out at the vast expanse of sand exposed by the retreating tide.

She'd almost reached him when he turned to look at her. She froze. His long black coat flapped around his legs, and he'd pulled the hood over his head. All that she could see were those pale blue eyes watching her.

"Zane? What're you doing here? Shouldn't you be trying to get away from Galveston?" No, no, that's not what she wanted to say. What he was doing on the beach was his business. "Have you seen Hope, the woman who was with me?"

"She was here with the demon for a little while, but they went back to the hotel in a hurry about ten minutes ago." Zane paused. "They were dancing on the beach."

Wait. How did he know Murmur was a demon? Now wasn't the time to ask.

Passion nodded. She'd worry about the dancing thing later. If there was a later. "Thanks." She started to turn away but stopped. She should at least try to save him. "Maybe you should get off the beach." His stare made her uneasy.

"I have something to do. Besides, it's too late to run." He pointed toward the Gulf.

She tore her gaze from his eyes and looked. What she saw closed her throat and froze all thought for a moment. *Terror. Panic.* Emotions—like so many others—that she'd never experienced before coming to the castle. They would probably be her final ones before she died.

The tsunami loomed on the horizon. A wall of water that seemed to reach into the sky rushed toward the shore at a frightening speed. No time to run. She'd never make it back to Edge before it swept her away. Funny that Edge, a virtual stranger, was the one person she'd choose to die with. Of course, he was immortal, so maybe he'd survive. *Unless Ganymede has already destroyed him.* No, she had to believe he still lived.

The shrieks from the people on the road above who'd just spotted the wave blended with the mad honking of horns. Where did those poor souls think they could go now?

She looked back at Zane. "I guess it's just you, me, and the wave." *Fatalistic, that's me.* Would Hope survive? She'd have some report for Ted tonight. Not that any of it mattered. Passion had wanted to experience what it meant to be human—the emotions, all the senses—and she'd certainly more than fulfilled her wish. *No, you haven't. You're dying a virgin.* Somehow, that was really important.

And then there was Edge. What had he been to her? A possibility? An experience that would have ended in disaster? She sighed. Passion would like to have found out.

The wave swept nearer and nearer, picking up speed, seeming to grow higher and higher. She moved closer to

Zane. In her final moments, she wanted to be near another living being.

The sorcerer's soft chuckle snapped her out of her pensive mood. "Something funny about dying?"

"You won't be dying unless the ones back in the castle don't get Ganymede under control."

Okay, he was crazy. "Uh, big wave coming our way?" She glanced at the massive wall of water. It was almost here. And no matter how calmly she wanted to meet her end, she couldn't control the mad pounding of her heart, the need to try to run from death.

Zane looked away from her to face the incoming wave. He didn't lift his arms, he didn't chant, he didn't do anything she'd expect a sorcerer to do in a last-ditch effort to survive. He just stood there. But even in her human state, Passion could feel the immense *something* flowing from him.

She looked up, up, up at the towering wave about to break over them, over all of Galveston.

Then . . .

The wave went away. It freaking just went away! One minute it was there, and then only a few gentle swells reached their feet. It was as though the wave had never been.

Passion breathed out on a shocked hiss. She hadn't even realized she'd been holding her breath. "What?" Words weren't coming easily. "*What* did you just do?"

He didn't answer her. He started to walk away.

She ran after him. "Oh, no you don't. You don't get to be Mr. Mysterious this time. What. Did. You. Do?"

Zane didn't stop walking, and he didn't look at her, but he did give her an answer.

"I made the wave go away."

"How?"

"Magic."

"You're human. Humans can't do stuff like that." Even black magic shouldn't have that kind of power.

His laughter was soft and mocking. "You're right. I

couldn't have stopped the wave. So I guess you didn't just see what you thought you saw." He glanced at her one last time. "Oh, and I suppose I also didn't wipe the minds of everyone who saw Ganymede doing his thing back at the castle."

"Why?" Her question was only a whisper.

But he heard her. "I have another two weeks of vacation time. I didn't feel like finding someplace else to stay."

Passion stood frozen in place as she watched him climb the steps, weave his way between the cars, and disappear toward the castle.

Then she was running. She would live! They all would live. *Please, please let Edge be okay.*

Edge felt like a dry husk, the last of his power draining away. Any minute now the squid's tentacles would fall away from Ganymede's mind, freeing him to destroy again.

Someone must've taken care of the tsunami, because it hadn't swept everyone and everything away yet. He didn't have the energy to figure out who would have that power.

The gargoyles had stopped roaring, but he hadn't heard shrieks of agony as they annihilated people. So that must mean Holgarth had succeeded in shutting them down.

Where the hell was Hope? And more importantly, to him, where was Passion?

He almost lost his focus as someone stepped to his side. Dacian spoke quietly.

"I finished helping Holgarth put the gargoyles back to sleep. Figured you'd need a shot of power about now. Bain looks done for the day."

"Yes. Now." Edge felt the instant relief as Dacian's power flowed into him. It wasn't much. Taming the gargoyles would've drained some of it, but he needed everything he could get. "Have you seen Hope or Passion?"

"Yeah. Passion woke me, and then she ran off looking for Hope."

"Damn. I told her to stay close by so that one of you could keep her safe." From the edge of his vision, he saw Dacian wrapped in a blanket. The vampire had pulled it forward over his head so it shadowed his face.

"Oh, and Hope is standing in the doorway."

"What?" Edge risked a glance toward the great-hall door. Sure enough, Hope stood there looking worried. "Why the hell isn't she out here trying to help?"

Dacian shrugged. "That's what I asked her. She gave me some story about Archangel Ted forbidding her to help any of the cosmic troublemakers. So there she stands."

"I never killed an archangel. Maybe it's time to experience the thrill." Edge couldn't believe Hope would allow thousands to die rather than disobey dickhead Ted.

God, he'd gone through Dacian's power fast. Edge could already feel himself fading again.

"Bain said you needed help."

For a moment, Edge didn't recognize the voice behind him. Then the man stepped up beside him even as Dacian moved away.

"Murmur?" He only hesitated for a moment. He didn't know why the demon was willing to help, but without a shot of something powerful, Edge was done. He nodded.

Murmur put his hand on Edge's shoulder, and the surge of power was like nothing he'd ever felt. Somewhere in the part of his mind responsible for keeping track of things, Edge made a note that the demon just might be powerful enough to twist the minds of cosmic troublemakers.

"Passion's here. She's arguing with Hope."

Dacian sounded relieved to see Passion. Edge must not be the only one worried about her. He suppressed a flicker of jealousy. Stupid emotion.

Just the thought that Passion was near kick-started his morale, which was at low tide right now. He'd always thought he had a shot at taking Ganymede in a fight. Not now. Ganymede's power was a roiling cloud around him, just waiting until Edge's strength gave out.

"Wow. Passion just knocked Hope on her ass. Now Passion is on her way over here." Dacian laughed. "Angels are more fun than I thought they'd be."

"No. She can't come near Ganymede. There's nothing she can do to help."

"I don't know about that. Check it out."

Edge just managed to turn his head. What the hell? Passion had Holgarth's staff in her hand, and she was helping Sparkle to her feet.

Propping Sparkle up, Passion dragged her toward Ganymede. When Passion got as far as she could without being drawn into the vortex of Ganymede's trapped power, she shoved the staff into Sparkle's hand and gave her a push.

"What's she doing?" Dacian leaned past Edge to get a better look.

"I'm not sure." Edge decided that Passion really didn't have an angel's power, because she had to let Sparkle go on alone.

Edge watched as Sparkle immediately fell down. But that didn't mean she was out. Slowly and painfully, she crawled toward Ganymede. It must be torture meeting Ganymede's power head-on.

Passion joined Edge. She laid her hand on his arm, and all the pain from maintaining his hold on Ganymede disappeared. He glanced at her.

"Thanks." He hoped she understood how much her touch meant to him, and not just because it took away his pain. Then he returned his attention to Sparkle.

She'd reached Ganymede. Gripping the staff in one hand, she used the other hand to reach up and grab Ganymede's arm. She hauled herself to her feet. Then she swung the staff against the side of Ganymede's head. The crack made Edge wince. Ganymede fell without a sound.

Relieved, he released his hold on Ganymede, and Murmur withdrew his power. Edge felt shaky and weak as he turned to Passion. "That was your plan?" He was amazed by the simplicity of it.

"Worked, didn't it?" She sighed. "I don't have the power that you guys have, so I had to think like a human. How could we put him down without anything supernatural involved? Now I've got to use my gentle power of persuasion. I'll be back."

She walked toward Hope, who'd climbed to her feet and was staring openmouthed at Passion. "Get your butt out there and help with Ganymede or I'll tell Ted that you were dancing on the beach with a demon." Passion didn't seem to care if anyone heard her.

It took a moment for the threat to sink in, but once it did, Hope rushed out to Ganymede. She put her hand on his chest and began the talking thing she did. This time Edge wasn't surprised when he couldn't understand her words, and he welcomed the sense of peace and contentment flooding him.

"Not only can she dance, but she has serious talent." Murmur sounded sincerely impressed.

Passion had rejoined them. "You will *not* lure her to her destruction with your demonic . . . skills."

"Skills? Really? Afraid to call them what they are? They're temptations, my innocent." Murmur laughed softly. "And I wasn't the one doing the luring, Passion. You have a dynamite name, by the way. Anyway, she came to my room and said she wanted to dance." He shrugged. "I never turn down a woman ready to dance."

Passion looked over at the other angel as though she'd never seen her before.

"We can all be tempted. Even you." The demon looked from Passion to Edge, and then walked away to join Bain.

Passion refused to meet Edge's gaze. "I have to help Sparkle."

By the time they reached her, Hope had finished talking and was sitting on the grass next to Sparkle. But she still kept one hand on Ganymede. Hope's thoughts seemed to be elsewhere, though, because she was staring at Murmur as he spoke with Bain. Sparkle was holding Ganymede's hand. She looked up at them.

Edge had expected tears, or maybe panic in the cosmic troublemaker's eyes. What he saw was fury.

"When I find out who's doing this to us, I'll take off my queen-of-sex-and-sin crown and borrow yours for a few minutes. I'm going to kill someone's ass for this. *No one* hurts Mede." She seemed to think of something. "What happened to the tsunami? It never showed."

"Zane stopped it." Passion raked her fingers through her hair. "He also wiped the minds of everyone except us who saw Ganymede in action."

Edge followed the motion with his eyes before forcing his attention back to the conversation. "The sorcerer? Where did he get that kind of power? No, forget that. I saw him bring a snowstorm to Galveston a short time after he lifted the freaking castle into the air." Was Zane really human? With that kind of crazy power, he could probably glamour them into thinking he was a turtle if he chose. "It's looking more and more like the enemy is either Murmur or Zane."

Passion seemed unsure. "I don't know. Murmur gave his power to you a few minutes ago, and Zane saved the whole island. Would they do that if they were guilty?"

Sparkle offered her own solution. "I'll kill both of them."

Edge was still thinking about what Passion had said. "Maybe the goal isn't to kill."

"What other purpose could there be?" Passion sounded frustrated.

Just then Ganymede groaned and Sparkle leaned over him. "Don't try to move, sugartart."

Sugartart? Edge would never get it with those two. He watched as Passion moved over to touch Ganymede, and his groan faded. Ganymede opened his eyes.

Edge tensed, ready to jump into action if Ganymede was still crazy. Okay, so he didn't have enough energy to jump anywhere. Luckily, the old Ganymede looked out from those cat eyes.

Ganymede didn't say anything for a moment. He looked around him, and Edge could see the realization sinking in.

"I checked out, didn't I?" He stared at his clawed hands.

"Completely." Sparkle leaned over to smooth his hair from his forehead.

Ganymede rubbed a hand across his eyes. "Anything major happen?"

Edge suspected that Sparkle would try to ease into the disclosure, but if he were Ganymede, he'd like to be told the truth straight up. So Edge told him. "A minor earthquake and a big-ass tsunami, but the sorcerer shut the wave down before it reached shore."

Passion added what she knew. "The news is reporting an earthquake along the Texas and Louisiana coast. Not much damage. We probably lucked out, though. Edge got to you before you could do any more major stuff. And scientists are already trying to figure out what happened to the tsunami."

Ganymede closed his eyes and muttered a long string of "shits." Then he opened his eyes. "The Big Boss will notice this."

"I suspect." Edge figured their boss had also taken note of *his* performance last night.

"What will happen?" Passion's question was almost a whisper.

Ganymede answered. "He'll probably show up any time now to take names and kick butts."

Sparkle sighed. "I'll have Bill reserve his room."

Passion looked suspicious. "Is that it? Nothing else you have to tell me."

Edge hesitated. "He might decide to destroy us."

9

She wondered what Hope would tell Ted tonight. Passion sat cross-legged on the mattress watching the other angel. The nightly lie-to-Ted ritual had turned into practically Passion's only entertainment.

She sneaked a glance at Edge. He lay on the mattress beside her, his eyes closed, waiting for Ganymede to finish his shower next door so that he could take his turn. Watching Edge wasn't fun anymore; it was torture.

A week had passed since Ganymede had taken his swan dive off Mount Sanity, and still nothing. No visit from the Big Boss, no more mental meltdowns by anyone, and no progress finding who was messing with their minds. Sure, they had suspects, but no proof.

During that long, long, *long* week, Passion had learned the nature of temptation. She'd had no problem resisting when there'd been nothing to resist. Heaven had been pretty much temptation-free. All she did was sit in her cubicle with her eyes closed—no windows in the room, so nothing to see anyway—and reach into human minds.

Their worlds were filled with colors and emotions, and she lived vicariously through them.

No, she didn't have to worry about crossing any lines in heaven. And when she'd first met Edge, she'd still had her feet firmly planted on the rules-of-heaven ground. Resistance had been a little tougher, but she'd still had some perspective. He was gorgeous but irredeemable. His lean-muscled body had made her want to touch, to taste, to do all sorts of interesting things to it, but she'd understood that what she was experiencing was lust. And lust alone wasn't enough to make her forget what he was.

Now? Lines were blurred and perspectives muddied.

With the fear that at any moment Edge or Ganymede could go on a mindless rampage, Passion and Hope had stuck close to them all week. After all, it was their duty as angels to protect the general population if they could. The sticking-close thing had been her downfall.

She'd had to talk to him. A lot. He was interesting. He made her laugh sometimes. He made her restless and hungry in ways she'd never imagined. He'd introduced her to junk food and *Star Trek*. She *liked* him. And she'd found herself skittering away from thoughts of his job. Plus, the lust thing? It grew with each minute, each breath she took.

But so far, she and Hope had managed to keep the nightly reports to Ted secret. That all might end in a few minutes if she couldn't get Edge to leave the dungeon.

"Ganymede is probably almost done. Why don't you go over and wait for him?"

Edge opened one eye. "Trying to get rid of me?"

"No." Yes.

Edge closed his eye. "I'm in no hurry. Sparkle's over there in case Ganymede blows again."

Fat lot of good that would do. But Passion understood that it was impossible for Hope to spend every second of every day with both Ganymede and Edge.

Passion looked at Hope again to see if she was getting nervous. But Hope was busy on the laptop that had pretty much taken over her life. Except when she went dancing with Murmur. Passion didn't even want to think about that complication.

Her final hope that Edge might leave the room before Ted checked in evaporated as the familiar cold wash of power hit. At least Ted only seemed to have audio, so as long as Edge kept quiet, everything should be okay on the archangel end. But Hope had to answer him out loud. Passion refused to look at Edge.

"What did you do today, Hope, to turn those in the castle away from evil?" Archangel Ted sounded distracted for some reason.

Hope sighed as she pulled up her list of lies on the computer. Passion felt sorry for her. There was no way Hope had time to do any soul saving when she was trotting around behind either Edge or Ganymede all day and dancing with the demon at night. None of which she could reveal to Ted.

Some of this was Passion's fault. She'd started Hope down this path when she'd blackmailed her into helping Ganymede. Hope had told Ted that yes, there'd been a little Earth shaking, but it didn't have anything to do with the cosmic troublemakers. That was the first time Hope had lied to Ted. Now it had become a habit.

Passion held her breath as she looked at Edge. His eyes were still closed. She relaxed a little. At least he didn't seem to be able to hear Ted's side of the conversation.

"I spoke with P!nk and convinced her that her so-what attitude wouldn't open heaven's gates for her. Next, I suggested to Lady Gaga that she walk away from her bad romance if she wanted to save her soul. She laughed at me, so I'll probably have to do a follow-up on that one. Then I told Britney Spears that saying, 'Oops! I did it again,' will *not* convince the Supreme Being she's ready to renounce sin. After that, I—"

Ted exhaled deeply. *"Enough. I'm not in the mood to listen to your endless list of petty sinners."*

Surprise. Passion thought Ted wanted them to concentrate on the petty sinners. He'd made it clear he didn't want them to go after the big guns. She glanced again at Edge. His eyes were open. Oh, crap. She put her finger over his lips.

And lost herself for a moment in the feel of them—the warmth, the softness, probably the only softness in his whole hard body.

"Have you kept an eye on the cosmic troublemakers?"

"Umm, yes." Hope sounded nervous for the first time.

"Have they shown any hints of violence? Have you heard them say anything that might make you think I should send down the avenging angels?" Ted sounded hopeful.

Passion widened her eyes even as she shook her head at Hope.

But Hope didn't need any coaching from the sidelines. "It's been peaceful here. And they really don't talk in front of me."

Even as Passion went weak with relief, she wondered about Hope. What had happened to Ted's model of the perfect angel? Hope had been the dedicated one. Now? She lied like a human and didn't seem to think that going out with a demon was a biggie. Worse than that, blue had begun to swirl around her. Lust. Murmur had a lot to answer for.

"What about you, Passion?"

"Well . . ."

"I have confidence you'll tell me what I want to know. After all, you do want to return home sometime before you die of old age. And make no mistake, if you stay in human form long enough, you will die."

Passion narrowed her eyes. Jerk. She hated being threatened. "I saw nothing. I heard nothing." Besides, even with all the bad stuff happening, she'd never felt so alive in her life. She was in no hurry to return to her home on the corner of Dull and Boring.

The air practically vibrated with his displeasure. *"Continue doing your works of mercy, but keep your eyes on the cosmic troublemakers. In fact, I give you permission to become friendly with them. Of course, you can't turn them from their wickedness, but if you hear any plans involving violence, I'll need to know. We have to stop them before they harm the human population."*

The coldness retreated. He was gone. And what was up with his obsession with the cosmic troublemakers? It sounded as though he was looking for an excuse to attack them. She sighed. And if she were a good angel, she'd give it to him. But she wasn't a good angel. So she was keeping her mouth shut.

Edge sat up. He was smiling. "P!nk? Lady Gaga? Britney Spears? You've been spending too much time with Murmur." His smile faded. "Who were you speaking to?"

Hope looked uncertain, so Passion stepped into the silence. No use trying to keep Ted's visits secret. "Archangel Ted checks in each night to find out what we've done during the day."

Edge shook his head. "I can't believe he bought your list, Hope."

Hope offered him a small smile. "Archangel Ted isn't into pop culture or music, so I was pretty safe."

His expression turned thoughtful as he looked at Hope. "Who are the 'they' you mentioned?"

"You and the other cosmic troublemakers. He wants to make sure you're not becoming too dangerous." Hope returned to the pleasures of Facebook.

Passion winced. So *now* Hope decided to be honest.

"Look, it's no big deal." Passion pasted on a fake smile. "Ted is a busybody. He wants to know everything, but it doesn't mean anything." Unless busybody Ted decided to send the avenging angels.

He didn't have a chance to comment because just then the dungeon door swung open and Ganymede, in his cat form, padded in. Sparkle trailed behind him carrying a hair dryer.

Ganymede's hair was wet and slicked back except where it stuck up all around his fuzzy face. Passion couldn't stop her grin. He didn't look like Mr. Destroyer of the Universe now. "You stayed in cat form for the shower?"

He glared at her. *"It takes too long to change forms. Besides, if I decide to misplace my brain again, you guys might have a better shot at subduing me in cat form. Of course, it would take all of you working together. I'm that powerful."*

"O mighty chaos bringer, if you reprise your role as deranged dude, I'll take up Holgarth's staff and bash you in the head again." Sparkle seemed to be enjoying the possibility.

Ganymede chose not to comment on that.

"I didn't think cats liked water." Passion tried not to laugh at his drowned-kitty look.

"I'm in cat form, babe. The real me enjoys a great shower. And Sparkle scrubbed my back." His cat eyes narrowed to slits at the remembered pleasure.

Passion thought of something she'd been meaning to ask. "Why do you stay in cat form at all? I mean, you make a great human." That hadn't come out exactly as she'd planned.

She caught the corner of Edge's frown. What was his problem?

"Cats do a better job of sneaking. No one notices a cat, so people don't filter what they say in front of me. It's more fun being a cat." He glanced at Sparkle. *"Most of the time."*

Sparkle snorted her opinion of that. "What he means is that he doesn't have any responsibilities as a cat. He can sit around all day watching TV and eating." Her expression softened. "When we make love, though, he'd better be in his golden-god form."

Ganymede leaped onto the table with the restraints attached to it, and Sparkle plugged in the hair dryer. This whole living space was just weird. Hey, how many angels ever got to wake in the morning to an iron maiden staring them in the face?

"Time for my shower." Edge rose in one lithe motion. He glanced at Passion. "Want to keep me company?"

The question caught her by surprise. She bit back her automatic yes. "I don't do backs."

Something in his expression promised that scrubbing his back would be one of life's highlights. "Not *in* the shower. You can stand outside to make sure I'm me when I come out."

"Fine." She grabbed her nightgown, robe, and slippers. She'd shower when he was finished.

Luckily, Dacian was still up in the great hall playing the big bad vampire in the last few fantasies. He wasn't irredeemable, so technically she should be trying to turn him away from evil. Right now, though, she didn't feel qualified to talk to anyone about making it through the pearly gates.

She settled onto a chair as Edge went into the bathroom. He didn't close the door, and she forced her gaze away from it. Too bad she couldn't do the same with her imagination.

Passion did some mental humming to drown out the sounds of him undressing and sighed her relief when she heard the shower door close. She looked around for a magazine to keep her thoughts busy.

"Come in here so I can talk to you while I'm showering."

The voice of the serpent in the garden. The big fat apple—juicy, sweet, and tempting. "I don't—"

"Afraid?"

The symbolic gauntlet. In her mind, Ted barked conflicting orders. *"They're irredeemable. Stay away from them. No, I want to know what they're planning. Act friendly."*

Even as she tried to pretend that strolling into the bathroom while he was naked was no big deal, her pounding heart knew what a liar she was. Sure, she'd slept on the same mattress with him for almost a week now, but this was different. Asleep, he wasn't actively tempting her. This was active and totally premeditated enticement.

"Close the door just in case Dacian comes home." He turned on the water.

She shut the door and then leaned her back against it.

"Explain again what your job was in heaven."

Passion swallowed hard. She could see him, hazy through the frosted glass. He was . . . She frowned. He'd asked her a question. "I soothed people's worries and gently guided them down the path to goodness."

"So you manipulated their minds?"

"What? No, of course not." But she had. It was for their own good, though. Didn't that make it okay?

"Did sex make it onto your sanctioned-by-heaven list?"

The long, unbroken line of his muscular body taunted and seduced her through the glass. "Not specifically. I guided people away from *all* excesses." Unease touched her. Now that she thought about it, Ted had demanded she only pass on thoughts he'd approved. Nothing wrong with that, though. He was just doing his job.

"Who checked up on you?"

She closed her eyes, but it didn't help. In her mind, there was no glass between them. Warm water sluiced over his gleaming body as she slid her fingers across . . . Taking a deep breath, she opened her eyes. "Ted. When I finished my assignments, he'd ask me for details about how things went."

"Did you choose the people you visited?"

Couldn't he just shut up so she could concentrate on the way his body twisted and bent, hard muscle moving beneath smooth skin . . . ? She tried to control the heavy feeling building low in her stomach. It felt so good, but she knew it was so wrong. Not here, not with this man. "No. Ted gave me a list of people who needed me." Thinking back, she realized Ted always sent her to people with power—politicians and military leaders. What was that about? Didn't the huddled masses need saving too?

"Were you happy in heaven?"

She watched him soap himself, sliding the washcloth

along his inner thigh, cupping . . . Passion gritted her teeth. He was doing this on purpose, and she didn't have the strength to open the bathroom door and leave. No wonder Ted had never been happy with her. He knew how weak she really was. "Of course I was happy. It was heaven." No, she'd always felt restless, unfulfilled. *And how easily the lies come to you now.*

"Who did you love there?" His voice had softened, but that didn't lessen the impact of the question.

"No one." Her answer was just as soft. She'd opted for telling the truth—to him, to *herself*. And that truth popped the bubble she'd built around her existence.

Mercilessly, he drove his point home. "Doesn't it seem strange that in a place supposedly dedicated to eternal love, there isn't any?"

She pressed her palms flat against the door as though she could keep the doubts and fears outside. But that wouldn't help, because all the uncertainties were already in here with her.

Passion watched unblinking as he turned off the water, opened the stall door, and stepped out. Steam filled the air with moist heat that made it hard for her to breathe. He stood too close, towered too tall above her. Wet, his tawny hair looked darker, and he'd slicked it back from his face. His bared body glistened as steam curled and flowed around him. She could almost believe he'd risen from the underworld, a beautiful demon sent to drag her from heaven forever. The worst part? She wouldn't miss Ted or any of the heavenly host.

Water beaded across his broad chest. One drop lost its grip on his nipple and wended a crooked path lower and lower, over his ridged stomach before coming to rest . . . She jerked her gaze back to his face.

"You excite me, maybe-angel. My body recognizes that and reacts accordingly." It wasn't an apology, just a statement of fact. He studied her from those gleaming amber eyes. "Do you understand?"

Passion shrugged in a pitiful attempt to seem casual.

"You're aroused. I've seen it before in humans' thoughts." Well, maybe not exactly like *his*. She controlled her need to glance down again, to scope out the exact length, breadth, and degree of hardness so she could have total recall when she was finally alone. Because never had anything she'd seen in people's minds lived up to this real-time experience.

Silence wrapped around her, made her want to squirm with her need to touch him. Passion knew that if she could see herself as she was able to see others, she'd be in the eye of a whirling blue hurricane of lust.

She had to say something. "I assume you had a purpose in getting out of the shower naked."

His sexy lips tipped up in a smile so sensual she had to force her hands to stay at her side. Awareness gnawed at her, exposing the gleaming bones of the real her that lay hidden within her angel shell.

"I want you to want me." He reached for a towel. "This was a cheap ploy to achieve that end." He stilled, his gaze sliding over her body. "Did it work?"

"Yes." But she wouldn't act on it. Not now, not here. She turned to open the door.

He didn't try to stop her. As she slipped from the bathroom, he threw a final few words her way.

"Think about your heaven, sweetheart. From what you've told me, I figure you've never been in heaven at all."

Passion shut the door before closing her eyes. She felt his comment as a punch to the stomach and almost doubled over with the pain. She had to believe that heaven was her home, because if it wasn't, her whole existence had been a lie.

She couldn't go back to the dungeon tonight and lie down beside him. Not after this. And she needed some alone time to think about the questions he'd raised about her home. None of what he'd said about heaven made sense, and yet the truth that lived in her said it made all the sense in the world.

She didn't dare discuss any of this with Hope. The other

angel would freak. Although from the way Hope looked at Murmur, Passion suspected she would find heaven pretty boring now.

Passion went back to the dungeon just long enough to tell everyone she'd be staying in her old room if anyone needed her.

Edge came back before she could leave, but he didn't try to stop her. He simply watched her from those eyes that saw too much.

She'd almost reached her room when she met Kemp Hardiway in the hall. He recognized her and stopped. Passion didn't have good memories from the last time she'd seen him, so she was tempted to say hi and keep on going. But that would be rude, so she paused.

He smiled, and it made a huge difference. Kemp would never look like the friendliest person in the world, but if he'd let his hair grow out, mess it up a little, and smile more, he'd be a great-looking guy.

"Did you ever finish your survey?"

He watched her with an intensity that made her uncomfortable, but that was probably just his way. "Yes." *Lies on top of lies on top of lies.* "I see that you stayed on after the earthquake." A lot of people had checked out, even though the hotel hadn't been damaged.

He shrugged. "It'll take more than that to scare me away. Besides, I have business in Galveston." He didn't mention what that business was.

Passion smiled. "Well, I hope the rest of your stay is less eventful."

He nodded. "Guess I'll see you around."

Just before he turned away, Passion caught the edge of his smile. Something about it looked a little too personal. And once again, she got the feeling she should know him from somewhere. She had other things to worry about, though, so she forgot about him once she stepped into her room.

She didn't stay long in the shower. The warm water and steam brought back images she could do without tonight.

Passion needed a clear head to think things through. Climbing into bed, she turned off the light.

A mistake. Because even as she tried to work through the muddle her life had become, she drifted toward sleep. Her last thought was how she really missed knowing that Edge slept beside her.

Edge sat at the foot of her bed and watched her sleep. Her pale hair was spread across her pillow and she'd pulled the sheet up to her chin.

He smiled. If that was her symbolic protection from him, she was in lots of trouble. His smile faded. So was he. Edge had no idea why he was sitting here when he should be on his way. A whim? Could be a costly one.

They would make love soon. He'd seen it in her eyes as she'd watched him emerge from the shower. She didn't realize it, but he did. And he wanted to bury himself deep inside her more than he'd wanted anything for a long time. But first, he needed to do this.

He said her name softly.

Startled, she sat up and looked wildly around the room. Her gaze fixed on him. "How did you get in?"

"Not much can keep Death out when it wants in." *It.* That's what he was, a tool of the Big Boss. Here, in this room, in the darkness with this woman, he could admit it. At least to himself.

"What do you want?"

She might sound calm, but he could hear the panicked pounding of her heart. Enhanced hearing was a bitch.

"The Big Boss touched base with me a little while ago. He has a job for me. I thought you might want to go along."

"Why would I want to do that?" She sounded horrified.

As she should. "Yeah, it was a dumb idea. Forget I asked." He started to rise.

She took a deep breath. "No, wait. I'll go." She climbed

from the bed, gathered her clothes, and disappeared into the bathroom.

What the hell was he thinking? She'd try to save the scumbag he was about to kill. That's what angels did, and she thought she was an angel.

And if he wanted to make love to her, this was a crappy way to try to win her heart. He quickly backtracked. Not her heart. He didn't want her heart. Just her body.

Then why had he made the offer? He raked his fingers through his hair. Damned if he knew.

He'd almost convinced himself that he should leave without her when she came out of the bathroom. Dressed in leather pants, heeled boots, and a sexy top, she was a walking ad for Sparkle. Edge smiled. God, he loved Sparkle's fashion choices.

"Ready?" He'd give her one chance to back out.

She nodded.

He beckoned her over to him. When she reluctantly stepped close, he wrapped his arms around her. She held herself stiff against him, but even as he prepared to dematerialize, he felt her soften, her body melding to his. And if ever he was tempted to tell the Big Boss to get someone else for tonight's job because he had better things to do, now was that moment.

Edge closed his eyes and savored her warmth, her *innocence*, because she *was* innocent or else she wouldn't be going anywhere with him. *Don't go crazy. She's just a blink of eternity's eye. Do your job.* Opening his eyes, he took them away.

They materialized on a dark street. A woman hurried along the sidewalk. Alone. It was late and everything was closed up. Behind her, slow steady footsteps stalked her. Edge pulled Passion into the shadow of an alley to watch.

"She's coming home from work at a bar. She didn't take a taxi because she doesn't have the money. She has kids waiting at home for her."

Passion remained silent.

"He'll kill her in the next block. She's caught one piece

of good luck, though. He won't rape her. He's only about the kill. She'll be his tenth. Fate has him slated to live forty more years. During that time, sixty more women will die. The law will never stop him." He smiled into the darkness. "But I will. Tonight."

"There must be another way." Passion's voice quavered— uncertain, torn.

"Give me another way that will save her life, Passion."

"Can't you just . . . stop him now and give yourself time to get proof to the cops?" She sounded desperate.

"There *is* no proof. And the Big Boss doesn't play that kind of game. Fate has decreed that he continue killing until he dies. 'Until he dies' is the operative phrase."

"I can't just watch and do nothing."

Was she trying to convince herself? What was he trying to accomplish by letting her witness his kill? She'd hate him for forcing her to make this kind of decision.

The man came into view, a darker shadow in a world of blackness.

"He doesn't look like a serial killer."

Edge could tell her a lot about serial killers and what they looked like. This one wore a suit, expensive shoes, and appeared to have just left his corner office. "See the knife in his hand, Passion? That's not a fashion statement. Clothes don't make the killer."

She grabbed his arm but didn't seem to know what to do beyond that. The man had almost reached them and was walking faster to catch up with the woman.

"Charles is a building inspector. He likes to dress well for his kills." Edge glanced up at the building the killer was passing. He focused.

Suddenly, the balcony on the fifth floor tore loose with a grinding screech and plummeted to the ground . . . with Charles crushed beneath it. Not one of Edge's more satisfying jobs, but he didn't think Passion would appreciate his wilder creative efforts. "Hmm, Charles inspected that building last week. Guess he missed something." Edge loved the irony of it.

Passion started forward, but Edge reached out to stop her. "He's dead."

She'd clapped her hand over her mouth as though to hold back a scream. Now she dropped her hand as she tried to free herself from his grasp. "I know, but . . . His soul is still there. I can feel it. I need to try . . ." She started to shake. "I think I can bring him back."

Edge frowned. "Explain." Luckily, the balcony hid most of the horror other than a thin trail of blood wending a path across the sidewalk.

"The night you fought Bain on the landing, you didn't see, but the woman was dead. Her neck was broken. She didn't have a heartbeat. But when I touched her, she just woke up."

Passion swayed, and he tried to pull her to him. She stepped away even though he still held her hand. That hurt. But what else did he expect?

"Maybe I didn't bring her back. I mean, Ted never said I had that kind of power. But if I try now . . ."

"If you try now and succeed, sixty women will die." He hardened his voice. No way was she bringing this bastard back.

Above them, someone opened a window and leaned out. "What the hell happened?"

"Time to go." Edge wrapped his arms around Passion and took them home.

Once back in her room, he released her. She stumbled over to her bed and sat down.

"Will you be okay?" Good time for him to be thinking about that.

She nodded. "How do you do it? Does killing just become routine? Do you ever wonder if the ones you killed could've been saved?"

Anger roared through him. "I remember the name of every person I kill. And no, I don't wonder if they could've been redeemed, because I can *see* their futures, and none of them would've ever regretted the lives they took. What I *don't* have to worry about are the ones I saved, because

I eliminated the predators that would've preyed on them. Think about the victims for a change, Passion." Why was he so angry? Did it matter what she thought? And if it mattered, why had he asked her to come with him in the first place? He huffed his disgust. He didn't know what the hell he was feeling.

"Do you ever wonder if you can be redeemed?"

Her question was so soft he almost didn't hear it. "I stopped wondering about that a long time ago. Redemption isn't part of my employment package."

"I don't understand you." She flung her hands into the air. "Do you really care about the ones you save, or is it just part of the job? Maybe you even enjoy the killing."

Coldness crept through him.

"I don't understand *any* of you." Passion sounded defeated. "I mean, have any of you thought about the people who lost their homes when Ganymede did his earthquake imitation? It's been all over the news, but I haven't heard anyone here talking about it, saying they were sorry it disrupted so many lives. All I've heard is worry that it might be traced back to the castle."

Edge actually felt his heart ice over. "Yeah, we're all bastards." It was better this way.

"I think I want to go to sleep."

Translation: get out of my room.

"Sure." He strode to the door and then paused. "But tomorrow we're going to talk about this bringing-people-back-from-the-dead thing."

Edge took the stairs down to the dungeon instead of the elevator because he needed to work off his mad. Passion wasn't the only target of his anger. He'd defended his job to her, but the truth was that after tens of thousands of years he'd had enough. There. He'd admitted it. No amount of creativity could make him less tired of the whole thing. He wanted out.

Guess he had a decision to make. Keep on killing or stop existing. Hell of a choice.

10

Passion had watched a man die last night, and her only regret was that she didn't *feel* any regret. Yes, the violence had horrified her, but beyond that . . . Where was the wrenching agony an angel should feel at the destruction of a life?

What if you're not an angel?

She could close her eyes and still see the black swirling around him. Irredeemable. As hopelessly lost as Edge. Then why didn't she feel the disgust for Edge that she'd felt for the man buried beneath all that concrete and metal? Would an angel play favorites? *No.*

She'd sensed when his soul fled. Somehow she'd known he was beyond her reach once that happened. And she'd been *glad* that she didn't have to save him. What did that make her?

Not an angel.

The whisper in her mind had no question mark at the end this time. But if she wasn't an angel, then what was she? Panic pushed at her. She had to be something, *somebody.* Her uncertainty had her teetering on the edge of a yawning abyss. She closed her eyes and stepped back from the chasm. She didn't have time for an identity crisis tonight. Passion glanced at the clock.

Time to go. She'd spent the day in her own room, away from the distractions of the others. Okay, away from the distraction of *Edge*. Besides, if she wasn't an angel, then she didn't have an obligation to trail around behind him and the others. Sure, she was being selfish, but logical thought escaped her when he was near, and she really needed to get her head together. But there was just so long she could hold her conscience at bay, so she'd agreed to meet everyone in the hotel's restaurant.

Passion took a last look at herself in the mirror. Each day she changed a little more. She wore Sparkle's makeup and clothes. She cared about how she looked. Hello, vanity. Fine, so she cared what *Edge* thought about the way she looked.

What will you do when Ted calls you back to heaven? Will you leave Edge? Will he care if you leave? And how could she return to a place that didn't feel like home anymore? All questions with no answers at the moment. Sighing, she headed for the door.

She was the last one to sit down, or almost the last. "Where's Hope and Ganymede?"

Sparkle shrugged. "She said Archangel Ted told her that since she wasn't doing a great job helping people in the castle, she needed to go out into the streets and see what she could do there. She wanted to hit Baybrook Mall on the mainland first because it would have lots of people all in one place." She looked puzzled. "Who goes to the mall and doesn't shop? She took Murmur with her to give her courage."

Sparkle narrowed her eyes. "Oh, and Mede isn't here because he was too lazy to take human form. I told him he couldn't set one paw in the restaurant if he stayed a cat. Cat hair in the soup doesn't amuse the Department of Health."

Passion decided not to comment on Ganymede. She

frowned. "Hope took a demon with her?" Okay, that was bizarre.

Sparkle's laughter was low and sexy. "Far be it from me to discourage her efforts, but if some stranger interrupted me while I was shopping for shoes . . ." She seemed to think about that possibility. "I'd hammer their heads into mush with the heel of the absolutely stunning stiletto I was holding. And I'm not a violent person." She thought some more. "Most of the time."

Unease touched Passion. Why would Ted contact Hope when Passion wasn't around? And why hadn't he included her in his go-forth-and-save message? *Because he knows you don't trust him anymore?* The thought startled her. Could he know how she felt about him? She relaxed a little. He couldn't know. Ted wasn't subtle, and if he suspected she had doubts, he'd be busy threatening her with more punishments.

But if she wasn't an angel, then that meant Ted was a big fat liar. She didn't need to move closer to the abyss because the edge was already crumbling beneath her feet. And speaking of Edge . . .

She looked across the table at Death. Or maybe she should call him Finis, since that was his real name. Unfortunately, changing his name didn't change her reaction to him.

Her heart did that strange *ker-thump* it only did when he got close. "So what do we think about what's *not* been happening?"

Edge shrugged. "Maybe the whole thing was an anomaly. Maybe no one caused what happened to Ganymede and me." His expression said he didn't believe that at all.

Holgarth tapped one long, thin finger on the table. "I tend to believe you might be right. After all, both of you have exhibited unstable tendencies in the past. Perhaps you both need counseling."

"And perhaps Wacky Wizard needs a kick in the butt."

Ganymede? Passion looked around.

A warning paw batted her ankle. *"Shh. Under the*

table. Don't look down. Don't want Sparkle to know I'm here."

What the . . . ? Okay, so if the cat was in her mind, he'd be able to hear her thoughts. *"Why are you here?"* She waited for his answer.

Bain seemed bored. "Personally, I think the solution is simple. We have three prime suspects. We take them down to the dungeon and torture them until one of them confesses." He shook his head. "Nah, that wouldn't work, at least not with Murmur. He'd sic his legions of demons on us and we'd be toast. At least you would. Me, I can take care of myself."

They all stared at Bain, and he stared back. "What?"

"I'm here because I sense someone powerful in the castle." Ganymede sounded impatient with the dinner conversation. *"Jeez. Demons never get that sometimes things need a little finesse."*

"And you're the king of finesse?" Passion almost said it out loud.

"Respect your elders, angel wannabe."

Bain evidently decided to change the subject. "Too bad Dacian couldn't join us. But Cinn just got back from her trip. Guess he has a lot of welcoming to do." He slanted a slow and sensual smile Passion's way.

Passion caught Edge's scowl out of the corner of her eye. Why was he mad? Bain's expression turned sly as he glanced toward Edge. What was that about?

"So do you think this powerful someone is to blame for what happened to you and Edge?" Passion tried to concentrate on Ganymede.

The waitress came to take their orders.

"Order two steaks. One rare. I like French fries. No veggies. I hate veggies. And, no, I don't think this person is connected to all the recent weirdness. Whoever I'm feeling has power like I've never felt before, and he or she is new to the castle. Makes me mad thinking about a stranger sneaking around. And I eat more when I'm mad, so get a double order of fries."

Passion avoided the puzzled stares as she ordered. *"Why me? Why aren't you bothering anyone else at the table?"*

"Because you're the biggest soft touch here." Ganymede made it sound like that was a good thing. *"And all the others would freak out. Sparkle would yammer on about the stupid board of health, Edge and Bain would insist on going with me, and Holgarth would piss me off with his snarky comments."*

"Going with you where? Explain." Thinking about another powerful being in the castle made her nervous.

"After you feed me some, okay, most of your meal—gotta keep up my strength—I'm going to search every room in the hotel. I can skip our three suspects. I already did them. This is a sneaky, one-cat job. Don't need any helpers. I'll check in with you every five minutes. If you don't hear from me, tell the others, because that means I'm in trouble. Not that I'm worried."

He was worried, and that upped Passion's unease. *"Sure."* She breathed deeply and tried to convince herself that this was a false alarm. *"They'll notice me feeding you."*

"No, they won't." Ganymede sounded amused. *"Trust me."*

Their food came and the tension lifted for a while. The first time Passion reached down with a piece of steak, she expected everyone to stop eating and peer under the table. No one did. Evidently, Holgarth wasn't the only magic maker at the table.

Everyone seemed to be relaxing . . . until Zane appeared at the table. Passion blinked. Where had he come from?

The sorcerer pulled out a chair and sat down. "Thought I'd check to see if you'd found whoever put the whammy on the cat."

"The cat has a name. Pass down some more fries. Easy on the salt. Got to watch my sodium intake." Ganymede sounded pretty mellow.

Edge narrowed his gaze. "What makes you think someone did?"

Zane raised one brow. "Oh, does he always stand naked in the courtyard spewing power to the universe? This place gets more entertaining every time I stay here."

"Smart-ass." Ganymede burped. *"Another piece of steak. Bigger this time."*

Holgarth glared at Zane. "I realize someone of your immense power must feel that actually asking politely if you may join us is beneath you, but it would make all of us lesser beings happy. So why not try it just to humor us?" Every sarcastic word oozed contempt.

"See, this is how Holgarth pisses off everyone. You're a little slow with the steak. Hungry cat down here."

Zane looked puzzled. "Why would I do that? You might say no." As if that settled everything, he leaned back to study them. "So which one of you searched my room?"

Silence.

"Come on, I know it must've been one of you. And whoever it was, you owe me a new carton of ice cream."

Passion controlled her impulse to glance under the table.

Zane stood. "Just so you know, I'm upping the power on my wards. Evidently, singed whiskers weren't enough to keep someone out." His lips quirked up in a smile.

Passion thought he should smile more often. It took him from scary magic maker to gorgeous guy who just happened to be a little terrifying.

"Don't send anyone to clean my room. I'll pick up my own towels from now on." He glanced at Holgarth. "And running a search on me won't do any good. Google doesn't know everything." He turned and walked away.

"That went well." Edge didn't try to hide his disgust. "Oh, and cats are supposed to be sneaky. What happened to our furry supersleuth?"

"No opposable thumbs, dumbass. I couldn't put all his stuff back exactly the way it was. So sue me. It was a waste

of time and whiskers anyway. Nothing there." Ganymede was silent for a moment.

Passion could feel the swish of air against her ankles as his tail whipped back and forth.

"I wonder why the Big Boss hasn't shown up. He's good at figuring out things like this. And he had to notice what I did. Sure, it wasn't as big as some of my more spectacular stuff, just lots of shaking. Yeah, a few buildings fell down, but they were shitty construction to begin with. And no one died. Not that I'm complaining. I don't want the Big Boss on my ass. But it seems strange he's not here protecting his interests."

Passion didn't have any thoughts on why the Big Boss wasn't there, but she did have a question for everyone. "I guess none of you have ever seen the Big Boss. What do you think he looks like?"

"Vin Diesel." Bain.

"The Rock." Edge.

"The guy who plays the vampire Eric in *True Blood*." Sparkle.

Holgarth gave it a little more thought. "Assumptions can be dangerous. Some of the most deadly beings I've ever known didn't look the part. That's why they were successful."

"Great. The Big Boss looks like Danny DeVito." Ganymede chuckled.

"I'm tired of this. Let's talk about something more interesting." Sparkle stared at Passion. "Have you and Edge had sex together yet?"

"Crap. I'm outta here. Even dessert isn't worth listening to this. I'll contact you in five minutes." And then Ganymede was gone.

Passion almost choked on her iced tea. "No. And I can't believe you just asked that."

Sparkle looked offended. "I'm the queen of sexual chaos. What did you expect me to ask you, what brand of cereal you ate this morning? I have a vested interest in your sensual well-being. I supplied the clothes, the makeup, and the opportunity." She shrugged. "Can I help it if you don't grab your joy where you can? From what you've told us about your heaven, you won't be getting any there."

Passion decided not to respond. That would only encourage Sparkle. And she wasn't ready to discuss the place she'd always called home. Luckily, Edge bailed her out.

He didn't look at Passion. "I thought we were meeting for dinner to discuss a plan. Guess not."

"If you have a plan, we'll discuss it." Holgarth's expression said that *he* was the only one with the brilliance to come up with a workable solution.

Bain shrugged. "We still don't know squat. Murmur plays loud music and dances with Hope. Zane and Kemp don't do much of anything that I can see. None of them have had any visitors. No one else in the hotel has been here long enough or has any real power."

"Mede checked out their rooms." Sparkle looked as though she was in a sulk about the diversion of the conversation away from sex. "Murmur has a sound system that would make even Satan run for earplugs, and Kemp has a few books. That's all. Mede didn't get much from their minds either. But they could've been planning death and destruction when he wasn't visiting."

Finally, Holgarth looked at his watch. "As fascinating as this conversation is, Edge, Bain, and I have to prepare for the night's fantasies." He scowled at Passion. "We can only hope that nothing unfortunate occurs tonight, since Hope has chosen to wander the mall in the company of a demon."

Passion scowled right back. "Hey, that isn't my fault. And if anything *unfortunate* happens, call me. I might not be able to stop it, but I can . . ." *What? Revive the dead bodies? Maybe.* "Well, I guess I can't do anything."

Edge stood, and Passion dared a glance at him. He was

watching her. She thought she saw a flash of angry hurt in his eyes, and her conscience poked at her. Sure, what he'd done last night had shocked her, but that was no excuse for the way she'd lashed out at him. She looked away.

"I bet you could do a lot." His voice was soft with controlled anger. "You mentioned something about bringing a woman back to life. What was that all about?"

He wasn't the only one angry now. "Is this payback? You don't like what I said last night so you blab what I told you to everyone?"

His smile was cold. "Well, I would've discussed it in private, but you didn't seem to be around today."

Passion took a deep breath to calm herself before looking at the others. They all stared back at her. "I'm not even sure if it really happened. It was the woman on the landing when Edge and Bain were fighting. I thought she was dead. I touched her and . . . she wasn't dead anymore." She shrugged. "Maybe I made a mistake. Maybe she was never dead at all. I mean, I couldn't do anything like that before I came here." Not that there'd been any dead bodies at home to practice on. Passion chose not to mention being able to see the colors of sin. Even Ted didn't know about that. "Besides, I wasn't important enough to have that kind of power." She narrowed her eyes at Edge. "Happy now?"

No emotion shone in his eyes. "I think everyone should put their talents on the table in case we need them. I seem to remember you healing me."

"I'm not convinced I did anything."

Bain stopped eating for a moment. "Death dude is right. Holgarth, print out a list of everyone's skills so we can all have a copy."

"Perhaps you've forgotten my regrettable history with electronics. Magic and computers tend not to work well together. But I'll write up a list and someone else can put it into the computer."

"Okay, I'll do it." Bain didn't sound enthusiastic. "My talents will take up lots of space, but that's all right because some of you have a short list, so it'll even out." He grinned as he glanced at Edge. "I can just put 'kills people' next to your name."

"Let's expand on that a little." Edge didn't smile back. "Conscienceless but creative killer. Also kicks demon butt when provoked." His gaze flicked to Passion and then away.

"Children, children." Holgarth heaved an exaggerated sigh. "It's fantasy time, so you'll have to put away your squabbles for the night."

Bain was laughing as he and Holgarth stood. They followed Edge from the restaurant.

Passion sighed.

"A sad sigh?" Sparkle looked curious.

Passion realized she wanted to talk to someone. She wouldn't ordinarily have chosen Sparkle, but who else was there? Hope? She didn't know Hope, never had. "Yes."

"You know I'm here for you." Sparkle's eyes gleamed with avid interest.

Okay, if Passion was going to say this, she needed to get it out now before she thought too much about it. "Edge took me with him last night. I watched him kill."

Sparkle pursed her lips. "Stupid, stupid man."

Illogical as it might seem, Passion had the urge to defend him. "He gave me a choice."

"Why did you go?" For just a moment, something incredibly ancient looked out of Sparkle's eyes. Then she laughed and was once more the Sparkle that Passion knew. "I mean, if you want to sleep with him, just do it. Don't muddle it up with all kinds of moral judgments."

Here came the hard part. "The man's death didn't horrify me. It should have. He was a serial killer, but I should've tried harder to save him."

"If you want me to tell you that your feelings were okay, then consider yourself told." Sparkle smiled. "But I don't think my opinions count for much with your boss." Her expression turned thoughtful. "Whoever that turns out to be."

Passion bit her lip. "You're right. It has to be me. *I* have to come to terms with my feelings." She sighed. "But there's more. I was mad at Edge for . . . everything, and I said some stuff about him not caring for people and maybe enjoying his job. I mentioned how none of you guys seemed upset about the people who lost their homes when Ganymede went crazy. That wasn't fair. I can't look into his heart to see his emotions."

Sparkle leaned back in her chair. She played with one glittery earring as she seemed to think about what she wanted to say. "Edge contributed a huge chunk of money for those people. Then he nagged us into doing the same thing. He even hired architects and contractors to help with the rebuilding. Of course, many of the victims had insurance, but Edge made sure any who didn't would have new homes." She speared Passion with her stare. "Edge cares more than he wants to. In his job, that's a liability. So he tries to cover it up with his I'm-a-cold-bastard act. And if you ever tell him I said that, I'll inflict female-pattern baldness on you for the rest of your short life."

"Okay, I feel so much better now." Passion felt lousy. But she didn't know how to make it better.

"Why did you come to me for this talk?" Sparkle sounded honestly puzzled.

"I didn't have anyone else to go to." That was one of the hardest things she'd ever had to admit. "I don't have a family. I don't trust Ted anymore. And I was never close to Hope." She shrugged. "I never made any close friends. Guess that left you."

Sparkle raised one perfectly shaped brow. "Umm, how about the Supreme Being? A logical choice. Love, forgiveness, compassion?"

Passion closed her eyes. "I've never seen the Supreme Being. I've never talked to the Supreme Being. I've only talked to Archangel Ted. And I don't think I believe in Ted anymore." She opened her eyes. "I don't know what I think." She started to get up. "This was a mistake."

"Sit down."

Passion sat.

"Two tortured souls. You're perfect for each other." Sparkle's eyes shone. "You're right. I was the wrong person to talk to. I've never had doubts about my place in the universe, about the things I do or don't do. I'm happy. You need someone who can empathize."

Passion just stared.

"You're a virgin, right?" Sparkle answered her own question. "Of course you are. What else could you be? I can't believe you've slept in the same bed with him for a week and nothing's happened. You need help, sweetie."

"I don't see—"

Sparkle held up her hand. "Quiet. I'm thinking. How can you make any decision about your existence when you've never really lived?"

Passion didn't see where Sparkle was going, but from her gleeful expression, Passion figured the trip would end badly. "Forget I even talked to you. I—"

"You want Edge." She waved away Passion's attempt to interrupt. "Don't feel bad, all women want him. But you have an advantage. He wants you back. I've seen the way he looks at you."

Passion's heart did the *ker-thump* thing.

Sparkle leaned forward. "I'm on a roll now. Don't stop me. You and Edge are the perfect storm—life versus death. Plus there's this total sexual attraction for each other. This is my moment in time. I can create sexual chaos on a scale no one could ever imagine." Her eyes seemed to grow unfocused with the sheer joy of the thought.

"One problem." Passion almost hated to wipe that joy from her face.

"What?" Sparkle didn't look as though she was paying much attention.

"We're completely wrong for each other."

Sparkle blinked. "That's the whole point, sweetie."

"And he hates me now." Sorrow pulled at her with each word.

Sparkle's smile was a slow slide of almost orgasmic pleasure. "I'm the queen of sex and sin, Passion. Remember that. I'm at my most powerful when I'm walking that blade's edge between love and hate. When you merge two powerful emotions, beautiful things can happen." Evil moved in that smile. "Or everything can go to hell. It's all about the game. And chaos can be . . . euphoric." She reached over to pat Passion's hand. "So sit back and enjoy the ride. Edge will teach you about life."

Sparkle was scary. Time to put a stop to this. "No. You're not going to meddle in my life, such as it is. And considering what Edge does for a living, he's not the best person to teach me anything. I think I'll go back to my room." *Running away?* Definitely.

She'd told Sparkle what Ted would expect one of his good angels to say. But Passion wasn't that person anymore. Did she want to make love with Edge? Yes. Not Sparkle's way, though. Passion never wanted either of them to feel manipulated.

Sparkle didn't react to her announcement. Instead, her gaze grew vacant as she began to hum a tune.

Passion frowned. "Light My Fire" by the Doors. She recognized it because Hope had downloaded the song from iTunes. It was one of Murmur's favorites.

"Jim Morrison of the Doors was one of my successes." Sparkle's voice had taken on a singsong cadence. "He was a beautiful, sensual powerhouse."

Passion pushed her chair away from the table and started to rise. "Thanks for listening to me, but I'll work things out on my own."

Without warning, Sparkle knocked her chair to the floor and stood.

Startled, Passion froze, her gaze riveted on Sparkle.

The cosmic troublemaker slowly rose into the air. Lightning flashed around her as her eyes took on a now-familiar amber glow. Her hair floated in the air, crackles of energy making the ends spark.

She began to hum "Light My Fire" again. The tune

echoed throughout the room, stilling everyone there, weaving a strange compulsion that pulled at Passion.

Ohmigod, no! Passion stumbled over her chair as she backed away. Frantically, she looked around the restaurant. No cosmic troublemakers, vampires, demons, or angels. No one powerful enough to help, including her. Passion would kill Hope for once again not being within easy calling distance.

Sparkle continued to hum, staring blankly from those glowing amber eyes. Someone else was sitting at her control panel while Sparkle took a coffee break. As she swept the restaurant with that eerie gaze, Sparkle toed off her shoes and then began to remove her clothes.

Erotic energy flowed from Sparkle in waves that grew stronger and stronger as she unzipped her black silk dress and let it slip to the floor. Her black bra and panties followed. She kept her earrings. Passion felt the waves of energy as phantom fingers touching her breasts and trailing down her body. Desire pooled low in her stomach.

Around her, men and women were stripping naked and turning to whoever was closest to them. Horrified, Passion watched a woman who had to be at least eighty tackle a buff twentysomething guy at the next table. They fell to the floor. Passion looked away quickly because some things once seen could not be unseen. Nope, didn't want that picture stuck in her mind forever.

Turning, Passion raced for the exit just as the chef dashed from the kitchen and made a grab for her. She dodged his flour-coated fingers and ran from the restaurant. As she fled, she glanced back to see Sparkle, naked and still floating above the floor, starting to drift toward her.

Once out in the hotel lobby, Passion looked around. Everything looked normal . . . until Sparkle floated out through the restaurant door. Passion ran toward the great hall even as the people in the lobby started to strip. It would only be a matter of time before Sparkle's sexual power overcame everyone in the hotel.

But what could she do? Instead of shouting "Fire!"

should she scream "Sex!"? Somehow she didn't think that would motivate people to flee in terror.

She had to find Edge before she ended up on the floor naked with some stranger. Passion didn't pause to think about why it had to be Edge. She was going with gut instinct.

So she ran. And as she raced toward the great hall, she glanced at her watch. Oh, crap. It had been a lot more than five minutes since Ganymede left, and he hadn't contacted her. He was in trouble. But she couldn't do anything to help him now.

Passion was out of breath by the time she burst into the hall. Sparkle's erotic pull was making it hard to think, urging her to tear off her clothes and join her body with whoever was nearest. Uh-oh. She realized she'd already unbuttoned her top while she was running.

It looked as though the first fantasy was about to begin. Panicked, her gaze skittered around the room. No Edge.

"I'm afraid if you wish to take part in the fantasy, you must purchase a ticket. Didn't we have this discussion before? And I'd suggest you wait until you reach the dressing room to disrobe." Holgarth's supercilious voice sounded right behind her.

She spun to face him. "Where's Edge?"

Holgarth narrowed his eyes. "Is something the matter?"

"Where. Is. Edge?" She just managed to control her need to shake the wizard until every bone in his skinny body rattled.

"He's in the dressing room. Now, what is the—"

"Sparkle. *Run.*"

She left him staring as the door between the great hall and the hotel lobby slowly swung open. Sparkle floated into view. The last thing Passion saw before she stumbled from the room was Holgarth methodically undressing. Ugh, gross.

Passion slammed open the dressing room door and rushed in. Edge turned to face her. He'd shed his shirt and was in the process of sliding his jeans down over his hips. "What the—"

She was gasping for breath, whether because of all the running she'd done or because Sparkle's sexual compulsion had found its target of choice.

Her gaze slid across his powerful chest, paused at his tempting male nipples—what would they taste like, feel like, as her tongue swept across them—before slipping down his hard stomach to where the bulge of his cock— wow, "cock," another word she'd never used—grew even as she stared.

Passion pulled herself from the brink. "Sparkle's lost control. Everyone in the castle is doing it with whoever is closest to them." She shuddered even as she plucked at her top, the need to rip it off almost overwhelming.

Edge watched her from hooded eyes, and for just a moment she thought she saw excitement flare in them. She must have been hallucinating, because when she glanced again they looked normal for him—cold, emotionless, and just a little amused.

She narrowed her gaze. "This isn't funny. We have to get out of here and find Hope. Unless you know a way to stop Sparkle before she leaves the castle and infects all of Galveston."

"Infected by sex?" He glanced at her open top and then looked away. He clenched his hands into fists. "Not the worst way to go."

Something primal stretched and licked its lips as she noticed his interest in the swell of her breasts where her top hung open. It purred its approval at his clenched fists, which hinted at control issues.

He took a deep breath. "You're right. We need to get out of the castle. Then we can try to figure out how to stop Sparkle." Edge didn't bother putting his shirt back on. He merely pulled up his jeans and quickly fastened them.

Passion was losing her battle with the sexual compulsion coiled inside her. Even as he grabbed her hand and pulled her toward the door, need uncurled, slithering along every nerve until it reached its target. There it expanded, filling her with hunger that was almost pain. She slapped her free hand over her mouth to stifle a cry.

And as Edge reached for the door, they heard it.

The soft echo of "Light My Fire."

Drawing closer.

11

Edge dragged her down a hallway leading away from Sparkle's eerie humming.

"Where're we going? We have to do something about Sparkle."

"Can't right now. Too distracted."

If he felt the way she did, then "distracted" was a really weak word. How about so overwhelmed with lust that all she wanted to do was drag him to the floor and then . . . *Think about something else, something* not *sexy.* Passion filled her mind with the image of a tuna and peanut butter sandwich.

"Ganymede could stop her. They have an emotional bond." He sounded reluctant to admit that. "But he hasn't shown up yet. That's bad news."

"Ohmigod! Ganymede. I forgot to tell you." She filled him in about the power Ganymede had sensed. "And he hasn't checked in with me."

Edge's muttered curse held all his frustration and worry. "Damn cat had to go off on his own." He raked his fingers through his hair. "Can't do anything about him now."

"Even . . . distracted, you should be able to stop the humming until we find Ganymede. You were able to hold Ganymede in check last week, and Sparkle isn't as powerful as him, is she?" Passion was gulping air, probably because of all her running. But the hunger clawing at her emotions, her body, was also taking its toll.

"Yeah, well, there're different kinds of power. Sparkle hits below the belt. Literally. Right now, I can't focus enough to stop anyone." He flung open another door. "Besides, what happens if I *do* stop her? I free a roomful of people from her compulsion, and they come out of it to find that, wow, they're naked and having sex with a stranger in the middle of the great hall. That'll be good for business."

Passion's steps were flagging. She just wanted to stop and . . . She shook her head. Couldn't think about that, *wouldn't* think about it. But her mind seemed to have absorbed Sparkle's humming, the tune repeating and repeating on an endless reel. She tried out a mental scream to drown out the sound.

For the first time, she noticed where they were. "A chapel? I didn't know the castle had one."

"Sparkle rents it out for weddings."

"Wait. Why aren't we going down to the dungeon or up to one of our rooms?"

"Too many crazy people and too easy to get trapped. We need to get out of the castle."

Passion had just about reached her limit. "Can't we stop for a minute?"

"Not unless you want to make love in front of God and anyone else who wanders through. The way I see it, we'll still be here when the next bride and groom walk down the aisle. They'll have to step over us on the way to the altar." He kept on going.

After a few more turns down hallways Passion didn't recognize, he pushed open a final door and they were outside. But before she could even sigh her relief, he'd pulled her into what looked like a small greenhouse.

"Weren't we safe outside?"

"You didn't take a good look. The courtyard's contaminated."

Contaminated? Passion decided that was one way of describing what Sparkle was doing. But the word sounded sort of cold, and she was burning up with her need for Edge.

"Why here?" Plants, some that looked a little strange, filled the room. There was a table in the middle of the greenhouse with even more plants.

"It's private."

Passion stopped her mental screaming long enough to really look at Edge. He practically thrummed with tension, and his eyes were dark with a hunger she recognized. "We're in trouble."

"Oh, yes." He smiled.

That smile burned along the same sensual path as her own. It looked as though they'd finish this trip together. Somehow the realization didn't horrify her. Not now, at least. Later, when Sparkle's humming wasn't coating her with its sexual compulsion, she might rethink things.

Passion dropped her gaze to judge the exact strength of his . . . contamination. Even a hazmat suit wouldn't help him now. And she didn't believe for a minute she'd ever do any rethinking.

She clenched her hands into fists to keep from ripping away his clothes. Passion didn't feel very virginal. But then, she'd visited the minds of a few virgins, and lust crossed all boundaries.

Where, where, *where* could they lie down? She raked her fingers through her hair. Her pounding heart felt as though it would explode through her chest at any moment. She glanced down at the floor. "The floor looks comfy. Nice soft dirt."

His gaze skimmed the room, passing over the table with its plants.

"How about the table? We could move the plants." Not one at a time either. They'd be gone with one desperate sweep of her arm.

Edge shook his head. "Wouldn't be very comfortable."

Comfortable? He was kidding, right? She was so hot for him that . . . "Hey, the wall seems pretty sturdy, we could—"

"No." He pointed. "Over there. Cinn keeps a cot here for the times when her plants need her."

These were Cinn's plants? And she slept with them? Okay, that discussion could wait for another time.

He frowned. "The cot's narrow. You won't be—"

She spoke through gritted teeth, because if she didn't keep her teeth under control she'd bite him. "Comfortable. I know. And. I. Don't. Care." Passion could still hear Sparkle's humming in her head. Mental screams weren't doing any good.

Edge placed his hands on either side of her face, forcing her to look at him. "Can you control what you're feeling? Can you stop this?"

"No." Why would she want to stop it?

He dropped his hands. "Too bad. Because I can't either."

What glowed in his eyes should have scared her. It was so sexual, so primal it made her shiver, but not with fear. She'd bet her eyes looked the same as his.

He started to speak, but she put her finger over his lips. "Don't. I can't wait any longer."

Passion followed him to the cot. With single-minded intensity, she began stripping. Before he could offer to help, she was finished. The black bra and panties Sparkle had given her went last.

She turned to find he hadn't offered to help because he was busy getting rid of his own clothes.

She'd seen naked men in the minds of those she visited, but she'd always kept an emotional separation. Before, it hadn't been her life or her fantasy. But this was hers, and he was . . . amazing.

There might be a moment in the future—if they had a future—when she'd be able to absorb the wonder of his body at her leisure. Sure, she'd seen him when he came out of the shower. But like now, there hadn't been enough time to truly appreciate all of him: the smooth flow of muscle beneath warm flesh, the shape of him—wide shoulders, hard thighs, and everything in between.

Right now? All she wanted to do was to *feel* him through every one of her starved senses.

Before she could spend any time trying to figure out what came next, he scooped her up and laid her gently on the cot. Then he knelt on the dirt floor beside her.

"If you've spent your life under Archangel Ted's thumb, I assume that this is—"

"My first time." She met his gaze. "Do *not* say the 'v' word. I'm not afraid—of you, of the pain, of anything. The only thing that scares me is the thought you might slow everything down so you can try to be gentle. *I'm* not feeling gentle."

Heat flared in his eyes. "Tell me what you want."

His expression along with—she glanced down—*everything* shouted, "Hurry, hurry, hurry."

She reached out to run her fingers along his clenched jaw. "I want you under me. I want my hands, my mouth on you. I want you inside me."

"Got it."

He nudged in beside her while she shifted so she was kneeling on the cot, straddling those lean hips. Her on-top position wasn't about control, it was about access to every inch of his body.

Edge lay quietly while she tried to slow her breathing, recapture a heartbeat that was running free. Couldn't do it. And so she stopped trying. She'd go with what her body was urging.

She reached down to slide her fingers over his smooth, warm chest, his male nipples, his ridged stomach, and then along the thick hard length of his . . . cock. She'd heard the word so often in the minds of the women she'd visited, but never understood the surge of hunger and emotion attached to it. She did now.

Her exploration drew a groan from him. And when he spoke, his words came in short gasps. "I can't give you slow and gentle for your first time, but I *can* give you control." He added in a harsh whisper, "Even if it kills me."

Passion grinned. "You won't have to suffer long. I'd like more time to touch . . ." She reached between her spread thighs to cup his sac. "To taste you." She leaned down to glide her tongue across one nipple and felt his whole body shudder. "But I can't wait any longer." Every moment since Ted had kicked her down here seemed to have been leading to this moment, and she wanted to savor it, but she couldn't stop her mad dash to the finish line of this particular race. Sparkle had a lot to answer for.

She started to scoot forward so she could plant herself on top of him. Surprised, Passion realized she was shaking. Nerves, eagerness? She didn't know.

"Wait."

Even through the full-symphony volume of Sparkle's humming in her mind, she heard him and paused. "I thought *I* was in control." Stupid, stupid thought. Her body had ripped control from her brain a long time ago.

"I'm just taking you on a little side trip to a scenic overlook. Trust me." His eyes glowed with wicked intent.

The promise in his eyes would always get her. And somewhere in the heat and desire of the moment, she realized her admission had closed the door to her past. "This had better be worth the risk."

"Risk?" He raised one brow.

"Of me dying from frustration." *Of me never being able to return to Ted's world.* When had she stopped calling it home?

His laugh was low and sensual. "Come here." He beckoned.

She slid up his body until he signaled for her to stop. Then he nudged her thighs farther apart and put his mouth on her.

Her world exploded with sensual overload. She tangled her fingers in his thick hair to anchor herself, but it didn't do much good. Bits of her flew off to disappear into the cosmos.

He slid his tongue back and forth across the nub of flesh that right now held all the secrets of her sexual universe. With each stroke of his magic tongue, everything became *more*. The scent of him, a blend of dangerous dark places and aroused male. The sound of his breathing, harsh with need. And above all else, the feel of each stroke—swirling, touching her whole body with just the tip of that tongue, driving her closer and closer to the edge of his scenic overlook where the air was almost too thin to breathe and just thinking about plunging off the cliff made her close her eyes and lick her lips.

Edge's sensual side trip ended here. Who knew she had a compulsion to jump from high places? She opened her eyes to stare down into the endless spiral of longing, lust, and—no, that last "l" word would remain only a possibility for now.

She hurled herself into the unknown.

Rising above him, she lowered herself onto his cock. Slowly, relishing the friction, the sense of being filled completely, she pushed past the brief pain—too far into her free fall to stop. Sexual hunger she'd never imagined feeling drove her toward that final impact. If she'd known falling would be so awesome, she would have jumped sooner. *But only with Edge.*

She stilled for a moment, her eyes closed, imprinting the glory of him deep inside her, making sure she'd never forget no matter where the rest of her life took her.

Then she began to move. She rose until only the head of his cock remained inside her before easing back down again. The heaviness built, strengthened, pushing toward . . .

Thought vanished and sensation took over as need twisted her into the shape of desire. She rose and fell, driving him deeper and deeper and deeper.

Somewhere along the journey, Edge joined her. He put his hands on each side of her hips and then drove up into her. And each time flesh met flesh, she thought it couldn't get better.

Closer, closer, closer. His groan blended with her small eager sounds. And suddenly, she was *there*.

Her orgasm took her even as Sparkle's song spun magic around them. Passion screamed Edge's name. He answered with one final thrust and a shout of triumph.

She held her breath as spasms of pleasure washed over her.

Never stop, never stop, never stop. But they did, the spasms growing weaker and weaker. And when stillness finally lay around her, she realized that she'd *never* regret closing the door to Ted's world and her past. This—even if it was all she'd ever have—had been worth it.

Passion felt Edge gently push the hair away from her face. She opened her eyes. For just a moment, his unguarded expression caught at her heart. But then it was gone, and he was once again what he'd always been—the cosmic troublemaker in charge of death.

"That was . . ."

Edge placed his finger over her lips. "Don't. Let it be what it was. We don't need words for it."

She nodded, and then slid off him. With her back to him, she quickly dressed. As her euphoria faded, reality set in. She was sore. She just hoped the hurt didn't spread to her heart.

Edge frowned. Did she regret making love with him? Damn. This was one time he wished he could slip into her mind. *No, you don't.* He wouldn't take it well if he found that what they'd shared hadn't meant as much to her as it had to him.

More slowly, he rose and dressed. She still had her back to him. Someone had better say something, because without Sparkle's humming in his head, the silence was deadly. He needed words, any words, to drown out his uncertainties. His doubts made him uneasy. He hadn't had many during his long existence.

"Are you okay?" *Right. How to be cool. Next you'll ask her if it was as good for her as it was for you.* He already knew the answer to that one. It didn't get any better.

Passion nodded and turned to face him. "I need a shower." She sounded distracted as she carefully avoided his gaze.

Oh, no, she wasn't going to get away with this. "Look at me, Passion."

Taking a deep breath, she raised her gaze to meet his. "What's wrong?"

She shrugged. "Nothing, I guess." Then she pressed those sexy lips together. "Fine, so that's a lie. I was just wondering if what we felt . . . Well, was it real? I mean, with Sparkle spinning her 'Light My Fire' craziness everywhere."

He tucked his emotions deep inside him where she couldn't see them. Sometimes, pride was all he had. "Do *you* think it was real?"

She studied him from those pale green eyes. "Yes, I do. For me." Uncertainty seemed to touch her. "I don't know about you."

"Couldn't get more real for me. Believe it." Intense relief almost made him weak. He didn't know where any of this would take them, but at least they had a chance. He pushed her hair aside and whispered his secret into her ear. "I've wanted to make love with you from the first moment I looked through the bars of that cage and saw you." Surprised, he realized it was true.

Before she could reply, someone flung the door open. Dacian and Cinn stumbled in. As soon as Dacian saw him, he peeled his lip back to show fang. Both of them had the same hungry look that Edge figured he and Passion had worn.

"Crap." Dacian pulled Cinn to a stop. "We came here looking for some privacy. No way would we have made it back to our apartment. What the hell are you doing here?"

"Leaving." Edge smiled. "It's all yours."

Cinn waved at Passion. "We spoke on the phone. I'd stop to chat, but . . ." She closed her eyes and took a deep breath. "I'm not standing strong against Sparkle's song."

"None of us are." Passion returned Cinn's smile. "We'll

talk later." She grabbed Edge's hand to urge him toward the door.

Edge paused just before leaving. "What's happening with Sparkle?"

Dacian made an obvious effort to focus. "Ganymede's still missing. Hope is nowhere to be found. In other words, we're screwed. So far, Sparkle has stayed in the castle, but her song has leaked out into the courtyard. I don't want to even think about what will happen if she takes her show on the road." He shook his head. "I can't stop her. I can't even stop myself." He pushed Edge out the door and slammed it behind him.

"What now?"

Edge smiled. Passion was having trouble making eye contact. She'd turned her head and aimed her question at the courtyard. But what she saw in the courtyard widened her eyes. She gasped and switched her attention back to him.

"I'm giving Sparkle a lot more respect after this." Edge felt equal parts amusement and horror. Naked bodies littered the courtyard. "I'm impressed."

Passion looked horrified. "They don't care that everyone can see what they're doing."

"And doing it with strangers. I don't know how we'll straighten out this mess once someone stops Sparkle."

Passion refused to glance to left or right. "Will this ruin the castle?"

Edge shrugged. "No one will be able to prove anything. But even if Ganymede, Dacian, or I take away their memories, we're still going to have to get them dressed and then make up some explanation for the missing time." He raked his fingers through his hair. Damn. This was getting complicated. "There's always the chance that someone will get pregnant. And if Sparkle takes to the streets, there's not much we can do to salvage the situation."

"Pregnant?" Her eyes widened. "I could be—"

He put his finger across her lips. "No, you can't. One of the perks of being me. I control my body." He thought about Sparkle's song. "Well, most of the time. Anyway, I wouldn't allow pregnancy unless it was mutually agreed upon."

"Have you and someone ever mutually agreed—"

"No." He sounded curt, but he couldn't help it. No way would he ever be a part of bringing an innocent life into his world.

She simply nodded.

"Let's find Sparkle." Passion turned and headed for the door they had come through a lifetime ago.

He took a step to follow her, and then he heard it. Sparkle was humming in his head again. After he'd made love with Passion there'd been blessed silence. He'd thought it had been one time and out. Wrong. Evidently, Sparkle's song sent you back for seconds.

Passion stopped. She looked back at him. "I hear Sparkle."

He knew his expression was grim. "We have to stop her before we end up in the greenhouse again fighting Dacian and Cinn for their cot." Under normal circumstances, making love with Passion over and over would be *his* idea of heaven, but compulsions wore out their welcomes fast.

Once inside the castle, he led her toward the great hall. If they didn't find Sparkle there, then they'd have to search the rest of the castle. And every minute spent looking for her brought them closer to . . . He narrowed his gaze. Not going to happen. The next time he made love with Passion, she'd have no doubt the feelings were their own.

They got as far as the chapel. That's where they found Murmur, feet propped up on a pew, head thrown back and long hair trailing over the back of the pew, earbuds in place, listening to music. He looked up when they entered, but he didn't remove the earbuds. He just smiled.

What the . . . Edge walked over to confront the demon. "What the hell are you doing here?"

Murmur didn't take out the earbuds. "I can't hear you, but I can read your lips. I went to the great hall looking for someone to dance with me, but all I found were a bunch of naked people having sex. I'm waiting here until the floating woman puts on a new tune. The one she has on repeat is getting old."

Passion joined him and got into Murmur's face. "Where's Hope?" She looked puzzled. "And I thought demons couldn't enter holy places."

He shrugged. "I left her at the mall. There's just so long I can listen to her message of love, redemption, and blah, blah, blah." His smile turned sly. "And I think you're asking how I can be here. Just because people call a place 'holy' doesn't mean it is." His expression turned dangerous. "I go where I want to go."

Edge was losing his temper. "Why don't you take out the damn earbuds?"

Murmur's eyes narrowed to slits of pleasure. "I like it when you get mad. What can I say to make you madder?"

Passion put her hand on Edge's arm. He took a deep breath and tried to calm himself.

"If I take out the earbuds, I'll be just like you." He shook his head in mock sympathy. "Compulsions are a bitch."

Passion looked thoughtful. She leaned close to the demon and spoke slowly so he wouldn't have any trouble understanding her. "Maybe you can help us. We need someone to hold Sparkle in check while we search for Ganymede. He can yank her away from whoever is controlling her. Edge would take care of Sparkle, but the compulsion makes it tough for him to focus. Do you have that kind of power? Could you stop what she's doing long enough for us to find Ganymede?"

Murmur looked amazed that anyone would ask his help for anything. "Why would I want to do that for you?"

"Because with everyone having sex, you won't find anyone to dance with you."

Murmur looked away, and Edge held his breath. He had no proof that Murmur wasn't the one creating the problem, but right now he had to take help where he could find it.

The demon nodded. "Let's go."

Edge decided that Murmur was smart to keep those buds in his ears. Sparkle's humming was starting to take its toll. He figured Passion was experiencing the same thing. They had to track down the cat fast.

They found Sparkle in the great hall. Evidently, she had enough power to spread her siren's song throughout the castle and into the courtyard. He just hoped it hadn't gone any farther.

Edge shook his head. "I've never seen this many naked people doing it in one place before. Not even at a Roman orgy."

"Ted would expect me to stop this." She kept her gaze fixed on him. "And when I couldn't, he'd use it as an excuse to send down the avenging angels."

"Avenging angels?" Edge and Murmur spoke at the same time.

She waved their questions away. "Later."

Murmur studied the situation. "I don't think I can stop her compulsion, but I can counter it with my own."

"Do it." Edge didn't even ask for details. "And do it fast." Or else he and Passion would be joining that crowd rolling around on the floor.

Murmur nodded. "You'll owe me for this. I'll have to stand here and watch all their jiggling and jumping bits. Humans shouldn't dance naked. It's an affront to music."

Passion frowned. "What're you going to—"

Edge grabbed her hand. "Doesn't matter. Get ready to run or else we might get caught by his compulsion."

She held back. "Wait. Just a minute. I want to see."

Murmur stood gazing out over the hall. Suddenly, power swirled around him. It pushed Edge back a step.

Then the music began. It came from nowhere and everywhere. Music like he'd never heard before. The rhythm lived and breathed, defying him to stand still. Sparkle's humming faded in the glory that was Murmur's music.

As if in a trance, everyone climbed to their feet and began dancing. They'd forgotten their partners of only a few seconds ago as they swayed, leaped, and twirled, held fast by Murmur's compulsion.

Edge didn't even realize he was dancing until Passion grabbed him. She'd latched onto a door frame, trying to hold herself still. She clung to him. Probably afraid he'd drift away to be lost in the dance. Hated to admit it, but it could happen. They might want to move the demon up on their suspect list.

Meanwhile, whoever was controlling Sparkle's humming must have noticed the competition. Sparkle's blank stare grew a little less blank. Her gaze narrowed on Murmur, and her humming grew louder. Murmur grinned. His music swelled and sped up. The dancers' frenetic motions became a blur.

"Great. Dueling compulsions." Edge forced his feet to shuffle and slide their way toward the door. He resisted his almost irresistible need to swing and sway. And he definitely would *not* twirl.

Passion threw one last question at Murmur. "How long will they dance?"

Murmur glanced at her. His eyes glowed red. "Until they die."

"No. You can't. That's wrong."

"I'm a demon. When did you forget that? Demons kill." His gaze shifted to Edge. "As do other beings."

Edge cursed as he danced back to grab her hand and yank her toward the door. "It's either dance, make love right here, or get out of Dodge. Your choice, but decide now."

She followed him from the room.

They didn't stop running until they once again were standing outside the castle. Even here, Edge had to focus on not dancing, on not dragging her back into the greenhouse.

"Where do we start looking for Ganymede?"

Passion was hopping and bopping to Murmur's music. Edge didn't think she even realized it.

"If I can get my head straight for a minute, I'll reach

for his mind." Why hadn't Ganymede reached for *him*? He didn't have time to sift through possibilities. He'd put a mental call out and hope Ganymede answered.

"Anything I can do?" Passion kept glancing at the naked humans and a few nonhumans dancing in the courtyard.

"Pinch me."

She abandoned the dancers in favor of staring at him. "Excuse me?"

"I need to get the compulsions out of my head for a few minutes while I search for Ganymede's mind."

Her smile looked a little too eager. "Pinch? Where?" Her gaze slipped to his butt.

As tempting as that was, her pinch would have to be in a spot that wouldn't aid Sparkle's cause. "Better make it my arm."

She didn't argue, just nodded.

The sharp pain cleared his brain for a few seconds. He reached for Ganymede. At first he got nothing. He listened harder. Then . . . There. A faint whisper. Edge focused harder. Almost, almost. Finally, he had it.

"He's in his apartment. Let's go."

They danced their way to Ganymede's door while visions of hot sex filled their minds. At least, Edge assumed Passion's mind was tuned in to erotic images too.

Time for more pain. "I need another pinch."

"Sorry. Can't resist." She pinched his ass. "So beautiful. So pinch-worthy."

He pushed aside visions of payback and concentrated on his mental message. *"What the hell is going on?"*

Ganymede's answer was immediate if faint. *"The bastard threw up some kind of spell around my room. Couldn't get out or reach anyone's mind. Son of a bitch will pay for this. Focus your power on your side of the door, and I'll take care of this side. If that doesn't work, we're shit out of luck until we can get Holgarth up here."*

Yeah, like that was going to happen. Holgarth was busy dancing naked to Murmur's compulsion. Anger drove Edge's power. Ganymede must've felt the same, because the door simply disappeared. Ganymede padded through the opening.

"You're in cat form?" Passion was doing what looked like a snake dance right now. Intriguing. Arousing. "Don't you think human form might be a better bet right now?"

Ganymede padded toward the stairs, ears pinned back and tail whipping from side to side. *"When I felt Sparkle get hit, it threw me out of cat form for a little while. I felt her compulsion. Fat lot of good it did me."* He sounded disgusted. *"Figured once I got out, I'd be able to resist the pull better in cat form."*

He wasn't resisting everything because Edge could see his tail beginning to wave in time to Sparkle's song while his front paws moved with Murmur's rhythm.

"What's the situation?"

Edge explained in as few words as possible.

"I can stop Sparkle. If Murmur is our guy, though, that changes everything."

Startled, Edge stared at the cat. That was a first. He'd never heard uncertainty in Ganymede's voice before.

"Maybe the Big Boss is your guy." Passion was now into a tango. She was beginning to breathe hard.

So was Edge.

Ganymede stopped to stare at her. Edge stared too. The implications were mind-boggling.

"Why would he mess with his own people?" Ganymede stated the obvious.

She shrugged. "Isn't there some quote about power corrupting and absolute power corrupting absolutely?"

"All that power could eat your brain. Maybe he's gone crazy?" Ganymede seemed to be considering the possibility.

"I don't think we want to go there yet." If the Big Boss had turned on them, then the world was in deep shit. Edge didn't think anyone would walk away from that.

They'd reached the great hall. For a moment, they just stared. Edge figured hell must look a lot like this. Only here there were dueling devils.

"Some of them are dancing at the same time they're . . . How is that physically possible?" Passion sounded horrified.

"Tell me that's not Holgarth over there. I can't look. I think I'm going blind." Ganymede turned his head away.

"Isn't that Bain?" Passion didn't look away from the demon, and she *didn't* look horrified. "What a beautiful man." Wonder moved in her voice.

"Demon. He's a *demon*. He sleepwalks. And he has weird friends. Didn't Murmur say that Bain is his friend?" The immediate stab of jealousy caught Edge by surprise. He wanted to tear Bain apart and then heave his pieces into the trash bin.

Edge had bragged about the control he had over his body, but he was doing a crappy job of controlling his emotions. What did that mean? He'd think about it later.

"Murmur needs to back off his power before I try to stop my sweetie." Ganymede padded over to the demon. *"Yo, demon, shut it down."*

Murmur stared at him from glazed eyes. "Why? Haven't had this much fun in centuries." He blinked. "Want to join them in the dance, but can't if I have to match power with the bitch over there."

Ganymede flattened his ears. *"If you weren't high on your own power, I'd take that comment personally."*

Edge and Passion joined Ganymede.

"So you're not stopping?" Passion cast Ganymede a worried glance.

Murmur grinned. "Hell, no."

Ganymede crouched, ears pinned and tail whipping. His power surged, creating a mini-tornado around him.

"Oh, shit." Edge made a grab for Passion in an attempt to get her out of harm's way before Ganymede went off on Murmur.

"Stop."

The one softly spoken word reached every corner of the great hall.

Everything stopped—Sparkle's humming, Murmur's

music, even Ganymede's power faded to nothing. The human dancers froze in place. The nonhumans looked around, dazed.

A man walked slowly across the great hall. Expanding power filled the room, pushing at the walls, and filling Edge with dread. He'd *never* felt power like this.

And even though the man had said only one word, Edge recognized his voice. A glance at the faces of the other cosmic troublemakers in the hall assured him that they did too.

The man heaved an exaggerated sigh. "I leave you alone for a few centuries, and look what happens." He smiled, a smile that promised someone would pay for this.

Edge stood straighter, shoving his fear and resentment into a place he hoped the man couldn't see. He lowered his head with the respect due his leader.

Sparkle, eyes wide with shock, said it for all of them. "Ohmigod! The Big Boss is here. And why the hell am I naked?"

12

The Big Boss, an ordinary human title for someone she couldn't imagine ever being ordinary *or* human.

Passion had rooted around in enough women's minds to suspect he'd never be able to walk down any street on the mortal plane without riots breaking out. She knew there'd be chaos in the cubicles back home if he appeared in their midst. The plane of existence didn't matter. Certain males just had "it." And females *knew*.

He wasn't as tall as Ganymede or some of the others. Probably not quite six feet. But he was eight feet tall when it came to impact.

She skipped over his broad shoulders and lean-muscled body in favor of studying him from the neck up. Black hair shot through with what looked like strands of gold fell in a shining curtain down his back. And his face . . . She'd never seen anything so beautiful in heaven or in the minds of mortals. Of course, she hadn't canvassed hell yet, so who knew.

Thick black lashes framed pale gray eyes, the pupils outlined in black. She'd bet Sparkle would kill for lashes that long. Passion wouldn't. Maim, maybe, but not kill. To top it off, his eyes had a slight upward tilt to them, giving them an exotic look.

He had a sensual mouth, and the angles of jaw and cheekbones were made to hold shadows and secrets.

Inexorably, her gaze returned to his eyes. They didn't lie. His comment might have sounded playful in a sarcastic kind of way, but his eyes didn't say playful at all.

They branded him as other. No human eyes could be that cold, that still, that *empty*. It wasn't the empty of nobody's-home. It was more the empty of I-don't-give-a-damn. Passion sensed she was getting a peek into the soul of a being who had existed for so long that all emotion, all *warmth*, had drained from him.

She'd never seen such cold eyes, sensed such an icy heart. Did he even have a soul? Maybe that's why she couldn't see *any* colors around him. Weird.

She thought about the no-colors thing. The angels didn't have any colors either, but that was because they didn't sin. She didn't think this man was sinless.

Then she realized he was watching her with those pale eyes. His lips lifted in a faint smile, and he nodded at her.

Something in the twist of his lips, the cold gleam in those eyes . . . He scared her.

She leaned into Edge. He might represent death, and black might be doing a jig around him, but he still had a soul, and he wasn't dead inside.

The Big Boss finally reached them. He leaned close to her for a moment. "All that from one glance? Damn, you're good." Then he looked at the others.

He'd been in her mind. Somehow that didn't shock her. It *did* make her mad, though.

"I am *not* happy. Look at this." He swept his arm to encompass the frozen, naked bodies. Cold power rippled away from him, slapping at all of them.

"We didn't cause it, Boss."

Ganymede didn't sound intimidated, but Passion

couldn't tell what he was thinking without a human expression to help her.

The Big Boss didn't acknowledge him. "How will we fix things?" He glanced at Edge. "What do you think, Finis? Should we kill them all?"

"I can't see that as fixing anything." No expression showed on Edge's face or in his voice.

"You don't enjoy killing anymore, do you?" The Big Boss smiled as though he'd just uncovered a wonderful secret.

Edge didn't answer him, just looked away.

"What about you, Ganymede? I could cut you loose. Wouldn't you like watching Galveston slide into a giant sinkhole? Your act would live forever on CNN, shown over and over again to horrified humans throughout the world. You'd have millions of views on YouTube. You always loved over-the-top performances."

For the first time since Passion had known him, Ganymede had nothing to say.

The Big Boss's smile was both a terrible and beautiful thing to see. "Oh, I understand. You've formed friendships here, grown to love the island. More than that, you have an emotional attachment to someone, and she wouldn't want you to destroy all those lives." He shook his head in mock sorrow. "You've let emotions creep into your existence. They weaken you. I should've come sooner."

He shifted his attention to Sparkle. "And what about you, Sparkle? Did you have a good time?"

While the Big Boss had been talking, Sparkle had found her clothes in the restaurant, pulled them on, and joined the group.

"I can't enjoy something I don't remember." She glanced around the hall. "But it must've been a hell of a party."

"You were magnificent. Just like the old days. Remember how it used to be? You'd choose two people who were completely wrong for each other. You'd manipulate their emotions until they fell in love. And then, you'd tear them apart without one moment of regret. You were pitiless. What happened to that Sparkle?" He stared unblinkingly at her. "Your success rate is in the toilet. It seems every couple you bring together lately ends up getting married. What kind of cosmic troublemaker is that?"

Passion could learn to hate this guy.

A low rumble filled the room.

The Big Boss glanced at Ganymede. "Stop growling at me, Ganymede. I'm only trying to understand what's been happening here."

There was silence for a moment, and then Sparkle spoke up. "Okay, you've made your point. You've made us feel like failures. But maybe you need to lighten up. I think I liked your rep better than you. He had that whole jolly ice-cream guy thing going on. He was fun." She smoothed down her hair and absently slipped on her metallic stilettos. "You're beautiful, but you need to warm a little before I can offer up some woman on the altar of your awesomeness."

Ganymede hissed and leaped in front of Sparkle. Edge crouched. Murmur looked amused, and Passion freaked.

Ohmigod, the Big Boss's eyes were glowing. He looked as though he was lining up Sparkle in his sights before blasting her out of the water. War would erupt. *Edge might die.* And why was that her first thought? Her primary worry should be that *she* might die.

Eternity seemed to hang on the Big Boss's reaction.

Then he laughed, a real laugh that actually warmed those icy eyes just a little. "I've always liked you, Sparkle." He looked out over the hall. "Even if you did make a mess here."

Passion could feel the tension easing. Edge came out of his crouch, and Ganymede sat down in front of Sparkle.

"I only see one solution for this." The Big Boss gave the naked people his complete attention. "I have to turn back time. When I release them, this never will have happened, and they'll continue doing whatever they were doing."

Passion's mouth opened and words came out before she thought about them. "That's impossible. Besides, I don't want to forget." Uh-oh. She'd called attention to herself. Not a good thing.

"Everything is *possible*, Passion."

Something about the way he said her name made it personal. And Passion didn't question how he knew who she was.

"I sympathize with why you don't want to forget." He didn't look sympathetic. "Don't worry, only the mortals will have no memory of what *didn't* happen. I'll leave the nonhumans with something to talk about."

Passion was confused. Not that she believed he could turn back time, but if by chance he could, then did that mean she was still a virgin?

"So if you're turning back time for everyone, then I guess you won't be here yet, and the rest of us won't be standing around with our thumbs up our butts." Ganymede looked disgruntled.

The Big Boss smiled, but Passion sensed darkness behind the smile.

"When I turn back time, I'll tweak the past for our little group here. So, yes, Ganymede, you will be standing around with your 'thumb up your butt.'" He shook his head. "Your use of language amazes me. Is 'thumbs up our butts' a Texas thing?"

Ganymede offered him a cat snort. *"Stick around and I'll teach you to talk like a human. And turning back time will have consequences."*

"There are consequences to everything we do. Time will change only for those inside the castle and out in the courtyard. I made sure no one entered or left the grounds once Sparkle started humming, so the damage was contained. For those who get home a little late or have someone outside the castle comment on the time lapse . . ." He shrugged. "It will simply be their unsolved mystery."

"Wait. Does that mean you knew what was happening from the beginning and didn't stop it sooner?"

Edge didn't sound mad, but Passion could sense his outrage, his need to strike out at his leader.

"Yes." The Big Boss's stare challenged Edge. "I wanted to see if the person orchestrating these events would make an appearance. Gloating is part of the fun. So while all of you were taking a sexual timeout, I was having a look around the castle."

Murmur had remained quiet, but now he spoke. "Look, I respect the hell out of you, but I'm getting restless. I've never seen anyone mess with time. Let's do it."

Bain had quietly joined the group. He'd pulled on his pants and boots, but he was still shirtless. "I'm going to kick your ass, Murmur, for throwing that compulsion at me."

Murmur grinned. "Hey, you had a good time. So let it go."

"Quiet." The Big Boss didn't turn to look at them. He stilled, and his gaze grew distant.

Edge clasped Passion's hand. She released the breath she hadn't known she was holding. Things would be okay.

"I'd suggest that everyone close their eyes. If not, once I begin you'll get the mother of all motion-sickness attacks, and I don't need to see you puking up your guts." He didn't shout, but once again, his voice seemed to fill the hall.

Passion immediately closed her eyes.

Even so, she knew the moment he began. It felt the way she imagined plunging backward down a roller coaster would feel, a free fall that left her stomach along with the rest of her world dropping away until she was sure her stomach had permanently lodged in her throat. Then it stopped.

"You can open your eyes."

When she opened them, it was as though she'd hit the pause button on a show while she ran to the bathroom. When she returned, she hit the pause button again and everything continued as though nothing had ever interrupted it. Everyone was dressed, and no one acted like anything unusual had happened.

Except for Holgarth, who descended on them with narrow-eyed temper written all over his face. "This is *not* acceptable. My fantasy schedule will be off by a half hour for the rest of the night."

Interesting. Holgarth remembered, so he wasn't human.

He glared at the Big Boss while Edge tried to make shushing motions at him.

From the Big Boss's expression, Passion guessed he was about to hit Holgarth with a deadly dose of snark, or something worse. She felt unwilling sympathy for the wizard. It didn't take much insight to figure out that the castle was everything to Holgarth. He was old, and no one had mentioned a wife or family. The fantasies were his children.

No matter how much of a butthead Holgarth had been to her, she found she didn't want his ego cut to ribbons, or worst-case scenario, *him* cut to ribbons. Still, she surprised herself when she impulsively put her hand on the Big Boss's arm.

When he swung to look at her, she saw the flare of shock in his eyes. How long had it been since anyone had touched this man?

She swallowed hard. "Please. Don't." That's all she could get out.

He held her gaze for a moment longer, then nodded. He turned back to Holgarth. "I apologize for disrupting your schedule. I realize how hard it is to keep this kind of operation running smoothly."

Passion wasn't the only surprised one. Even Holgarth looked shocked. She'd bet his insults weren't often met with an apology.

Holgarth nodded stiffly. "All right then. If Sparkle can keep her clothes on, and time doesn't make a habit of running backward, then I can maintain my schedule. And since *finally* someone strong enough to protect us all has arrived"—he glared at Ganymede and Edge—"I assume I can reclaim the dungeon as part of the fantasies." He even managed a tight smile.

Well, well. Passion thought the Big Boss had won over at least one person tonight. If he was capable of an act of kindness, maybe she'd have to rethink her soulless judgment.

Holgarth walked away with no comment about how he'd spent his time while Sparkle hummed. Passion, for one, never wanted to find out.

"He's right. You can move back to your own rooms." The Big Boss glanced at Edge, Ganymede, and Sparkle. "I'll meet you three in the lobby after the last fantasy." His narrowed gaze skimmed Passion, Murmur, and Bain. He offered them a brief smile before starting to walk away.

"What should I call you?" Passion hoped he got the unspoken message. He wasn't *her* boss.

He paused. "Bourne? I loved the movies. And I've never been a Bourne before." He turned away and kept walking.

"Fine. Bourne it is." Passion pulled her hand from Edge's grip without meeting his gaze. "I'll move my stuff out of the dungeon."

She knew she sounded stiff, but now that everything was sort of back to normal, she felt uncomfortable with the whole sex-by-compulsion event. The part of her conscience that still answered to Archangel Ted thought she was trying to use Sparkle's humming as an excuse. She wasn't. She'd wanted to make love with Edge, with or without a compulsion.

Passion started to walk away. Murmur and Bain followed close behind. Edge didn't try to stop her.

"Intense dude." Murmur smiled. "Dangerous but cool."

Bain didn't comment.

She hurried to put some distance between them. Passion wasn't interested in talking with anyone right now. She'd headed toward the stairs leading down to the dungeon when she spotted Hope entering the castle. Hope waved at her. Passion groaned. Looked as though she wouldn't get any alone time.

Passion stepped into a small alcove to wait for Hope to reach her. For the first time, she thought about not telling

Hope what had happened here. Sure, she'd tell her about the Big Boss showing up, but not all the other stuff. What if Hope felt obligated to tattle to Ted? There were some things Hope might think were too evil to keep from him. Passion didn't want a visit from the avenging angels if she could help it.

Just then Murmur and Bain walked past her alcove. They were headed toward the courtyard. Passion didn't pay much attention to them until she caught a little of what they were saying.

"This is getting ugly, Murmur. I've covered for you so far, but I won't put my job here in danger because of you. What's the holdup?"

Bain's voice had a dangerous edge that Passion hadn't heard before.

"What's the matter, Bain? Afraid I'll screw up your vengeance plan?" Murmur smiled. "Don't worry, I'm almost ready to make a decision. But I won't lead my demons into battle until I'm sure I'm on the right side."

Bain laughed. "You mean the *winning* side."

Murmur's smiled widened. "I'm totally self-serving. And any side I support will always be the winning side. Not many can stand against me or mine. Remember that."

Whatever else Murmur and Bain said was lost as they moved away from Passion. What was that about? She drew in a shaky breath.

But she didn't have time to think about whom to tell because Hope had reached her.

Passion stepped out of the alcove. "Nice of you to stop by the castle once in a while." Sarcasm was useless with Hope, but Passion kept trying.

Hope stopped. "I'm so glad you're here. I have a bunch of stuff to tell you." She was like a can of soda someone had shaken, all fizzy with excitement.

Passion controlled her urge to stomp all over Hope's obvious happiness. "Where were you?" She continued toward the stairs. Hope walked beside her.

"Baybrook Mall on the mainland." She almost glowed.

"I talked to a lot of people about turning away from darkness until mall security interfered." She frowned. "They threatened to make me leave the mall if I didn't stop bothering people."

"Then why didn't you come back sooner?" *In time to stop Sparkle.*

Hope's glow returned. "I ran into Kemp in the mall."

Kemp? "The guy from here? The one with the buzz cut and the bad attitude who wouldn't talk to us?"

"Yes. He's really nice. He believes I'm doing the right thing. Murmur left right after we got to the mall. He's not very open to goodness and light." Murmur's desertion didn't seem to bother her. "But he's a great dancer. Anyway, right after Murmur left, Kemp showed up. I was going to get a cab back to the castle, but Kemp offered to take me to the movies. After the show, he drove me home."

If Kemp hadn't kept Hope at the movies, she might have gotten back in time to do some good. Passion hated the way she was starting to suspect everyone. Pretty soon she'd be sitting on her own little desert island surrounded by a shark-infested sea of suspects.

"That's great. I'm glad you had a good time." Did she sound sincere? "Well, we don't have to stay in the dungeon anymore. The Big Boss showed up, so he'll take care of his people. We can go back to our room."

"The Big Boss?" Hope's eyes lit with interest. "What's he like? Did he have the colors of sin around him?"

"He's . . ." How to describe someone who was so much more than his physical appearance? She shrugged. "You'll meet him. His name is Bourne. And I couldn't see any colors around him."

"But you always see—"

"Not this time."

"Why couldn't you—"

"I don't want to talk about it."

Hope got the message and lapsed into silence.

Once Passion reached the dungeon, she threw her things into her bag and left quickly. She didn't want to run into

Edge until she'd figured out how she felt about him, about her, about *them*.

Instead of going directly up to her room, she got off the elevator at the lobby. The restaurant stayed open late because of the fantasies, and she decided she needed some comfort food to take back with her. A burger and fries sounded good. She was learning things she never knew about herself. In human form, she became an eating machine when she felt stressed. She'd probably be heaven's first fat angel. If she *was* an angel.

Passion was thinking about Edge when she slammed into someone as she left the restaurant. Clutching her to-go box tightly, she rushed into an apology. "I'm so sorry. I wasn't looking where I was . . ." Then she recognized the person she'd bumped into.

"You're still here?" The old woman looked horrified.

"I thought you left." Passion had seen Bill help her out of the hotel on that awful day.

The woman sniffed. "I paid for a month, and I'm not leaving because of a false alarm." She narrowed her eyes at Passion. "What happened to that man? He should be locked up in a loony bin somewhere. Scared me out of a year of my life. And at my age, a year is important."

"He's still here."

The woman looked more outraged than scared. "He's a danger to everyone in this hotel. I saw his eyes. Killer's eyes."

"He's doing better now." *Lame, Passion.*

"Well, he made a big dent in my trust. Don't think I'll be helping any strangers for a good long time." Her stare was a little creepy.

The woman pursed her thin lips. "You were trying to help him too. Maybe you should stick to helping people who deserve it." Then the woman walked away. She had a determined stride. Nothing old or doddering about it.

Passion blinked. What was that rant about? The woman's last comment hit a little too close to home. Ted didn't think she should be trying to help the irredeemable ones either. She pressed her lips together. Ted would call it her mutinous expression. To hell with what Ted thought. She didn't believe Edge was beyond redemption. He didn't kill innocents. *Listen to yourself. You're pitiful. Murder is murder.*

Okay, enough soul-searching. It just made her crazy. Maybe she should've bought two dinners.

When she let herself into her room, Passion found Hope already there. She'd unpacked her few things and was propped up in bed with Sparkle's laptop.

"I have twenty-three new friend requests." She didn't look up from the screen. "I told everyone what heaven looked like, and now they all want to argue with me." She shook her head. "Why can't humans accept the truth?"

"Because they don't know you're a real angel."

"I told them I was."

"Humans need proof, Hope. Besides, your truth doesn't line up with what they want to believe, so they dismiss it." In a moment of unclouded-by-lust clarity, she realized that was true for her too. She wanted to believe in Edge's innate goodness, and so she ignored everything Ted said. Because she *really* liked Edge. She might even be getting close to loving him. Passion closed her eyes. And how stupid was that?

Someone knocked on the door. Since Hope didn't make a move to answer it, Passion did. Kemp was standing on the other side. His hair was still in a buzz cut, and his eyes were still almost black, but he was smiling this time.

"Could I talk to Hope?"

Passion started to turn toward Hope.

"Oh, and I'm sorry about the first time I saw you. I was doing something important and . . ." He looked embarrassed. "You guys interrupted."

"It's okay." And it was. The survey had been a crazy idea. Once again, Passion noticed that Kemp was a great-looking guy when he smiled. He still wasn't human, though. She didn't have the nerve to ask him what he was.

A few minutes later, Hope left with Kemp. Passion was alone. With her thoughts. Of Edge. Damn.

A hot shower didn't do a thing to cool down those thoughts, so she changed clothes, grabbed a light jacket, and headed for the door. No way was she staying here to stare at her bed.

Passion left by the hotel entrance so she wouldn't run into him and wandered through the park. The cool air didn't do much to clear her brain. She ended up sitting on a bench in front of where the pirate ship was moored. The pirate fantasies were done for the night, so it was just her and a bunch of tangled thoughts.

Passion was so busy picking through her conflicting emotions that she didn't realize someone had sat down next to her until he spoke.

"Nice night."

Startled, she almost jumped off the bench. "Zane?"

He wore a hoodie, and his face was in shadow. He nodded. "Mind some company for a few minutes?"

Passion shrugged. Fear pushed at her, but she ignored it. If he wanted to hurt her, he probably wouldn't choose to do it while they sat in full view of anyone still wandering the park.

He didn't say anything and the silence began to wear on her. Finally, she asked a question. "Why are you so angry?" She winced as soon as the words left her lips. Impulsive questions got her in trouble.

His hood was pulled too far forward for her to read his expression, but she sensed surprise. "What makes you think I'm mad?"

She shrugged. "Just a feeling. I'm good at reading emotions." *And besides, red, the color of rage, is doing the cha-cha around you.*

"Lots of things make me mad." He didn't offer any specifics.

"Mad enough for you to manipulate the cosmic trouble-makers' minds?" Passion got ready to run like hell. She must have a death wish.

He laughed. "Relax, mystery lady. I'm not angry with them." His laughter faded. "I'm saving all my rage for someone else."

"Are you human?" Since he hadn't gone ballistic with her last question, she took a chance on asking another.

"What do *you* think?" He didn't seem upset.

"All I sense is human, but logic says it would be tough for a human to do the kinds of things you can do."

She could see a flash of white teeth within the depths of the hoodie. "Anyone with enough power could cloak what they were."

Passion huffed her frustration. Why wouldn't he just answer the damn question?

"I have a confession."

Uh-oh. She got ready to run again.

"I sat down here because I have some questions for you."

She relaxed a little and smiled at him. "I'll probably be as straightforward with my answers as you were."

"I guess that's fair. Disappointing but fair." He leaned back against the bench. "What are you?"

Passion sighed. She was getting tired of that question. She should lie to him, but she couldn't summon the energy. Tonight had worn her out. *Edge* had worn her out. "I thought I was an angel, but now . . . ?" She shrugged. "I don't know what I am."

"Interesting." He sounded sincere. "So what powers do you have?"

"I'm not supposed to have any while I'm on the mortal plane. I'm being punished. But I can still see the colors of sin. You're surrounded by red. Lots of rage."

She could feel his tension. "I see. What else?"

Passion hesitated. "Nothing." She'd blabbed enough.

"I get it. You don't trust me. Smart lady."

The question-and-answer session had gone on long enough. Time for her to go back to her room where she could trade glares with her big empty bed. She stood. "I think I should—"

He put his hand on her arm. "Wait. I have one more question."

She resisted the urge to move out of reach. "Sure."

"What do you know about Holgarth?"

She blinked. "Holgarth?" Where had that question come from? "Not much. He's a wizard, and he rules the castle with an iron fist. Oh, and he's the master of snark. Why?"

He shook his head. "Nothing. Just wondering."

Liar. As much as she didn't want to talk to Holgarth, she should probably tell him about Zane's interest.

A final question popped into her head before she could walk away. "Why are you staying here? I mean, all of this must be boring to you when you could be in Vegas draining the casinos dry. You could even have your own Vegas show. Criss Angel could only wish he was as good as you."

"I'm waiting for someone." He didn't sound amused.

Was he waiting for the person causing all that red? Maybe he wouldn't answer, but she had to ask. "Who?"

His smile was a flash of white in the darkness. "Think I'll let that be a surprise."

13

Edge had wanted to follow Passion. He'd wanted to carry her off to *his* room—because no way was he giving Hope something juicy to post on Facebook, or worse yet, blab about to this Archangel Ted person—and show her that Sparkle had nothing to do with the sound-and-light show they'd created together.

He couldn't, though. Holgarth was waiting to start the next fantasy, and Edge was his evil vampire of choice. And since this would be the last fantasy of the night, Edge would have to meet with the Big Freaking Boss, aka Bourne, afterward.

Edge got through the fantasy and headed for the lobby. The others were already there. Bourne had found them a table tucked into a shadowed corner. They all had drinks. God, that's exactly what he needed. He thought about Passion. Okay, maybe not exactly.

He slipped into the one empty chair. His drink was already on the table. "Whoever got the drink, thanks."

Ganymede was in human form and looked pissed about it. He glared at Edge. "That would be Sparkle."

Sparkle sighed. "Big, blond, and sulky here didn't like being dragged off his fat cat butt and away from the TV and ice cream."

Ganymede narrowed his eyes to slits. "I'd DVR'd *Top Chef*, and I was just getting into it. This better be worth it, Boss."

Bourne looked bemused as he stared at Ganymede. Edge didn't blame him. Death and destruction could rain down on Ganymede, and he'd simply sit in the middle of the storm with his ice cream and TV remote. He wasn't normal.

Ganymede turned his bad temper on Sparkle. "And she's acting as though I'm the only one who wanted a little downtime after the night we had. Ask her what she said when she had to leave in the middle of doing her nails to come down here?"

"I. Don't. Care." Bourne had evidently had enough. "All I need are a few troublemakers who can work up a decent bloodlust, who want to go out and tear someone apart for the sheer joy of it, who love coming home covered in the blood of their enemies. Is that too much to ask for?" He exhaled deeply. "But I guess I'm old school."

Edge felt his rage building. How long had he wanted to put his fist into the face of the Big Boss? But up until now, their leader had been this faceless power who'd manipulated their lives without regard to what *they* wanted. Bourne had a lot to answer for.

Don't say it. Keep your mouth shut. Edge knew what Bourne was capable of, knew he could destroy without moving a muscle. But something in Edge wouldn't be denied.

Yeah, this was about Passion. Up until now, he hadn't much given a damn about anything, couldn't work up a decent mad about his existence. But he'd finally found someone . . . *Don't wimp out on me now. Say it.* He'd found someone who felt right for him, who felt like his *mate*.

And he couldn't have her. He was tied to forever as Death. Edge could imagine a typical day at their house.

"Thanks for making breakfast for me, sweetheart. I'll be home late. Tough day at work. Three drug lords, two serial killers, and a partridge in a pear tree. Don't wait up for me. Love you." Yeah, Passion would be happy with that kind of life.

Knowing his next words might be his last, Edge let his feelings rip. "If you want a bunch of man-eating tigers, you don't declaw them and pull their teeth."

Bourne stilled, his eyes fixed unblinkingly on Edge. "I sense some hostility."

His voice was so soft that Edge had to strain to hear it. "You think?"

Sparkle tried to defuse the moment. "Don't listen to him, Bourne. He doesn't mean anything."

Bourne never took his attention from Edge. "Oh, I think he does. Why don't you lay it out for me, Finis."

God, he hated that name. "No one ever asked me what *I* wanted to be. I was born, I killed. And for tens of thousands of years I was okay with that. I was like a child. I didn't reason out anything. Then I got older, hungrier. Killing had become a compulsion. I destroyed whole villages, hundreds of people at a time. Finally, I hit the big time. I took out Pompeii. Oh, you covered it up. Ganymede made the volcano blow, and you planted new memories in the minds of those who escaped. But it was then you realized I was off the leash."

Any moment now, Edge expected Bourne to wink him out of existence, but the fucker just sat there staring at him.

"Go on. This is fascinating."

Edge wondered what it would take to shatter Bourne's deadly calm. Well, there was still time to find out, because he wasn't done yet.

"After Pompeii, you started to rein me in. Only one kill at a time. Finally, I did some maturing. I accepted the limitations you imposed." He looked away from Bourne. "But things haven't been great with me and my profession for a long time. I coped by not feeling. Guess what? I'm feeling again. And I can't stop it."

"Anything else?" Bourne's voice gave nothing away.

"Yeah. Why did you send me here to work?" He glanced at Sparkle. "And make Sparkle my boss? You had to know that would piss me off."

Bourne turned from Edge without answering him. "How about you, Ganymede? Want to pile on?"

"You know how I feel. You've been putting the brakes on me for a long time." Ganymede looked at Sparkle. "How about you, honeyfluff?"

"Honeyfluff?" Bourne sounded disbelieving. "A chaos bringer doesn't call *anyone* 'honeyfluff.' It's just . . . wrong."

Sparkle shrugged. "I'm happy. I'm doing what I was meant to do. And you haven't put any limits on me. Yet."

"That's because you haven't stepped over any lines. Yet. Tonight might've done it, though." Bourne stood. "Look, I need some air. Let's walk on the beach for a while."

It was too soon to relax, but so far Bourne didn't seem really ticked. Although Edge didn't trust him. He could be waiting till they got outside to cull his herd.

Bourne led them onto the beach. There was no moon tonight, and a chill wind had whipped up. The sound of the surf soothed Edge. For a moment, he allowed himself to think of Passion. What was she doing? And when would Bourne let them go so he could find her?

"Hey, Boss, we have a tail. They were hanging in the lobby when we were there. Two big dudes. Want me to find out what they're after?" Ganymede showed some enthusiasm for the first time.

"They're working for me."

Edge turned to stare at the men trailing them. "Vampires?"

"Specialists. Those are Listeners. Very rare, and very expensive to hire."

"What do they do?" Sparkle glanced back. "Holy stereotypes. Please tell me they're not both wearing black dusters. After this is over, I absolutely must conduct a clothing intervention with them."

Bourne looked pained as he rubbed the crease between his eyes. Edge didn't blame him. Sparkle had that effect on people.

"The Listeners can monitor multiple minds at once. So back in the lobby, they were tuning in to everyone in the room. If anyone had been paying attention to our meeting, they would've alerted me." Bourne stopped walking. "Okay, I've conquered the desire to disintegrate all of you and scatter your molecules throughout the universe. So we can continue talking."

Edge wanted to make a sarcastic comment, but he didn't. As much as he resented Bourne, he had to remember that they had a common enemy. Now wasn't the time for personal grudges.

"Here's what I got from your little moments of truth. You all hate me except for Sparkle, but she's really disappointed with my security detail's clothing choices. Did I miss anything?" Bourne's expression gave nothing away. No anger, no hurt feelings. He could have been discussing getting together to watch a game. Cold son of a bitch.

"For the sake of fairness, I'll share a few of my feelings. First, I'm not apologizing for anything. I've always done what I thought was best. Second, I'm paranoid, and I see enemies everywhere. Sometimes I've been wrong, but a few times being distrustful has saved my ass and yours. So understand where I'm coming from when I say I don't trust anyone." He speared each of them with a hard stare. When he reached Sparkle, his lips lifted in a faint smile. "All right, I don't suspect you, Sparkle."

Bourne's gaze rested on Ganymede. "You're probably the closest to me in power. I've felt your resentment when I limited your . . . activities. Yes, I'll admit I'm glad you're here with Sparkle. I figured she'd distract you from thoughts of the throne."

Ganymede made a rude noise. "Who'd want the job? I'm into creating chaos, not ruling."

Bourne shifted his attention to Edge. "I sent you to work

under Sparkle to teach you some humility. Too much arrogance can be dangerous. To me." His grin was rueful. "Didn't work. It just pissed you off."

Edge needed to hear it put into words. "So you thought Ganymede or I might be behind what's happening?"

"It crossed my mind." He held up his hand before Edge could say anything. "Take it as a compliment. If you weren't so powerful, I wouldn't have given it a second thought."

"I hate walking on the beach." Sparkle slipped off her stilettos and emptied the sand from them. "And I hate talking around a problem. Here's what I see. Someone's been trying to draw you to the castle by attacking each of us until you couldn't ignore the situation any longer. So what do we do about it now that you're here?"

Bourne laughed, and there was no underlying message in it. "You amaze me, Sparkle. Ganymede can topple mountains, and Edge can visit death on the deserving, but you . . . You could lead."

Edge grinned, and everyone seemed to unwind a little. "She's right. What's the plan?"

"Whoever's in charge of this couldn't overthrow me because they didn't know where I was. Now that I'm here, he or she will try to kill me and take over the top spot. This isn't the first time this has happened. I've survived other attempts, and I intend to survive this." He glanced back at the castle. "I've called in all the cosmic troublemakers I trust. The most powerful ones will stay in the castle. I've gotten rooms for the others in nearby hotels. They should be arriving tomorrow. I don't know what forces the enemy has, but I guarantee they're out there. We'll get some rest and then we hunt."

Edge nodded. He glanced at his watch. Hell, it was too late to bother Passion.

"Edge?" Bourne's voice was close.

"What?" He looked up in time to see Ganymede and Sparkle walking away. Bourne stood next to him.

"Passion and Hope aren't angels. We don't know what

they are, or who they answer to. Be careful, no matter how you feel about Passion."

Edge's first instinct was to protect her. "She's not the enemy."

"Think. The three attacks came right after they arrived."

"Yeah, but Hope stopped both Ganymede and me."

"The point wasn't for you to die; the point was to make the situation so bad that I'd have to show myself. It worked. Whoever's in control of this wants to be the next Big Boss. It doesn't make sense to destroy his soon-to-be most valuable assets."

Edge could only nod. He refused to suspect Passion. And yes, he was being stubborn. So what?

Bourne turned to walk away, but Edge had one more thing to ask.

"Was it worth creating me?"

"I didn't create you."

"You pointed the gun. You pulled the trigger. Same thing."

"I gave you a purpose in life. There's a balance in everything, even death. Most murders are committed by malevolent forces against the innocent. You destroy those malevolent forces. You balance death."

It made sense in a weird sort of way. Edge followed Bourne back to the castle.

Passion was so tired she could sleep standing up. Once back in her room, she looked long and hard at her bed, the one *without* Edge in it. She wasn't *that* tired. Hope hadn't come back yet, and the phone's red message light was on. Passion would bet the two were connected.

The message was short and not so sweet. Hope was spending the rest of the night with Kemp. Sometimes Passion didn't get her roommate. Hope stood firm on some of Ted's rules, but then when temptation beckoned, she flung everything aside to chase it. Go figure.

Passion had almost decided to crash on Hope's bed when she remembered. She had to tell someone about the conversation she'd heard between Bain and Murmur. And what was with Zane and Holgarth? Oh, and she couldn't forget Zane's mysterious visitor.

She looked down at the phone. Passion would dance naked with a demon—okay, so if the demon was Murmur it wouldn't be too awful—before she'd wake Holgarth up. But someone had to know immediately about Bain and Murmur. She never considered calling anyone but Edge. Taking a deep breath, she picked up the receiver.

Edge took a while to answer. Asleep. He wouldn't be thrilled to hear from her.

"What?" He sounded groggy.

"I have to talk to you."

"Passion?" Suddenly, he sounded alert.

"I can't talk on the phone." Sure she could, but she didn't want to. She wouldn't even try to pretend she didn't have an ulterior motive.

"No problem."

He gave her his room number and hung up without asking why she couldn't talk on the phone. She didn't take anything with her because she didn't want this to look too obvious. But she had no intention of coming back here to sleep alone with nothing but her frustrating dreams for company.

Edge opened his door before she could even knock. He'd pulled on his jeans but nothing else. His hair was mussed, and he was the sexiest thing she'd ever seen.

"Come in. Sit down." He closed the door behind her.

She dropped into a chair and waited for him to take the chair across from her.

"What's up?"

His gaze was clear and steady, but Passion wanted to believe she saw something hot and hungry in those amber eyes. Wishful thinking? She hoped not.

"I'm sorry I dragged you out of bed." She wasn't. "But I heard a few things tonight you need to know about."

Passion hoped he didn't ask why she hadn't gotten Bourne out of bed instead of him.

He didn't.

"Let's hear it."

He leaned forward, and her gaze dropped as she admired the way his muscles flowed beneath smooth skin as he moved.

"Passion?"

She could hear the amusement in his voice. Passion glanced away so he wouldn't notice her flush. And she knew it was there because she could feel the heat creeping up her neck and into her face. *Think thoughts of icebergs and blizzards.* Damn Ted for turning her into a blushing virgin. *Hello, you* are *a virgin. Technically.*

Feeling cool enough to continue, Passion looked back at him. "I was in the great hall waiting for Hope when Murmur and Bain walked past. They didn't see me." She quickly told him what she'd heard Murmur say. For whatever reason, she kept Bain's comments to herself.

By the time she'd finished, he was already standing. "I'm going to have a talk with our music demon. Now." His voice was flat—no rage, no emotion.

And that scared her more than if he'd ranted and threatened. "Maybe you should wait until the others are with you."

"What others?" Edge looked insulted. "I'm Death. I don't need any help." He pulled the door open and strode into the hallway.

She ran after him. "This isn't about needing help. It's about thinking things through and coming up with a strategy."

He didn't even look at her. "Nothing to think through. He's threatening us with his demons."

"He didn't exactly say that. It sounded as though someone tried to hire him, but he still hadn't made up his mind." She was having trouble keeping up with his long strides.

"What do you know about war, Passion? Nothing. And

make no mistake, this *is* war. You never give the enemy time to prepare. A preemptive strike saves a bunch of headaches later."

"Preemptive strike? Are you crazy?"

For a moment, his shoulders stiffened as though from a blow.

Edge finally glanced at her. "Relax. I'm not going in with guns blazing."

Passion didn't believe him. The realization made her stomach churn. Where was her trust? How could she think about a future with him when something that important was missing? *Listen to yourself. You have* no *chance of a future with him. You* never *had one.*

"But if you don't trust me, then I guess you should go back to your room. Thanks for passing on the information. I'll take it from here."

Shocked at his icy tone, she stopped and stared as he walked away from her without a backward glance.

Only after he disappeared up the stairs leading to the tower did she move. Trying to push aside her hurt, she raced up the stairs after him. Thank heaven he didn't take the quick way up to Murmur's room and dematerialize. But maybe he was trying to save all his energy for the demon.

Passion had a bad feeling about this. She was gasping for breath by the time she reached the top of the stairs. As she hurried toward Murmur's room, she could hear voices coming from his open door. Passion ran.

She stopped in the doorway. Relief washed over her. They weren't trying to kill each other yet.

Edge stood a few feet into the room. From the looks of the door, he hadn't knocked. He looked relaxed, but tension rolled off him.

Murmur stood beside his bed and was calmly pulling on his pants. "See, this is why Mom always told me to wear pajamas to bed."

"You didn't have a mother." Edge spoke through clenched teeth.

"Right. Well, if I had, she would've said that. But sleeping nude feels so much more sensual, don't you think?" Murmur's gaze went past Edge to Passion. He smiled at her.

Edge didn't turn to look at her. "You won't have to worry about what to wear to bed if you don't answer my question. Are you bringing your demons against us?"

Murmur finished fastening his pants before meeting Edge's gaze. His eyes had changed, become the eyes of a cat with no white and a pupil that was nothing but a vertical slit of black. The rest of the eye was glowing red.

Passion sucked in her breath. If she'd forgotten at times to fear Murmur, to forget what he was, those eyes were a stark reminder.

"I don't answer to you or yours." His smile was a mere twist of his lips. "When I decide, you'll be the first to know." He reached behind him.

Was he reaching for a weapon? "No!" Without stopping to think, she flung herself past Edge to put herself between them. "Please, Murmur, don't do anything stupid. We can talk—" Everything stilled.

"Passion. Get out of the way." Edge's curt order shattered the moment.

Instinctively, she stumbled to the side, just as power blasted past her. The force of it knocked her to her knees. She looked up in time to see Murmur's shocked expression along with the gaping hole in his chest. Blood poured from the wound, running down his body to pool at his feet.

The demon's gaze locked with Edge's. "I'm disappointed in you. I'd heard you killed with style. This is just sloppy." His voice died away as he collapsed onto the floor and lay still.

Passion shifted her stare to Edge. She didn't try to hide her horror. "You killed him." She struggled to her feet.

"I thought he had a weapon. You were in danger." His voice was too quiet, too calm, too this-is-just-another-dead-body.

She choked back a sob as she forced herself to look at

Murmur and what had fallen from his hand when he fell. "God, no. He was reaching for his freaking iPod. He must've been going to put it in his pocket. You know he always had music with him."

Edge glanced away. "It was a mistake. But what's done is done."

"No, it isn't." She felt the familiar surge of power blaze through her as it rushed down her arms, along her fingers, and collected in her fingertips. Passion scrambled to her feet, obeying the need to reach for Murmur, to fill him with life. Evidently, the power didn't play favorites, or else it didn't realize he was a demon.

"Don't do this, Passion." Edge's voice had softened. "Whose side do you think he'd fight for after this? How would you feel if he killed someone you knew?"

"That's not fair. You don't get to make me change my mind by laying a guilt trip on me." She'd made her decision. "If you want to stop me, you'll have to use force."

Passion dared to look at Edge, at his narrowed eyes, at his lips pressed tightly together, at his implacable expression, and said what needed saying. "I understand something now. There has to be a balance. I balance you, Edge. You're death, and I'm life." *And never the twain shall meet.* She didn't have time to think through the ramifications of what she'd just said, but she'd bet they wouldn't make her happy.

In two staggering steps she fell to her knees again beside Murmur. She tried to ignore the wet, sticky realness of his blood. Passion forced back nausea as she laid her hands over his torn chest. Her fingers glowed, heat searing each tip.

Then she closed her eyes and released her power, willed life back into him, and tried not to think about Edge standing behind her.

Silence filled the room. She was almost ready to believe it was too late for Murmur when she felt him move. Passion opened her eyes and gasped.

The wound had closed. But even though the terrible

tear in his flesh was gone, he still shouldn't be looking up at her. Not with so much of his blood smeared on the floor beneath where she knelt. Without thinking, she put her hand across her mouth to stop from crying out. When she dropped it, she knew she'd left his blood on her face. It didn't matter.

"What did you do?" Murmur looked up at her wonderingly.

"She brought your ass back to life. Against my express wishes, I might add."

Edge didn't sound happy or sad. He sounded . . . empty. Passion kept her attention on Murmur.

"How do you feel?" She shuddered as she looked at all his beautiful long hair fanned out around his head and soaked in blood.

Murmur didn't answer her question. "My ass thanks you for a second chance at life. You're a special lady, and I owe you a special favor for what you did."

Passion didn't have to think about what she wanted. "Don't fight against the Big Boss. Walk away from the battle."

Murmur pushed himself to a sitting position. He looked at Edge. "You didn't kill *me*, you killed my body."

"I knew that." Edge's voice was still strangely flat. "But you would've had to return to the underworld. It would've taken you out of the fight."

"You knew he wasn't dead?" Passion felt outrage.

Edge shrugged. "His body was dead. Same thing for our purposes."

"For *your* purpose, not mine." She looked back at Murmur. "I'm sorry. I thought you were reaching for a weapon, and Edge believed I was in danger. My mistake, because all you wanted was your music."

Murmur slowly struggled to his feet. "First, I'm glad you saved my body. I like it, and I'd hate to have to search for another one." He grabbed her hand and pulled her to her feet.

Passion swallowed hard. "Where did this one come from?" Did she really want to know?

Murmur shrugged. "One of the fey was kind enough to vacate it, and I moved in. I don't often get a chance for something this perfect."

Edge moved closer. "Just idle curiosity, but why did you grab your iPod? Doesn't seem like the logical thing to reach for in that situation." His gaze rested on her for a moment— cold, expressionless. "Even though Passion didn't find it surprising. It wouldn't be *my* weapon of choice."

Murmur's smile was hard, taunting. "Yes, I got an up-close view of your weapon. I won't forget." His smile softened as he shifted his attention to Passion. "Music increases my power. That's why I always have it with me."

"Who wanted to hire you and your demons?" Passion refused to think about Edge right now.

"I don't know." Murmur answered Passion but kept a wary eye on Edge. "Someone of power summoned me here. He made no attempt to bind me—not that he could have—but he also didn't show his face. He proposed a deal. I would help him overthrow the Big Boss, and he'd pay me with a favor owed. Very tempting. I don't need money, but a favor owed by a powerful being is worth a great deal."

"And he didn't give you a name, or *something*?" Edge sounded disbelieving.

"I told him I would stay here to look the situation over. He said if I decided to help him, we'd talk. Well, I've been looking the situation over. You didn't endear yourself to me tonight, Death."

"You know, somehow that doesn't bother me." Edge moved a little closer, but the tension was gone from his body. "What about Bain? What does he have to do with this?" His gaze shifted to Passion. "I noticed that she didn't give much information about his side of the conversation."

Passion stiffened. *She?* He wouldn't even say her name now?

Murmur's expression hardened. "Maybe you should ask him about it."

Passion would never know what Edge would've said because someone spoke from the doorway.

"I'd really like to know what the hell is going on here." Bourne stepped into the room.

14

You're death, and I'm life. Passion had laid the truth out. Not that he hadn't known it before, but somehow having her say the words made it real.

Even with Bourne standing behind him, Edge couldn't ramp up the old adrenaline rush. He felt dead inside. Fitting.

This was his fault. He'd overreacted to Murmur. Not his usual style. He went for cold, calm, and rational. The demon had said it. He'd been sloppy. But something had happened when Passion flung herself between them and he'd thought Murmur was reaching for a weapon. Fear for her had wiped away all reason. He'd simply reacted. Stupid. He *knew* Murmur didn't need a physical weapon to fight him.

She'd reduced him to a brainless caveman mentality. And he'd probably horrified her for all time. *Way to win her heart, dumbass.* He turned to face Bourne.

"Well, I'm waiting. Let the story begin." Bourne leaned against the wall with his arms crossed over his chest.

The bastard was fully dressed. Figured. "I killed the demon. Passion brought him back to life." Edge glanced at Murmur. "Want to tell your side?"

Murmur raised one brow. "An assassin of few words." He shifted his gaze to Bourne. "Your loose cannon here blew in my door and then accused me of selling my services to your enemy. When I reached back to pick up my iPod, Passion thought I was going for a weapon. She stepped between us. Then your cosmic troublemaker in charge of idiocy went all Neanderthal and killed me." He paused for effect. "But luckily, there was an angel of mercy—God, I love clichés—on hand to save me. I have 'You Raise Me Up' on my iPod if you'd like to hear it. Music always adds atmosphere to the drama, don't you think?"

Passion looked shocked. "You can say God?"

The demon exhaled wearily. "Yes. God, God, God, God."

"*Are* you selling your services to the enemy?" Bourne pushed away from the wall and dropped his arms to his side.

Murmur shrugged. "He made the proposal, and I was considering it. But you can relax. I promised Passion I wouldn't fight against you or yours. My thank-you to her for saving me." He held up his hand to stop Bourne from interrupting. "And no, I don't know your enemy's identity. He didn't show himself when he spoke to me. But I felt enough of his power to know he could kick most butts. I think I'll stick around to watch the show."

Bourne turned to Edge. "How did you find out about this, and why did you come to his room without me?" He didn't look happy.

Edge searched his mind for a way to protect Passion, but she didn't give him time to answer.

"I heard Murmur and Bain talking. Maybe I should've come to you with what I'd heard, but I don't know you." Her expression said she didn't trust him much either.

"Bain is involved in this?" Real anger moved in Bourne's eyes. "Guess we'll have to get his take on things."

Bourne said no words, didn't even blink, but suddenly Bain appeared in midair and crashed to the floor with a startled grunt. He at least wore pajama bottoms. Good thing. Edge didn't think he could take the sight of another naked demon.

"What the hell . . . ?" Bain rose to his feet in one fluid motion. His eyes glowed red and his fingertips had sprouted claws. He bared his teeth. Edge didn't remember them being that sharp. "I'm going to kill someone."

"Calm down." Bourne didn't sound worried. "I just need to ask you a few questions."

Edge tried to send Bain a warning glance. Bourne sounded calm, but that meant nothing. The demon might not have long to live if the Big Boss didn't like his answers.

Bain met Edge's gaze and gave a brief nod before concentrating on Bourne. "What happened to the old-fashioned way of communicating? It's called a phone."

Bourne's cold smile should've iced over the walls. "This kind of summoning has more impact and usually gets me the answers I want." He shrugged. "Yes, I like to intimidate. It's a weakness."

Bain had taken a moment to glance around the room. His gaze lingered on the blood-soaked floor and the equally bloody Murmur. He looked worried by the time he returned his attention to Bourne. "So ask."

"We know why Murmur is here. How do you figure into it?" Bourne signaled his complete unconcern with his safety by sitting on the nearest chair. "Oh, and before you try to lie your way out of this, know that Passion heard the two of you talking."

Passion winced, and Edge wanted to hammer Bourne into the floor. He could've done this without bringing her name into it. How much did Edge really know about Bain? What if the demon was into revenge? Almost every time the Big Boss opened his mouth he reinforced Edge's belief that he was a cold, unfeeling bastard. Of course, before Passion those same words would have described him.

Bain stared at Passion. Edge could imagine the demon's thoughts. How much had she heard? How little could he get away with telling Bourne?

She must've understood his look, because she spoke up. "All I heard Bain say was that he'd covered for Murmur so far, but he wouldn't put his job in danger because of him."

"You know, I really would've liked *Bain* to answer that question." Bourne's expression said he knew exactly why she'd answered. Now Bain knew he could keep quiet about everything else he'd said.

Bourne drew in a deep breath, and Edge figured he was trying to hold on to his temper. "So you knew Murmur might be a danger to the castle, and still you kept quiet. Why?" Left unasked was why Bourne shouldn't fry Bain's ass.

Edge gave Bain credit. No matter what he felt inside, he kept everything cool on the surface.

"I've known Murmur a long time, a lot longer than I've known everyone here. And he understood we'd be fighting on different sides if he went with the enemy. And he definitely knew I'd tell you if he made the wrong decision."

Bourne narrowed his eyes. "I suspect that's not all of it." The glance he threw at Passion wasn't friendly. "But I guess that will do for now." His gaze turned thoughtful. "At least we now know whoever's doing this is trying to bring in outside forces." He looked at Murmur. "Did you hear his voice? Was it definitely a male voice?"

Murmur nodded.

"Okay, so we're probably looking for a man, although with his power, he could appear as whatever he chose."

"What will you do with Murmur and me?" Bain subtly changed. Power flowed around him, and he bent his knees in the beginning of a crouch.

Edge moved closer to Passion, ready to get her out of here if violence exploded. Not that he thought either Murmur or Bain could take the Big Boss. But then, who knew? He'd never seen Bourne in a battle. But he was a legendary figure. The few who had witnessed him in action spoke of his power in whispers.

"What do *you* think I should do?" Bourne aimed his question at Murmur.

Murmur shrugged. "I think Frank Dane had it right. 'Love your enemies just in case your friends turn out to be a bunch of bastards.'" His gaze slid to Edge before returning to Bourne. "Hey, it could happen. But it's your call. I might mention, though, that if you manage to destroy Bain and me, legions of demons will descend on this castle. I don't think you can afford a battle on two fronts. Maybe I'm wrong and your power is limitless. In which case, we're shit out of luck."

"Are you my enemy?" Bourne still wore no expression.

"I could be." Then Murmur smiled. "But right now Mercury is in retrograde, so I don't think I'll begin any new enemy-making ventures for a while."

Edge might not trust demons as a whole, although he sort of liked Bain, but he had to admit that Murmur had balls. Not many would give attitude to the Big Boss.

Bourne seemed to consider his options. Then he shook his head. "Against my better judgment, I'm walking out of this room without doing anything." He turned to leave but then paused. "That doesn't mean I won't be watching." It looked as though he included all of them in that. He glanced at Edge. "Would you give me a few minutes of your time if you're through killing demons?"

Edge hated his sarcasm, but he nodded. He stared at Passion. She wouldn't meet his gaze.

"I think I'll head back to my room." She didn't look at anyone as she left.

Murmur walked over and sat in a chair. "Conflict is stimulating. I'm not even tired anymore."

From the expression on Bain's face, Edge figured Murmur was about to get a little more stimulation from his old buddy.

Edge followed Bourne out of the room. Bain slammed the door behind them.

Bourne walked in silence for a few moments before speaking. "What if that had been a trap? What if Passion had lured you to the demon's room and he'd attacked you the moment you stepped through the door? What if Passion had joined him in the attack?"

Rage flared. "Passion is *not* the enemy."

"How do you know? Tell me what she is, where she came from. Tell me anything that you know about her other than what your cock is telling you."

Edge wanted to slam his fist into Bourne so bad that— He took a deep breath. If he lost his temper, Bourne would have something else to bitch about. Why couldn't he stay calm when Passion was the object of the conversation?

"I don't have any proof. I just *know*." Yeah, that would convince the Big Boss.

Bourne shook his head. "I can't fight emotion. Just do one thing for me, keep your eyes and ears open when you're around Passion and Hope. Oh, and don't try to face down a powerful demon alone when help is near. That's just stupid."

Edge opened his mouth to argue that he hadn't gone to Murmur's room looking for a fight. He closed it. The truth? He'd been itching to kick some ass. Besides, from the expression on Bourne's face, arguing would just ring the bell on Bourne's personal piss-o-meter. He'd pushed his leader as far as he was going to go tonight.

"One thing I need to know." Edge figured this question wouldn't jiggle any of Bourne's hot buttons. "How did you know what was going on in Murmur's room?"

"The universe gives off vibrations. You and Murmur disturbed those vibrations."

What did that mean? "Yeah, but how did you know we were the ones doing the disturbing?"

"You and Murmur are not exactly common folk. You give off a hell of a powerful vibration. I sensed the disturbance and followed it to Murmur's room." He smiled ruefully. "Okay, I know you don't get it. You'll have to trust me on this."

The word "trust" triggered other thoughts—of Passion's lack of trust in him, of Bourne's lack of trust in her, of Edge's lack of trust in the universe.

A few minutes later, Edge was back in his apartment. He raked his fingers through his hair. She wouldn't sleep in his bed tonight, maybe never. If she were smart, she'd wash her hands of all of them. The only good thing about that was he wouldn't have to act the part of a spy. No, he was wrong. There was nothing *good* about what had gone down with them tonight.

Passion dropped into the nearest chair while being careful not to make eye contact with her bed. What a disaster. She didn't know which one of those guys had ticked her off the most. Okay, it was Edge. Because she cared for him more. Yes, yes, she was to blame too. She shouldn't have acted on impulse and jumped between them. She'd love to believe Edge reacted the way he did because of how much he cared for her, but that was probably wishful thinking on her part. More likely, he would've blasted away at Murmur with or without her blocking the way.

Time to stomp on any and all dreams that included Edge. His boss didn't trust her, and Edge was, in the end, accountable to Bourne.

She pushed herself out of the chair and was just reaching for her nightgown and robe when someone knocked. Passion closed her eyes. No, no, no. She didn't want to talk to anyone else tonight. It was almost dawn, and she was drained.

But the knocker didn't give up, so finally she went to the door. She was wiser now than a week ago, so she asked the all-important question. "Who is it?"

"Cinn. Could I talk to you for a minute?"

Surprise. Passion opened the door.

Dacian's wife stood holding a big bushy plant in her

arms. With her warm brown hair, big hazel eyes, and friendly smile, Cinn didn't look like Passion's personal image of what a vampire's mate should look like. But then, Dacian with his puny circle of sins wasn't exactly what she'd expect from a big bad vampire.

Passion waved her in. "I'm surprised to see you. It's almost dawn." She automatically checked her out for sins. Nothing but a little pale blue. Lust. Not unexpected if you were anticipating curling up next to someone as yummy as Dacian.

Cinn walked over to the arrow-slit-slash-window and set the plant on the floor. "After what happened tonight, I wanted to make sure I got Sweetie Pie to you right away."

"You wanted to bring me a plant?" Nice lady, but she probably needed to know that Passion was death to plants. Everyone else's cubicle had a leafy friend to keep them company. Not Passion's. Every plant she touched went to the great potting shed in the sky.

Cinn sat on one of the chairs and motioned for Passion to take the other one. "You probably should know a little about me so you can understand Sweetie Pie."

Sweetie Pie needed understanding? Looked like your typical leafy plant to Passion. Nothing exotic about it.

"I'm connected to Airmid, the goddess of all healing plants. So I've inherited a certain . . . talent with them. You saw a few in the greenhouse."

Passion couldn't tell her that she saw *nothing* but Edge in that greenhouse.

For the first time, Cinn looked a little uncertain. "I guess there's no easy way to say this, but my plants are sentient."

Passion stared at her and then slid a quick glance at Sweetie Pie. "Umm, explain."

Cinn grinned. "If you have a few minutes someday, I'll introduce you to all of them. But Sweetie Pie's claim to fame is that she feeds on sexual energy."

Well, at least Cinn had come up with a statement guaranteed to take Passion's mind off of her troubles for a few minutes. Passion couldn't think of one thing to say about Sweetie Pie, so she said nothing.

Cinn's uncertainty returned. "I know this is tough to believe."

"Not at all. If I can believe in cosmic troublemakers, vampires, and demons, then I can believe in Sweetie Pie." Not completely. A plant that fed on sexual energy was just weird.

Cinn's smile said she recognized and understood Passion's doubt. "So here's why I've brought my plant to you. As you and Edge were leaving the greenhouse, I noticed Sweetie Pie."

Passion grinned. She'd bet Cinn didn't notice the plant for long.

"I couldn't believe it. She'd grown at least six inches during the time you were there."

"And that means?" Passion thought she knew.

"Sweetie Pie had been depressed for weeks. We'd tried putting her in a few of the guests' rooms, but nothing helped."

"That means the guests weren't . . ."

"Not even a little." Cinn smoothed her finger over one of the plant's bright green leaves. "Sweetie Pie was devastated."

Uh-oh. Passion saw where this was leading.

"And now, look at her. She's all perky and bright. She loved you and Edge. I hate to ask a favor of you, but would you keep her for the rest of the time you're here?"

"Sure." One thing she had to know. "She can't see, can she?"

Cinn laughed. "No, nothing like that. She just absorbs all those delicious sexual vibrations."

Passion sighed. "Afraid there won't be much of that around here."

"Anything you want to share?"

Passion didn't, but before she could send the message to her mouth, it was off and running. She told Cinn everything that had happened.

"Let me get this straight. Edge was mad because he thought you didn't trust him not to go ballistic on Murmur. Which he did. Then you pointed out what total opposites you were. Not a smart move. And Bourne doesn't trust you. Did I miss anything?"

"I think that's enough."

"Hmm."

Passion thought that said it all. She couldn't think of anything that would mend the tear in the tenuous strands she and Edge had begun to weave between them.

"Tough case. Edge always wears this iron shell around himself, so it's hard to tell what's going on inside sometimes."

"You think?" But Passion *had* seen cracks in that shell.

"Maybe it's just me, but I've gotten the feeling he doesn't love his job that much. Don't get me wrong, he does it, but there's no real enthusiasm there." Cinn smiled. "Thank God."

"Edge thinks if he stops killing, he'll cease to exist."

"Who's going to make him go away? Bourne?"

Passion nodded. "Most likely."

Cinn looked thoughtful. "I'll have to see what I can do to change the Big Boss's mind."

"You'd help Edge?" A spark of hope turned the blackness to at least a dull gray. No matter what happened between them, she wanted Edge to have a choice in his life.

"Why not? He's family. The Castle of Dark Dreams takes care of its own." She seemed to already be thinking. "I'll get back to you. Meanwhile, I'll leave Sweetie Pie here." She stood.

Once Cinn had left, Passion climbed into bed. *Her* bed. If Edge and she weren't meant to be, then she'd better get used to sleeping here. She didn't think Hope would appreciate sharing her bed once she got back.

Just before turning off her light, she looked at Sweetie Pie. "Sorry, girl, but you'll have to go to bed without supper tonight. Get used to it."

She dreamed—of a tawny-haired man with magic

hands who made love to her in every single one of the park's attractions. She lived the fantasy right up until the moment Bourne showed up dressed as the Wicked Witch of the West. On that bit of silliness, she woke . . .

To the sound of Archangel Ted's voice in her head. She shivered in the suddenly icy room.

"Something happened last night. I felt it. Explain." He didn't even pretend to care if she'd saved any souls.

Not that she'd saved even one since she'd been here. She couldn't be an angel, because an angel would've been prostrate with guilt. But then, she was beginning to doubt Ted's identity too. "Umm, I guess Sparkle got a little carried away and—"

"I know about that. I mean, what happened close to dawn?" He sounded impatient.

"Wait. How do you know about Sparkle?"

"Hope told me."

"Hope wasn't here when it happened."

"But a friend of the man she's sleeping with was."

The most shocking part of his response? He didn't seem horrified with what Hope was doing. Passion glanced at Hope's bed. Still neatly made, but some of Hope's clothes were flung across it. So she'd come back to the room and then left again while Passion slept. No one would accuse Passion of being a light sleeper.

What lie to tell him that wouldn't sound like a lie and wouldn't have him running for the avenging angels? She opted for a version of the truth. "I heard the demon Murmur talking about leading his demons into battle. I mentioned it to Edge, and he went to confront Murmur. Nothing big happened."

Ted was silent. Did he know she was only telling part of the truth?

"I'm glad you're keeping your ears open. But don't carry anything you hear to Edge or any of them from now on. Remember, they're irredeemable." And then he was gone.

What was that about? He couldn't wait to get away from

her. She didn't question her good luck, though, as she got ready to leave the room. She'd find Holgarth and tell him about Zane, and then get something to eat in the restaurant.

Passion glanced at the clock. Wow, two o'clock. Sunlight was streaming through the narrow window, so the world hadn't ended while she slept.

Sweetie Pie still sat on the floor beneath the window. She looked a little droopy. One leaf had fallen off. That one leaf made Passion feel guilty. How stupid was that? "Forget it, Sweetie Pie. I am not bringing home random strangers just so you won't lose leaves. Suck it up." *Just like I'm doing.*

Passion found Holgarth in the great hall talking to Edge. Her first thought was that she had to get control of her heart. It did this funny hop and pause before racing like mad whenever she saw Edge. Her second thought was that maybe she should eat first and then come back to speak with Holgarth. When he was alone.

You are a giant squishy wuss. Just because things hadn't ended well last night—okay, so they'd been a big pile of poop—didn't mean she couldn't walk right up and talk to Holgarth.

Flying high on false courage, she sailed across the room and planted herself in front of them. They stopped talking to stare at her. Her courage melted and trickled down her back, leaving a shivery trail of sensual need behind. She clenched her hands into fists. She would *not* allow Edge to affect her this way.

Holgarth coughed. Even his cough was supercilious.

"Feel free to interrupt. I was just explaining to Edge the importance of making sure his apocalypse lasts no longer than an hour. The fantasy schedule will be destroyed if it lasts longer."

Passion wasn't sure how to respond. Was he kidding? He had to be. But then, maybe not. "Holgarth, I need to talk to you." She refused to look at Edge.

"Talk away." The wizard glanced at Edge. "You stay here. I'm not finished with you."

Edge wore a pained expression, but he didn't leave.

"I have to talk to you *alone*." She really didn't, but if it got rid of Edge, she'd go for it.

"Nonsense. What could you possibly have to say—after all, you're not exactly a font of fascinating information—that would warrant Edge's exclusion?" He'd drawn his lips into a thin line, indicating that this was payback for interrupting his conversation.

She huffed her annoyance. "Fine. I spoke with Zane last night. He asked what I knew about you."

"He knows I'm a wizard. What else is there to know? If this is all you had to tell me, then I fear you've wasted my valuable time."

Now Passion was getting ticked. "Not quite. He's got a lot of anger bottled up inside. If that anger is aimed at you, then maybe you need to take notice." What she was about to say next was petty and small, but it would make her feel so good. "After all, from what I've heard, your talent doesn't match up very well against his."

His expression turned thunderous.

She smiled as she started to turn away. "Oh, and he said he was waiting for . . ."

Zane was striding toward them. A woman walked beside him. Edge's soft "wow" said it for both of them.

She was tall, almost six feet. Slim, elegant, and gorgeous didn't begin to describe her. Long black hair, straight and shining, flowed down her back. Her large, dark eyes were outlined in black that emphasized the power glowing in them. She wore a long gold gown that clung to her curves and shimmered as she almost glided beside Zane.

Not human. Definitely and positively.

She stopped when she reached them. She said nothing, only glared at Holgarth.

Holgarth was the first to speak, and Passion almost didn't recognize his voice.

"Isis."

15

"You have aged, wizard." Her voice was cold, angry, and as beautiful as the rest of her. With a casual wave of her hand, the hall emptied except for their small group.

"The centuries weigh on me, goddess. You, on the other hand, look exactly as you did the last time I saw you."

Holgarth might sound calm, but his eyes told a different story. Edge watched emotion flood them—disbelief, sorrow, pain, and . . . fear.

"Wait. Goddess? *Goddess?*" Edge tensed as he drew his power to him. "Friend or enemy, wizard?"

"I'd say she's not happy with me. I suppose I'd have to discover the exact degree of not happy in order to answer your question."

"You're the goddess Isis?" Passion looked puzzled. "Someone fill me in. Ted never said much about the ancient deities."

"She's the Egyptian goddess of magic, among other things." Zane sounded proud of her.

Edge frowned. "What's your connection to the goddess, Zane?" This had bad written all over it. Had Isis decided to take a shot at being the next Big Boss? Didn't seem likely, but he'd better err on the side of caution. He put out a mental call to Bourne and Sparkle. Ganymede had blocked him. Probably tied up with *Top Chef* and a bowl of popcorn.

Zane was looking at Holgarth when he answered. "She's my mother."

Holgarth shook his head. "No, you can't be. You're not Horus, and Isis had only one child."

Isis's laughter was ice shattering. "How little you know of me, wizard. Zane is mine."

She pointed at Holgarth, and light radiated from her. Edge had to cover his eyes to protect them from the glare.

"And *yours.*"

Edge dropped his hand from his eyes. Holy hell. He didn't know what shocked him more: that Holgarth had actually fathered a child, or that Holgarth had fathered a child with a woman who looked liked Isis.

Holgarth swayed, his eyes wide and disbelieving. "No. It can't be. I would have known."

This was a Holgarth Edge had never seen, stripped of his self-importance, his sarcasm.

"How could you know? You surrounded yourself with magic to keep me from finding you. If you didn't want *me*, then why would I believe you wanted our son?"

"I didn't know. I didn't realize . . ." Holgarth's gaze went to Zane. "I never suspected. You don't look like . . ." He seemed unable to finish a thought.

Zane's smile was filled with malice as his face subtly changed. His blue eyes became gray, the exact shade of Holgarth's. His facial structure and mouth shifted until his resemblance to his mother was obvious. "You never saw past my glamour."

"I thought he was human." Passion sounded offended that she hadn't realized what Zane was.

Zane's expression softened as he looked at Passion. "We all hide behind something."

Edge felt as bemused as Passion looked. He stared at

Isis, trying to make sense of what she was saying. "So you and Holgarth . . . ?" It seemed *he* couldn't finish a sentence either.

Some of the anger faded from her eyes as she smiled at Edge. "I always had a weakness for short men with big egos and attitudes. Genghis Khan was merely five foot one, but he was a giant in so many other ways and a magnificent lover." She looked back at Holgarth, and the cold returned to her eyes. "I met the wizard when he was Napoleon's advisor. He was not then what he is now: shriveled and bitter."

Holgarth finally seemed to find his voice. "If I'd known . . ." He never took his gaze from Zane. "The pride you so admired, Isis, caused me to run, to hide myself. I knew what I was, what you were, and that there could be no lasting relationship between us. Osiris was your only love." He tried to shrug but didn't quite carry it off. "I wanted more than you could give."

"You presumed much, wizard. How could you possibly know what I was willing to give? And because of your cowardice, your son grew to manhood never knowing his father."

Edge felt Bourne's presence behind him a moment before his leader spoke.

"You sided with Dacian's maker and the rogue cosmic troublemaker Rabid in the last battle here, Zane. Now you've shown up again. Is this just about your father or something more?"

Exactly what Edge would expect Bourne to ask. He only cared about rooting out his enemy, and all the emotional crap be damned. Before Passion, Edge would've agreed with Bourne's approach. But now? He felt bad for Holgarth.

Zane turned to Bourne. "Once I found my father, I wanted to hurt him." He shrugged. "Fighting against him was a way to do that. But in the end, I couldn't kill. I bailed." He looked uneasy. "I don't know why I came back. I had no intention of revealing my identity. But then Mom found out and insisted on confronting him. So here we are."

Isis's smile was coldly pleased. "You have a former guest to thank for my visit. I sat next to Asima, the messenger of the goddess Bast, at a recent theater performance. She told all."

"I always knew Asima was a bitch." That from Sparkle, who had quietly joined the group.

Bourne didn't seem interested in Asima. He was focused on Zane. "And this time, Zane? Will you fight against him *this* time?" His voice was at its softest, its most dangerous.

Isis evidently recognized the threat. "Zane is done with this place. There is nothing or no one he cares about here."

"Zane?" Holgarth looked at his son from stricken eyes.

Edge could hear all of Holgarth's agony in that one word.

Zane didn't meet his father's gaze. "I've paid my money, so I'll stay. I kind of want to see how everything shakes out with your Big Boss." He turned and, without a backward glance, walked away.

Isis studied Holgarth. "Perhaps all is not lost between you and our son." For the first time, something other than anger touched her eyes. "But you might have to disrupt your precious schedule to make the effort."

Holgarth didn't question how she knew about his obsession with schedules. Edge figured Zane or Asima had filled in the details.

Isis's expression softened. "And you were probably right, wizard. Osiris was my only love after all." And then she was gone.

Shock held everyone still.

Tears slid down Holgarth's face, but he made no attempt to wipe them away. "I . . . I believe someone else will have to run the fantasies tonight." He looked like a tired old man.

Sparkle stepped forward. She put her arm across Holgarth's thin shoulders. "Come with me. We'll go to your apartment, and I'll make you a cup of your favorite tea."

She shook her head. "Forget the freaking tea. I'll have Mede bring down the strong stuff. We'll wallow, and cry, and then we'll make plans to win back your son." She matched his slow steps as they left the hall.

In that moment, Edge realized what Ganymede must have always known. All the surface stuff—the shoes, the nails, the sex—didn't mean squat, because Sparkle Stardust was at heart a kind lady no matter what her job demanded.

"All that pain because Holgarth ran from the woman he loved."

Edge could hear the tears in Passion's voice.

Message received. "Have you eaten?"

She shook her head.

"Let's go to my apartment, and I'll order room service." Edge waited tensely to see if she'd go for eating alone with him.

Bourne never gave her a chance to answer. "Before you eat I have to talk to you." He fell into step beside them. "*Both* of you. We'll go to my room."

Edge didn't bother to argue. He glanced at Passion, and she nodded. They followed Bourne up to the top tower suite. No one spoke until Bourne closed the door behind them.

"Wow. I'm impressed." The suite had to take up the entire floor. Passion scanned the huge room—period pieces in rich, dark wood, Oriental rugs on hardwood floors, a dining area set with gleaming crystal, an honest-to-goodness window instead of an arrow slit that looked out over the Gulf, and a short flight of stairs that led up to the bedroom and bath. "It must be nice being you."

Bourne shrugged. "Name recognition has its perks." He motioned them to sit down.

Passion sat on the couch and Edge joined her. She knew she should put some space between them because . . . Passion tried to dredge up her former anger, all the reasons they shouldn't be together. Only she couldn't *think* when he was this close. All she could do was allow the rising tide of her senses to roll over her and hope she didn't drown before he moved away.

"Here's what's happening. I shut down Ganymede's TV and put him out on the street to check up on our suspects. I'm pretty sure we can cross Murmur and Zane off our list. Kemp is still a maybe." He glanced at Passion. "Ganymede convinced a few angels to talk to him. None of them had ever heard of an Archangel Ted."

Passion should have felt shock. She didn't. She'd pretty much admitted to herself that she'd never been an angel. But knowledge didn't make the giant empty space inside her go away. "Who am I then? *What* am I? And who is Ted?"

Bourne didn't answer immediately. And when he did, it wasn't comforting. "I don't know."

"Okay, so Ted is a phony. The bastard lied to Passion. She isn't responsible for his scam."

She resisted the urge to lean into Edge. He'd defended her. No matter how lousy she felt about everything else, he'd *defended* her.

Bourne nodded. "I think you're right. Then if that's true, we have to ask why he lied to her? How many fake angels does he control, and does he have an ultimate plan for them other than 'doing good'?"

"Why didn't I know? Why didn't I question my existence? I just sat in my cubicle and did what Ted asked." Shame filled her. How could she have been so dumb? "None of us ever asked Ted questions."

"He must've been in your head." Edge's voice was quietly dangerous. "Exactly what kinds of help did he tell you to offer?"

"I usually went to people who were wrestling with tough decisions or didn't know who to trust. Ted told me what decisions they should make or the names of people they could confide in."

"And I just bet most of these people were in positions of importance." Bourne sounded grim.

"Yes." An ugly picture was emerging. Ted must've been

manipulating her thoughts from the beginning, but somehow knowing that didn't lessen her feelings of guilt.

"So he's been setting up his power structure on the mortal plane for a long time. Looks like Ted just moved to the top of our list." Bourne leaned forward.

"But Ted's not here. I would've seen him by now if he was."

He dismissed her comment. "Just because you haven't seen him doesn't mean he's not here. How many fake angels does he control?"

"I don't know. I never saw them all at once. Just the ones who worked with me and some of the avenging angels . . ." *Avenging angels.* Suddenly, she knew. That nagging sense of familiarity had been tugging at her since she first met *him*. "Kemp is one of the avenging angels. I only glimpsed him once or twice, so I didn't recognize him when I saw him here. But thinking about the avenging angels must've jogged my memory. And now Hope is with him." Had Hope been part of the conspiracy all along? Passion hated her suspicions. Would she ever trust again?

Bourne nodded. "I'll have to pay Kemp a visit." His expression said Kemp wouldn't enjoy it.

Edge looked confused. "If Ted's our guy, why the hell did he make his army believe they were angels?"

"I think I get it." Bourne's lips lifted in a frightening smile. "He needed an army committed to destroying me, an army truly convinced I was the enemy. They could never question their moral obligation to fight against evil because they were *good*. And who better than angels to defeat the leader of the cosmic troublemakers." His smile faded. "But there's something I'm missing. I'll have to think about it."

He looked at Edge. "Oh, forgot to tell you, I—"

Bourne didn't finish. He narrowed his eyes as he stared at the door. Passion turned to see what had put that expression on his face.

White nothing was flowing under the door and seeping

around its edges. Really. Nothing. Everything it touched disappeared, leaving emptiness behind.

Edge leaped to his feet dragging Passion with him. He glanced at Bourne. "We're outta here."

He held her tightly to him. She knew he was about to do his dematerializing act that would take them away from the danger. But when nothing happened, she stared up at his horrified expression.

Bourne stood, but more slowly than Edge. "He's made sure none of your powers will save you." His smile was a mere baring of his teeth. "He'll find shutting down my powers a little harder."

Even as they watched, the nothingness started sliding in around the window. *Trapped.* Panic pushed at her. She pulled out her cell phone. No bars. Shit.

Without warning, a shimmering space about the size of a door appeared in the middle of the room. Passion could see vague shapes on the other side of its rippling surface.

"I always have a portal for emergencies. This one leads to one of my homes." Bourne watched the advance of the nothingness with seeming unconcern. "You'll go through it. Make yourselves comfortable. When this is over, I'll reopen the portal so you can return."

"Aren't you coming with us?" Why would he choose to stay? The strength of Edge's body pressed firmly against her back kept unthinking panic at bay for the moment.

Bourne looked surprised at her question. "Why would I? This is his first challenge. I have to shove it back into his teeth. Now go, so you're not here to distract me."

Edge clasped her hand tightly as they ran through the portal. When she glanced back, it was gone.

They were standing in a large room. She couldn't see much detail because it was night. But it wasn't completely dark. A wall of glass looked out on a moonlit lake surrounded by forest. The calm beauty of it pushed back her fear.

"If something goes wrong and Bourne can't reopen the portal, you can zap us out of here." Passion didn't want to think about Bourne losing the battle, but she had to face the possibility.

Edge moved closer to the window. He remained silent for a little too long. "That might not be an option."

"You think you might not have your powers back? Well, I guess we could hike out if we have to." She looked at her cell phone. Still no bars. "Where do you think we are?"

He reached back for her hand and pulled her closer to the window. "Look up."

"What?" The night sky was too bright to see many stars because of . . . she blinked . . . the two full moons shining there. She swallowed hard. "At least now we know why Ted couldn't find him." Was that breathy voice hers?

"He won't leave us stranded." Edge sounded sure of that.

"If he's dead—"

"He won't die. He's survived as our leader for tens of thousands of years." His voice was tight as he moved around the room. "Where're the freaking lights?"

After watching Edge circle the room in a fruitless search for switches, Passion decided to try something else. "Lights on." Surprised, she watched light flood the room.

Edge gave only a cursory glance at the huge room with its soaring ceiling, fireplace big enough to double as a guest bedroom, and beautiful furnishings. Passion took a few more minutes to admire everything before following him.

The kitchen was futuristic-scary. But Edge had found this planet's version of the fridge and was rooting around in it. "There's enough food in the kitchen to feed us for probably a month." He sounded relieved.

Passion left the kitchen first in search of a bathroom. Along with a bathroom that could have doubled as a Roman spa, she found the master bedroom. Edge joined her there.

"Our fearless leader knows how to live." Edge walked

over to the bed and lay down. "All those sleeping-on-a-cloud mattress ads? This one actually delivers. Come on over and try it." He patted the spot beside him.

"We can't just kick back and relax. We have to do *something*."

He raised one brow. "Suggestions?"

She waved a hand toward the wall of glass that looked out on nothing but forest on this side of the house. Bourne evidently wasn't into privacy. "We should go out and take a look around." Passion stared at him, as if her glare had the power to remove his yummy body from the temptation of that damn bed. Now wasn't the time for . . . *If not now, when?*

Edge looked past her at the window. "I don't really think you want to do that, sweetheart."

For a moment, she thought he'd read her mind. And then she turned to follow his gaze.

Three very big, very red eyes stared back at her from the other side of the glass. She blinked. They blinked back at her. "Umm, exploring can wait till morning." She looked around. "No window coverings." She was afraid to give a verbal command for fear the window might open. No way did she want to see what owned those eyes.

When she looked back at Edge, he was smiling. "Ready to join me?"

She nodded. Once on the bed beside him, she forced herself not to look at the window. Closing her eyes, she tried to relax. He was right. She'd never lain on anything this comfortable. Then she thought about stretching out on top of his naked body. Who wanted to sleep on a cloud anyway?

Passion allowed the silence to build until she decided to say what needed saying. She opened her eyes. "What I said about you being death and me being life? Dumb."

"But true." He didn't turn his head to look at her.

"You didn't pay attention to the rest of what I said. We balance each other. And that's a good thing." That's not what she'd thought at the time, but she did now. And there was something about recognizing the balance that was important. The meaning was just out of reach, though.

"You didn't trust me not to kill Murmur."

"No, I didn't." Couldn't deny that.

"You were right."

His lips tipped up in that smile she loved.

"I never lost it like that before." He turned his head to stare at her. "But I was so afraid for you that I couldn't think about anything except stopping him. *You* make me lose control."

Passion understood the gift he'd just given her. He'd made himself vulnerable, admitted that she weakened him in some way. But that wasn't right. "I always want to make you stronger. And being willing to defend someone you . . . care for is a strength."

Once again, the silence weighed on them.

Finally, he spoke. "You know I want to make love with you? Right now, right here."

Took the words right out of my mouth. She nodded.

"We can't, though." He sounded pained. "Bourne. The portal. We have to be ready."

She nodded again.

"There must be a TV or something in this damn room." He scanned the area.

Passion agreed. She needed a distraction before she said to hell with Bourne and ripped Edge's clothes from his luscious body.

He picked up what looked vaguely like a remote from the bedside table and began pushing buttons.

"Don't push anything that says Open Windows." She still refused to look at the wall of glass.

A few minutes and a lot of muttered cursing later, the far wall suddenly became a giant screen.

"Yes." Edge pushed his success by pressing more buttons.

"Describe what you wish to view." The sexy female voice gave no other instructions.

"Avatar," Passion offered.

"We're on an alien planet. Why would we want to watch a movie about another alien planet?"

The sexy voice overrode his complaint. *"Describe* what you wish to view." She almost sounded a little impatient.

"Hey, how about showing us making love on a roller coaster? Is that description good enough for you?" Edge's frustration was leaking out.

Passion laughed. "It's a machine. It doesn't register ticked-off or sarcasm. Besides, they probably don't have roller coasters on this planet. Maybe we have to actually describe the plot of the movie."

Edge made a rude sound, but he didn't get a chance to make any snarky comments because suddenly a title scrolled across the screen. *Sex on a Roller Coaster.*

"What the hell . . . ?" Edge sat up.

"Ohmigod!" Passion popped up beside him.

They both stared at the screen.

"Since you did not describe any specific actions, the Fantasy Fulfiller will generate random sexual acts." The female voice sounded smug.

Shock, horror, and yes, fascination held Passion's gaze riveted to the screen. She should've been shouting, "Turn it off!" but it was all too . . . She licked suddenly dry lips.

Beside her, she felt Edge tense, but he didn't say anything. Definitely no "shut it off" shouts from him.

Then the first scene appeared on the screen. She gasped. "That's us. How?"

Even though she knew the images weren't real—okay, so they looked darn real to her—she frantically scanned the screen, and then sighed her relief when she didn't see anyone else on the coaster, didn't see any shocked onlookers staring up from the ground.

They were both naked. She sat straddling his thighs facing him as the car hauled itself up the steep incline. His mouth was on hers, and Passion could practically taste the long, drugging kiss. Sweat sheened his perfect body, delineating his hard muscles. Her gaze dropped to between his legs, to the long, hard length of him.

She gripped the comforter until her knuckles turned white as he broke the kiss and slid his tongue down the side of her neck. Passion tried to unclog her brain. No, not *her*, the woman on the screen who was the pretend her. But she could swear she felt the warm glide of his tongue, and her nipples tightened into hard nubs of overexcited nerve endings as he teased each one with the tip of his tongue.

Passion closed her eyes and tried to get her breathing under control. *Not me, not Edge.* Those people on the screen weren't them. But every second that passed seemed to make it more them.

Passion didn't dare look at Edge. She kept her gaze focused on the screen where her alter ego had shimmied as far down as she could given the car's confines and was showing him what the tip of *her* tongue could do.

He groaned as she circled his cock and then closed her lips over the head. Passion felt that groan all the way to her toes.

Edge had tangled his fingers in her hair, guiding her talented mouth up and down on him. Who knew she was this good? Warmth and heaviness gathered low in her stomach. Fantasy and reality fused. She couldn't believe how just watching his body respond to her mouth made her damp, made her body clench.

Passion wanted to reach down and touch herself, relieve the frustrated urgency quickening her breathing and heartbeat.

Okay, so she did feel a little embarrassed as she watched her screen image's bottom waving in the air and bouncing with each up-and-down motion of her mouth.

Passion chanced a quick glance at Edge. He was staring straight ahead, but he wasn't making any attempt to hide his arousal.

Then the car reached the top of the hill. At the same moment, she moved forward and planted herself on him. Passion imagined the stretching sensation, the friction, the joy of being filled. As the car paused, she began raising and lowering herself onto him.

Finally, Edge took over. He grasped her hips and drove up into her at the same moment the car began to hurtle down the other side.

Edge's hips became a blur of motion as he slammed into her over and over. She screamed her ecstasy as she threw her head back and spread her arms wide. Passion thought she sort of looked like the woman on the *Titanic* who stood at the front of the ship with her arms held out. In real life, Passion would have had a death grip on his wide shoulders.

The hurtling car seemed to be taking a long time to reach the bottom. Long enough for both Edge and Passion to reach orgasm. Very loud orgasms.

In the final throes of obviously mindless pleasure, Edge gave one final mighty thrust, lifting her high into the air, and . . .

Flinging her out of the car. She disappeared, her scream fading until it suddenly stopped.

Passion froze. Did she just see . . . ? "You killed me? How could you kill me? What kind of rotten fantasy is that?"

The screen faded to black as the female voice offered a few closing comments. "But you died happy. Sadly, our hero was devastated. Grief over the loss of his love drove him crazy. He went on a mad spree of destruction, dynamiting roller coasters across the country. He was finally caught and spent the rest of his miserable life in a mental health facility." Huge sigh. "I love tragic love stories."

There was dead silence in the room until the sound of applause turned both of their attentions to the window.

Red eyes looked back at them. Not just three eyes. *Rows* of red eyes. One on top of the other.

"It looks like they set up freaking bleachers out there." Edge looked down at the remote. "There has to be a button to . . ."

"Don't bother looking. They'll go away now that they've seen the show."

Bourne's voice caught them by surprise. He stood in the bedroom doorway, one shoulder propped against the frame. He shook his head as he laughed softly.

"Too bad I didn't have time to fill you in on a few things before sending you through the portal. First, the green button at the bottom would've given you a selection of movies. You activated the Fantasy Fulfiller. You have to give her an exact description of what you want or else she improvises. She's not good at it."

Bourne pushed away from the door and moved farther into the room. Passion didn't notice any blood or obvious wounds.

"Second, my semicivilized neighbors like to watch the movies with me. They're too big to fit in here, so they watch from outside. You made their night. They've never seen a fantasy like that before."

Passion felt the heat rising in her face. This was way beyond embarrassing. "Edge didn't really want that fantasy. He said it to be sarcastic. He didn't know about the Fantasy Fulfiller. He—"

"I think he gets it, Passion."

Edge's voice sounded weird, all tight and deep and raspy. She chanced a glance at him.

Hunger so powerful it shook her glowed in his eyes. His hands were clenched into fists, and it was obvious the Edge on the screen was the only one who'd gotten a release.

Time to change the subject. "You survived." She watched Bourne walk over to the window and wave at the dozens of eyes before they faded back into the darkness. She didn't ask what owned those eyes.

"You had doubts?" Bourne stood watching them.

Passion wondered how much of the fantasy he'd seen.

"I cleared my suite of his pitiful attempt at intimidation and then came for you."

"Pitiful attempt?" Why wasn't Edge chiming in? "It sure got my attention."

Bourne's expression turned grim. "He was just playing this time. I don't think he seriously thought his invasion of my space would destroy me. He wanted to annoy me. He did. Now it's time to take the fight to him." He waved them toward the door. "Let's go. I have some people I want you to meet."

16

Edge walked back through the portal with Passion and then stopped. Every inch of Bourne's suite was packed with big, dangerous-looking men and women who he knew could kick major butt. All cosmic troublemakers.

And in the middle of the mob, seated on the couch, were a terrified Hope and a pissed-off Kemp.

"Before I came for you, I took time to collect our resident angels." Bourne smiled at Hope and Kemp.

Hope cringed, and Kemp scowled. They weren't restrained in any way, but they weren't making a break for it either. Edge didn't blame them. Too many badasses in the room to take a chance.

Edge figured he'd better clue Passion in. "These are Bourne's deadliest troublemakers."

"Where's Sparkle?" Passion looked uneasy as she glanced around.

"My sweetie's the best at what she does, but this job is going to need more of the physical stuff." Ganymede sat on the arm of the couch, still in cat form.

Passion didn't look convinced. "I'd put my money on

Sparkle. I *saw* what she could do. There're different kinds of 'physical stuff.'"

No one paid any attention to her.

Bourne walked over to stand in front of Hope and Kemp. "Now. Let's have a talk. Where is Archangel Ted?"

Hope's eyes widened. "I don't know. I don't know *anything*." Her gaze skittered to Kemp. "Why didn't you tell me?"

"Because you might've told *her*." Kemp sent Passion a glare that said traitor.

Bourne's voice softened a little. "You *did* know Kemp was one of the avenging angels, didn't you?"

Hope nodded and then looked down at her clasped hands. "I just thought Archangel Ted had sent him to check up on us, to make sure we were really trying to save souls."

"I believe you, Hope."

Bourne patted her hand, and she visibly relaxed.

He turned his attention to Kemp. "Where is Ted?"

Kemp said nothing.

"How many angels does he have?"

More silence.

"When will he attack?"

Silence.

"Want me to twist his balls, Boss?" This from one of the troublemakers standing in the crowd.

Kemp winced, but Edge gave him credit for not putting his hands over the body parts in question.

"Torture won't make me tell you anything."

Kemp sounded calm, but Edge watched him swallow hard.

Bourne didn't address the ball-twisting offer. "Kemp, why do you want to overthrow me?" He seemed sincerely interested.

"Archangel Ted told us about all the evil you've visited on humanity. It's our duty to destroy you so he can redeem your misguided followers and bring peace and goodwill to the world."

A smile tugged at Bourne's mouth. "Wow. Anyone who

thinks they can do all that doesn't really understand the situation. And I hate to break this to you, but he's no more an angel than I am. He's just another power-hungry immortal hoping to take over my job. Oh, and you're not an angel either. Sorry."

Kemp glowered. "I *am* an angel. He told us you were the voice of the devil, that you'd try to turn us against him."

"Kemp, Kemp, we've talked to several real angels. None of them have ever heard of an Archangel Ted." Bourne looked as though his patience was wearing thin. "And what self-respecting angel would admit to the name of Ted?" He waved the comment away. "Never mind about that."

"Are you going to kill us?" Kemp seemed resigned to martyr status.

Hope gulped. She stared at Passion. "Please help me. I forgive you for going over to the dark side. I'll go too, but I don't want to die."

Kemp shot her a poisonous glare.

"Neither of you are going to die." Bourne glanced at the still-open portal. "Unfortunately, I don't have time to convince you you're wrong, so I'm just going to take you out of the equation until I'm finished with Ted."

Everyone's gaze shifted to the portal.

"When you go through, you'll be in my house. There's plenty of food. And if you use the Fantasy Fulfiller, make sure the fantasy is something you won't mind my neighbors seeing." Bourne waved them toward the portal.

Neither Hope nor Kemp moved.

Bourne exhaled wearily. "Why must I do everything myself?" He beckoned to them.

An unseen force lifted both Hope and Kemp from the couch and floated them over to and through the portal. Hope's screams were the last thing Edge heard as Bourne closed it.

Passion stated the obvious. "Kemp didn't answer any of your questions."

Bourne smiled. "Oh, but he did. Every time I asked a

question, he thought the answer. And I was in his head to hear them."

"And?" Edge was starting to feel claustrophobic with all the power pressing in on every side.

"He doesn't know where Ted is. His leader has been communicating in the same way he did with Hope and Passion. So no mental picture."

"How many of the bastards are there?" Now that the couch was empty, Ganymede leaped down and stretched out on it.

Bourne didn't look concerned. "About fifty avenging angels, along with the office staff that worked with Passion. The office staff won't be a threat."

Edge could see Passion bristle.

"Excuse me? Everyone in that office has skills." She narrowed her eyes. "Have you forgotten what I can do?"

Bourne smiled. "I apologize. Of course you have amazing talent, but I'm thinking in terms of the ones who could rip our heads off."

"Fifty doesn't seem like much of an army." A female troublemaker Edge didn't recognize, but who had to be at least six-five, spoke for the first time.

"There only have to be enough to keep you at bay while Ted kills me. I'm sure he thinks that's more than enough to take care of twenty-five of you. Of course, his fifty haven't been forged in the fires of chaos, destruction, and general crappy attitudes. They'll be way out of their league." Bourne's smile turned into something much darker. "And so will Archangel Asshole."

"Since Ted didn't have any luck getting Murmur's help, do you think he found someone else to pad his forces?" Edge couldn't imagine who he'd get on short notice.

"No vampires. No demons. No fey. What's left?" Bourne shrugged. "Maybe a few dumbass shifters."

"How do you know none of those beings will be helping him?" The voice of doubt came from the middle of the troublemaker mob.

"My last fortune cookie?"

No one had the nerve to call Bourne on his nonanswer.

"When's the attack coming?" Ganymede didn't seem to be experiencing any kind of adrenaline rush. The cat yawned, his eyes slowly drifting shut.

"Ted told Kemp to be ready at seven tomorrow morning. If they strike at dawn, they take away any help Dacian could give us. And there won't be a bunch of humans up to get in the way."

Passion widened her eyes. "We have to get the humans to safety."

Before being drawn into Passion's angelic orbit, Edge wouldn't have given a damn about human collateral damage. But this was his woman—jeez, had he just thought that?—and he needed to back her up. "Humans will be a distraction. Passion's right."

Ganymede opened one eye. *"Sparkle can take care of that. She's good at those kinds of things."*

Bourne glanced at his watch. "I want all of you to get a good night's sleep. I'll call you in time to eat before the battle."

Ganymede gave a cat snort. *"This is too civilized for me. Why aren't we rampaging through the castle dragging the freaking winged wusses out of their hiding places and sending them to their real maker?"*

There was a rumble of agreement from most of the other troublemakers.

Bourne cast Ganymede a stare guaranteed to drill a hole right through his fuzzy head. "Because the 'winged wusses' aren't here yet. I'd know. Besides, your goal will be to disable, not kill them. They honestly believe the lies Ted has fed them."

"Not kill?" Ganymede's disbelief was echoed by the rest of the troublemakers.

"Feel free to pummel, pound, and punish. But no killing." Bourne's tone said he was throwing a bone to the bloodthirsty masses.

Ganymede didn't look appeased.

Edge was enjoying Bourne's put-down of Ganymede, but he had to ask a question. "When he realizes Hope and Kemp are gone, won't Ted suspect you know about his plans and change them?"

"Probably not. He's overconfident or else he wouldn't even be attempting this. He can't do anything until his forces are here, and he still won't want to take a chance of Dacian weighing in. So he won't attack before dawn." Bourne thought for a moment. "As soon as you leave, I'm calling in Holgarth and Zane. They can wake the gargoyles and command them to stop any incoming nonhumans. I suspect Ted has enough power to shut them down, but not before they sound a warning."

Passion looked doubtful. "Good luck getting Holgarth and Zane to work together."

Bourne smiled. "Oh, they'll work together." His smile didn't bode well for Holgarth and his son. "They'll also be warding all of your rooms. No one will get in while you're sleeping." He turned to Edge. "You'll have to stay in Passion's room tonight. I've put three of the men in your apartment."

And that was that. Everyone left his suite, but Passion held Edge back till last. She wanted to ask Bourne something.

"Edge has said he doesn't know who created him. Do you know?" She felt Edge's surprise at the question.

Bourne dropped onto the couch. "No. I found each of them wandering the cosmos like lost children. They were primal and savage, and like children, they had no focus for their power. I gave them that."

She took a deep breath. Now for the scary question. "Why guide them along the path to chaos? Why not turn them into agents for good?" Passion hoped he wouldn't use her body to open a new portal.

But all he did was shrug. "Their power was what it was. I couldn't change it, only channel it into less destructive paths."

Edge finally spoke up. "Less destructive? Have you

looked at what Ganymede's been doing for the last few millennia?"

"Change takes time. Ganymede's power is under control." He frowned. "Except for sporadic outbursts."

"What if one of us wanted to change, to be something other than what we've always been?"

Edge sounded casual, but Passion could feel tension thrumming through him.

Bourne raised one brow. "Like into an angel?"

Edge looked horrified. "Crap, no."

"Then I guess he'd have to talk to me about it. After we eliminate Archangel Ted." Bourne closed his eyes, signaling that the conversation was over.

Edge paused once they'd left Bourne's suite. "I have to get some clothes and things from my apartment. Go right to your room and lock your door behind you."

"Is that an order?" Passion forced the frown from her face. He just wanted to keep her safe. That was endearing in a bossy kind of way.

He laughed. "It's a suggestion. I'm not stupid. But Ted's out there somewhere, and I don't want you taking any chances."

She dismissed his worry. "I'll be careful. But Ted won't be focusing on me. I don't have any fighting skills, so I won't be a danger to him." Passion did want Edge to know where she'd be, though. "I have to talk to Sparkle for a few minutes, and then I'll go to my room." She smiled. "We'll call room service and eat in. Then . . ." Passion let the possibilities simmer.

"Got it."

Without warning, he pulled her into his arms and covered her mouth with his. He tasted of elemental male and sensual promises. She deepened the kiss and hoped he sensed how much she wanted him. When he finally broke the kiss, he was breathing hard.

She watched him walk away, and then went in search of Sparkle. Passion found her in Sweet Indulgence, yawning as she leaned on her candy counter. Sparkle's eyes lit up when she saw Passion.

"You've saved me from terminal boredom. I can count my customers on one hand tonight. What's up?" Sparkle narrowed her gaze on Passion's hands. "Chipped nails. We'll take care of those tomorrow."

Passion perched on a stool across the counter from Sparkle. "I have a problem."

Sparkle's smile was so potent that Passion was surprised it didn't send out sex signals to all males within a ten-mile radius.

"Dare I hope you're coming to me for advice on how to drive Edge into an erotic frenzy?" She slid the tip of her tongue across her bottom lip.

"No."

"No?" Sparkle didn't try to hide her disappointment. "But I have so much to offer." It was just shy of a whine.

"Maybe some other time." Passion knew she had a lot to learn about all that was sensual, and she had no problem with sitting at the designer-clad feet of the mistress of sex and sin. But just not tonight.

"First, did Ganymede tell you that Ted will probably launch his attack tomorrow morning?"

Sparkle frowned. "No. He has a nasty habit of assuming I don't have any interest in 'manly' things. Usually he acts like a jerk when he's in cat form. I wonder why?"

Passion forced Sparkle out of her musing about cat-versus-golden-god forms. "Can you do something that will get rid of the humans in the castle? Once the fighting begins, I'm afraid no one will care if they die."

"I'm on it." She pulled out her cell phone. "Holgarth, take care of something for me. Have Bill notify every human guest that a massive bedbug infestation is about to overrun the castle." She listened for a moment. "I don't care *what* you say. Improvise. Tell them bedbugs ate the guy in room 140. Warn them to get out of the castle now. We'll refund all their money."

Sparkle made a face as she listened to Holgarth. "It isn't stupid. No one wants to take home hitchhikers who bite." She thought about that for a moment. "Unless they're superheated gorgeous vampires."

Finally she sighed. "Just do it." And she hung up.

She smiled at Passion. "Done."

"Thanks. One more thing." Passion hesitated.

Did she have the right to ask this of Sparkle? What would Edge say if he found out she was doing this? Okay, so he'd be ticked. But she cared enough to want him to have a shot at something other than being Death for the rest of his existence.

"Has Bourne ever released any of the cosmic trouble-makers from their assignments?"

Sparkle didn't answer immediately. "A few have been destroyed like Rabid. And some have been busted down to less important jobs because they weren't good at what they were doing." She shook her head. "But I don't remember anyone asking for a different position and getting it."

Passion wouldn't give up that easily. She got right to the point. "If Edge didn't want to be Death anymore, what would give him the best chance of convincing Bourne to go along with it?"

"Does Edge know you're doing this?"

"No." Passion held her breath.

"Good for you. I love women who take control. It's sexy. Let me think." She pushed a box of chocolates across the counter to Passion.

And while Passion waited for Sparkle's thoughts, she scarfed down the candy.

Finally, Sparkle spoke. Good thing. Passion was well on her way to devouring every chocolate and then starting on the box itself.

"I think Bourne might be open to switching Edge with someone else. If I can come up with the name of someone who'd do a good job as Death and who wants out of his assignment, Edge might be able to make a deal." Sparkle looked motivated. "Now, in return for my help, you have to learn a new sensual skill."

Uh-oh. "I really don't have time to—"

"Sure you do. This is just a little foreplay thing. You'll learn it in a few minutes."

Passion sighed. "Fine. Show me."

When the first panicked evacuee from the bedbug invasion drove past Sweet Indulgence a half hour later, Passion was still practicing Sparkle's Dance of the Seven Hershey's Kisses. Who knew the things you could do with a Hershey's Kiss.

A short time later, Passion was in the hall headed toward her room with a gift bag of Kisses from Sparkle in her hand. She was smiling. Sparkle had jump-started her sexual creativity.

Suddenly, one of the doors opened and a woman sporting a halo of white hair stepped out. Passion recognized her. This was the woman Edge had terrified when he'd lost control. She'd returned to the hotel after Ganymede's power surge, and Passion had seen her once more outside the castle's restaurant. She remembered the woman telling her she should be helping people who deserve it. Obviously, the woman hadn't meant cosmic troublemakers.

She looked frightened, and Passion figured if Edge and Ganymede hadn't scared her away, then whatever was happening now must be a biggie. "What's the matter?"

The woman's hand shook as she reached out to Passion. "There's a huge bug in my room. I've never seen anything like it. Will you come in and kill it?"

Passion frowned. After all she'd survived, an insect was scaring her? Suspicion touched Passion for a moment, but then she dismissed it. Different fears for different folks. She stepped into the woman's room. "Where is it?"

The woman pointed into the bathroom.

Passion sighed as she walked into the bathroom. She looked around. "I don't see it."

"Sit down on the floor, Passion." The voice was angry, dangerous, and *familiar.*

"Ted?" She couldn't even turn to look at him. As her mind screamed for her to turn, to fight, to run, her body obeyed his command. She sat on the floor.

"You may look at me, but that's all."

Passion raised her gaze to meet his, but she couldn't speak.

"If you could talk, I'm sure you'd ask where the sweet old lady went." His smile chilled her. "She's still here." Too fast for Passion's eyes to follow, Ted became the old woman. "I can be whatever I need to be. You never suspected." Triumph filled his gaze as she changed back to Ted's form.

There was nothing angelic about him now. The black swirling around him was just as dark as what surrounded Edge. His brown eyes had always seemed filled with love for everyone. Now? They gleamed hard and cruel. He looked bigger, menacing.

"I won't need to tie you up, Passion, because I'm powerful enough to hold you here until I've finished with Bourne. You've been a great disappointment to me."

"You too, jerk." Passion wondered if he could read her thoughts. He hadn't when he'd made his nightly mental visits to Hope.

Passion got her answer in a startling way. Without warning, something slammed into her mind. It was the equivalent of taking a battering ram to a castle gate. If she could have moved, she would've pressed her hands to her temples to keep her brain from leaking out, because she just knew there had to be a giant hole in her head.

"There. I'm in your thoughts now, Passion."

That's how he did it? Ganymede had entered her mind with not even a ripple.

Ted scowled. "I could have been gentler, but traitors must be punished. You deserve to suffer after abandoning your brothers and sisters."

"Well, if you can read my mind, then read this. You've been handing all of us a load of crap since we came into being. Bastard. Wow, cursing really does make me

feel better. If I'd known what a wing nut you were, I would've cursed a lot more a lot sooner."

There was no warning. Ted simply leaned down and punched her in the face. Her head rocked back and hit the wall hard. Momentary dizziness made her close her eyes.

Passion felt as though someone had sucked all the air from her lungs. Her stomach heaved and she had to force back the nausea. It wasn't the pain that made her want to throw up—although the side of her face hurt like hell—but the realization that this was the first time anyone had ever struck her in anger. And she never would have guessed that the blow would come from the man who'd controlled— yes, she could now admit he'd controlled all of them— everything she'd said and done . . . forever.

All the wasted time, all the lives she might have ruined by intruding on people's thoughts. She opened her eyes and stared at him. Passion hoped he saw all the disgust and contempt she felt for him.

He smiled. "You have no idea how long I've wanted to do that. You've always been a pain in the ass. I wasn't really surprised when I realized you were helping them."

"What are you?"

He widened his eyes in mock surprise. "I'm an angel, just as I've always claimed." Ted straightened and leaned against the bathroom door frame. "Of course, I fell a long, long time ago."

Fallen angel. Horror tore at her. Not only because of how easily he'd fooled her, but because she feared not even Bourne could stand against one of the Fallen.

Ted smiled. "That's the first thought you've had that has pleased me. And you're right, of course he can't stand against me. By tomorrow night, I'll be the new Big Boss."

He pushed away from the door frame and moved a little closer. Passion hated her instinctive fear.

"Now that I'm in your head, I think I'll see what you know about Bourne's plans."

If Passion could laugh, she might be a little hysterical by now. Bourne had used the same method with Kemp, only Bourne had been smart enough not to warn him beforehand. And Bourne had evidently slipped in unnoticed, because Kemp had never suspected he wasn't alone in his mind.

Ted's expression didn't change, but Passion sensed his anger, his need to hit her again.

"So Bourne has Kemp. What did Kemp tell him about my plans?"

Now was Passion's chance to test her theory that Ganymede had jumped into her mind so easily because she hadn't seen him coming. She was ready for Ted. She retreated to a corner of her mind where she built her mental wall high and thick, imagined solid steel. Then she hunkered down behind her wall and made her mind a blank.

She could feel Ted probing, trying to find a way past her defenses. The wall held.

"You can't keep me out, little girl."

But she did. And sometime in the next few minutes Ted's probing became painful pokes. It felt as though he was sticking a needle into different parts of her brain. Passion kept her mind a blank even as she kept her wall strong.

"I'll ask the question in a different way. Maybe you'll like this version better." His voice was low and ugly with anger. "What are Bourne's plans?"

The pain increased. Forget the pins. Now he was using a jackhammer on her brain. If she could've screamed, she would have. The pain went on and on. Her wall started to bend and buckle.

"I'll be in soon. You can't keep me out."

He was right. Even her steel wall was collapsing under so much agony. The worst part was that she couldn't keep her mind blank. The pain wouldn't let her. So before he blasted through, she focused all her thoughts on Edge, on what she intended to do with her bag of Hershey's Kisses.

"Yes!"

Ted's exclamation of triumph was accompanied by a

stab of pain so intense she thought she'd pass out. She didn't. Too bad.

"Now for Bourne's plans or anything else of importance you'd like to tell me."

And in her fantasy, Passion performed her Dance of the Seven Hershey's Kisses for Edge. Over and over and over again, each time with a slightly different variation.

The pain escalated in direct proportion to Ted's curses. She wanted to reach up and rip off her head.

But something almost as good started to happen. Darkness crept into the corners of her vision, unconsciousness slid closer and closer. And when blackness finally descended, she welcomed it.

It only took a few seconds after waking for Passion to realize that Ted's Torture Show had only taken a commercial break. He was standing by the bathroom door, frowning, and the side of her face was throbbing in time to her heartbeat.

She'd wanted to believe she was mentally stronger than he was. Passion now knew she wasn't. If he started doling out more of the same, she'd cave, and then hate herself. Probably not for long, though, because he'd kill her.

"I don't have time for this." He almost sounded petulant. "I have to summon the avenging angels."

Passion didn't know why he still called them that. They weren't angels. They were . . . Whatever she was. But she wasn't going to ask him any questions because she had to start building her mental wall all over again.

"I'm leaving you here, Passion. When I come back, I'll see if you're ready to answer my questions." His expression promised more pain if she remained stubborn. Then something seemed to occur to him. "While I'm gone, think about those answers. Once Bourne is gone, you'll be an important member of my empire."

Empire? Had he said *empire*? Oh, boy.

His gaze turned sly. "You're surprised. You probably thought I'd just kill you after I got my answers and that would be the end of it. But you'll be working for me for a very long time, Passion. You're *Life*, much too valuable to destroy."

He'd known about her power?

It mustn't have been hard for him to read her outrage. "I've always known you could restore life. Why do you think I allowed you to stick around to annoy me? And if you're interested, I have enough power to cloak the colors of sin you're able to see." He lowered his voice. "You have no idea how powerful I am. Just hope you never find out."

He started to turn away. "Oh, and don't waste your time sending out mental calls for help. I've layered enough spells around this room to block anything you try to send. And even if someone tried to ride to your rescue, my wards would keep them out." He smiled. "Try not to miss me too much."

She listened until she heard the front door close. There were plenty of people who could hear a mental SOS if she had the power to send it.

Wait. Why wouldn't she have the power? Passion had learned a lot about her mental strength as she'd spent night after night in the minds of others. Maybe Ted had never taken it away at all when he kicked her down here. He hadn't shut down her other power, the ability to see the colors of sin. She'd just assumed she no longer could enter others' minds and so hadn't tried.

But before she could search for someone, she'd have to get past Ted's spell. She'd learned the best way to reach into a mind wasn't the swallow-it-whole method. That spread the power over too wide an area, weakening it.

Passion had always gotten better results by slipping through the tiniest possible opening in a person's thoughts. The more nonintrusive the better. Then she'd direct all her power through the small opening, hitting her targeted area with the power of a laser.

Praying that she still had her power, Passion focused. Then she began to drill a mental hole in Ted's spell.

17

Death walked the Castle of Dark Dream's halls, and tonight he'd live up to his title without any regret.

Passion was missing. No one had seen her after she left Sweet Indulgence. She'd been wrong. Evidently Archangel Ted *did* have an interest in her.

Edge reached the last door in the long hallway. He focused his power and blew it off its hinges.

Bain winced. "You know, Sparkle's going to be pissed about having to replace all these doors."

Edge glared at him. "I'm going to find Passion if I have to tear down the fucking castle." He strode into the empty room, and after checking in the bathroom and closet, returned to the hallway where Bain waited. "You said all the humans are gone?"

Bain nodded. "Every one. They ran like rabbits. Afraid of a bunch of small insects." Contempt for humans oozed from him.

"Bedbugs bite. Don't think you'd hang around long either if they targeted you as their demon dessert." Edge didn't give a damn about bugs. He wanted to find Passion. "Is Murmur still here?"

The demon cast him a wary glance. "Yes. Why?"

"He's not going to sit on his ass doing nothing. He's still in that body he loves so much because of Passion. So I'd say he needs to shut off his music and help find her."

"You might not be the best person to ask him."

"I'm the perfect person. He hates my guts. I'll promise him a favor. It'll make his century." Edge took the stairs up to the tower and Murmur's room.

He knocked on the door and then waited. Bain stood out of the line of fire.

Murmur finally opened the door. He didn't smile, and his eyes had that red glow going, but he also didn't come out blasting. "You left my door on its hinges. You're maturing."

Edge controlled rage that was too close to the surface. He needed the demon. "The guy who tried to hire you is named Ted. He's been masquerading as an archangel. He's Passion's boss. Now she's missing. I'd like you to help find her." What he *wanted* to say was, "I'll rip your head off if you don't get your butt out here." Way to sweet-talk a demon. Edge thought about also asking if he could search Murmur's room but decided against it. No need to antagonize him more.

Murmur relaxed enough to nod at Bain and then to lean his shoulder against the door frame. "And why should I do this?"

Edge knew better than to appeal to a demon's better nature. They didn't have one. "I'll owe you."

Excitement glowed in Murmur's eyes. "A favor? You'll owe me a *favor*?" He did everything but lick his lips.

Edge took a deep breath. "Yes." The demon looked so gleeful that he wanted to punch the smile off his face. For Passion's sake, he didn't.

Murmur went back inside his room to get his key and then returned. He joined them in the hallway. "What have you tried so far?"

"Violent door removal." Bain sounded resigned.

"Why am I not surprised?" Murmur kept smiling, though. "Who else is hunting?"

"Everyone." Edge knew he sounded grim. "She's either unconscious or not in the castle because Ganymede and Bourne have been putting out mental calls." It still bothered Edge that Ganymede had been able to reach into her mind but he hadn't. His disappointment wasn't because it showed that Ganymede had more power, but because Edge was jealous of anyone who could touch her in a way he couldn't.

He wouldn't even consider that she might be dead. If he believed that, nothing could save the castle or the city. And she'd never want to be the catalyst for his deadly rampage.

Bain spoke up. "I talked to Bourne. He doesn't think she's dead. This Ted wants to reign over his own little kingdom of powerful nonhumans. He won't have a kingdom to reign over if he destroys his minions."

Edge tried to calm his breathing. He hoped Bourne was right.

"Makes sense. Have you thought about a portal?" Murmur seemed interested.

"Bourne was able to open one in his suite." Hope stirred in Edge. "From what we've seen so far, Ted has the power to do something like that."

"How much of the castle have you searched?" Murmur looked bemused as Edge blew away the only other door on his floor. "You know, there're easier ways to open doors."

"Yeah, but this takes the edge off my need to maim, murder, and mutilate."

Murmur waved him on. "Then by all means blast away."

"We've searched all of it. This was the last room." Edge went inside and did a quick search. Nothing. Frustration and fear pounded at him along with a rising sense of time running out. Where the hell was she? He rejoined Bain and Murmur in the hallway.

"Bain said he'd only checked out one floor with you." Murmur followed Edge down the stairs.

"At first Bourne sent Edge off to search on his own. But then he decided I might see something Edge missed." Bain stopped at the bottom of the stairs and pointed down the hallway. "I only helped with this floor."

Murmur nodded. "Let's go back over all the places you searched."

"Why?" Before seeing the demon in action, Edge might've dismissed his suggestion. But Murmur had crazy skills, and Edge would use anyone or anything to help Passion. He had no pride where she was concerned.

"I have the power to see past glamours that would probably fool you. Things aren't always what they seem." Murmur took the lead as they retraced the steps Edge and Bain had already taken. He stopped at the end of the hallway. "Nothing here. Let's go down to the next floor."

That's when Edge heard it. Passion's voice. Faint and cutting in and out like a bad phone connection.

"Edge. Help. Ted . . ."

Ted what? He was missing words.

The others sensed something happening and stood frozen. They didn't ask questions.

"I'm . . ."

Where? Edge strained to hear.

"Bathroom."

What bathroom? But he'd missed that important info.

"Can't move. Can't talk."

Her voice faded away and Edge wanted to break something, preferably Ted's head. Through his haze of fear and fury, he felt wonder that she'd reached out to him, *only him.* How had she managed it? Then he remembered her job description. She was used to touching the minds of others. But something was stopping her from maintaining a strong connection.

He waited a few moments, hoping she'd return. Nothing. But at least she was still alive. Relief left him weak.

Finally, he turned to the others and told them what she'd said. "Where the hell could she be? I've searched the halls up here, and the others have covered the rest of the castle."

"We'll retrace your steps, and then we'll retrace theirs. We'll hunt for glamours and any sign of a portal."

"I'm impressed, demon." And he was. "I should've put some thought into the search instead of just becoming a human wrecking ball." Reason had packed its bags and taken a fast flight out of town once he realized she was gone.

Murmur shrugged. "You care for her too much. Love rots the brain."

Edge's response was automatic. "I'm not—"

"You are." Murmur sighed. "Denials bore me, so don't bother with them. Let's go down to the next floor."

Edge didn't pay much attention as he followed the demons down the stairs. He felt his way around the word "love," poking at it in the same way he would an aching tooth. The pain felt way too good. He was glad to reach the bottom of the stairs.

He scanned the length of the hallway. Every door hung open, even Passion's. Okay, so his temper had been off its leash by that time. "Nothing here. I searched inside every room."

Ignoring him, Murmur walked slowly down the hall, staring intently at every door. Finally, he stopped in front of an open door about halfway down the hallway. "This door is still closed."

Bain nodded his agreement.

"How?" Edge trusted the demon's judgment enough not to argue.

Murmur moved closer. "Very nice." He reached out to what looked like open space where the door had been, but it was obvious he was touching something solid. "A very strong spell. As soon as you touched the door with your power, the spell made you see what you expected to see— a door blown open. I can see what *is* because I have no expectations." He cast Edge a sly glance. "And, of course, I have a variety of amazing skills while you have only one."

Edge ignored the taunt. "But I went into the room, searched it." He knew the spell was possible, but it was still hard to swallow.

Murmur nodded. "The spell sold you a bill of goods. You *thought* you'd opened the door, and you *thought* you'd searched inside. Actually, you never left this spot in front of the door. Once the spell had seized your mind, it allowed you only to see what its creator wanted you to see." He looked at Edge, all slyness gone. "The battle between your Big Boss and this Ted will be epic." Anticipation glittered in his eyes.

Edge's first instinct was to blast away at the door he couldn't see, but that hadn't worked the first time. "Can our combined powers take the door down?"

Bain shook his head. "Along with the glamour, there's a ward shielding the door from attacks. Removing spells isn't one of our talents. You need someone with more magical skills." He glanced at Murmur. "Agreed?"

Murmur nodded. "I wonder if your Ted is inside?"

"It doesn't matter." If he could get through that door, no one would stop him from reaching Passion.

"It matters to those of us who care about keeping our asses." Murmur backed away from the door. "I bet if you manage to get past *this* door, the door to the bathroom will have enough wards to fry you to crispy-done if you disturb them."

Bain added his thoughts. "Plus, Ted might be sitting behind that door like a big fat spider waiting to pounce."

"I don't think so." Even as he talked, Edge reached out to Bourne's mind. He'd thought about trying to get Zane up here, but with Passion's life on the line, he wanted the best. "His avenging angels aren't here yet. He's not ready to face Bourne."

He had barely finished his mental shout-out when Bourne appeared. Edge didn't waste words. "There's a cloaking spell and the door's warded. Passion got through to my mind, but her thoughts kept breaking up. She's in a bathroom. Said she couldn't move or talk. I'd guess she's in there." He nodded at the door.

Bourne took a moment to study Murmur. "You decided to help?" He looked disbelieving.

Murmur grinned. "Death now owes me a favor."

Bourne shook his head as he glanced at Edge. "Foolish."

"It's for Passion." Edge thought that said it all. He held up his hand to stop his boss's comment. "I know. Love rots your brain. Can you take care of this?"

Bourne put out his hand and rested it against the door. Edge still thought it was freaky that he couldn't see anything solid there.

"Hmm. I suppose I'll have to stop thinking of Ted as an object of contempt. This is incredibly complex." Bourne dropped his hand.

"Can you get rid of it?" Edge did *not* want to leave Passion inside that room one more second while Bourne admired his enemy's work.

"Of course."

Bourne's expression never changed, but suddenly there was a quiet pop and it almost looked as though the area in front of the door rippled. Finally, Edge could see the closed door.

Bourne glanced up and down the hallway. "You're responsible for all the other doors?"

"Absolutely." Edge refused to apologize for the destruction. Sparkle could take it out of his paycheck.

"I took care of the ward too. Feel free to complete the demolition." Bourne nodded at the door.

Within seconds, Edge had blown open the door and was striding into the room. He headed for the closed bathroom door.

"Wait."

Bourne's sharp command stopped him.

"The whole damn exterior of the bathroom is warded—

door, walls, and probably floor and ceiling." He scanned the room. "At least I don't sense a portal."

"We need to get Passion out of there now." Edge spoke through clenched teeth, even as he admitted to himself that he might not be quite rational about things at the moment.

"Those wards will light you up like a Christmas tree. And they're too powerful for me to take down safely." Bourne looked as though he hated admitting that. "This is bad. Even if I take them down from a distance so *we're* safe, the concussion will kill anyone inside that small bathroom." He moved closer.

Edge's mind circled the problem, studying it from every angle. "Could I bypass the wards by dematerializing and then materializing inside?"

Bourne shook his head. "The wards wouldn't let you through."

Murmur summed it up. "So we have to find a way into the bathroom without touching the outside of the warded door, walls, floor, or ceiling."

"That's about it." A crease had formed between Bourne's eyes.

Edge rubbed his forehead, as though that would jump-start his brain. "Okay, so the only empty spaces going into that room are the vents, drains, and faucets."

Bourne threw him a sharp glance. "That's it. I have an idea." He spoke to Murmur and Bain. "You two wait outside in case Ted shows up. I'd guess he already knows we're in his room, so he won't come back to it, not without backup. But I don't want to chance any interruptions."

Edge wished the son of a bitch *would* return. Ted needed to sit down for a long talk with Death.

Once Murmur and Bain had left the room, Bourne turned to Edge. "Do you trust me?"

"What's that have to do with anything?" Edge didn't trust anyone, except Passion. But he didn't think this was the moment to admit it, not when he wanted Bourne to help him free her.

Bourne smiled. "You don't. Fine, so let me reword the question. Do you trust me to get you and Passion out of there alive?"

That was easy. "Yes." Edge didn't doubt Bourne's immense power.

"Good. Because you'll have to put your life in my hands. No doubts."

"Let's do it."

Bourne nodded. "I'm going to turn on the shower in the bathroom. Then I'm going to control your dematerialization and send you into the bathroom through the showerhead. The *water* isn't touching the wall, just the outside of the pipe that goes through the wall. If all goes well, you'll materialize in the bathroom. Then you can carry Passion out through the door since the wards are only meant to keep people out."

And if something goes wrong? Edge didn't ask the question, because he didn't want Bourne to back away from this. He'd take his chances. If things went bad, he'd never know because his molecules would be floating free forever. *All the king's horses and all the king's men, et cetera, et cetera, et cetera.* "Sounds like a plan."

Bourne's gaze grew unfocused, and a few seconds later Edge heard the shower water running. He took a deep breath. Edge would never be comfortable with someone else controlling his fate, but he had to push his feelings aside and concentrate on Passion.

Dematerializing was like falling asleep. One minute you were there and then nothing. He didn't know when it happened, but suddenly he was standing in the shower with cold water streaming over him.

He stepped out of the shower, dripping all over the floor. Passion sat with her back pressed against the wall near the door. She didn't speak, she didn't move, she only stared at him from wide eyes filled with . . . Edge had expected fear. What he saw was one ticked-off lady. He grinned. *That's my woman.*

His woman? Edge stopped smiling. He'd turned into

what he'd always derided—a man ruled by his feelings for a woman. *And you know, it feels damn good*. He reached her in one stride.

Then he saw her face. Fury made him shake. "The son of a bitch hit you."

Passion had never heard such murderous rage, such an unspoken promise of retribution in anyone's voice. He touched the side of her face with gentle fingers. She winced.

"He *will* pay, and it will be my debt to collect." His eyes darkened.

She believed him.

Then he scooped her up, kicked open the door, and strode from the bathroom.

Murmur and Bain stood in the hallway, but they didn't follow Edge back to her room. Bourne didn't comment on her face, but she'd heard his swift intake of breath when he first saw her. "I'll join you in a few minutes. I have to take down the bathroom wards and make a few calls."

Edge nodded and then carried her to her room. He gently laid her on the bed.

Passion stared up at him—unable to speak, to move. She only hoped he couldn't read what was in her eyes. She didn't want to burden him with all her emotions, especially one he wouldn't welcome. She tried instead to concentrate on how she wanted to kick Ted's butt all the way back to his fake heaven, wherever that had been.

Edge murmured words of comfort until Bourne walked into the room.

"Zane will be up to free you, Passion. I'd do it myself, but wielding any more magic would drain me. I have to be at full strength when Ted makes his move. Sparkle is on her way with someone to fix the door and something to help with the swelling. I'm sure she'll be her usual sympathetic self. At least with *you*." Bourne glanced at Edge. "If you want something to eat, order it right after Zane finishes because in about an hour he'll be warding the doors and no one will be able to get in."

Passion would have frowned if she could. What magic had Bourne wielded? She'd already gotten that something was going on when Edge came out of the showerhead instead of through the door. Damn, the side of her face was throbbing.

"Why bother? Wards didn't keep *us* out." Edge never took his gaze from Passion.

"Taking down wards uses energy, especially when there're lots of them. He won't want to deplete his strength any more than I do, so I don't think he'll bother you."

Edge finally dragged his attention from her. "Thanks. For everything. I'll find a way to pay you back."

Bourne smiled. "I'm counting on it." Then he left.

A few seconds later, Zane walked in. He looked grumpy. "I feel like indentured labor here. I paid for my room—even though some bastard ripped my door off—but I'm still expected to be at the beck and call of your Big Freaking Boss." He stopped at the foot of the bed and stared at Passion. "Who hit you?"

She couldn't answer him, but she appreciated the outrage and anger in his voice.

Edge answered for her. "Ted. But I'll make sure she's the last woman he touches."

Zane nodded and then got to work. He studied Passion for a few minutes, ignoring Edge's impatient mutterings. Then he reached out, touched her hand.

Power radiated from his touch, and suddenly she could move. Relief washed over her. "Ohmigod, thank you." She stretched her arms above her head and tipped her head back. "I'll never take the power to speak and move for granted again."

Then she remembered. "Ted is a fallen angel. He admitted it. Someone has to tell Bourne."

"Interesting. I'll let Bourne know." Zane turned to leave.

Talking made her face hurt more, but Passion had to ask. "How are things going with you and your dad?"

Zane winced at the word "dad." "He's trying, but the

snark keeps escaping when he's not paying attention. I'm convinced that my fatherless childhood was a blessing. If he'd been around, I probably would've committed patricide by the time I turned five. Or worse yet, I would've turned into a mini-Holgarth." The thought seemed to horrify him. He left.

Passion didn't have time to say anything to Edge before Sparkle showed up. It didn't matter what part she was playing—Nurse Sparkle or Sparkle the Handyman—she always dressed to impress. She wore black leather pants, black boots with four-inch heels, and a silky green top that was only half there. Glittery green earrings dangled almost to her shoulders.

Sparkle beckoned, and a man stepped into the room. The stones in her rings caught the light and almost blinded Passion. "This is Dan. He's going to fix your door." She speared Edge with a hard stare. "Along with all the other doors. *Expensive* doors." She waved Dan to work.

Then she walked over to the bed. For the first time, Passion noticed she was carrying a small tote bag.

Sparkle narrowed her eyes as she studied Passion's face. "Ted hit you?"

Passion nodded.

"Remind me to separate his sexual organs from his body the next time I see him."

Passion got the feeling she wasn't kidding.

"Is anything broken?" Sparkle touched her face with light fingers.

"I don't think so, but it hurts like a bitch."

Sparkle smiled. "I like how you're expanding your store of colorful language."

"I'm not in heaven anymore." Passion glanced at Edge, and something in his gaze promised that she could be. Very soon.

"I have an ice pack to help bring down the swelling. Don't leave it on your face too long." She dragged it out of her tote bag. "I also have some painkillers. Use them. And

I'll stop in the restaurant and order something good that won't require any serious chewing. Someone will bring it up." She dropped the pills on the bed. "Now, I have to find Mede and explain to him that even though I might be his cute little peppermint patty, and even though I live in terror of breaking my nails or scuffing my awesome designer shoes, I can fight like a berserker, and I fight dirty." She turned and swayed toward the door. She paused just before leaving. "Of course, you know that sex is a natural painkiller." On that final note, Dr. Stardust left.

"Go, Sparkle!" Passion smiled up at Edge. "Why don't you order room service for yourself? I guess Sparkle is taking care of me. I'll take the pain pills right before I eat."

He nodded, his expression thunderous. "If it doesn't hurt your face too much, I'd like to know what happened."

Passion widened her eyes. "You just reminded me. I forgot to tell any of them that Ted was the old woman who tried to help you the night he ramped up your urge to kill Ganymede. That's how he fooled me. He came out of his room, and all I saw was the old woman. He lured me into his room by telling me there was a bug inside he wanted me to kill." Quickly, she told him everything else.

When she finished, he simply nodded. "Ted had wards on the front door and all around the bathroom. Bourne was impressed with his magical talent." Edge's tone suggested that none of Ted's magic would save him in the end. "Let me order my food and tell Bourne about Ted's glamour. Not that he'll use the old woman one again. Then I need to get out of these wet clothes and take a shower."

When Edge emerged from the shower, he wore only jeans.

She tried not to stare. Her throbbing face didn't lessen her appreciation of that wide expanse of sculpted pecs and smooth muscle.

Passion forced her attention away from his body. She met his gaze. He grinned at her. She looked away. "I need a shower too."

After assuring Edge she was fine other than a sore face, she went into the bathroom—okay, so the bathroom creeped her out—and took a hot shower. Then she pulled on her nightgown and put on her robe. Those homey touches, along with feeling that she'd washed off all of Ted's evil, made her feel almost normal again.

Trying to ignore Edge, who lay sprawled on the couch staring at Sweetie Pie, she climbed into bed and propped herself up with pillows.

Edge glanced over at her. "The plant looks a little wilted."

Passion refused to meet his gaze. "Guess she hasn't been getting her plant food of choice."

The food arrived a few minutes later, and Edge joined her in bed to eat his. Passion took her pills and finally acknowledged that she felt safe—from Ted, from the avenging angels, and from her own fears. Because of Edge.

She watched as he took their plates and piled them on the coffee table. Then he returned to the bed. She stared unblinkingly at the smooth play of muscles beneath all that gorgeous skin as he moved. He stood beside the bed and pulled off his jeans before climbing into bed beside her. She enjoyed that too.

He reached out to turn off his light and she did the same. Then they lay there in the middle of all that silence. Finally, she couldn't stand it anymore. She turned onto her side facing him.

"Did I ever tell you about Sweetie Pie?" Even with the pills, she felt too wound up to sleep.

The noise he made could've been laughter. "Yes, I know about Cinn's plants. Is that Sweetie Pie over near the window?"

"Yes. She lost four more leaves."

"That's sad."

His soft laughter was a sensual back rub. She relaxed into it.

"I feel guilty."

"Hmm? I can see why you'd feel that way. Keeping her healthy is a serious responsibility."

"That's what I thought." Long, long, long pause. "I figured maybe we could try Sparkle's natural painkiller."

18

"What about this?" Edge rolled onto his side, facing her. He gently cupped her cheek.

She sighed. "All of me wants you, but my mouth will have to take a rain check for the night. No heavy lifting. I guess some delicate nibbling will be okay, though." If she had anything to say about it, her mouth would be all over him next time. *Next time?* Would there be one? "At least the pills are starting to kick in."

"What else do you want, Passion?" He tugged at her nightgown. "This is a token covering. Take it off."

"What else do I want?" She did some creative wiggling until he was able to slip the nightgown over her head. "How about making love with you at every attraction in Live the Fantasy?"

His soft laughter touched her with deliciously dark excitement.

"The scope of your wants boggles the mind, but I'm nothing if not accommodating. We can check the castle off your list tonight." He pushed the covers aside, his gaze sliding the length of her bared body. "I'll be the savage laird of the castle, and you can be the helpless maiden captured as you stupidly wandered the dark forest picking berries."

"Wait, wait." She tried to marshal her thoughts, but they kept scattering in the face of all that hard male flesh. "That is so sexist. How about me being the lairdess of the castle and you're my captured warrior?"

"There's no such thing as a lairdess." He punctuated his argument by cupping her breast and rubbing the pad of his thumb back and forth, back and forth across her nipple.

"Well, there should be." She almost hummed with sensual bliss at the warm friction of his skin against hers. Her nipple was a super-sensitized nub of pleasure/pain. "Oh, and there's one more thing I want."

"Hmm?" His concentration seemed to be wandering from the conversation.

"Pay attention." She leaned close and kissed a path along his jaw to get him back on track. "This time I want it to count. No false starts. That means no turning back time, or Fantasy Fulfiller stealing our images and slapping them onto the big screen."

His smile was a flash of white in the darkness. "It will definitely count, sweetheart."

"Good. Too bad we're stuck in here. A castle love scene should have lots of atmosphere. You know, knights in armor, the clash of swords, a deadly villain. That kind of stuff. One of Holgarth's fantasies would be fun." Having the freedom to touch any part of his body was even more fun. She reached down to stroke his muscular bare-bare-gloriously-bare thigh as she considered fantasies. But it was growing harder to concentrate on much of anything other than her exploding senses.

He raised one brow. "With all that going on, wouldn't our lovemaking get lost in the action? I warn you, I'll never blend in with the secondary characters." His smile widened. "I love playing deadly villains, though." He leaned close to kiss the sensitive spot right behind her ear.

"Villains are more creative, more compelling, more interesting than plain vanilla heroes."

"Oh, yes." She breathed out on a shuddering sigh. The touch of his mouth on any part of her body flipped on her sensory switch.

"You know, Murmur thinks I'm a one-trick pony. But I have skills he doesn't know about." Edge kissed the corner of her mouth and then slid his tongue across her lower lip.

He tasted of all that was wild and untamed, of things wicked and wonderful. She opened her mouth as he kissed her lips softly and then moved on. "I love a man with skills. Show me." *Everything. Now.*

"We'll need protection against the thing that's attacking the castle."

He covered her breast with his mouth and flicked the nipple back and forth with his tongue. She forgot all about the big bad as she stifled a moan.

"Castle gates badly in need of shoring up should do it. What's the fun if they're strong enough to withstand anything? Danger is the red pepper we sprinkle on our pizza." He kissed a path over her stomach, pausing to swirl his tongue in her navel.

Castle gates? What the heck was he talking about? She blinked. No, those were definitely not castle gates at the foot of the bed. Castle gates that were already partly open and looked as though they would fall over at any minute. "How did you—"

"Shh." He placed his finger across her lips.

Well, if he was going to wave temptation right in front of her face . . . She glided her tongue the length of his finger. Then she glanced at him from partly lowered lids. "That's just a coming attraction. My mouth might not be fully functional right now, but my tongue is just fine."

"Give me a minute to remember what I was saying." He traced ever-widening circles on her hip with the tip of one finger. "Oh, yes, danger. Something big, something powerful is trying to get past those gates. Our minutes of pleasure are numbered, so we'll have to cram every sexual nugget we can into our lovemaking." He shifted his gaze to the less-than-sturdy gates.

Passion followed his gaze. She sucked in her breath on a terrified gasp.

A dragon peered in through the cracks in the gates. Glowing golden eyes the size of saucers looked as though they were sizing her up for tonight's appetizer. "Please tell me that's an illusion." Frantically, she searched for the door. It wasn't there. The part of the room beyond the foot of the bed was hazy and indistinct except for the monstrous dragon.

"It's real."

The dragon blew out a puff of smoke to emphasize how real it was.

"Relax. It's a construct of my mind. I control it." He paused. "Probably."

Her heart rate slowed slightly. "I get it. This is our own Castle of Dark Dreams fantasy. You're the heroic warrior who will slay the dragon and save the laird's daughter—who is perfectly capable of saving herself—before giving her an orgasm she'll remember until she dies and even beyond." For a moment, she thought longingly of her bag of chocolates. No, not this time. The dragon's breath would melt them all before she could even begin her Dance of the Seven Hershey's Kisses.

Edge inched toward the foot of the bed, a journey marked by exploratory kisses that touched her flesh with heat and filled her lower stomach with heavy anticipation.

He must have touched her "open" button with those sensual lips, because she instinctively rolled onto her back and parted her legs. She was ready, had been ready for her entire existence. He leaned over her to nibble the flesh of her inner thigh. Her legs trembled.

"That would be too stereotypical. No, actually the dragon is your shape-shifting mother who thinks no mercenary warrior bastard would ever be good enough for her daughter. She plans to fry me to a crisp. She's right. I'm evil to the core, and I plan to seduce you over and over and over." His breathing was growing labored.

Passion bit back laughter. "So does Mama get you?"

"I haven't decided yet."

The dragon roared, but Passion wasn't paying attention.

Edge rose over her in one smooth movement—straddling her legs, slipping his hands beneath her bottom, and lifting her to where he could use his mouth to full advantage.

Had he done this the first time in the greenhouse? The first time that officially had never happened but would always mark the beginning of her real life? She didn't try to remember, because she knew that every time with him would always be the first, the best, the one carved into her heart forever.

He drew a pattern of almost unbearable sensation along her inner thigh with his tongue. She whimpered encouragement as he neared . . . What? The epicenter of every nerve ending in her body? That's what it felt like. Passion simply stopped breathing as he slid the tip of his tongue over that super-sensitized nub of flesh, *over every emotion she'd never felt, would only ever feel with him*. She clenched around her need. And when he finally slipped his tongue inside her, twenty fire-breathing dragons could have been tearing down the castle gates and she wouldn't have cared.

Not enough. She wanted more. Mind and body were in perfect sync. *Never* enough. She wanted her hands on his body, her mouth touching his skin.

It almost killed her to do it, but she tangled her fingers in his hair and tugged him back up to where she could reach him. He cupped her bottom, massaging a message of fast-fading control into her flesh as she ran her fingers over his smooth-muscled chest.

She followed her fingers' path with her tongue and swore she could taste his desire on his damp, sweat-sheened skin. The scent of the soap he'd used in the shower clung to him, some sort of citrusy smell. She'd find out what it was and buy cases of it, because the scent would always bring her back to this moment, this man.

Mama Dragon's roar lent urgency to her fingers, her mouth. She didn't even pause to enjoy each ridged stomach muscle. She spent all of her remaining time torturing him with her tongue. Who knew she had a talent for this? There, right at the base of his cock, when she pressed her tongue to that particular spot, he groaned. And when she swirled her tongue around the head and then gently nipped, he shuddered and gasped. She wished she had more time to discover all his sexual hot spots, but she didn't.

Passion could feel pressure building, warning that a slow and relaxed loving wasn't going to be an option. "Why can't we slow things down, make it last longer?" She ran her hand over his inner thigh in a frantic effort to feel all of him. At once.

"Maybe because a dragon is about to crash through those gates. More likely because I want you too much. I'm a greedy bastard."

His breath was warm on her neck and sent sensual shivers skittering down her spine.

She moaned as he nibbled a path around her breast before closing his lips over the nipple. At the same time, his fingers slid once again between her legs to tease and torture.

"I can see the colors of sin." Passion gasped as he pushed one finger into her. "But not my own. Lust is blue, greed is yellow. Right now I bet bright green is spinning around me at warp speed." Her laughter was choked off as he gently nipped her nipple.

"What color am I?" He seemed to be having trouble breathing between each word.

Rational thought was tough right now, but she still knew she didn't want to tell him. She could lie, she could . . .

Passion cleared her mind for the moment it took to really look at what swirled around him. She blinked. Dark blue. *Blue?* Passion stared harder. Blue with only a few streaks of black. Ted had been wrong. Edge wasn't irredeemable. Tears filled her eyes. Something hard and brittle shattered inside her, allowing relief to seep through. The relief wasn't for her, because she was way beyond allowing a color to stop what she felt for him. Her relief was for the man she . . . loved.

"You're blue. Deep, deep blue. Lots of lust going on."

Her emotions spiked at the same time as her hunger— for the feel of him buried deep inside her, for the heat of his body pressed against hers, for the knowing that it would never get better than this.

"Now would be nice." Translation: *I'll die right now if you don't.*

He didn't waste energy answering her. Instead, he once again knelt above her. She raised her hips to meet his expected thrust.

Edge grasped her hips, but just as he pressed the head of his cock between her thighs, just as she spread her legs wider and felt her body opening to him, just as she knew that waiting even one more second would shatter her . . . He paused.

Damn, damn, damn. "What part of now wasn't clear?" Hyperventilation was a real possibility.

"Bourne turned back time. No matter what you *remember* happening, it never happened in real time. You're a virgin again." His explanation was a harsh rasp.

"So I'm unique. I get to be a virgin twice. Please, please, *please*." She was beyond more coherent conversation.

He eased into her, the same remembered sensation of stretching, being filled. And when the pain came, it didn't matter because the sky was falling, the ground opening, the earth shattering around her. The thunder booming in her ears was her heartbeat, and lightning flashes zigzagged behind her closed lids. It was her sexual apocalypse. This was how it felt for the world to end, not with a bang but a giganormous orgasm.

She opened her eyes as it rolled toward her—a Mount St. Helens of erotic ecstasy, gathering speed and power, pressure building right before it blew. Passion wanted to see his face when it happened. Edge's movements grew more urgent as his body's rhythm took over—almost drawing out, plunging back into her, repeat and repeat and repeat. Faster, harder, and she arched to meet him with each thrust. Everything blurred—his face, her thoughts, life as she knew it.

Pleasure exploded. She froze in mid-arch, stopped breathing, her existence shrinking to the indescribable sensations of spasm after spasm after spasm.

Somewhere on another planet, she heard Edge's shout of release. But she could only focus on her own spasms as they slowly faded. She was probably working on some yellow in her personal sin rainbow, because she was definitely greedy. Something that felt this good shouldn't end so soon.

Passion collapsed back onto the bed. Edge rolled onto his back beside her. She rested her head on his chest, feeling his heartbeat slowing, his breathing easing, and said the words she'd never planned on saying. "I love you."

He remained silent for so long that she thought her words might've been muffled against his chest, that he hadn't heard her.

Finally, he drew in a deep breath. "Sometimes when people make love, they say things they wouldn't under other circumstances."

She took a moment to think that through. "You believe what I said was the orgasm talking?" Okay, that made her mad. "Ask me an hour from now, a month from now, a year from now and I'll say the same thing." She shouldn't have said it at all. He obviously didn't feel the same way, and now she'd put him on the spot. "Just forget it."

The dragon roared. That was it. She might not know how to handle the situation she'd just created with Edge, but she could deal with one freaking dragon. Crawling to the foot of the bed, she rose to her knees and punched the dragon in the nose. "Back off, Mama."

The dragon along with the castle gates disappeared. Behind her, she heard Edge's laughter. But now that she could see the rest of the room again, something else caught her attention. "Edge, look at Sweetie Pie."

"What the hell?"

The plant was at least a foot taller than before they made love. It was a bushy burst of sensual satisfaction. "We did that." Passion couldn't help her spurt of pride.

"Come back to bed. And, no, we can't take her with us to wherever we plan to make love."

Happy, she returned to his side and snuggled in. He planned to make love with her again, and Sweetie Pie was healthy again. Maybe she should keep her mouth shut for now. Why take a chance of ruining her present glow?

Edge evidently didn't have any qualms, though. "What kind of existence would you have with me, Passion?"

She'd like to find out.

"Would you spend each night following me around so you could bring the people I killed back to life? How long before you hated me? Your hate is the one thing I couldn't stand." He smoothed his hand over her hair.

"We are what we are, Edge. You weren't given a chance to choose your path." She allowed the steady rhythm of his heart to lull her. "I couldn't *not* love you. When I was in Ted's bathroom, I only thought of reaching out to one person. You. It would always be you."

She felt his sigh.

"I knew why I was created, but emotions never entered into what I did. I killed, but I didn't *feel*. When the Big Boss stopped me from slaughtering whole villages so that I could destroy one person, I didn't understand. I was Death in its purist form—merciless, focused on the act not the person. Now? I remember the name of each person I destroy. I kill from a distance whenever I can. Sometimes I have . . . regrets."

Passion reached out and clasped his hand.

"For you, and *only* for you, I'll stop killing no matter what the consequences." He held up his hand to stop her instinctive denial. "Don't try to talk me out of it. Let me do this for us." Edge took a deep breath. "Please."

He hadn't said he loved her, but he'd said much more. If he was no longer Death, he was of no use to Bourne. Would Bourne destroy Edge? He might feel he had to make an example of Edge so that others wouldn't walk away from their assigned paths too. Was Bourne that heartless? Passion realized she really knew nothing about who the Big Boss really was.

"We'll face Bourne together. And don't give me an argument or else you'll get some of the same that I gave to Mama Dragon." Did she sound fierce enough?

His soft chuckle warmed her heart as he pulled her into the curve of his body.

"Let's get some rest while we can." A few minutes later, his breathing slowed. He was asleep.

Passion stared into the darkness and made a promise to the man sleeping beside her. Neither Ted nor Bourne would take Edge from her. She might be Life, but if she had to kill for her man, so be it.

19

The roar jerked Edge from a dream of making love with Passion. Beside him, he felt her sit up.

"What's that?" Sleep still roughened her voice.

Edge was already leaping from the bed. "The gargoyles. Get dressed."

Even as he pulled on jeans and a T-shirt, the roars stopped. "Ted must've shut them down, but they did their job. They warned us." He yanked on his boots.

Suddenly, Bourne was in his head. From the shocked look on Passion's face, he was in hers too.

"I was wrong. He decided on a preemptive strike. It's two hours until dawn, so Dacian will be awake to fight with us." Bourne didn't sound happy about being wrong. *"His avenging angels are in the castle. I was also wrong about something else. He did find demonic help. He's brought twelve hellhounds through the portal."* There was a pause. *"I don't have to tell you what to do. Spare the angels if you can, but feel free to send the hellhounds home with their tails between their legs."* Another pause. *"If Ted wins, don't let him talk you into joining him. Leave the*

castle and regroup. Choose a smart leader. Don't regret me. I've had a helluva run." Then he was gone.

The scariest part of Bourne's message was that he'd even consider the possibility of losing. He must have upped his estimate of Ted's power.

As much as Edge sometimes railed against Bourne, he couldn't imagine Ted taking his place. The Big Boss was, well, the Big Boss. No cheap phony archangel could replace him. Bourne had survived for tens of thousands of years. Edge couldn't conceive of him no longer existing.

"What's a hellhound?" Passion was almost dressed. "Ted doled out information on a need-to-know basis."

Edge strapped his sword to his waist. With the power he wielded, he didn't need any other weapons. "Demonic dogs. Huge. Black fur, glowing red eyes, super strength and speed. They can get into your mind. Do not, I repeat, do *not* stare into their eyes. Meet one's gaze and you die."

What he didn't say was that she wouldn't have to worry about the hellhounds. He'd leave her safely in Dacian's apartment with Cinn behind a locked and warded door.

Within ten minutes after being jarred from their sleep, Edge and Passion were racing down the stairs. He could hear the sounds of battle rising from the great hall before he even reached it.

Once on the ground floor, Edge took a side corridor that bypassed whatever was happening in the hall, and then led her down the stairs to Dacian's apartment.

"What're we doing here? Why didn't you give me a weapon?" She sounded suspicious.

Dacian opened the door before Edge could answer. The vampire backed away so they could enter and then closed the door. Cinn sat on the couch, glowering.

Edge couldn't put off telling Passion any longer. "You and Cinn don't have the battle skills to survive out there. Stay here. Lock the door behind us. We'll send Zane to ward the door. Cinn will give you a weapon." Not that it would do any good if Ted got past the wards. But he had to believe that wouldn't happen.

And in probably the first cowardly act of his existence, Edge turned and strode toward the door where Dacian waited.

Cinn got off a parting shot. "I love you, vampire, even though you're being a domineering jerk about this. Don't lose your head, or else I'll have to turn my plants loose on all those losers up there."

As much as Edge wanted to escape before Passion could weaken his resolve with an argument, he paused before closing the door.

Tell her. Say the fucking words. He couldn't. If he didn't make it through this fight, he didn't want her saddled with his final words of love. Better that she think he never cared that much. "Don't leave the room." He recognized the outrage in her eyes. "Please. I'll be able to focus on keeping Bourne alive if I know you're safe." Then he closed the door behind him. He didn't wait to hear if one of them locked it.

He raced up the stairs with Dacian. The great hall was a mass of bodies locked in battle. Edge saw Zane nearby. The sorcerer had three of Ted's angels suspended in midair. Their curses didn't include words like "heck" and "darn." They'd shed their angelic natures pretty fast.

Edge managed to catch Zane's attention and nodded at him. The sorcerer left the three hanging in the air while he headed down to ward Dacian's door.

Sounds of battle reached him from other parts of the castle, but he'd stay here because Bourne was here. It was his job to help keep the Big Boss alive.

Bourne stood on the raised platform that normally held the long banquet table. He didn't wave his arms, didn't yell or chant, didn't do anything but stand there. And still *things* happened. Edge hated to admit it, but his leader had always been there for his people even when said people were busy cursing him out. Once again, Bourne had their backs.

A hellhound that had managed to sneak up on Holgarth

as the wizard was busy knocking an angel over the head with his staff—there were times when magic wasn't nearly as much fun as an old-fashioned beat down—suddenly exploded in a shower of blood, fur, and other unidentifiable bits.

Four angels who thought they had the numbers in their favor as they leaped on Dacian ended up bouncing off the wall at the opposite end of the hall. Meanwhile, Bourne stood staring into space—silent and untouched.

Ganymede, who'd chosen to fight in human form, was near the courtyard door. He was pulverizing five angels at once with bursts of energy that flashed and boomed. Looked like he was having a blast.

Near Ganymede, Sparkle fought in her own way. An angel, who'd evidently fallen to her special brand of magic, sprawled on the floor at Sparkle's feet. He looked up at her from sex-glazed eyes while he clasped her ankle in a desperate grip. Edge snorted when the guy licked her ankle.

Sparkle was into multitasking. Ignoring the man at her feet, she was pummeling another angel with the stiletto she'd slipped from one foot. Primitive but effective.

Bain was methodically destroying the hellhounds one by one. Edge had always suspected that Bain logged lots of frequent-flier miles to and from hell. So who better to kick demon butt?

Edge continued to scan the hall even as he fought his way toward Bourne. Where the hell was Ted?

A man standing in a corner, one shoulder braced against the wall, caught Edge's attention. Murmur. The demon was smiling. This was entertainment to him. Bastard.

Edge punctuated the opinion by flattening an angel who tried to tackle him. The guy was lucky he wasn't warmed up. Edge hadn't even drawn his sword yet. He stepped over his enemy. Bourne had said not to kill them, but Edge was making sure they'd stay down for a long time.

The enemy who challenged Edge next wasn't as easy to dismiss. He didn't fling energy blasts or shout challenges as he swung a big-ass sword. He stood in front of Edge with no weapon. Creepy. But a hostile was still a hostile, and Edge got ready to take him out of the battle.

Then Edge felt it. *Love.* An almost physical ache. It flowed over him, around him, coating every part of his body and soul. Not sexual. It was the feeling you had for a parent—not that he'd ever had one. The man was big, like all the cosmic troublemakers, and Edge knew they'd make an unbeatable fighting team. This guy would always have his back. The angel smiled, promising that they could be buddies forever if Edge would just fight at his side tonight.

Edge almost did it. But something stopped him at the last minute. He wasn't one of the most powerful trouble-makers for nothing. He grabbed on to the thought fighting to surface, the warning to wake up and smell the trap. He backed away.

The angel's smile died. "How did you know?"

Edge didn't answer, but asked his own question. "What are you? Not an angel, but there's something about you . . ."

The angel tensed. "My power is love. I can make anyone love me." His expression turned sly. "Or someone else." He shook his head. "Except you, evidently." He drew his sword. "I guess I go to Plan B now. It's called tough love. But first, tell me who you are."

Edge knew his smile was slow and evil. "I'm Death." Then he slapped the guy's sword away and punched him so hard that he hit the floor and lay still. "See, love *doesn't* conquer all."

Something bothered Edge as he continued to battle his way across the hall. These phony angels all seemed to fight just like the cosmic troublemakers. They were big, tough, and seemed to have lots of different skills. Why was that knowledge important?

Edge noticed a lot of blood, but only two dead bodies. They were both troublemakers he didn't recognize, and it looked as though the hellhounds had gotten them. Not that there weren't a bunch of bodies littering the room, but none of them were dead. Okay, so Ted must've told his guys to disable but not to kill. Made sense. Ted wouldn't be much of a Big Boss if he didn't have anyone to boss. He wouldn't be happy about the kills, but Ted couldn't control demons the way he had his . . . His what? The fake angels were powerful, but they didn't seem to have any real battle experience.

All thought vanished as he saw a massive black body hurtling toward him from the corner of his eye. At the same time, a voice spoke in his mind.

"Look into my eyes, Death. We are the same, you and I. We kill, and we enjoy it. Look at me and see the truth."

"Don't think I'll do the eye-staring thing." As Edge pivoted to face the hellhound, his sword was already raised. "And wrong, dickhead. I don't enjoy it. But, hey, I might enjoy *this*." His swing completed its deadly arc and took the hound's head with it. At the same time, Edge loosed a flare of power that incinerated the remains. "I'd forgotten how much fun a good decapitation was."

The fighting had reached a ferocious peak. Edge tried to keep from slipping in the blood or tripping over unconscious bodies. The three guys whom Zane had left flailing in midair were still there. Where was Zane? A prickle of unease tried to surface.

This would be over soon anyway. Sure, there were lots more of the bad guys. But except for the hellhounds, the rest just didn't seem to have the savagery, the killer instinct that the troublemakers had. *Bad for them, good for us.*

Edge didn't have long to savor thoughts of victory, though. He'd kept an eye on the stairs leading down to Dacian's apartment throughout the fight. No matter how much he tried to tell himself that Passion was safe, he still worried.

So he saw the exact moment when Ted appeared at the top of the stairs with Cinn and Passion. He knew it was Ted because power rolled off him in waves. Both women had the same frozen look that Passion had worn when he'd found her in the bathroom. Only this time Ted was allowing them enough movement to walk.

Fear clawed at his gut. He'd left Passion in a safe place, only it hadn't been safe from Ted. Where was Zane? Edge could see Holgarth fighting his way toward the stairs. He was worried about his son too.

"Stop." Once again, Bourne silenced everyone with one word.

Ted grinned. "You're good. I usually have to shout a few times before everyone shuts up."

Fury pushed aside fear. Edge clenched his hands into fists. This was the asshole who'd hurt Passion. Now he was standing there with a grin on his face like he'd won the battle because he held two women hostage. And one of those women belonged to Edge.

Something moved in Edge, something he thought he'd left behind thousands of years ago. Bloodlust. Blind, merciless, *hungry*.

"So while the rest of your people were fighting, you were looking for someone to hide behind." Contempt dripped from Bourne's words. "Looks as though you found two of them. I suppose a big man like you *needs* two women to shield him."

Ted's expression turned ugly. "You don't deserve to be boss. Here's what I'll offer. Tell your people to stand down while you and I battle it out. Because in the end, it isn't about them. It's only about who is strong enough to lead."

Bourne shrugged. "Fine. They won't interfere." Anticipation gleamed in his eyes.

Ted looked almost gleeful. "I'm Fallen. Have you ever battled one of us?"

"No, I haven't." Bourne looked unimpressed. "But then, you haven't fought anyone like me either."

"How do you know?" Ted's belligerence was leaking through.

"Because there *is* no one like me."

"What the hell are you, anyway?" Ted waved that away. "Never mind. It doesn't matter. Let's do it."

Everyone else except for probably Dacian and Edge were watching Bourne and Ted. Edge was staring at Passion. She stared back at him, and something in her eyes made him narrow his. She kept rolling her eyes toward the ceiling of the great hall. Over and over. What the . . .

He looked up. Just in time to see five angels suddenly appear in midair. They floated just below the ceiling. Too late, Edge realized what had happened. Ted had held back his most powerful angels. This wasn't going to be a fair fight.

But he reacted a second too late. All five angels loosed energy at Bourne in deadly waves. Edge could hear what sounded like a sonic boom as each blast hit him. Bourne staggered as he looked up, trying to fight back, but that was the moment Ted had been waiting for. Power poured from him, coalescing into a shimmering ball of killing force that he launched at Bourne.

The deadly ball exploded on impact with Bourne's body. For moments that seemed to stretch on forever, blinding light enveloped Bourne. And when the light faded, he lay on the floor.

Edge *felt* him die. The tearing of the bond that had connected him to the Big Boss since he first emerged from his primeval past almost brought Edge to his knees. Agony and an aching emptiness where the bond had rested made him gasp for breath. He'd never known, never realized that Bourne had filled so much of him, had meant so much to him.

"All of you are now mine. I'm the strongest among you. None can challenge me." Ted waited only a moment, secure in his belief that he was the most powerful in the hall. "Both forces combined under my leadership will shape this planet into something better." His voice was filled with triumph.

Self-important prick. *Something better?* Edge didn't think so. He was only saying that to maintain the charade for the dumb angel wannabes who followed him. Ted was all about power for Ted.

Hunger for vengeance was the lit match held to the primal fury boiling in Edge. His woman, no, his *love*, was frozen beside that bastard. His leader was dead because Ted had no honor, couldn't beat Bourne in a fair fight. And it all would stop.

Now.

Edge glanced at Ganymede. The chaos bringer nodded, giving his okay for Edge to avenge Bourne. He understood that it was Edge's right to punish the one who'd hurt Passion.

"You cowardly son of a bitch, you only *think* you're the most powerful here." Edge stepped forward as he issued his challenge.

Ted glanced at the ceiling, ready to order the hovering angels to strike Edge down, but another voice interrupted.

"I love games as much as the next demon, but this cheating has to stop. Takes away from the fun. So I'll just even the playing field a little." Murmur sounded mildly annoyed.

The demon pushed away from the wall long enough to focus on the five angels. "Come on down with the rest of us."

Edge wasn't sure what happened next, but for a moment weird music seemed to fill the hall. Then it did what music shouldn't be able to do. It almost sounded as though it compacted into a thin stream of screaming sound aimed at the five.

They shrieked as they clamped their hands over their ears, and then they fell. Everyone scrambled to avoid being hit. When the angels landed, they lay still.

Murmur shook his head. "See, no one appreciates good music nowadays." He nodded at Edge. "Do what you have to do."

"Thanks." Edge was starting to see the benefit of demonic connections.

For a moment, there was silence. And then all hell broke loose. Fury at their leader's death drove the cosmic troublemakers. They fought now with deadly intent, not much caring if they killed every one of Ted's fake angels.

"It's just me and you now, Ted." Edge started toward him.

Fear tore at Passion, but she couldn't move, couldn't do anything to stop it. Ted would kill Edge. She could see Dacian fighting his way toward them, but he wouldn't be any match for Ted either.

Then she took a deep breath and tried to calm herself. How did she know Edge would lose? He was Death. She had to believe, to have faith, that he'd survive this. But God, she was sick of being helpless.

She watched Edge draw closer, moving in confident, deliberate strides. Silent screams filled her mind as Ted drew his power around him. She wanted to close her eyes, but that would be the coward's way. If Edge had the courage to fight Ted, then she had the guts to watch. And if Ted killed the man she loved, Passion would find a way to destroy him.

Edge stopped a short distance from his enemy. Ted started to glow with the power he was drawing to himself.

"Give it your best shot, because one shot is all you'll get." Edge seemed amused.

"Surrender." Ted nodded toward where Bourne's body still lay on the platform. "He was the only one who might have matched me. If any of you were stronger, you would've overthrown him long ago."

"Maybe none of us were power-hungry bastards who cheated because they couldn't win in a straight-up fight."

Ted laughed. "My motto? The end justifies the means. Always."

Suddenly, Dacian was beside Passion. She realized that while Edge and Ted had riveted her attention, the vampire had carried Cinn away. Now, Dacian scooped her up and moved her to where he'd deposited his wife. Ted didn't notice.

Zane was there. He looked a little beat up and a lot

embarrassed. "Ted took me down before I could get the ward up. I'm sorry he got to both of you."

"Just break the spell," Dacian ordered.

Nodding, Zane touched both Cinn's and Passion's hands. Like the last time, suddenly she could move and talk.

"Ohmigod, we can't let Edge fight Ted." What could she do?

Dacian shook his head. "He wouldn't want anyone to interfere." He offered her an intense glance. "He's doing this for you as much as for Bourne."

Passion blinked. "Why?"

"Ted hurt you." The vampire seemed to think that said it all.

She didn't have time to sort through that statement now. Passion stood. If she couldn't help Edge, then she'd help someone he cared about.

Passion looked with despair at the mob she'd have to fight her way through. She'd never get to Bourne in time.

"I think this has gone on long enough."

Startled, Passion turned to see Sparkle beside her. "What?"

"This crap." Sparkle waved at the men still fighting. "Look." She held up one of her stilettos. "I broke the heel on the head of the last dumbass I fought." She shook the offending shoe in front of Passion's eyes and then narrowed her gaze. "You need to get to the Big Boss."

"Fast."

Sparkle faced the room and shouted, "Everyone fighting for Ted just got kicked in the nuts."

Shocked, Passion widened her eyes as every one of Ted's men dropped to the floor clutching themselves and writhing in agony. Only Ted's women remained standing. It didn't take long for the troublemakers to overcome them.

Passion stared at Sparkle. "You could've done that at any time? Why didn't you?"

Sparkle sighed. "I'll explain about men and their egos at another time. Let's get to Bourne."

A few seconds later, as Passion knelt beside Bourne with her hands on his chest, she watched the man she loved face Ted.

"You assumed that no one but Bourne could destroy you. You were wrong." Edge's voice had changed, grown deeper as it filled the hall. "I am Death. And tonight I claim you." The words had the ring of ancient ritual in them.

Passion shuddered.

For the first time, Ted looked a little unsure. He covered it with bluster. "I guess I'll have to find a new Death now."

Edge said nothing. He stood there as Ted prepared to destroy him.

Terror lived and breathed in Passion as she reached out to Edge's mind. *"I love you. Don't you dare die."*

She watched his lips quirk up.

"I love you too, angel. Should've admitted it before this. And if you have to write my epitaph, don't forget to say what a great lover I was."

"That's not funny." She knew her smile was watery.

He *loved* her. The knowing was a warm and joyful fulfillment. Tears filled her eyes. She would *not* lose him. Instinct told her he would be the only one to complete her life, no matter how long that life lasted.

Then everything happened at once. Ted tried to reprise his glowing-ball act. He watched with smug satisfaction as the ball exploded against Edge the same way it had with Bourne.

Passion knew she screamed, but she couldn't stop it. And when the glow died, she expected to see Edge lying on the floor.

He wasn't. Edge stood staring at Ted, a half smile on his lips. "Oops. It's a little harder when you don't have five of your people helping you."

Ted looked shocked. He narrowed his eyes and glared at Edge. Passion figured he was either trying to put the big freeze on him or control his thoughts like he'd done in Sparkle's store.

"Not working, Ted. I feel you tapping on my mind, but I'm not opening the door. You caught me by surprise the first time. But I'm not surprised anymore. Too bad for you." Edge's smile widened. "Now it's my turn."

Passion could almost see Ted assessing his chances. He'd already expended a lot of energy, and his forces were beaten. She knew what his next step would be. Passion waited for him to dematerialize. He didn't, and she could tell from his expression that he'd tried.

"Oh, no, Ted. You're not leaving until I'm ready." Edge stepped into Ted's space. And before Ted could react, he'd picked the other man up with one hand and held him suspended in the air. "You hurt the woman I love. You murdered Bourne. And for these crimes, you're history."

Ted struggled in Edge's grip, but he didn't seem to have any strength left. Panic filled his eyes. "Let me go. I'll leave and never come back. I'll—"

"Oh, yes, you will definitely leave and never come back."

And suddenly Ted disappeared.

"Where'd he go?" someone asked.

Edge turned to search for Passion just as Bourne's body jerked. He drew in a deep breath. Passion closed her eyes, relief washing over her. Both Edge and Bourne were alive.

Bourne stared up at her. "Thank you."

For just a moment, Passion *saw* him. Not physically, but as a brilliant energy burst in her mind. And the seeing took her breath away. "What are you?" She could barely force the words past her lips.

His gaze never left her even as his answer filled her mind. *"What you would never imagine."*

She waited.

"But some things should remain unknown."

She nodded.

Edge reached them and crouched down beside Passion. He put his arm around her and pulled her close. His answer was more for Bourne than the troublemaker who'd asked the question. "Ted dematerialized, but I made sure he'll never materialize anywhere else. All that he was is scattered across the universe now."

"Good." Bourne sat up. "I'm getting too old for this. Help me up."

Ganymede had joined them. He pulled Bourne to his feet. "What do we do with all Ted's people?"

Bourne scanned the room, his gaze resting on the two bodies of his own people. His expression was grim. He glanced at Passion.

She shook her head. "Sorry. Their souls have left."

He nodded. "I don't have the energy to deal with Ted's people right now. We'll send them through the portal to join Kemp and Hope until I've recovered. The worst they can do there is trash my home." He didn't look happy at that prospect.

Bourne looked at Ganymede. "You have the power to open the portal and send them through."

Ganymede nodded. "We need more nights like this, Boss. You know, sort of recreational periods where we can cut loose and kick ass."

"Glad you enjoyed it." Bourne still looked weak. "Take care of Ted's people and then join me in the meeting room. I want Edge, Passion, and Sparkle there too."

Then he raised his voice so everyone in the room could hear him. "I'm proud of you. I know I don't praise you often . . ."

"Like never," someone in the crowd muttered.

Everyone laughed.

Bourne laughed with them. "Okay, I'll try to do better from now on. But know that through all the centuries, I've recognized your greatness. And if I'd died permanently tonight, I know that you would've carried on because every one of you is that strong."

He waited for the cheers to die down. "Now bring our fallen comrades to me."

Silence fell as they gently laid the two men at his feet. Sadness wrapped around her. She hadn't saved them.

"You can't save everyone."

Edge's whispered comfort warmed her, eased her guilt.

Bourne crouched beside the bodies. Sorrow seemed to reveal the ancient being Passion knew lived behind that beautiful face. "Thank you for your sacrifice. I release you from your service, and I send you to your reward. We will always honor your memory." The bodies disappeared. He lowered his head, and everyone waited in silence.

Finally, he straightened and looked over the cosmic troublemakers watching him. "Go. Relax and celebrate." He seemed to consider his words. "Don't celebrate too much. I want Galveston to still be here tomorrow."

Passion felt the release of tension. Except for the ones who would help Ganymede get Ted's people to the portal, the troublemakers left the hall.

Bourne looked at the others who'd fought with them. "Dacian, it's almost dawn. Get some sleep. I appreciate what you did tonight." His gaze moved on to Bain, Zane, and Holgarth. "I'll remember all of you."

They nodded. And Passion noticed that Holgarth's gaze kept returning to his son. She hoped they could work things out.

Edge spoke up. "Murmur brought down the five floating bastards."

Bourne smiled. "I owe you five floating bastards, Murmur."

Murmur's eyes lit. "This is the second favor you guys owe me. I'll have to visit more often."

Passion let everything drift past her while she thought about the monumental event that had happened tonight. *Edge loved her.* He really loved her. She rolled the words around in her mind and felt them melt into her heart. He'd said them, and she'd never let him take them back. She clasped his hand. "Let's get to the meeting room and see what Bourne wants. Then I'll tell you what I want."

His smile was a slow slide of sensual promise. "No matter how much you want, sweetheart, it'll only be a speck in the universe compared to my list."

20

Bourne sat at the head of the table in the small hotel meeting room. He waited as the last person took her seat. Sparkle.

"Where were you?" Ganymede was still in human form, and he didn't look happy to be here. He glanced at the others in the room. "Let's get this over with. I'm hungry."

Sparkle speared him with a death stare. "Hey, I sacrificed my favorite shoes to the cause tonight. I had to get another pair. So stuff it, Mede."

Edge smiled at Ganymede. "Looks like you've lost your honeybunny status."

Bourne took over. "I'll keep this short. I failed tonight."

"It was six against one. And they were all-powerful. Don't beat yourself up over this." Ganymede whispered an aside to Sparkle. "Have any candy in your purse?"

"No." Sparkle didn't look forgiving.

"Still, I should've anticipated that Ted would cheat." Bourne shook his head. "It'd been a long time since anyone challenged me. I'd grown complacent."

Edge voiced his thoughts. "Ted was strong, but you

could've taken him in a straight-up battle. I've been wondering . . ." He didn't quite know how to explain his thoughts. "His phony angels were as powerful as us. The one edge we had was our fighting experience. What are they?" He glanced at Passion. "What are you?" *Besides the woman I love.*

She leaned toward him. "I remember something I said to you a while back. We balance each other. I'm Life and you're Death. Do you think . . . ?"

Edge got it at the same time everyone else seemed to.

"They *are* us? Only instead of being cosmic trouble-makers, they're cosmic do-gooders?" Sparkle sounded horrified. "Oh. My. God. That means there's some tight-assed bitch in that crowd ready to undo all the bad I've accomplished. She'll bring together couples who're perfect for each other and encourage them to fall in love, marry, and only have sex in the missionary position. I feel like puking."

Ganymede shrugged. "I don't feel threatened."

"Not until one of them starts following you around to calm all that beautiful chaos you love so much. He'll probably try to put you on a diet, take away your ice cream, and encourage you to exercise." Sparkle looked as though the thought intrigued her.

Ganymede's eyes narrowed to dangerous slits. "Then he'll have a really short life span."

Bourne's gaze turned thoughtful. "You're right, Passion. It all makes sense now. I wondered why everyone I found instinctively chose chaos when I knew the universe always balanced things in some way." He looked excited. "They belong with us."

"Speak for yourself." Ganymede poked Sparkle. "Look in your purse. Maybe you have a pack of Life Savers in there somewhere."

With a resigned sigh, she peeked inside. "One Life Saver with lint stuck to it."

"I'll take it."

Bourne seemed to make an effort to pull himself away from thoughts of his new recruits. "I have two more things to discuss before I let you go." He focused on Edge. "Cinn's been nagging me about allowing you to resign from your position as Death."

Startled, Edge glanced at Passion.

She shrugged. "I might've mentioned that I'd appreciate her help." Then she returned to watching Bourne.

Bourne raked his fingers through his hair. "I've known for a while that you weren't happy with the job, but I have a problem. Death is an important position. If I let you walk away, who takes your place?" He looked troubled. "I owe you for tonight, and if I could, I'd give you something else to do."

Sparkle jumped to her feet. "Canis."

"Who?" Bourne sounded puzzled.

"Passion came to me for help in finding a way to free Edge. So I did some research. I found Canis, and I've already talked to him. He's powerful, and he's chomping at the bit to be Death." Sparkle glowed with triumph.

Edge looked at Passion. He raised one brow. "Is there anyone you *didn't* ask?"

"Well, I wanted you to be happy." She fidgeted. "And I couldn't do it by myself. So I went to the people I thought would be the most help." She looked up at him from beneath her lashes.

He tried to look pissed, but his lips lifted into a smile in spite of his best effort. Would he ever be able to stay mad at her? He hoped not.

"It might work." Bourne sat thinking. Finally, he nodded. "I'll do it. Edge, you can trade places with Canis."

Now for the big question. Edge took a deep breath. "So what does Canis do?"

Bourne looked amused. "Canis is in charge of fomenting chaos in the government. But he's been bored for a long time. Seems as though the politicians have done such a great job of creating their own chaos that he hasn't had anything to do." Now Bourne was openly grinning. "In fact, you can probably keep your job here. And if the two parties ever start agreeing with each other about anything, you can take a quick trip to DC. But I wouldn't count on that happening anytime soon."

"Thank you." Edge closed his eyes and allowed the joy and relief to roll over him. He felt Passion's hand clasp his. He tightened his grip. Never letting her go, *never.*

When he opened his eyes, Bourne was leaning back, a bemused expression on his face. "I've been the Big Boss for a long time. But after tonight, I've decided I need some help."

Startled, everyone leaned forward.

"I died tonight. And if not for Passion, you'd all be chasing your tails trying to figure out what to do. I've always handled everything myself, and I never planned for an emergency like this."

He paused so long that Edge wanted to drag the words from him.

"So I've decided to appoint a second." Bourne allowed the implications to sink in. "I'll personally train this person to take over in case I'm dead or unable to be the Big Boss anymore. They'll know all that I know."

"No one could take your place." Ganymede glanced away.

Edge grinned. Ganymede felt embarrassed spouting anything that sounded even vaguely like affection for his leader.

Bourne steepled his fingers and stared over their heads. "I appreciate the compliment. This person might not be your ultimate choice for leader, but at least you'll have someone smart, with common sense to move you forward. Let me say first that sheer physical power wasn't my first consideration."

"Edge proved tonight that he's strong enough to defeat almost any challenger. And I've always suspected you could kick my butt, Ganymede, if you felt motivated."

He shrugged. "This appointment is also a little selfish. Even if I'm the Big Boss for thousands of years to come, I need someone to help me. Especially now with the new ones."

"Who is it?" Passion asked for all of them.

Bourne smiled. "Sparkle Stardust, do I have a job for you."

Passion stood on the deck of the pirate ship, staring into the darkness, aware with every cell in her body of the man standing beside her. It was cool, but not cold. She reveled in the night and what it would bring.

After sleeping the day away, she'd wakened to the news that Sparkle was keeping the park closed for a week until everything was straightened out.

That meant . . .

She turned to Edge. "We have seven days to make love at every attraction." Passion reached up to slide her fingers along his jaw.

He angled his head to kiss her fingers. "An exhausting assignment, but doable."

His smile was so sensual she wanted to throw him to the deck and rip his clothes from his perfect body. She drew in a deep calming breath. No, they'd already done the fast and furious twice before. This time she'd draw out the pleasure until neither of them could wait another moment.

"I'm very good at organizing things. During the day we can talk about our wedding . . ." The poor guy hadn't even gotten all of the words to his proposal out before she'd shouted yes and pounced on him. Okay, so she was pretty eager. "And at night we can . . ."

His smile widened, a little savage and a lot predatory. "I like the nights best." He pulled her away from the deck and guided her into the captain's cabin. Then he reached for her.

"Wait." She pushed him toward the captain's bed. "Make yourself comfortable, because I have something planned for you."

Passion watched with avid eyes as he pulled his T-shirt over his head and then slid his jeans down his narrow hips. She had to remind herself to blink.

When he was done, he sprawled across the bed, almost convincing her to abandon her plans. No, she was made of sterner stuff.

She smiled at him and then began to undress, drawing the torture out by going very, *very* slowly. His low growl made her shiver.

When she stood naked before him, she bent to draw the small bag from the pocket of her jacket. She straightened and offered him the sexiest smile she had.

"I'm going to dance for you. You like chocolate, don't you?"

And she began her Dance of the Seven Hershey's Kisses.

Turn the page for a preview of Nina Bangs's
next Castle of Dark Dreams novel . . .

Wicked Whispers

Now available from Berkley Sensation!

The music pressed against the inside of his skull, a melodic migraine pounding out a deadly rhythm in his head. Murmur resisted the urge to just let go, to free his songs, to stop their ice-pick notes from jabbing at him. Pain-free seemed like a good place to be.

He gritted his teeth against the agony. "I need to do a pressure release before my head explodes. I don't think vacuuming up demon brains is part of the maid's job description." Even pacing this hotel room would work off some of the tension buzzing in his brain, but moving hurt too much, so he simply sat as still as he could in the chair facing Bain.

"Control it. If not, they'll kick you out of the castle, and I need your help." Bain leaned back in his chair and watched his friend from hooded eyes.

Murmur took a deep breath. "I *never* lose control. So to keep my record intact, I'll have to take my show on the road. Where can I go to defuse?" The castle-slash-hotel might specialize in fantasy role-playing, but Murmur didn't think they were ready for what he'd deliver.

Music was his power, but it was also his weakness. If he kept it captive for too long, the pain crippled him. And at some point it might even drive him crazy. What the world did *not* need was a mad music demon.

Bain shrugged. "It's late, so I'd try the beach. No one there to hear you. But if some of your music does creep back into the castle, no big deal. Remember, I saw you in action here a few weeks ago. You pissed me off with that compulsion you laid on everyone, but we all danced and had a good time. No harm." He shrugged. "And sure, you were a little scary in the final showdown with Ted, but all demons ramp up the terror." His grin promised he could take scary to a whole new level. "It's what makes us beloved by all."

No harm because I stopped the dance in time. But I didn't want to stop it. I wanted it to go on and on and on . . . Murmur knew his smile was bitter. He winced. Damn, even that small use of facial muscles upped the agony. "Don't be an ass, Bain. You know what would happen if I lost control, so don't act as if it's nothing." He stood and walked slowly to the door, each tortured step sending new vibrations rattling around inside his aching head.

"Fine. Do your thing." Bain's tone said he still didn't get it. He glanced at Murmur's music system. "This is a pretty fancy setup for just a hotel stay. Maybe you should turn it on and relax with some mellow tunes instead of dragging yourself to the beach."

"I have a 'fancy setup' because I *need* the music." He and the other demon had been friends for millennia, but that didn't mean they knew squat about each other. Demons weren't social creatures, and being friends simply meant they didn't try to tear each other apart when they met. All right, so Bain and he were a little closer than that, but Bain had only experienced Murmur's music on a small scale. He'd never really seen what happened when Murmur got serious.

Bain heaved an exaggerated sigh and rose to follow

him. "Then I'll leave you to your midnight concert. I'm due for my last fantasy performance of the night in about ten minutes. Give a shout if you need me." He paused before heading for the winding stairs leading down to the great hall. "And thanks for sticking around. I appreciate it." Then he was gone.

For a demon, Bain's words were the same as a big hug and a sloppy kiss from a human. Demons didn't display emotions. Most of the time, they didn't have any to display. Okay, so maybe there were occasional outbursts of rage leading to mass destruction. But that was about the limit to their softer feelings.

Murmur took the elevator. No way would he survive the explosion of pain as each foot landed on those stone steps. From there he staggered out of the castle, his hands over his ears, trying to block all the human voices adding to the din in his head.

He stumbled across Seawall Boulevard and down the steps leading to the beach. This was all Bain's fault. The other demon had called Murmur to help with some yet-to-be-explained vengeance plot. Since then Murmur had been stuck on Galveston Island, unable to find a place far enough away from people to free his music.

Sure, he could've abandoned Bain. But Bain was a friend. His *only* friend. And wasn't it pathetic that Murmur actually cared? Not a positive demonic character trait. He'd have to shore up his I-don't-give-a-damn wall of indifference.

Right now, though, he needed to stop the pain. When he'd put some distance between himself and the Castle of Dark Dreams, he glanced around. Not far enough away from humanity to cut loose completely, but he could at least siphon off some of his music and relieve the agony for a while.

A moonless night, but there was some light filtering down from the streetlights across the road. No one on the beach. That's all he had to know. The pain was almost to the point of exploding from him. That would be a bad thing for everyone in Galveston *and* for him. He wasn't ready to leave the castle yet.

Drawing in a deep breath, he allowed his music to escape in a slow, controlled flow of sound. It mirrored his mood of the moment—dissatisfied, confused, and even a little sad. Murmur let the intertwined melodies build to a crescendo of angry frustration. Why the hell was he feeling these emotions now after so many thousands of years?

He closed his eyes at the remembered bliss of times long past. Times when he'd released the fury of his songs on entire villages, watching as everyone within the sound of his music died screaming. Or, if he was in a more play-ful mood, they'd die dancing, unable to stop until their puny human hearts gave out.

Murmur hadn't done that in a long time. He wasn't ready to examine the reason why.

Ivy stepped onto the beach and wandered toward the water-line, where gentle waves lapped at the sand. The Gulf was quiet tonight. The lights from the street didn't do much to help her see where she was going. Symbolic? Maybe. Because three days ago she'd made the first impulsive deci-sion of her adult life.

She'd taken a job at Live the Fantasy, an adult theme park where people could unpack their dreams of being more than they were, dust them off, and play the part for an hour. Tomorrow she'd meet her boss for the first time. Ivy glanced back at the castle. Still time to run.

Before she could begin to obsess about the insanity of accepting a job as the personal assistant to someone named Sparkle Stardust, she heard the music.

It came from everywhere and nowhere. The melody wrapped around her, tendrils of compulsion that seeped into her soul and made her—she widened her eyes—want to dance.

Ivy didn't dance. Ever. She had no rhythm. But she was okay with that. Dancing didn't further her life's goal—a solid, well-paying job so she could build her own white picket fence around a home in suburbia. She'd never depend on a man to do her picket-fence building.

But suddenly, for no apparent reason, she wanted to dance, *had* to dance. Without her permission, her feet began to move with the throbbing beat. Closing her eyes, she let it happen. If she really concentrated, she could almost hear words—of futility, frustration, *need*.

Ivy realized she was dancing farther and farther away from the castle, but she didn't seem to care. All that mattered was the music. Its bass pounded out an ever more frenetic message of anger and so much need that it brought tears to her eyes. She swirled and leaped on waves of emotion, even as the Gulf's waves curled around her ankles before retreating.

The person she'd always been—logical, grounded in reality—screamed, "What the hell are you doing?" But nothing mattered. Everything she was floated away on the compulsive rhythm urging her to dance and dance and dance . . .

And then she saw him. He stood in the darkness, waiting as she danced closer and closer. At first he was only a shadow among many shadows. But as she drew nearer she saw him more clearly. Tall, elegant, with broad shoulders and a body that she imagined would be powerful and lean-muscled beneath his black boots, black pants, and what looked like a black silk shirt open at the throat. All that unrelieved black only served to lead her gaze upward to . . .

Her heart was a frantic drumbeat, her breathing a harsh rasp in her throat, and it had nothing to do with exertion.

His face. She gathered all of her willpower and forced her feet to still while she studied him from only a few feet away, too close for safety.

Shining blond hair fell in a smooth curtain to halfway down his back. He watched her from eyes framed by thick lashes. She couldn't see the color of those eyes in the dark-

ness. The angles and planes of his face cast shadows high-
lighting male beauty that seemed impossible, but obviously
wasn't. Her gaze drifted to his lips, full and so tempting
that . . .

He smiled. Ivy felt that smile as an ache that started in
her chest but moved rapidly south. This was *not* good. She
glanced away and tried to recapture her sanity along with
her breath. "I wonder where that music is coming from."

He ignored her comment. "Dance with me." His
voice—husky, compelling, but with a harsh rasp of some
emotion she couldn't identify—hinted that unspeakable
pleasures awaited anyone who danced with him.

No. She didn't dance with strangers she met on the
beach. It absolutely wasn't going to happen. "Sure."

And so they danced. Together. Touching. Not what she
thought she'd ever enjoy, because with his arms around
her she'd have to follow his lead. Ivy knew from experience
that she couldn't match her steps with a partner. But
she did.

It was like floating. She swayed in time with her silent
partner as he swept her into the dance. Everything seemed
supersized. The sand felt deliciously cool beneath her bare
feet. When had she kicked off her shoes? The water sparkled. There was no moon, so how could it sparkle? When
she tipped her head back to allow her hair to float in the
sudden breeze, she saw a sky filled with millions of glittering stars. Not real, *couldn't* be real. But the impossibil-
ity of all those stars didn't bother her. Only the man and
the dance mattered.

He'd pulled her close, and she felt the realness of him
as surely as if he wore nothing—the hard planes of his
body, the pounding of his heart where her head rested
against his chest. And when he cupped her bottom to tuck
her between his thighs, she had proof that the dance was
affecting him in the same way it was her.

Desire clenched low in her stomach. Shock made her
miss a step. She drew in a deep, calming breath and tried
to recapture the magic of the dance. But she couldn't. This

wasn't her. Ivy didn't go around wanting to throw men to the ground and then ride them until a screaming orgasm shattered her.

The music stopped. Ivy just stood there breathing hard. Exertion or hyperventilating? Didn't matter; the result was the same. She felt light-headed.

"Thank you." His words were cool, his tone distant. He turned and disappeared into the darkness.

Ivy stood staring at the water that no longer sparkled. When her dizziness finally passed, she found her shoes and then walked slowly back to the Castle of Dark Dreams. Aptly named, as it turned out. If anyone qualified as a dark dream, her unknown dance partner did.

She decided to wait until she got back to her room before thinking about what had just happened. There was always a logical explanation for everything. *Except when there wasn't.* Ivy pressed her lips together. Of course there was an explanation. She just had to find it.

Ivy paused before entering the castle. For a moment, she thought about going around to the great hall entrance and taking a look at the ongoing fantasy. No, she didn't need another shot of make-believe after what she'd experienced on the beach.

Was he staying at the castle? Would she run into him again? Ivy narrowed her eyes as she strode through the door leading into the hotel lobby. He didn't matter. What did matter was her new job. She needed to concentrate on that.

She stepped into the elevator still wrapped in thoughts of what tomorrow's meeting with Sparkle Stardust would bring. Someone stepped in with her. Ivy dragged her thoughts away from her new job long enough to notice the man sharing the elevator.

She blinked. He was short and squat with dark hair that stuck out everywhere and looked like steel wool. He had a nose that seemed to swallow his face, and his wrinkled skin was the color and texture of a walnut shell. He stared at her from beneath bushy brows the same color as his eyes. Black. Did anyone really have shiny black eyes? He didn't look friendly. She prayed the elevator door would open and spit her out onto her floor.

"You took my job, human." His voice was a dark threatening rumble.

Human? Ivy stared gape-mouthed at him. "Your job?"

The elevator door slid open. But shock rooted Ivy in place.

"I would have made a better assistant than you. What do you know about the needs of a person of power?" On that contemptuous snarl, he stepped from the car, and the doors silently closed behind him.

Okay, that was just bizarre. Ivy took a deep fortifying breath before pressing the button to open the door again. She stepped out. Thank God, the strange, and yes, disturbing man was gone. He must have a room on her floor, though. That made her uneasy.

Trying to shake off the encounter, she unlocked her door and stepped inside. She sighed her relief as she turned on the light. And froze.

Her room was crawling with spiders. Thousands of them. Big, fat, ugly spiders. They crawled over her bed, up her walls, and across the ceiling. They watched her from gleaming eyes that oozed malice.

Another woman might have screamed and run. Ivy just pressed her lips together, narrowed her eyes, and strode to the phone on her night table. She swept spiders from the receiver before making her call, even as she mentally chanted her personal mantra: no black widows, no brown recluses, no *fear*. Then she went back to stand at the open door and wait.

She tried not to think, to conjecture, to *panic*. Ivy had built her entire life on the premise that any problem could be solved if approached in a calm and rational way. There was always a logical explanation for things. Okay, so the man on the beach was an anomaly.

At least she didn't have long to wait and stew. She heard steps behind her and turned.

A wizard? Would the weirdness never end? He was about the same height as her, and she wasn't tall. Thin, gray-haired with a matching long pointed beard, his narrowed gray eyes promised that she'd be sorry if she'd brought him here on a fool's errand.

She scoped him out from head to toe and thought of the spiders to keep from chuckling. He was a walking stereotype. His gold-trimmed blue robe was decorated with glittering suns, moons, and stars. He wore a matching tall conical hat. It added almost a foot to his height. And he carried a strange-looking staff.

"Holgarth, I presume?" It had better be, since that's who she'd demanded to see when she'd called the desk. Ivy moved aside so he could step into the room. "Unless you intend to beat them to death with your staff, I'd suggest you call in the exterminators."

He pursed his thin lips, his cold stare saying that she wasn't amusing him. Ivy decided that not much *would* amuse this guy.

"How unfortunate." He sounded as though a plague of spiders were nothing more than a minor irritation. "I'll get rid of them and then you can—"

"Uh, no, to the rest of what you were going to say. I mean, you can certainly get rid of them, but I won't be here to see the miraculous event. I want another room and . . ." She thought about the man in the elevator. "And I want one on a different floor."

Holgarth sniffed. "Hired help used to know their places."

Ivy widened her eyes. "Oh, I absolutely know my place. It's in a new room not infested with spiders." Was she trying to get fired? Maybe. All the weirdness that had happened so far didn't bode well for her new job. "*You're* the one who hired me. I'd think you'd want me to be happy."

"I did *not* hire you." He seemed bitter about that. "I wanted someone more tractable, but Sparkle insisted that you were right for the job."

"'Tractable'? Does anyone even use that word in everyday speech? Well, if wanting a room where I won't wake up every ten minutes imagining spiders two-stepping across my face makes me intractable, then so be it. I want out of here."

He pressed his lips into a thin line of disapproval. "Come with me."

She frowned as another thought surfaced. "I never spoke with Ms. Stardust, so how did she know I was right for the job?"

For the first time he looked as though he approved of something she'd said. "Exactly the point I tried to make." He glanced at his watch. "Enough useless chatter. My time is valuable."

"What about my things?" She moved into the hall and stopped to wait for him.

"Someone will bring them to you." He lingered in the doorway, mumbling something to himself.

And just before he joined her, closing the door behind him, Ivy got a peek into the room. The spiders were gone. She blocked the sight from her mind. The unexplainable was piling up at an alarming rate, and her brain couldn't handle it all at once.

Holgarth led her down the winding stone steps. "I prefer to avoid the elevator. It performs in an erratic manner when I use it."

Hey, Ivy understood completely. She'd probably perform in an erratic manner too if she spent much time around him.

He didn't stop when they reached the great hall but took another flight of stairs down. Pulling out a bunch of keys on a large ring, he used one to open a door. "Your new room, madam." He didn't try to hide his sneer.

Ivy had a few questions. "There aren't any windows on this level. And the sign over that door across from me says DUNGEON. Why am I on the dungeon level?"

Holgarth raised one brow. "You're not on the dungeon level. You're on the vampire level. The dungeon just happens to be here. We use it in our fantasies." He paused for effect. "Except when we're using it to hold a recalcitrant creature."

She glared at him. "Now you're just being annoying. Fairy tales don't scare me. You didn't answer my question. Why am I here?"

His lips twitched. She had a feeling this was Holgarth's version of a belly laugh.

"A fairy tale? Yes, the fey sometimes visit us. But we haven't had to incarcerate one yet." He looked thoughtful. "They would present some unique difficulties." Then he widened his eyes. "Oh, but you asked about this room. The hotel is full right now. You could, of course, return to your old room." He looked hopeful.

He'd like that. Ivy prided herself on being even-tempered, but Holgarth totally ticked her off. "Fine. I'll stay here." Not waiting for his reply, she walked into the room and shut the door in his face. Then she leaned against it and closed her eyes.

Finally, she sighed and walked over to one of the chairs in the small sitting area. The big four-poster bed called to her, but if she gave in she'd be out as soon as her head hit the pillow. She had to stay awake until someone delivered her things.

She tried not to think. Attempting to figure things out when she was so tired wouldn't work. Tomorrow morning, when her mind wasn't a mushy banana, would be time enough to think about the weirdness.

Instead, she studied the room—dark period furniture, a stone floor covered with what looked like Oriental rugs, and jewel-toned tapestries on the wall. Hello, Texas Gothic. The only thing missing was an open window with white sheers blowing gently in the night breeze and the scent of honeysuckle. Okay, so maybe that was Southern Gothic.

A knock interrupted her thoughts. She pried herself from the chair and opened the door. Holgarth stood there beside a man loaded down with her things. The wizard watched as the man dumped her clothes on the bed, her shoes on the floor, and everything else on the coffee table in the sitting area.

Love the five-star treatment here. But Ivy didn't voice her thoughts because she wanted Holgarth to answer a question for her. She waited until the man left.

"I was on the beach tonight and I heard music. I don't know where it was coming from, but it seemed . . ." What? Tempting, arousing, compelling? "Strange. Then I met a man—tall, long blond hair—and he asked me to dance with him." This was dumb. Holgarth would just make fun of her. "I danced."

She watched Holgarth's face, expecting to see his usual disdainful expression. "Do you know if he's staying in the castle?" Not that Ivy really cared. Okay, maybe she *did* care. A little.

The wizard stared back at her from eyes that gave nothing away. "If you hear the music again, cover your ears. And *never* agree to dance with him." He sounded completely serious.

"Why?" *There's always a rational reason for everything.*

Holgarth's gaze speared her. "Explanations would be useless. Remember, you don't believe in fairy tales." He turned and walked away.

Well, that was totally unsatisfying. She closed the door and got ready for bed. After searching under her pillow for spiders, she relaxed enough to fall asleep.

And dreamed of the man, the music, and the dance.

Welcome to the Castle of Dark Dreams,
where private pleasures and devilish fantasies come true,
and where the men who breathe life into women's ultimate
desires burn with their own supernatural fire . . .

FROM *USA TODAY* BESTSELLING AUTHOR

NINA BANGS

THE CASTLE OF DARK DREAMS NOVELS

Wicked Edge
Wicked Fantasy
Wicked Pleasure
Wicked Nights

PRAISE FOR THE CASTLE OF DARK DREAMS NOVELS

"Demons, vamps, angels, and wizards make for one ex-
hilarating ride!"   —*Fresh Fiction*

"Fabulously wicked."   —*Midwest Book Review*

"Paranormal romance filled with humor and sex...and
with the right touch of suspense . . . Action packed."
                                        —*The Best Reviews*

ninabangs.com
facebook.com/NinaBangsAuthor
facebook.com/ProjectParanormalBooks
penguin.com

M1168AS0912